A Soldier's Final Journey

A Soldier's Final Journey

Gerry Feld

Copyright © 2019 by Gerry Feld

All rights reserved. No part of this book may be reproduced or transmitted in any form or by any means, electronic or mechanical. This includes photocopying, recording or by any information storage and retrieval system without permission in writing from the owner.

This is purely a work of fiction. All names, characters places and incidents are the product of the author's imagination or are used fictitiously. Any resemblance to any actual person living or dead, events, or locals is totally coincidental.

Cover Design and all art work supplied by: R.L. Sather
Interior layout by Roseanna White Designs

Print Paperback ISBN # 978-0-578-45387-3
E-Book ISBN # 978-0-578-45395-8

TABLE OF CONTENTS

TABLE OF CONTENTS

PREFACE

My first novel, *A Journey into War*, followed Steve Kenrude, a quiet farm boy from Minnesota through the turbulent years of World War Two. Steve evolved into a confident leader and good friend to all the men who served with him. As with most heroic soldiers, Steve returned home to a welcoming family. But what happened to him then? Was he successful? Did he enjoy life and those around him? And how did he cope with returning to civilian life?

As I answer all those questions in this novel, I do not forget all the brave men who served with Steve such as Harry Jenson, Francis (Franny) Martin Doogan III, Captain Fontaine, Father O'Reilly and many more. We shall explore how these heroes from the greatest generation were affected by time and changes in a world they could have never predicted.

As you will see, not everything went smoothly for the brave warriors of Charlie Company. The Korean War would take each of them to the limit of their faith and endurance once again as they endure the horrors of war, the loss of friends and comrades, and the evil that lies in the hearts of men.

Their families will struggle as they send their loved one off to war yet again, and strive to overcome the yet unknown challenges that will plague their lives.

As a historian of World War Two, I had tons of information to work from, as well as interviews I had completed with veterans over the years.

When it came to Korea, I knew the basics regarding the war, but that was never enough to write a story. I ended up doing a tremendous amount of research to get the facts and information I needed. As with most historical fiction writers, I have used literary license to create scenes in actual battles, where I could place my characters into those situations based on actual historical accounts. In one case I created an entire military operation to enhance the story. While it has no historical background, it does accurately represent the period and describes what I imagined such an operation would be.

So, come along and join the heroes and their family members from *A Journey into War,* as they go forward into the brand new world found in my new book, *A Soldier's Final Journey*.

ACKNOWLEDGEMENTS

I must thank Mark and Katie at Computer Dynamics for all their help and patience. Midway through the project my old computer failed and I had to transfer to a new machine I knew nothing about.

Prior to this book, I had never worked with a professional proof reader/editor before. I was pleased to have worked with Lori Hawkins, who was understanding, and made the entire process much more painless than I thought it would ever be. She was a joy to work with.

DEDICATION

The most important and perhaps most difficult aspect of writing a book is the dedication. There are so many people who impact one's life, it is impossible to mention them all. Of course my parents impacted me the most. Besides giving me life, they taught me about living and inspired me to dream and never stop searching for what I believe in.

It is my belief that no author writing about our nation's wars should ever forget the men and women who put their lives on the line and sacrificed so much to keep our nation free. As the poignant saying goes, "All gave some, some gave all." As General George S. Patton Jr. once said, "It is foolish and wrong to mourn the men who died. Rather we should thank God that such men lived." So in their memory, I also dedicate this book to them.

However, no dedication could be complete unless I include my wife JoAnn. She stood beside me during my first novel when things got a little crazy. She inspired me to forge on and never give up. Though at times it was more like, when you find yourself in hell, keep going. However, she never read the manuscript prior to the publishing of the book, so she had no idea of what the story was about or what my writing style was like, until she read the finished product.

This time she was anxious to be involved in the undertaking, and volunteered to take on the arduous task of proofreading and correcting my manuscript. Throughout the project, she gave me plenty of good advice as we discussed every aspect of the story line.

JoAnn has been a tremendous inspiration, and has given me overwhelming support in this new undertaking. Thanks JoAnn, you are the best—love you always.

CHAPTER 1
DEVASTATION

The smoldering ruins of trucks and tanks littered the snow covered hills of South Korea. Half burned naked corpses were draped over the sides of gutted turrets, a graphic testimony that massive armor was no protection in this type of warfare.

Frozen bodies lay in grotesque shapes just under the light snow that fell during the night. Arms were frozen in upward positions as the suffering men reached for help during their last agonizing moments of life. It was a ghastly scene no man should ever have to witness.

After emerging from his foxhole cold and stiff, Sergeant Steve Kenrude walked slowly across the battlefield searching for men from his command that had perished during the horrifying battle. Americans lay on top of North Korean Soldiers where they had died in hand to hand combat after running out of ammunition. Some were missing arms and legs as high explosives from tanks and artillery had raked the formerly peaceful valley for hours on end. Some were crushed by the treads of monster tanks that rumbled about the valley dueling one another in deadly mortal combat.

Walking to the top of a small rise Steve scanned the area below in all directions. "My God," he uttered in a low voice as he took in the carnage that surrounded him. He had seen devastating combat during World War Two, particularly in the winter battles of Bastogne, Belgium in 1944, but what he witnessed today horrified him. It would take days just to remove the bodies that littered the valley and sort them out by nation. There were Americans, South Koreans, North Koreans, Chinese, British, Canadians, Dutch, and men from several other small countries that chose to join the United Nations Forces in this war.

Yes, the top commanders in Japan would surely claim a major victory from the carnage here last night. They were asked to stop a North Korean drive which threatened to push U.N. forces all the way back to the southernmost tip of the peninsula, effectively ending the war, and they had succeeded. Both sides continued to throw in every reserve unit they had including cooks, truck drivers and office clerks, all necessary to stem the merciless attack.

The fighting had started about noon the day before and ended somewhere around two this morning.

The 187th Airborne had been thrown into the battle to help bolster the line, although every upper echelon officer knew it was a waste of the highly trained airborne soldiers. Nevertheless, without their expertise with close in combat, the line might have collapsed.

Slowly, Steve began descending the hill towards the spot where Alpha and Dog Companies made a heroic last ditch stand around midnight to block an end-around maneuver by the North Koreans. It had been ferocious and bloody but the tenacity of the airborne soldiers won the day.

Steve knelt down by the first airborne soldier he found. Brushing snow from the overcoat he recognized the D-Company emblem, so it wasn't one of his men. Just four steps later Steve recognized the body of Private Sid Nelson from his First Squad. A Russian bayonet was still embedded in his chest.

As Steve examined the face of the young soldier he heard footsteps come up behind him. Looking over his shoulder he saw Sergeants Eddie Shrider and Harry Jensen walking toward him.

"One of yours?" Harry called out.

"Yeah. Sid Nelson, first squad," Steve replied, as he stood up.

Shaking his head Eddie Shrider placed his hand on Steve's shoulder. "A lot more out here. Lost all of my second squad, and some from every other squad. Damn waste of good men."

Harry continued on for a few feet until he came upon two men that were twisted together in a fight to the death. Kneeling down he attempted to pull the frozen bodies apart. "It's Krueger, from my fourth squad. Son-of-a-bitch! He was a good man. I just had him assigned from Benning a week ago. Funny, I knew he was a hero the minute I laid my eyes on him. He had that do or die attitude you couldn't miss, you know?" Harry placed his hands on the man's head as he said a silent prayer.

Standing up he looked at Steve. "What the hell, Stevie boy, what the hell! What are we going to do, bleed America white for this God forsaken country? This has to end, Steve! We can't keep throwing America's best into the fire like this. It has to end!"

Before Steve could respond, Eddie Shrider walked over to Harry. "Hell Harry, we saw this every day in Europe. I just don't think it got to us the way this war is. We're older now and understand what it's like to have a home, a family and someone to love. We didn't understand all of that back in forty-four. We were kids. We just fought like we were told."

Steve nodded his head. "A lot of truth in that, Eddie. Plus, now we have more men under our leadership and it just plain hurts when they die and we can't do a thing about it."

The three veterans stood quietly for several moments as they took in their grim surroundings. More light snow began falling over the battlefield as Major Fred Monk walked up to them. "You guys from Alpha Company?"

"Yes sir!" Harry responded with a salute.

The Major shook his head as he gazed about the valley floor. "I never thought it would end last night. I thought we'd run out of men to hold the damn place. What heroics must have played out! But we'll never know what all happened out there." After taking a deep breath he turned toward the three sergeants. "Col. Fontaine was looking for all the platoon Sergeants and officers. He wants to hold a meeting at the Command Post at 0800. You guys better make your way back. There's not a damn thing you can do out here anyway. Those poor bastards are all in God's hands now."

After Major Monk walked off, Harry turned back toward Steve. "Remember when we sailed back into New York in '45. We questioned a lot of things, like what was it all about, and what kind of a difference we made. I don't know Steve, did we make a difference? Here we are doing it all over again, and for what? To stop Communism, protect South Korea? Is the price even worth it Steve?"

As the men began walking back up the hill, Steve pondered everything his best friend had said.

"I can't answer that, Harry. I wouldn't even know where to begin. Last night drained everything out of me. All I had left. Sometimes I wonder how I can go on myself, much less lead anybody else. I just want to go home, hug Karen and hold the kids as tight as I can. That is the only thing that makes sense to me anymore."

As they reached the top of the hill, Col. Fontaine approached from the battle line they established after the battle had ended last night.

"Are you men alright? I was looking for all my platoon leaders, but you guys were missing." The Colonel studied the faces of his tired platoon leaders.

"Nodding his head Steve responded. "I had to go look for my guys. I found one, so I have a good idea where the rest are. Harry and Eddie were out there doing the same."

The Colonel nodded his head. "Well, meeting at 0800 at my C.P. After that we'll load up and pull back. We need to regroup and re-equip. Alpha, Charlie and Dog Companies are ineffective as they stand right now. Easy and Baker Companies are a bit better off. See you at the meeting, gentlemen." As the Colonel turned to leave Harry spoke up. "And our dead, sir?"

"Graves Registration is on the way. They will search over the battlefield to find them and bring them back. Sorry men, but we have been ordered back by I-Corp," Col. Fontaine responded as he departed.

Eddie drew in a deep pull from the cigarette he had just lit. Exhaling the smoke he looked at his two partners. "Someday this war will also end. We may see the end of it or we may not. But I'm afraid the folks back home and the rest of the world will never really know or understand what the hell we did over here. If they did, would they have allowed it?"

Steve looked intently at Eddie and Harry. "You may have a valid point Eddie. But who are we to decide what the world should or should not know. We are just soldiers, doing our jobs the best we can. The politicians back in Washington will play that game whether we like it or not, or agree with anything they say.

All I want is to get home to Karen and the kids and never have anything to do with war again. I'm tired and my soul aches for peace. I just want to go home."

CHAPTER 2
RETURN TO GLENDALE, 1945

As World War Two came to an end, the citizens of Glendale, Minnesota took time out from their busy schedules to celebrate and remember those who fought and died. Eight young men from the surrounding area were either killed in combat, or listed as missing in action. Mayor Morris and the town council approved the final design for a dark gray granite monument honoring the dead, to be placed near the city cemetery.

West of town on the Kenrude farm, plans were being made to expand their operation. Steve was working out details for purchasing the old Donnelly farm from the current owners. The G.I. Bill was giving Steve all the help he needed in procuring the loan. Combining the two farms would allow Kenrude Farms to have nearly three hundred acres under plow. Steve's father Alex nervously wondered how they were going to prepare all the land with the little machinery they owned. Nevertheless, he was proud of his son's initiative, and believed in the overall plan they had drawn up. Karen, Steve's wife, quit her job in town to become their sole book keeper.

Nancy Kenrude was just thankful to have her eldest son home from the war. Steve appeared to be doing well, with no real lingering results from the harsh combat he had seen. Although, she was the first to admit his temper was much shorter than before he left, she prayed he would mellow with time. Nancy was also excited about their plans for creating Kenrude Farms,

Inc. It would be great to have her entire family so close again, once her youngest son Mike was mustered out of the Army. Although, that could be a few more years down the road, she was happy there was no more war to fight. Alex and Nancy's youngest child, Christine, was really happy to have her big brother back home. She loved the attention and affection Steve showed her now, though she didn't understand why he was treating her as if she was so special all of a sudden. But she didn't care why, it was just great to have him home safe and sound.

Karen Donnelly was really excited about the plan to move back into her childhood home on the Donnelly farm after she and Steve were married. She knew a tremendous amount of work would be required to bring the house back to the condition she remembered. The years since her family had last lived there had been hard on the place, the house and yard were sorely neglected.

She also knew she could count on her mother to give her a big hand in reclaiming the old family home. Janet Donnelly, Karen's mother, still loved their old farm very much and was excited to think of her future grandchildren growing up in the comfortable and roomy old farm house.

Although the war in Europe was over, Mike Kenrude was still stationed in Germany. His unit had spent months rounding up German war materials and munitions. From time to time they still captured high-ranking officers, or S.S. members attempting to hide from the new military government. They learned quickly not to drop their guard while detaining these men. All too often they would pull hidden weapons and shoot anyone nearby before killing themselves.

Mike had seen several men from his company killed or wounded by those fanatics. He was really looking forward to getting leave in September, so he could be home for his brother's wedding.

The main focus of the Kenrude and Donnelly families throughout the summer months was the endless list of details for Steve and Karen's wedding, scheduled for the second Saturday in October. The new minister in town, Peter Warner, had been busy with weddings, as many returning veterans were marrying their long suffering sweethearts. Still, he easily worked the Kenrude-Donnelly nuptials into his schedule without a problem. Of course Steve contacted Harry Jensen, his best friend from the war, to make sure he could come and be his best man. Harry responded excitedly, "Wild horses couldn't keep me away."

In mid-August, Steve was able to close on the farm. After leaving the bank, he drove Karen to the farmhouse. Taking the keys from Steve, Karen walked slowly up the stairs to unlock the front door. Stepping inside, her head swam with visions of her wonderful childhood. As tears rolled down her cheeks, she wrapped her arms around Steve's neck. "Thank you, Steven. I've always dreamed of living here again. You have made me very happy." Steve held her tightly for a moment then released her. Looking at her with a smile he asked her a question. "Well, is this the end of an era and the beginning of another all over again?"

Karen laughed excitedly, "Oh gosh, you remembered my words after all this time. You are so special!"

"How could I forget? It was such a sad day when we moved you and your mother out of here after your father's death. I felt horrible when we walked out the back door and you said those words. I couldn't imagine how terrible you must have felt. Actually, something that kept me going during the entire war was the promise I made to myself that somehow I was going to make it right for you. I wasn't sure how, but I knew I would find a way. When I heard the Wilson's were losing the place, I worked as fast as I could to put it together."

Looking about, Karen sighed. "There is a lot to do. Everywhere I look I see work. But I know in time we'll have this house looking as good as new again. Then we can have babies running around and Christmas dinners for the family. We'll fill it with holiday smells just like when I was a child. I love it."

"That all sounds wonderful, sweetheart. We're going to have the best life together. Nothing is ever going to take me away from you again. I mean it, nothing!" Steve replied firmly.

The Kenrude family celebrated on September 30th, as Mike returned from Germany for his first leave since running away to join the Army during the war. No one brought up the unfortunate incident, making it a splendid homecoming for him. He was amazed at how much the farm had changed since Steve and his father had started implementing the expansion plans, and it was looking like the business would be everything he hoped it could become.

Two days before the wedding, Harry Jensen and his fiancee Marylyn arrived in Glendale. It was a joyous reunion for the two men, made even better when Karen and Marylyn hit it off instantly, quickly becoming good friends. That night after a tremendous meal at the Kenrude home, Mike informed them of Russia's belligerence and lack of cooperation regarding the occupation of Germany. He warned everyone that the time would come when we would have to deal with them as an enemy.

After listening to Mike's somber report, the three men entertained every one with some of the lighter moments from their military experience. Harry explained how hard he had worked to surprise Steve by getting Franny home for the wedding, but things just hadn't worked out. Marylyn then announced they were going to be married the first weekend in December, and everyone was invited. Harry reminded Steve that he had to be there, as he was still needed to be the best man. Steve and Karen heartily agreed.

As the festivities wore on, Steve couldn't remember having such a fantastic evening in his whole life. Finally, his family was reunited, and the man who had been by his side through all of the horrors of war they had experienced was now sitting beside him enjoying a peaceful evening with the women they loved. He felt truly blessed.

Saturday dawned sunny and unusually warm for October in Minnesota. The beautiful fall foliage coupled with the crisp morning air made an exceptional setting for a wedding. The church was packed with relatives, neighbors and friends as the young couple exchanged their vows. A reception was held in the church basement which had been decorated beautifully by Christine and several of her friends.

After the wedding, Steve and Karen drove north, stopping in the small town of Richmond, Minnesota, where they rented a cabin for several days on what is called the Horseshoe Chain of Lakes. Karen enjoyed having Steve row her around in a small boat, as they explored the many small inlets and islands. On their second outing, they packed a small lunch and picnicked on an island they had visited the day before. It had a small rocky outcropping where they could sit and enjoy the beauty of the cold blue water and colorful trees.

That night as they sat on the dock back at the resort, Karen finally coaxed Steve to talk a little about the war. At first he was reluctant and attempted to change the subject, but Karen didn't let him off the hook that easily. Slowly, Steve began talking about his experiences in the states before heading off to England. These things were easy and sometimes comical to explain. He knew that stories of England and the war would be much tougher to talk about. Karen listened intently, gently asking questions from time to time. She didn't expect her husband to explain everything in one night. After all, they would have a lifetime together to talk about it, and she understood it would take time.

Returning home after the honeymoon, Karen set up a small office in one of the spare bedrooms, where she was able to work on the bookkeeping for the farm while still attending to her daily homemaker routine. Steve vigorously threw himself into the fall harvest since he'd fallen a bit behind while they were away on their honeymoon.

The Jensen wedding in December was a large event, as many relatives from Sioux Falls came to celebrate with the happy couple. Steve once again enjoyed being with Harry. They had not lost the magic that made them such good friends and combat leaders. At times, all they needed to do was look at each other and they knew what the other was thinking. Before the reception ended, Harry informed Steve and Karen how many Charlie Company members had responded to the New Year's Eve party invitations they had mailed out. Harry laughed as he recounted Major Fontaine's note replying to the invitation.

"Jensen, can't believe you actually followed through with the party. I guess you still must hang around with Kenrude or you have a great wife to get things organized. You could never carry this out on your own. You're too much of a bull in a china shop."

Everyone had a good laugh, most of them agreeing with Major Fontaine. Harry then related the story of how the party idea came to be as the men prepared to ship home. Steve and Harry were very excited about seeing some of their buddies again, and their wives were interested in finally being able to put faces to the names of men they had heard so much about.

The New Year's Eve party at the Central Hotel in Des Moines turned out to be a great success. The two men were excited to see Mike Anderson, Josh McGruder, Phil Brant, Karl Drussing, Oscar Joblinski, Billy Juarez, Ben Rabinowitz, Major Fontaine and especially Franny, who was now stationed at Fort Benning, Georgia. Karen and Marylyn enjoyed finally meeting these men that had almost become legends in their minds, while excitedly entertaining their wives. It was a festive celebration for everyone. Before leaving Des Moines on New Year's Day, Karen told Harry and Marylyn that she was pregnant and due in July. They were both very excited to see their good friends begin a family. Knowing his turn was coming, Harry encouraged Steve to make notes on how to handle a baby properly, it was clear he would need all the help he could get when the time came.

As the spring of 1946 moved forward, Steve and Alex purchased a used but much larger plow from an implement dealer in Willmar. They were excited, as it would cut their plowing time nearly in half. Karen's pregnancy was going well, and Christine waited on her every chance she could. They had become as close any two sisters could be.

As Christine graduated from high school in June, Nancy found herself unprepared. Although feeling very excited for her only daughter, she was already feeling a huge loss, as Christine would be moving to Minneapolis. She had received a scholarship to attend nursing school at the University of Minnesota in September. From the time she was a little girl, Christine loved to play nurse with her brothers, and worked at bandaging the dog and cats whether they liked it or not. The scholarship had fulfilled Christine's dreams for her future.

The highlight of the summer came in July when Karen delivered Thomas Alexander Kenrude, right on schedule.

There was no prouder papa in the county than Steve. Christine spent hours with Karen, getting practice bathing a new born, changing diapers and helping any way that she could.

As the fall semester of school was set to begin, Nancy and Alex had a really tough time driving Christine to her dorm in Minneapolis. After they had unloaded everything and got Christine settled, they stood around the car. Nancy hugged her daughter tightly, asking again, "Do you have everything you need, honey?"

"Yes, Mom. I'll be just fine," Christine responded. "After all, you checked and rechecked everything at least three times before we left home, and again a time or two here."

Alex broke out laughing. "Yup, there's not much chance of anything being missed when Nancy Kenrude is on the job."

"Hush now you two. I just wanted to make sure my baby has what she needs. I couldn't do anything for the boys, and had to leave it up to Uncle Sam to take care of them. I sure wasn't going to miss the chance to make sure my daughter had the best," Nancy remarked, wiping tears from her face.

After kissing Christine once more, Alex finally coaxed his wife into the car for the long drive home. Neither of them spoke much for the first half hour. Then Alex turned toward Nancy. "You know sweetheart, we did a really good job of raising those kids. They are all smart, well-adjusted and ready to take the bull by the horns as necessary. I'm damn proud of every one of them."

Nodding her head, Nancy choked back a few more tears. "I agree. But now all my little ones are gone. It plain breaks my heart, Alex. I don't know who I should be anymore. I have no children to take care of."

Alex smiled tenderly at his beautiful wife. "You have Thomas to work with you know. Karen will let you come over, or bring him to our house nearly any time you want. She lost Christine as her helper, too, so you should grab the opportunity and jump right in."

Smiling at her husband, Nancy said, "Actually, Karen said the other day how much she was going to miss all the help Christine had given her. You're right. I'll talk to her tomorrow and see what I can do to help. That would be nice. I really do need a little one around to make me feel worthwhile."

All Alex could do was smile, understanding Nancy's strong maternal feelings. The ride back to Glendale seemed longer than normal, but they still managed to get home before nightfall.

In January of 1947, Mike's unit was disbanded in Germany. He came home on leave for several weeks before reporting to Fort Hood, Texas. About six months into his assignment he met a young beautician named Glenda. They fell head over heels in love with one another. Although Mike wanted to get married right away, Glenda was more on the cautious side and wouldn't be rushed. She was well aware that Mike was completely hooked on her, so time really didn't matter.

Several major events took place in 1947 for the Kenrude family. First, Mike was promoted to Staff Sergeant in February. Now with a larger income, Mike and Glenda decided it was time to get married.

So on a warm April morning surrounded by many friends, Mike and Glenda were married in a small service at the base chapel. After the wedding they planned a honeymoon back to Minnesota so the family could meet Glenda.

Then, on September 23, Karen delivered a baby girl named Abigail Janet. Depending on who you spoke to in the family, the baby had different names. Some called her Abigail, others called her Abby, while, Alex insisted on calling her A.J. She never minded how anyone in the family addressed her beautiful new daughter, however Karen preferred Abby.

Harry contacted Steve in mid-October with some sad news. He heard from Franny that Larry Woodward committed suicide. According to Larry's father, he had a tough bout with depression when he first came home. But after meeting a very nice young woman, everything appeared to be going his way. He got a promotion at work, and the couple began making plans to purchase a home. Unexpectedly, one morning he failed to show up for work. Two days later, his father found him, hanging from a beam inside a storage shed on their farm. No one could understand why he killed himself. He left no note or explanation, and understandably, his new wife was devastated. Steve took Larry's death extremely hard. All Steve could remember about Larry was the hard charging, brave, resilient, ready for action soldier he could always depend on. Larry was liked and trusted by everyone in the unit.

In January of 1948, Mike and Glenda had their first child, a son they named Mathew David. In late April when the roads were safe, Mike and

Glenda drove to Glendale to show off their new son. Alex and Nancy were totally enamored by this third grandchild they had been blessed with.

During that summer, Steve was paying close attention to rumors regarding the sale of the Miller farm that sat directly south of his folk's place. If indeed it went up for sale, there was no doubt they were going to buy it. Adding that parcel to what they already owned would give them slightly over five hundred acres. That would make Kenrude Farms, Inc. one of the largest operations in the area. Steve worked out the financing at the bank well in advance, so he was ready when the time came.

Just after Thanksgiving, Alex and Nancy received a call from Glenda, explaining that Mike had been seriously injured in a training accident and was in the hospital. Steve and Karen caught the first flight they found from Minneapolis to Texas. Arriving at the hospital, Mike looked pretty tough but he was glad to see his big brother and sister-in-law. After shaking hands, Steve inquired as to what had happened.

"Let me tell you Steve, it happened so fast I couldn't believe it. There had been rain for several days when we went out on a night maneuver. We were attempting to get our vehicles across a slow moving stream when one of the trucks carrying ammunition got hung up in the mud. The driver of the vehicle in front was backing down the bank so we could attach a tow chain when suddenly all hell broke loose. Someone gave one of the mortar teams the wrong coordinates and they started dropping those damn things all around us. The truck we were going to use for the tow was hit first. It sent me flying back across the stream bed. The next two rounds straddled the ammunition truck.

"I yelled for everyone to run as far away as possible, but it was too late. The next round landed directly on top of the ammunition truck. I had barely run maybe ten feet when I was picked up and tossed like a rag doll. I landed on a pile of rocks probably thirty feet away. I had a concussion, four broken ribs, fractured shoulder, broken pelvis, punctured lung, punctured ear drum, cracked femur and internal bleeding from my spleen. The surgeons repaired my lung, removed my spleen, and took out the shrapnel on my backside. Remarkably, after a long stay in the hospital they say I'll be just fine. Damn Steve, we lost three good men that night, all because of somebody's stupidity. Those guys never had a fair chance. It all happened so fast. You know firsthand what mortars are all about."

"Did they figure out who was responsible?" Karen inquired.

"Our Company Commander told me this morning that it's still under investigation. He says he won't rest until they resolve the issue. And let me tell you, I would not want to be on the wrong side of Captain McCreery in a case like this. That Irishman has a temper, and right now, he wants blood!"

Steve smiled as he handed Mike a glass of water. "So, I guess we can report to Mom that you will be fine, other than your baby soft butt may not be as cute as it used to be. Sound about right to you?"

Mike laughed a bit. "Man, it hurts to laugh. Cut it out, brother."

The next day as Steve, Karen and Glenda arrived at the hospital, they found Mike severely depressed. At first he asked them to leave, as tears streamed down his face.

Glenda leaned over giving Mike a kiss. "What's the matter, honey? What happened?"

After taking Glenda's hand he drew in a deep breath. "The doctor told me about an hour ago that I will be discharged from the Army when I'm released from the hospital. He said since I lost my spleen and had so many broken and cracked bones, the medical board found me unfit for military duty. After all I gave them, now they find me unfit to serve, those son-of-a-bitches!"

"That's terrible," Glenda said softly, as she began to cry. "What will we do now?"

Before Mike could respond, Steve stepped forward. "That's not a problem if you're willing to move to Minnesota. I heard just before we left that the Miller's are definitely putting their place up for sale next month. Dad and I are going to buy it, we've got the money, and we sure as hell could use another partner in the corporation. And the Miller house is in real nice shape. You could move right in if you're interested. It has a new well and the roof was just replaced. It's ready to go!"

Karen placed her arm around Glenda. "Yes, and think how nice it would be for all our little children to get to know each other and play in the great outdoors of Minnesota."

Glenda smiled as she wiped a tear from her cheek. "Is this a serious offer, Steven?"

"You bet it is, Glenda. Mom and Dad wanted me to bring it up to you just in case something like this happened. How about it Mike? You would never need to look for a job again?" Steve explained.

Mike looked up at Glenda. "So Glenda, are you saying you would be willing move to Minnesota with our snow and cold winters?"

"Yes darling, I would. Wherever you are is the place I want to be," Glenda responded, hoping Mike would accept the offer.

"Alright then. Guess you got yourself a new partner. Sounds like it will be sometime after the first of the year before I get discharged, but we'll be ready to move home," Mike responded, as the two men shook hands.

After the purchase of the Miller farm was completed, everyone went to work cleaning, hanging drapes and painting the inside of the house so it would be totally ready when Mike and Glenda arrived in January. Nancy and Alex were especially happy to have all their children and grandchildren close by.

After a house warming party welcoming Mike and Glenda home, Steve excused himself to get some fresh air. As he walked slowly down the snow covered driveway, he thought back to the war and everything that had happened since. He felt truly blessed tonight. His family was together, the farm was growing by leaps and bounds, and the next generation of Kenrude's was beginning to take root. Although he felt extremely happy, there was a nagging fear in the back of his mind. He wasn't sure what it was or why it was there. He dismissed it for a moment as he thought about his family again. Nevertheless, as he reached the county highway a cold north wind chilled him to the core. He hadn't felt this way since the night they jumped into Normandy. Walking briskly back to the house, he found Karen outside waiting for him.

"Is everything alright, Steven?" Karen inquired nervously, as she took his cold hand.

"Yes, sweetheart. Everything is fine. I just needed some air, but it's too damn cold out here. Let's go back inside," Steve responded, after giving Karen a soft kiss.

After putting the kids to bed, Steve and Karen retired to their bedroom. Karen fell asleep nearly instantly, but Steve lay wide awake. His warrior intuition was back, and it was working overtime. He just knew something bad was coming their way. He could feel it in his bones and it wasn't good. What could it be? Who could attempt to tear his family apart? Steve looked over at his sleeping wife. There was no way he was going to let anyone hurt her. The howling winter wind sounded sinister. It sounded like an angry wolf looking for vengeance. Somewhere out in the dark night, evil was lurking, and it was right outside their door, just waiting to pull him and his family into a fiendish plot.

CHAPTER 3
KOREA BOILS OVER

Having Mike back on the farm made a big difference in the workload. For spring planting, Steve only had to hire one extra worker. It was evident Mike had missed working on the land and with the animals, and he more or less took charge of all the new calves that were born which was a huge help.

After much thought, Alex decided their farm operation required a larger tractor. So in June he purchased a brand new 1949 Farmall model M, from an implement dealer in Willmar. It was a very powerful tractor capable of pulling huge loads and moving lots of snow. Alex was the envy of the neighbors for some time, as he rode proudly across his newly plowed fields.

Nevertheless, news broadcasts from Asia had everyone on edge throughout the year. The Korean peninsula was in constant turmoil. North Korean incursions across the 38th parallel resulted in continuing battles with South Korean forces. Kim Il-Sung, the North's self-proclaimed dictator, vowed he would unify the North and South Korea into one country under communist rule. Syngman Rhee, President of South Korea, vowed he would battle to the death to keep South Korea free and independent. As Russia backed the North, the United Nations with support of the United States firmly backed the South.

As Korea became a major topic of discussion around Glendale, most citizens felt the United States would never get involved in what they considered the civil war of another nation. Steve and Mike new if a full-fledged war began, the United States would once more send American boys to fight and die. Few people around Glendale understood the horrors of war better than Steve. Mike reminded everyone what he had predicted in 1947, that one day we would meet Russia on the battle field one way or the other, and it appeared his prediction was going to become a horrible reality.

The winter of 1949 was long and hard for Minnesota residents. Unending storms dumped record amounts of snow throughout the state. Alex Kenrude swore he had not seen snow piles this high since back in the twenties. Sadly, many farmers had cattle starve or freeze to death.

Consequently, the spring of 1950 came late. Due to a slow melt and very wet conditions, farmers were kept out of their fields until late April, and in some cases early May. Once field conditions improved, farmers rushed to plant as the growing season was going to be nearly a month shorter.

Alex breathed a sigh of relief when their field work was completed. Even though planting had been delayed, Alex and Mike were still predicting a banner year for their operation. Those predictions included the new crop of calves, born from their growing herd of registered Holsteins, the calves had thankfully survived the harsh and unforgiving winter, thanks in part to good preparation and a lot of hard work. Alex was proud of their operation and felt positive that everything was looking up. Everywhere he looked he saw progress, and it made him feel blessed.

However, Steve was not so sure. Although he fought hard to disregard a persistent feeling of doom, it continued to creep into his mind and heart when he least expected it.

On the evening of June 24, Steve sat on the front porch with Karen as their children played in the yard. It was a classic Minnesota summer evening, as warm air ripe with the smell of blooming clover was stirred gently by a soft north breeze.

Looking up from her mending, Karen caught Steve dozing off. "Hey, Mr. Kenrude, don't fall asleep now or you won't sleep at bed time."

Steve looked over at his beautiful wife. "Yeah, I know. But it was one busy day. Dad and I fixed all the fences on the east side, besides moving some of the old hay down to the south pasture. We still have more hay to move as the new crop isn't ready to cut. We're going to be busy the next few weeks."

Karen smiled. "Well, at least I'll know where to find you."

"That's for sure. Every night I'm going to come home with tractor butt." Steve replied with a grin.

Karen studied Steve's face for a moment. "Honey, is there something wrong? Lately, you seem to have a worried look on your face sometimes, just as you did right now."

Steve wasn't sure how to answer that question. He surely didn't want to scare her with his premonition of doom, but he also knew he had to level with her. "Listen to me carefully, sweetheart. For over a year now I have had this strange feeling that something bad is going to happen. I just can't shake it, and I sure as hell don't like it. The problem is, I just can't put my finger on it yet."

"Well, if it has been over a year, it can't be much. Honey, come on, you can see everything is just fine. We are all doing great, the farm is better than ever. I think you just have too much on your mind. Maybe once the crops are in this fall, we should take off with the kids for a few days and just relax. It would be good for all of us," Karen said with a smile.

"Yeah, maybe you're right. We've been so busy expanding this operation, seems like I always kind of wonder when the roof's going to cave in. Maybe that's what it's been all along, I don't know," Steve responded, just as Abby ran up onto the porch and climbed into his lap.

Steve rocked her slowly as he watched Tommy chase their black lab Bosco around the swing set he and Alex had built for the kids.

As they settled into bed for the night Karen looked over at Steve. "Is your mind more at ease now that we talked about your worries?"

"Yeah, I guess a little. I just love you and the kids so much, I don't want anything bad to ever happen to any of us," Steve replied, as he took her into his strong arms.

"Hey, we'll all be fine, honey. Now get some sleep, alright," Karen said softly before kissing her loving husband.

Nodding his head, Steve closed his eyes before slowly drifting off to sleep. Around midnight Steve jumped violently before sitting straight up in bed.

Karen quickly sat up beside her husband taking him by the hand. "Are you alright? You haven't had a nightmare about the war in a long time. Tell me what's going on?"

As sweat poured down Steve's face he shook his head. "No, it wasn't a nightmare. It happened. I'm telling you, it happened," Steve responded, as he trembled.

"What happened, honey? What are you talking about?" Karen inquired, as Steve's behavior was starting to worry her.

Steve threw back the covers and took Karen's hand. "Come with me, please." Walking into the kitchen, Steve turned on the radio, attempting to tune in an all-night station from the Minneapolis area. After several attempts, he found one just starting the news.

"It's been reported from General MacArthur's command in Japan and confirmed by the White House, that North Korea has launched an all-out assault against the South. South Korean forces are in full retreat, unable to stem the tide of the onslaught against them. A high White House source tells CBS News that Seoul may easily fall in the next forty-eight hours. President Truman has assured President Rhee the United States will do all we can to help his beleaguered nation. In more news—"

Steve turned off the radio before slumping down into a chair as Karen stood near the sink gasping for air. "How? Tell me, how did you know?" Karen asked, sitting down beside Steve.

"I didn't know Korea was going to be the thing I was scared about. But when I woke up I knew the worst had happened. I could sense it," Steve explained, holding Karen's hand. "I'll be gone with in a month."

"What? What do you mean you'll be gone in a month? You've done your duty. You don't need to go back again. No! I won't let them do this to you. No! It's not right." Karen stated in a loud voice.

Before Steve could answer, Tommy came wandering into the kitchen. He walked over to Karen, taking her by the hand. "Mommy, is everything alright? Are you and Daddy mad at each other?"

Karen picked up her son and kissed him. "No. Daddy and I are just fine. Some terribly bad men did something really bad today and we were discussing it."

"Will the bad men come here?" Tommy inquired, as he gazed somewhat fearfully toward Steve.

"No son, the bad men won't come here. They're a long ways away, half way around the world actually. So buster, you have nothing to worry about. Okay?"

Tommy nodded his head with a smile. "That's good, Daddy. I'm going to go back to bed then."

"Do you want me to tuck you in again? " Karen inquired.

"No Mama, I'm alright," Tommy replied, as he walked back out of the kitchen.

After discussing the situation for a few more minutes, Steve and Karen went back to bed. Neither of them slept well for the balance of the night.

Around six-thirty in the morning, Mike and Alex drove up the long driveway to pick up Steve. Karen walked out to greet them as they climbed out of the truck. "Good morning. Coffee's on," Karen called out, as she waved them toward the back door.

As they entered the kitchen, Steve was just turning off the radio. "So you heard the news about Korea?" Alex inquired.

"Yeah. I don't like it one damn bit. A lot of young guys are going to get killed over this. I don't even know what to say about the whole mess," Steve responded, before taking a drink of coffee.

Shaking his head, Alex looked at his two boys. "Well, at least this time I know my boys will be safe. You guys already paid your dues and I'm damn proud to say it."

Steve looked quickly toward Karen, shaking his head. She caught Steve's gesture and gently nodded. After finishing their coffee, Alex and Mike walked toward the back door. Steve kissed Karen then whispered. "Thanks for not saying anything. It would kill dad."

Karen replied softly, "I know, I know. It's killing me to think of it. Do you really think you could be called back?"

Nodding his head, he looked intently at his wife. "I'm afraid so. We've let our military suffer since the war ended. They're going to need men with technical skills like airborne operations."

On July 10th, Karen watched the mailman drive up into the yard as she hung wet clothes out on the lines.

"Hey, Mr. Randolph, how are you doing today?" Karen inquired walking toward his car.

"Oh, not so bad. If I could get rid of this arthritis in my back I would be a whole lot better though. But, being sixty-four what can you expect." Slowly he removed a letter from a stack on the dash of his car. "I have a special delivery for Steve. You can sign for it, Karen."

After signing the form she looked down at the envelope and gasped. Instantly, she became light headed before dropping to her knees.

Roy Randolph quickly knelt down beside her. "Girl what's the matter with you? You look like you've just seen a ghost."

Without saying a word she pointed toward the return address on the envelope. It read, "Department of Defense, Washington D.C." Under Steve's name and address, was printed, *'Reply Immediately.'*

Puzzled, Roy was not sure what to say.

After a few moments, Karen caught her breath and struggled to stand up with Roy's aid.

"Steve's been worried about being called back up to fight in Korea. I'm afraid this is his notice," Karen explained, as tears rolled down her face.

"No, they wouldn't do that to Steve. Here, give me the envelope and we'll open it to see exactly what they have to say. Then you can put your heart to rest." Roy suggested, reaching for the envelope.

"No. Thank you, Mr. Randolph," Karen replied, as she drew in a deep breath, "but we need to let Steven open this. He's working on a tractor at his folk's place. I'll take it over to him," she explained boldly.

Nodding his head in agreement, Roy walked back to his car, a little shaken by what had just transpired. After watching Karen walk back into the house, Roy returned to his route.

Since Nancy had picked up the kids earlier in the day, Karen jumped in the car and drove quickly over there. Driving into the yard she saw Tommy sitting on a wooden stool beside the tractor, as Steve and Mike worked on the hydraulic pump.

"Hey, what brings you over here?" Steve called out as Karen stepped from the car.

Before answering Steve, she kissed Tommy on top of the head. "Go tell grandma you want a drink of water. And tell her I'll be in to see her in a few minutes."

Without a word he jumped off the stool, racing toward the back porch.

"What was that about?" Steve questioned, wiping hydraulic fluid from his hands.

After taking a deep breath she held out the envelope.

Steve looked at it for a moment before taking it from her hand. After carefully tearing it open he removed a two page letter. Shaking his head he looked toward Karen.

"I have thirty days to report to Fort Benning in Georgia."

Karen threw her arms around Steve's neck, sobbing intensely.

Mike took the letter from Steve's hand, reading the contents before placing it back in the envelope. Alex told Tommy and Abby to sit on the porch before he and Nancy joined the others near the tractor.

"What is it?" Nancy asked Mike, a worried look on her face.

"The Defense Department has called Steve back to active duty. They want him at Fort Benning in thirty days."

Nancy looked at Alex in utter amazement. "Can they do that? Can they really do that? I mean he has served his country, he almost died. Can they really do this, Alex?"

Alex took his near hysterical wife in his arms. "Yes, honey. I guess they can if it's an emergency. As horrible as it sounds, they can call him back."

That evening Steve received a phone call from Harry. With a sobbing Marylyn in the background, Harry told Steve he had also been called up. Unlike Steve, Harry was angry. No matter what Steve tried to tell him, Harry was totally beside himself. There was no calming him down tonight. Steve felt helpless. He couldn't do anything to calm his best friend's feelings. The next evening Steve called to see how Harry was doing. Marylyn was totally relieved to hear Steve's voice. Before putting Harry on the line she assured Steve he had calmed down and was now making all the necessary preparations.

The two men talked for several minutes, working on travel plans so they could meet before getting to Fort Benning. The next thirty days went by way too fast for everyone. Steve and Karen tried their best to explain what was happening to the children. They prepared wills and filled out financial paperwork in case anything happened to Steve.

There were times that Steve felt his head was about to explode, and he didn't know what to do about it. One afternoon he drove the tractor down toward Eagle Lake. Jumping off, he walked over to the large rocks near the shore. Looking up toward the sky he shook his head. "Well, here we are again Lord. I never thought in all my wildest dreams I would be heading back to war. But this time it's so different. Dear God, I have a beautiful wife and two fantastic children. Why, why are you doing this? I was angry with you when I left for Europe, and I had no right to be. After all, you were always good to me and my family. And in the end, you brought me back home safe and sound, and I appreciate that very much. But, I just don't know if I can handle all the killing and misery, the destruction and total waste. Just tell me why? Give me a reason why it has to be me again? What's your plan for me? Is war all that I'm good for?"

Steve looked at several geese swimming on the lake for a few moments. "I know you aren't going to answer me. You didn't last time either. This is so hard. I don't want to leave my family behind. I have responsibilities, you must understand that." After several moments of silence, Steve turned back to the tractor. He sat on the seat for a moment before looking skyward again. "I guess it's like Mom always said, your will be done no matter what. Alright, that's where we will leave this." Taking a deep breath he started the tractor and drove slowly back to the barn.

Alex and Mike quickly hired a new employee named Frank Schuster to help take up the slack soon to be created by Steve's absence. He seemed to be a good worker and was always willing to take on extra responsibility.

A week before Steve left, Tommy crawled up in his lap. At first he just played with a stuffed dog he received for Christmas. After handing the dog to his father he asked, "Daddy, what is war?"

Steve was taken aback. They had been so careful trying not to scare the kids or talk about where he was going. Gently, Steve brushed at his son's messy hair with his hand. Before he could speak, Tommy turned, looking up at his father with his big green eyes. "What's war, Daddy?"

Karen stood a few feet away, trembling as she desperately fought back her tears.

Steve looked down into his son's questioning eyes. "Tommy, sometimes the men who run countries don't get along. When they can't work out their differences they decide to fight one another."

Tommy nodded his head. "Like when Timmy Smith hit me when I wouldn't give him part of my cookie at the church picnic?"

Steve nodded his head with a slight smile. "Yeah, something like that, son."

"If they are fighting each other why do they need you?" Tommy asked.

"Well, when leaders of countries fight, they don't do it like you and Timmy did, just one on one. They have their whole country fight the other country. They put together armies of men, and those men fight one another with bad weapons. And when they need help, they call on their friends."

"What kind of bad weapons do they use, Daddy?"

"Really bad ones, Tommy, guns, planes, tanks—" Steve began to explain when Karen stepped forward, scooping Tommy out of Steve's lap. "Time for bed young man, you need a bath. I'll get your water ready; you go toss your dirty clothes in the hamper."

Once Tommy was in the bathtub, Karen walked up to Steve. "No more. There will be no more of that. That boy does not need to know that his daddy could be blown up or injured by hideous weapons and never come home. Please, no more talk like that. He's way too young. He'll be hearing about Korea no matter how much I try and keep it from him. I don't want him terrified that you may not come home every time he hears about the war. Let me deal with all of that after you're gone. Do you understand? He's too young to understand all of that."

Steve took Karen in his arms. "I'm sorry honey, I was trying to explain as best I could. I knew there would be questions, hard questions, but that caught me by surprise. No parent should ever have to explain to their children about war."

"You needn't be sorry, sweetheart. You were doing what you thought was best. I just don't want our children scared to death all the time," Karen explained softly as she held her handsome husband.

Departure day was a very emotional one for the Kenrude family. Putting on his bravest face, while fighting back tears, Steve hugged and kissed his children. He assured them he would be back soon. Walking outside he gave his mother-in-law Janet a huge hug. "Please help look after Karen and the little ones," Steve asked intently. "I'll get back here as soon as I can."

Janet Donnelly held her son-in-law with every ounce of strength in her arms. "We love you Steve. Karen and the kids need you. Please be careful, and yes, I'll be with them every day."

Wiping a tear from her cheek, Steve gave her a gentle kiss. "I love you Janet. I know this will be really difficult for Karen. Thank you for everything."

Slowly, Steve turned toward the car where his parents and Karen were waiting to drive him to the train station in Minneapolis.

Arriving at the rail depot, they strolled down the platform without saying a word. When they got to gate seven, Steve hugged his parents. "I know you will do everything you can to help Karen and the kids. Listen, if worse comes to worst, never let them go without. They deserve the best."

"You know we would never let that happen, son. They are our family and we Kenrude's take care of our own, come hell or high water," Alex said, with a forced smile.

Then Nancy kissed Steve on the cheek. "Just come home, Steven. Just come home. Your little ones need their papa."

Finally Steve turned toward Karen. "I just can't believe this is happening again. I am so sorry, sweetheart. Who could ever have guessed that war would rip us apart again?"

"I know. And this time it's not just me that will be impacted by your absence. Abby and Tommy are going to miss you so terribly. I promise I will do my best to let them know every day that you love them and want to be with them," Karen explained, as she kissed Steve. "I can't help remembering when we bought the house. You stood there and said you would never leave me again. Now here you are having to go, and there is nothing any of us can do to stop it."

"I thought of that too sweetheart, and it breaks my heart. I just wish this were a bad dream and we would wake up and have it over with. But I know that's not going to happen. Please take care of yourself and the kids. I'll be home soon as I can," Steve said, as he kissed Karen one more time.

As the conductor pulled at Steve by the arm, he finally stepped aboard the train. He stood in the doorway, waving as the train gained momentum, pulling away from the three crying people at gate number seven.

As Steve settled into his seat he watched the Minnesota country slowly pass by. He remembered the train ride with Harry as they left for Fort Leonard Wood nearly eight years ago. None of the men on that train knew what to expect when they arrived at the Fort, or what would become of them in the war. To most of them, it appeared to be just one big adventure. He wondered how many of them never made it home, or how many came home shattered and hurting forever. Today, Steve knew what was waiting for him at Fort Benning and eventually in Korea. He hoped desperately that he and Harry could be together once again. If it had not been for Harry, Steve knew he would have cracked under the pressure many times. Harry was always his rock.

But could the two of them survive another war? The odds were totally against that happening and he knew it. He remembered Harry's words before parting in Chicago on their way home just five short years ago, "We couldn't continue to be so lucky. Eventually one of us was going to get it."

Steve slept off and on as the train rumbled across Wisconsin and northern Illinois. When the Porter called out, "Next stop Chicago, windy city coming up folks," Steve wiped his eyes and sat up straight, looking out the window.

As they rolled into the station, Steve began scanning the platform for any sign of Harry. Just as the train came to a complete stop, he observed Harry running alongside the car. He was waving wildly trying to get Steve's attention. Moments later he joined Steve and they hugged each other for a moment before the Porter asked them to move out of the aisle.

"Wow, did you ever imagine this in your wildest dreams? Did you ever think we would be heading back to another damn war? I was livid when I received my notice. I couldn't believe it. I think for a while Marylyn was actually scared of me. She just stood there in the kitchen backed into a corner bawling her eyes out. Man, I scared that poor gal and I've never been so sorry in my whole life," Harry explained, as he hung his head.

"Is she alright now, or do you want Karen to talk with her?" Steve inquired of his best friend.

Smiling Harry shook his head. "No, everything is fine on the home front now. Though, I think she's going to call Karen and see if she can come up for a few days and visit. She knows she's going to be lonely."

"Hey that's great. Karen would love to have Marylyn and the kids come for a stay. That would be good for all of them." After a moment of silence Steve continued, "So Harry, what's your take on this damn recall. Do you think we might just train new men and never see combat?"

"No. I think we'll end up over there. I just don't know what to tell you, Steve. This Korea thing, it sure sounds like an entirely different kind of war than we're used to. Sounds like these guys are kind of like the Japanese. They have those damn human wave attacks where they charge until either they are dead or you are. I really don't like those odds at all."

Steve nodded his head in agreement. "I sure hope we can stick together like we did before. I know with you by my side we can pretty much get the job done, and get home in one piece. I'm just not sure the odds of that happening again are very good though."

"Yeah, I've thought of that too. They're going to use us old guys anywhere they can to bolster all the new men. We have the experience no one else has. But let's make a pact right here, right now. When we get to Benning we fight like hell with any one we need to, so we can stay together. Brig or no brig," Harry replied with his cunning grin.

"What the hell. Why should this war be any different than the last one. You got yourself a deal, Harry," Steve replied with a laugh.

The men were more than ready to get off the train when they finally arrived in Columbus, Georgia. There were several Sergeants standing around the platform holding clip boards.

Approaching the oldest looking one of the group, Steve spoke. "My name is Steve Kenrude, and this is Harry Jensen. We've been recalled for active duty. Where do we report?"

The sergeant looked through several sheets of paper before coming to a stop. "Alright, here you guys are. Head out front and jump on a military bus, there are a couple out there. Go ahead and climb on either one. We should be out of here in a few minutes. Welcome back… I guess," the sergeant stated with a wry grin on his face.

About five minutes later, both buses pulled out, headed for the base. Looking over the men it was easy to see that they all were new airborne recruits, fresh from basic training.

"Man, I hope we don't have to work with these guys, Steve. They're all too young and dumb looking. We would have to start from scratch, and that's not going to work," Harry whispered.

"Yeah, you're right, Harry. But if we do need to train these guys it might mean we don't go overseas at all. We might just stay here and train new recruits in the fine art of combat," Steve replied, actually hoping that might just be the case.

"Good point, good point, Stevie boy. Let's keep our fingers crossed on that idea," Harry quickly replied, nodding his head, though inside his feelings were far different.

Arriving at the base, all the new men were dropped off at a reception station. Steve and Harry were driven to another set of buildings several blocks away. As they exited the bus, Harry pointed toward a sign. *'All veterans report here.'*

Walking into the building they observed two young lieutenants working behind a counter. One of them signaled the men over to his station, "Names please."

"Kenrude and Jensen," Harry informed the officer.

Quickly he pulled out two files. "Sit over there and fill out these forms. When you're done bring them back here and I'll assign you a barracks for the night."

Returning the files, Steve said, "May I ask a question, sir?"

"Sure, ask away. I'll tell you whatever I can, and it ain't much," the lieutenant answered earnestly.

"What are we going to be doing here? Are we training new recruits or are we going to end up in combat? What's the scuttlebutt at this point?"

"Man, I wish I could answer that for you guys. Honestly, I don't have a clue. Everything is in such a state of disarray, I'm not sure anyone really knows what the hell is going on. Hell, we got people coming and going worse than Grand Central Station. This comes under the heading of SNAFU if you know what I mean," the lieutenant replied shaking his head.

Nodding in understanding, Steve thanked the lieutenant for his honesty.

"Alright guys, follow me," the young lieutenant said, then led them out the back door. "I'm going to turn you over to Lieutenant Jones in Building 45. He'll take care of you for the night and get you all settled in tomorrow."

Arriving at Building 45, Lieutenant Jones was sitting at a desk just inside the door. He took the files from Steve and Harry then stood up. "As you probably know already, I'm Lt. Jones. I'm assigned to you retreads. I don't need any lip from you guys on how tough you had it or how tough you think you are. Just go inside, find a bunk, and I'll deal with you tomorrow."

Harry was about to let the officer have a piece of his mind when Steve took him by the arm. "Yes sir. We're on our way. Come on Harry, let's not end up in the brig tonight, huh?"

Laughing, Harry turned to Steve. "Yeah, we can wait until after we get a good night's sleep for that."

Inside the barracks there were about twenty other men, most either playing cards or writing letters.

Some of them said hello, others just looked up for a moment before returning to whatever they were doing.

"Let's take these bunks in the corner, Steve. They look just fine to me," Harry called out, tossing his bag on the bottom bunk.

The men had barely sat down when a tall thin man approached them. "Hey, I remember you guys. You came into Beuzeville right after D-Day. You helped us clear out that building full of krauts on the town square while we attacked the bastards in the church. I'm Sgt. Shrider. Well, now it's Eddie Shrider, America's best sports broadcaster in Philadelphia."

"Hell yeah, I remember you. So you got recalled too?" Harry said, as they shook hands.

"Yeah there are a couple other 82nd men in here, but no one from the 101st that I know of. Guess we'll find out tomorrow what all's going on. Sounds like they get a small group of us in here every couple days. They clear us out then bring in the next bunch. So, I guess we'll see what happens."

"Yeah, that's a fact, Eddie. Man it sure is nice to see another familiar face. Even if you were in the 82nd, right?" Steve responded with a smile.

Before they could say another word, a commotion broke out in the office area. Everyone stopped to hear what was happening. Suddenly the door burst open, and Lt. Jones was walking backwards trying to stop a Captain from entering the barracks.

"Look Lieutenant, if you don't get out of my way I'm going to see that Lt. Colonel Fontaine jacks your sorry ass up in the morning. Is that what you want?"

"No sir. But these men are assigned to me, and I was told no one but—" the Lieutenant began to declare, before the Captain cut him off.

"If you don't like what I'm doing here write a letter to Truman or maybe even MacArthur himself, just get out of my face!" With that, Lt. Jones stormed out of the room.

"Alright, I have a list of men I need to follow me right now. When I call your names grab your bags and check in with Staff Sgt. Doogan out by the truck."

Harry poked Steve. "Did you hear that? Staff Sgt. Doogan! How many Doogan's can there be in this damn army? This has got to be some sort of a set up to get us old guys together in one big group. If anyone could pull that off it would be Franny."

"Not only that, but did you hear him say, Lt. Col Fontaine?" Steve whispered back.

Steve smiled as the Captain took the list from his pocket, "Shrider, Edward; Jensen, Harold; Kenrude, Steven; Sanchez, Israel. Fall out."

As the men left the building, Franny let out a hoot. "Damn, we rescued you boys from a fate worse than death. Welcome to Alpha Company, Third Battalion 187th Parachute Infantry Regiment boys. Climb aboard and we'll be on our way to your new home."

As the Captain strolled from the building he yelled at Franny, "Get this truck started before all hell breaks loose."

"Yes, sir!" Franny responded, jumping behind the wheel. Seconds later they were rolling down a quiet tree-lined road heading south. Several miles later they pulled into a brightly lit courtyard and stopped. The men jumped from the truck, forming a circle around Franny and the Captain. After shaking hands, the smiling Captain addressed them.

"I'm Captain Fargo, your company commander. Some of you may already know my able assistant tonight, Sgt. Doogan. He will get you settled in my NCO barracks behind the truck. Get some sleep and we'll discuss matters in the morning. Doogan, when you get them settled in we have one more thing to accomplish tonight. Don't take long."

"Understood, sir," Sgt. Doogan responded with a salute.

Franny quickly walked the men to their quarters. "Look guys, I can't stay as you heard. Get some sleep and you'll get the full buzz in the morning. We've got a great mess hall here, breakfast starts at 0500 and runs until 0630 for right now. Sleep well guys, we'll talk tomorrow."

"Good night, Franny. Thanks for everything," Steve said, slapping his old buddy on the shoulder.

About 0530, the four men walked to the mess hall. The smell of fresh coffee and bacon filled the courtyard. Since Steve and Harry hadn't eaten that much since they left home, they were ready for a good solid breakfast. They had barely started eating when Franny came over with his tray. "How are you sad sacks doing this morning?"

"Sad sacks? Well, you can knock that crap off, Doogan. We may have been out for a while, but now we're here to straighten out the mess you created," Eddie Shrider responded, smiling.

"We're all good, Franny, real good. Did I hear Fontaine is a Lieutenant Colonel now?" Harry inquired.

"Yeah, he got the promotion right when the war broke out. They pulled him from his cushy job at the Pentagon and sent him here to get things rolling with the 187th. Believe me, things aren't good here or anywhere else in this man's army. Everything has kind of gone downhill since the Pacific

War ended, it's a damn shame. You'll be shocked as you get into things. All the politicians, all the brass, they figured we would never get into another war since we have the A-bomb. So our troop levels are terrible, they suck, and what we do have are ill-equipped and poorly trained. Many of our vehicles are in tough condition, too. Our mechanics have to cannibalize parts from one truck to keep another going. We don't have ammunition to do much training, and the same goes for our artillery and tanks, too. That's why the North Koreans are kicking our butts so badly," Franny explained to the four stunned men.

"So, how did we end up here with you?" Steve inquired with a smile.

"Well, I was involved with jump training before the war broke out. And believe me, I was getting pretty sick of some of the attitudes I was running into with recruits and brass. I was thinking of getting out. Then Fontaine shows up and asks me to join the 187th, so I've kind of been his aide, the 'get things done, or else' NCO. He told me to watch the list of veterans coming back and to snatch up anyone I thought would be good for the regiment. Well, when I saw your names, it was time to screw with Lt. Jones, and steal you away from that idiot. But believe me, this is no cake walk, and it starts right after we get uniforms and talk to Col. Fontaine," Franny explained with a very concerned look on his face.

"This is going to be dead serious, and we don't have much time," he added.

After breakfast, the men were fitted for uniforms. They were all surprised to see they were wearing Staff Sergeant stripes. Franny then delivered them to headquarters to see the Colonel. After several minutes, they were ushered into a small meeting room where Col. Fontaine was waiting. After shaking hands and exchanging a few pleasantries, he told the men to have a seat.

"Men, the army as you knew it has fallen apart to a dangerous degree. Men seem to lack discipline and training, and most of all leaders that can get them ready to fight this damn war. We need to be ready to ship out by mid-September. Right now, I would guess most of these men will throw away their weapons and join the South Korean Army in full retreat. That's a fact men, it's that bad! We have filled most of the positions we need except for A-company, which is a disaster.

Kenrude, you will have first platoon. Jensen second, Shrider third, Wentworth fourth and Sanchez will have our new fifth platoon. You met your company commander last night, Capt. Fargo. Your First Sergeant will be Sergeant Francis Doogan, Franny, who you should all know. As you are aware, both of them were airborne men in Europe so they know the score. Any questions?"

Steve raised his hand. "Sir, are these men parachute ready?"

"Good question, Sgt. Kenrude. Yes, they are all certified paratroopers. However, they lack every aspect of being a soldier that made you men great. Dig into them and make them learn. Give them some sort of chance to stay alive when we get to Korea. You need to understand, today's army was not ready to go to war. Right now we're scrambling for men, equipment and weapons, weapons that work. We have men busting open crates of World War Two weapons, degreasing them and getting them ready to be used, and some of them were in tough shape when they were crated. Some of our men haven't done much firing with the weapons they have, due to lack of ammunition. I had a truck load show up yesterday, though, so get these guys out on the range. Get these guys in the shape you were in when we left for France. If they're dead they don't do us any good, you all know that." Col. Fontaine looked the men over for a minute before leaving the room.

"That's it in a nut shell, men, just like I told you earlier. Let's get to work now," Franny declared, and stood up to go. "One more thing, just like in Europe we all want to come back alive. If we fail these guys here today, most of them, plus ourselves, will come back in a box, and I ain't letting that happen."

Steve looked at the rest of the men. "Franny is right. This is our one and only chance to make a real difference. Let's do the job to the best of our ability. These guys deserve that much from us."

Franny led the men from the meeting room to his office, where he gave them lists of the men they would have in their platoons. For the next several hours they toured some of the training facilities they would be using over the next few months. Franny took notes as the men threw out suggestions for improvements, and ideas to stiffen up the training and make it more realistic.

CHAPTER 4
THEIR WORK BEGINS

Around 0800, a convoy of trucks arrived in the company area. As the men unloaded, Franny's staff assigned them to barracks. After stowing their gear, Sgt. Doogan ordered an immediate formation. As the men fell in, the five Staff Sergeants took charge of their platoons. They spent the balance of the day on physical fitness drills and the art of preparing a proper jump pack. Steve found out that Franny had been correct, some of his men did not have weapons. Others had weapons that failed to function properly. He quickly found out that was the case with the rest of the company as well.

After conferring with Col. Fontaine, several phone calls were made. The next morning the entire company was marched down to weapons procurement where the sergeants made sure everyone received an operational weapon. They also took time to make sure each squad had one man with a Browning automatic rifle, and each squad leader had a Thompson submachine gun. Once this was completed, they marched to the firing range where they spent the rest of the day sighting, practice firing, and qualifying with their new weapons.

That evening after chow, Steve met with his four squad leaders. "As you know, I was given permission to pick my own squad leaders, but I decided to leave things as they are unless I feel you're not doing your jobs.

So Kilburn you keep first squad; Martinez, second; Whitebear, third; and Hagen, fourth. I want discipline and Army regulations enforced to the letter, and I'll expect reports on those who don't comply. We'll drum those men out and bring in new people who give a damn. I want our barracks ship shape every morning before we fall out for training, and I want the grounds around the buildings kept clean and orderly as it should be. I don't want to find one cigarette butt anywhere. If I do, that means a five mile run and extra calisthenics for a week. Everyone falls out with their basic paratrooper pack with weapon each morning, no excuses. We run before chow every day. We'll be eating lots of C-Rations in the field. These men need to learn how to exist on the bare minimum while in combat. Any questions? Anybody want to resign?"

None of the men said a word at first, then Sgt. Whitebear stood up. "Sgt. Kenrude, I have one man who needs to go. He disrupts the entire squad and challenges me every day in front of the men. His name is Demytrie. He's a real loser. I'm afraid he'll just muck up the works and get these good men killed."

Steve nodded his head. "Let me have a crack at him for a few days and we'll see how things go from that point. Is that workable for you?"

Smiling while nodding his head in agreement, Sgt. Whitebear sat down.

The following day during weapons and bayonet training, Steve kept a close eye on third squad. The second time he observed Demytrie arguing with Whitebear, he walked over to the men.

"Demytrie, let's go for a walk," Steve yelled at the insolent soldier.

"Why, Sergeant? What's up? You got some sort of bee in your bonnet for a poor Greek kid?"

The rest of the men laughed as Steve stood silently in front of him, shaking his head.

"What's the matter Sergeant? Cat got your tongue?" Demytrie added, causing howls of laughter from among the ranks of the squad.

Before Demytrie even knew what happened, Steve grabbed him by the arm, spun him around and threw him to the ground.

"You can't do that, Sergeant. I'll have you up on charges!" Demytrie cried out.

"Yes, I can do that, Demytrie! I was using you as part of a demonstration to show the rest of your squad how to take down an enemy in hand to hand combat. Now get your sorry ass off the ground, grab your gear and follow me," Steve demanded sternly, staring at the impertinent young Greek.

After they had walked about a hundred yards from the squad, Steve turned to face Demytrie. "Listen to me young man. This is not a game. Men like you screw up in combat all the time. Personally, I could give a shit if you get your sorry ass blown away. But I don't want anyone else killed because of your stupidity. The life of every soldier is precious to me. It should be that way for you, too. Now, if you want to be a screw up, you can kiss those jump wings goodbye and I'll send you off to some ground pounding infantry unit where you can be on latrine cleaning duty a couple times a week. How does that sound to you?"

After taking a deep breath, Demytrie looked Steve squarely in the eye. "I don't think you could transfer me out. I won these wings fair and square, same as you did. I'm here to stay and that's that. There ain't any crap you can do to me that I can't take. I grew up in a pretty tough neighborhood where you had to kick ass or get yours kicked. I don't think you would have survived, Sergeant. And that's a fact." Smiling, Demytrie spit right next to Steve's boot.

"Alright. I accept your challenge. Drop your pack and weapon right here. I want you to run laps on that service road until I tell you to stop, get your ass moving right now," Steve ordered angrily.

Once more Demytrie spit on the ground, nearly on top of Steve's boots before beginning his run.

Harry walked over to Steve. "Get rid of that son of a bitch. He's not worth the time. We need to get these men kicked into shape. He'll just gum up the works like Whitebear said."

"I don't know, Harry. I think the little bastard has potential. He's never had discipline in his life. He's just like a wild horse that needs to be broken." Steve wore a sly smile as he spoke.

After an hour of jogging around the service road, Steve held out a canteen to Demytrie. He just turned his head to continue running. "Have it your way, tough guy," Steve yelled, as he emptied the cool fresh water from the canteen onto the red Georgia clay.

About an hour later, completely soaked, Demytrie fell to the ground and stayed there. Steve ordered everyone to stay away from him. Defiantly, Demytrie worked his way back to his knees before standing erect. With his knees still shaking, he began running, very slowly. After about twenty yards, he collapsed again. This time Steve and Whitebear walked out to him. Kneeling down, Steve handed him another canteen. "Slowly soldier, drink it slowly."

"Screw you, Sergeant. I don't need it. Just give me a minute and I'll be ready to go again." As he pushed Whitebear away, he struggled to his feet. He staggered for about ten feet before falling face first to the ground.

One more time Steve handed the canteen to Demytrie. "Drink, son. You're finished."

After a few minutes, Demytrie finally sat up. "What's next, Sergeant?"

"Glad you asked. We're all being driven back to the cantonment area, as it's been a long day. You, my friend, get to hike back. You can have this canteen and a candy bar I have in my pack. Report to me as soon as you get back. Oh, and by the way, it's supposed to rain. I'll be taking your poncho," Steve added, before he stood up and walked away with Whitebear.

Around eight that evening, soaked and muddy, Demytrie walked into the orderly room. Steve was sitting in the office discussing training projects with the other squad Sergeants.

Timidly, Demytrie walked up to the door, "Reporting as ordered, Sergeant."

"Good job, soldier," Steve called out, as he looked over the bedraggled man. "Head over to the barracks. Whitebear has a bag lunch for you. Take a shower and get that weapon cleaned. You have guard duty at 2300. Any questions?"

Without a word, Demytrie turned and walked away.

The following morning the company went out on a field march, with each platoon going their own way. About midday, Steve stopped his company along a ridge-line overlooking a small valley. Taking out his binoculars he scanned the area closely.

After several minutes he called his squad leaders together. "Alright, we're going to dig in along this ridge line. I want third and fourth squads to dig in on the south side of the road. Whitebear, you are on the end closest to the road. Make sure Demytrie is on the far end of your line. First and second platoon, dig in on the north side of the road. Martinez you are the far west squad."

Immediately, the squad leaders put their men to work. Steve stood back watching his men. Some of them began digging good deep shelters that could save their lives in a mortar attack. Others dug semi-deep holes that would never offer much protection in combat. A few others screwed around, never actually digging any type of proper protection, despite what they were told.

About two o'clock, Steve observed two planes circling the area. "Take cover!" He called out from the road so both teams could hear him. The planes dove on the ridge line, dropping bags full of powder as they screamed overhead. After circling around, they made a second pass pummeling the area again. As they flew off, Harry's platoon attacked from the valley, using cover and concealment to work their way up the steep bank. Simultaneously, Sgt. Shrider's third platoon attacked the far eastern side of Whitebear's defensive line. Total chaos ensued as the line collapsed.

In no time, Harry's platoon had over run third squad and most of fourth squad. Shrider's men took prisoners and captured weapons. Once Steve was completely satisfied, he blew a whistle ending the attack. Sgt. Doogan had come along to watch the exercise. He was angry beyond words as he watched the disaster unfold. The platoon Sergeants had their men sit on the bank in the shade as Sgt. Doogan prepared to address them.

Before he could speak, Sgt. Whitebear informed Steve that Demytrie was missing. "That's fine, Whitebear. He was probably captured by the enemy. He's most likely dead somewhere in the woods. You can go join your men. It's all good," Steve replied, with a slight smile.

Looking confused, and a bit concerned, Whitebear nodded his head before walking off to join the others.

"Well gentlemen, you've had an eye opener today," Franny began. "You saw what can happen if you don't follow orders. Most of you from the south side of the road would be dead or captured. You would have left a hole in the line for the enemy to flow through, and move against your rear areas. In other words, you would all be dead. You best get your act together because you won't get a second chance in real combat. I've seen it happen and it happens fast. No one, and I mean no one, gets a second chance when the shit comes down. You either do it right or you die"

As the men prepared to march back for evening chow, Whitebear reported that Demytrie was still missing.

Once again, Steve told him to forget about it.

About ten o'clock that evening, Demytrie walked into the orderly room. He was a sight, mud from head to toe.

"Where have you been, troop? I have you listed as AWOL. I've already called the MP's to arrest you on sight. Want to tell me where you've been?" Steve inquired, as he leaned back in his desk chair.

"I was taken prisoner, Sergeant. The bastards threw me in a swamp, they tied my hands and feet and dragged me through a damned briar patch. Then they tied me to a tree and left. I must have been there three hours or more. When it got dark, they snuck up on me and set the grass around me on fire. Sergeant, I was so scared I pissed my pants." With that he began to cry. After a few moments, he looked up at Steve. "I'm ready to take that transfer now. I want out of the airborne. I quit. I don't want no more of this game playing shit. Send me on my way, please."

"No! You can't quit, Demytrie. You just found out what it's like to be a man and be scared as hell. You learned tonight what can happen if you screw up in combat. I'm depending on you to help get these men ready for Korea. I'm depending on you to take Whitebear's place if something should happen to him. You're my ace in the hole, soldier. Do you really want to walk away from all you've worked for? Because if you do, I have a transfer order right here on top of my desk. Sign it, and just like that, you're on a bus heading to Leonard Wood and Combat Infantry School first thing in the morning. Your call soldier, you can be a man or you can be a quitter. Which is it gonna be?"

Taking a deep breath, Demytrie replied quietly, "No sergeant, I don't want to quit. I need the extra fifty-five dollars a month to help my mom and little sister back home."

Steve felt real compassion for the young soldier standing in front of him. There was no doubt they had broken him tonight. Now it was time to build him back up. "Glad to hear it. Go get cleaned up, son. Whitebear has some chow for you and a new uniform. Go ahead and toss that one. Get a good night's rest. Tomorrow's a new day, soldier. I can guarantee the sun will be much brighter."

Nodding his head, Demytrie began walking away. Slowly, he turned to face Steve. "I won't let you down, Sergeant. Not tomorrow, not ever. You can count on me."

"I know I can, son. Now go take care of yourself," Steve replied, knowing he now had one solid trooper he would always be able to depend on when the worst came down.

Over the next few weeks, all the hard work began to pay off. Quickly, the men were becoming a well-oiled machine. They worked as a team while looking out for each other. Their jumps went smoothly with very few problems. Harry began to see them more like the Charlie Company of World War Two every day. It was great to see them maturing into tough airborne soldiers.

The brass at headquarters decided one more major full equipment jump was necessary before they would be comfortable enough to send the 187th off to Korea. The jump was scheduled for early morning August 20th. During the early morning hours, Steve was awakened by heavy thunder storms rolling across Fort Benning. Wind driven torrents of rain mixed with light hail created a tremendous clatter against the windows of the barracks. Rolling from his bunk at 0430, he was sure the jump would be canceled. Quietly, he began reorganizing the training program for the day on a clip board next to his bed. However, at 0450 a runner from battalion headquarters arrived, informing the platoon sergeants that the jump would go as scheduled. Somewhat upset, Steve looked over at Harry who was lying awake on his bunk.

"What kind of bullshit is this? We both damn well know how to fight battles in all kinds of weather. But the possibility for injuries goes way up when we jump for no reason in weather like this."

"I know, Stevie boy. You're preaching to the choir over here. But orders are orders. Let's just get the men ready and get it done," Harry replied, pulling on his boots.

At 0500, the men were assembled in the courtyard. After roll call, First Sgt. Doogan told the men to stand at ease. "Alright men, listen up. We're not running this morning because the jump is on as scheduled. Eat breakfast then report back to your barracks and suit up. Trucks should be here about 0630." With that Franny turned the men over to their platoon sergeants.

Steve told his men to form a circle around him. "Okay everybody, I need your total attention. As you know everything is wet. Be cautious when you land so you don't slide and break any bones. With the rain and humidity, you may run into a thick haze on your way down. Keep your eyes open for trees and other obstacles that may hurt you. Most of all, use your best common sense. Now fall out and get some chow."

As the men headed toward the mess hall, Demytrie walked up to Steve, "Sergeant, have you ever jumped into a heavy haze or fog before? It just looks a bit scary to me."

Steve looked at the worried paratrooper. "Oh sure, we jumped several times in England, and believe me you can get some real fog over there. It rolls back and forth and mucks up everything. I landed in a tree once I never even saw. Luckily, my chute shredded and I just slid to the ground like an angel until my toes were firmly implanted in the mud."

"So, no big worries then, Sarg," Demytrie inquired nervously.

"Nope, you'll do fine. Like I said, keep your eyes open and be prepared to reposition at the last minute if you need to. Remember, T-7 chutes don't adjust well at low altitudes. So, just keep your wits about you and you'll look like a pro." Steve reassured the paratrooper with a slap on the back.

By 0900, the men were beginning to load aboard their C-47 Skytrain's as the sky began to darken.

Captain Jellison, the pilot of Steve's plane came down from the cockpit. "Sarg, what's the latest word on the weather? It's starting to look pretty damn threatening off to the southwest."

"It's not supposed to rain, last I heard, Captain. But I'm not so sure the weather people know what the hell they're talking about. In Minnesota, you think of taking cover when you see skies like this at mid-morning," Steve replied, scanning the fast dark moving clouds.

"Yeah, I'm from Kansas. I know storm clouds when I see them, and this doesn't look like good flying weather to me." The pilot agreed, shaking his head.

Steve pointed to a Jeep that was coming down the taxiway, stopping at each aircraft. "Well, looks like we're about to get orders to abort, Captain."

Seconds later the Jeep pulled up to Steve and his pilot. "Headquarters wants you moving in fifteen minutes. Saddle up and get the show on the road, boys." A young second lieutenant called out to them.

"Hey, what the hell, Lieutenant? Have you seen those damn clouds? The wind aloft has to be in excess of fifty miles an hour. There's no way we'll keep these lumbering over weight Skytrain's in any kind of formation without cracking into one another. Did anyone think of that?" Capt. Jellison barked back at the lieutenant, who was already shaking his head.

"Just do your job, Captain. That's what the army is paying you the big bucks for," the lieutenant snapped back before racing off to the next plane.

"Well, you can bet I'll be dealing with that little smart ass weasel when I get back. That was about as insubordinate as you can get. You heard him, Sarg. I'll be calling you in to testify," the angry Captain shouted before walking back over to his C-47.

As the jump master secured his door, the massive Pratt and Whitney engines spun to life. After adjusting his sitting position, Steve could easily make out dark blue flames emanating from the exhaust ports. Sometimes watching the flame filled Steve with excitement and courage. Other times it was more like a bad omen just waiting to take revenge on the paratroopers inside. Today, there was sort of an ominous look to it. Once in a while the flame broke into several longer tongues that seemed to curl and dance in the air behind the engine. It unnerved him a little today.

Finally, the plane began rolling down the taxiway. Steve looked down the middle of the plane. The men from first and second squads appeared to be at ease. They were all taking this as just one more routine jump the army wanted them to experience before moving on.

Minutes later, the massive C-47 rose into the menacing sky. The turbulence reminded Steve of the D-Day jump into Normandy. The weather had been pretty lousy for several days, giving them a very rough flight across the English Channel. But that was World War Two, and this was just training. He felt the aircraft circling the airfield to gain altitude as the pilot turned his cumbersome transport southwest toward their drop zones. The pilot had been accurate about the wind. The plane bounced and weaved like a bobber on rough water. Several men began to get airsick, even Steve had to force down his breakfast a couple of times. This was the worst flying weather he had ever experienced. A bright flash to their left followed by a tremendous roar shook the aircraft. It was immediately followed by another flash to the right and a bolt of lightning streaking across the ever darkening sky.

Instantly Steve's mind yelled out, *'Flack! Flack damn it.'* Sweat ran down his face. But there was no flack here in Georgia. This was lightning. They had flown directly into a thunderstorm. The plane shook violently as the air surrounding the lightning bolt became electrically charged. Steve closed his eyes, waiting for the burst of thunder that was only seconds away. The concussion was incredible. It felt like a two hundred pound bomb detonating right outside the thin aluminum skin of their C-47. Quickly, Steve sat forward staring out the window across the aisle. Bright blue flames roared from the wing of an aircraft slightly above them in the formation.

Apparently it had been struck by that last bolt of lightning. Whose men were on that aircraft? Were they his third and fourth squads? Was it Harry or Franny? Suddenly all the fears and trepidations of World War Two filled Steve's mind. It was really happening all over again. Men were dying and others were going to be injured for life. What the hell was he doing here? "Jump, someone jump! What are they waiting for? Where the hell are they?" Steve watched frantically for signs of life in the other aircraft as sweat ran down his forehead.

Seconds later, he could see parachutes opening as men dove from the crippled aircraft. Steve closed his eyes, letting out a sigh of relief. Reopening his eyes, he watched flames spread inward toward the fuel tanks. Before he could brace himself, the plane disintegrated in a massive ball of flame. But that was not the worst of it. As their plane rocked wildly, jagged debris ripped holes in the fuselage. Flames roared from their left engine as the bent prop gyrated, spinning uselessly on the engine. Men screamed and swore as panic overtook the otherwise calm paratroopers. They all wanted off the plane as they knew their aircraft was in serious trouble. The jump master swiftly stood up, opening the door and yelling, "Hook up, and get out!"

Instantly, the men began moving to the door as Steve helped the jump master into his parachute.

"Go, go, keep going," Steve yelled, as one man froze in the door. He couldn't understand what was keeping the man from jumping. In a rage, Steve approached the frozen man. "What the hell are you waiting for? These men will die if you don't go!"

The soldier pointed to large tongues of yellow and orange flame roaring back along the fuselage. Looking down, Steve could see several parachutes quickly being consumed by flames.

Nothing like this had ever happened before in all of Steve's jumps. His mind spun uselessly for a moment, not sure of what to do. But he had to do something quickly, or he and all his men were going to die a horrible death. "Drop your chutes and weapons. Free-fall away from the plane before you pull the reserve!" Steve called out to the remaining paratroopers. "Now, go!"

Immediately, the men followed Steve's command before bailing out the door.

After dumping his main chute, Steve followed the jump master, Capt. Jellison and his co-pilot out the door. Counting to ten, Steve pulled the rip cord for his reserve chute. It opened flawlessly, but did not slow him down as much as the T-7 main parachute normally would. Looking down, he saw a large opening, a grassy looking field where several other men had already landed. He aimed for the edge of the field to avoid anyone on the ground. Landing with a solid thud, he felt pain in both his knees. After dropping the remainder of his gear, Steve walked slowly toward the middle of the field. The pain subsided as he continued walking, which was encouraging.

"Form on me! Form on me!" Steve called out through the driving wind.

Instantly, Sgt. Martinez arrived with ten men. "We lost at least three, Sarg. I saw their chutes on fire as they came down. For some reason they never opened their reserves. One is right over there near the wood line. I think the others are somewhere in the woods behind him. Do you want us to have a look?"

"Yeah, that would be great. You saw them, so direct the men where to look. Bring their bodies back over to that broken tree near the wood line," Steve instructed his efficient young squad leader.

After completing a head count with Sgt. Kilburn, one more man was unaccounted for. Steve was about to organize a search party just as their pilot, Captain Jellison, came walking toward them. "Sarg, I found one of your men over there by that small clump of trees. He's had it. His neck is broken." Sgt. Kilburn instantly took three men to collect their comrade's remains.

After the bodies were collected and carefully wrapped in parachutes,

Steve checked his compass. "Alright. We'll walk back toward the northeast. If I'm correct on our position, we should soon come across a north-south road. Let's move out!"

Within minutes, they came across survivors from the aircraft that had been struck by lightning. Steve approached the bewildered looking group. "I'm Staff Sergeant Kenrude, A-Company. Who are you guys with?"

Several men spoke out at once, "Dog Company, third platoon."

"Any cadre left among you guys?" Steve inquired of the dejected band of paratroopers.

"No, we haven't seen anyone, Sarg. We've looked all over. We have two dead over there near the power pole, and one over there by the drainage ditch. But we haven't found either of our squad leaders yet," one of the paratroopers explained.

"Alright, take three men with you to gather up your dead. Wrap them in chutes and place them on the bank of the drainage ditch. I'll take the rest of your men with me. When you're finished, follow us," Steve instructed the private before signaling everyone else to follow."

In about twenty minutes, the paratroopers came across the north-south dirt road Steve had counted on. In the distance they could make out a Jeep coming toward them from the south. The driver of the Jeep pulled to a stop in front of Captain Jellison.

"Are you guys all survivors of those two planes?"

"Yes Corporal, we are. Are there any other vehicles coming out this way?" Captain Jellison inquired.

"Yes sir, four deuce-and-a-halfs and three ambulances are just a short way behind me. Lt. Brigham is leading the search party in his Jeep," the corporal explained, as he looked back down the road.

Minutes later the convoy arrived just as the corporal described. Captain Jellison walked up to Lt. Brigham. He explained the location of the bodies along with information regarding the two missing squad leaders.

Once the search party emptied the trucks, Steve directed the paratroopers to climb aboard. They drove roughly half a mile before coming across one of Dog Company's squad leaders, who was sitting alone alongside the road.

Steve jumped out of the truck to speak with him. "I'm Sgt. Kenrude, A-company, are you all right?"

"Sgt. Johnson from Dog Company. I'm not sure where anyone else is right now. I kind of twisted my left ankle when I landed on a tree stump. It hurts pretty bad. So I made it to the road and figured eventually someone would come along and pick me up."

Smiling Steve replied. "Good move. We have everyone except your squad leaders. You have three dead for sure. They are being loaded up by a search party as we speak. Have you seen any of your squad leaders?"

"Yeah, I don't think Sergeant Thorpe made it out of the plane. The jump master was hurt bad, Thorpe was trying to slip a chute on him. I tried to help but he screamed at me to go. I couldn't have been out of the plane more than fifteen seconds when it went up like the fourth of July. I'm sure he went down with the wreckage. What a damn waste of good men. Did we prove anything to anyone today, Staff Sergeant?" The dejected paratrooper inquired sarcastically.

Steve put his arm around the shaking squad leader. "Yeah we did, Johnson. We proved good men will do whatever they need to do to survive in war. No matter how bad today feels, there will be worse ones down the road. I promise you that, as sure as we're standing here. Chalk it up to whatever you want Johnson, but keep one thing in mind. You and every man on these trucks lived to fight another day. It may not be much, but it's something worth hanging on to."

After taking a deep breath, Sgt. Johnson nodded his head. Steve and another paratrooper helped Sgt. Johnson climb aboard one of the trucks.

Thirty minutes later, the rescue convoy rolled up to the cantonment area. As the men jumped down, Harry and Franny came running through the crowd.

"Thank God!" Harry exclaimed, as he grabbed hold of Steve. "You alright, Stevie boy?"

"Yeah, my knees are a little sore. I landed pretty hard with my reserve chute. But I think they'll be alright in a couple of days," Steve responded, shaking hands with Franny.

"Man, we have been worried sick. When shit started happening they called off the damned jump and flew us back here. A third plane was damaged by lightning on the way back. One guy was killed. How many did you lose, Steve?" Franny asked, as the men walked slowly toward their barracks.

"I lost four and Dog Company lost three for sure, maybe four. We're not sure about one of their squad leaders right now. He may not have made it out of the plane before it went down. But, our plane crew survived. Again, we don't know about the other crew. Damn! We lost nearly a squad of men over some stupid-ass training session that meant absolutely nothing. What a damned shame. What is wrong with those fools attempting something like this?" Steve demanded angrily.

After several days Steve was still experiencing quite a bit of pain in his right knee, so he signed up for sick call. The doctor examined Steve's knee before rolling his stool back towards a small desk. "Well Sergeant, I think we need to get a good x-ray of that knee to determine what kind of damage you might have. This is your lucky day. If I find anything wrong, you won't be going to Korea. You can stay here to train new paratroopers as they arrive."

"No, we won't be doing any x-rays then, Doc. I'm not backing out on my men this late in the game. As far as I am concerned it's nothing more than a slight sprain. I'll be just fine," Steve responded as he stood up from the exam table.

The doctor shook his head as he peered over at Steve. "I can have you medically held you know. You came to me, I didn't come to you. I think you have a problem and I am not sure how it will affect your performance in combat. My instincts are to notify your commander that you're unfit for any more jumps until we work on that knee."

Steve grew angrier than he had been in a long time. "Listen to me, Doc. I'm going with my men. I don't give a damn how you feel about anything. Without a leader they know and trust, many of those boys will die. I will not have it on my conscience that I abandoned them when they needed me most! Is that clear, Doctor!"

The door to the exam room swung open. A large male nurse walked in. "Is there a problem, Doctor?"

The doctor shook his head. "No, the Sergeant and I are just having a lively discussion on the subject of responsibility. You can go."

After the nurse left, the doctor cleared his throat before looking up at Steve. "Responsibility! That word covers a lot of territory when it comes to leading men into combat. I'm sorry, Sergeant, but I'm just not sure you're up to what may be necessary in a tough situation. However, on the other hand, I do understand your concerns for your men. That is admirable to say the least. So I will write on the chart that you have a sprained right knee and should be on light duty for a week. I'll give you several wraps you can place on the knee as long as you think you need it. I just hope neither of us regret this decision, Sergeant."

Taking a deep breath, Steve nodded his head. "I'm sorry for losing my temper, Doc. But these men mean the world to me, and I don't want them going into combat without me. Thanks for what you're doing. I promise you won't regret your decision. I've been hurt worse."

As the doctor prepared to leave the room, he smiled and patted Steve on the shoulder. "Bring them home alive, Sergeant."

Entering the cantonment area, Steve ran into his favorite first Sergeant.

It was Franny and Col. Fontaine, out making inspections. "What did you find out about your knee, Kenrude?" the Colonel inquired.

Quickly Steve handed over the form he had received from the doctor. "Light sprain, sir. I'm on light duty for a week. He also gave me a couple of wraps I can put on it for strength."

"Fabulous, that's just great," Col. Fontaine responded with a smile. "As terrible as it sounds, we can replace the men who were killed easily enough. But a combat veteran like you is irreplaceable. We need all the experienced men we can get if we're going to pull this off. You had me worried there for a moment, Kenrude. Glad you're still with us."

Sir, I have a serious question to ask. How are we going to replace the men we lost, it's going to be tough jumping into battle short-handed," Steve inquired.

The Colonel looked at Steve and Franny. "We have some older paratroopers training in Hawaii. They are going to be shipped over to Japan to join up with us to fill the vacancies. They are good men, and it should all work out well. Believe me, if that wouldn't have been possible, I would have fought like hell to get our orders changed until we were up to par."

After thanking the Colonel for the information, the men walked away in different directions. Steve blew out a deep breath of air, just hoping he had made the right decision. If the knee were to go during a combat jump, he would kick himself the rest of his life. But for now he would take it easy and hope it was nothing more than a serious sprain.

That evening, Franny and Steve sat outside the operations room enjoying a cold beer after a long day. "That knee going to be alright, Stevie boy?" Franny asked as he looked at the ice bag Steve had wrapped around it.

"Oh yeah, don't worry about me, Franny. I'll be just fine in a week. My squad leaders will get the work done until I get moving full speed again. We'll be ready to go when General MacArthur calls for us," Steve replied with a confident smile.

Franny nodded, feeling good with Steve's response. "So how has civilian life been, Steve? Ever miss the army? I'm damn glad I stayed in. I found a great gal and she'll move anywhere the army sends me. And my little girl is my pride and joy. Truth is, I couldn't think of anything else I'd rather do."

"You know Franny, I miss guys like you and the camaraderie we have. But on nights like this, I miss sitting on the back porch with Karen and the kids. We have a great life. I miss them so much. The letters, they just don't do it for me this time. Not like back in Europe when a good letter from Karen kept me pumped for a week. No, this time it's different. I worry every day about Karen and the kids. I was really happy and things were going well. I just pray I can get back home again. This is not what I wanted to be doing this time of year, or ever again, actually. But, being with you and Harry again is the best. If I have to do this all over again, I wouldn't want to do it with anyone else. I trust the hell out of you guys."

Franny smiled. "You know, I told Darcie the other night I had to be the luckiest guy in the world. I have two of my best buddies in my company. What more could a guy ask for? These may not be the best conditions to be together, but I sure enjoy being with you."

Steve smiled. "You know that actually sounds a bit crazy. When I think of the crazy Francis Martin Doogan III that I first met, holding that damn big B.A.R., I have to laugh. But thinking of you holding a small child makes me want to laugh all the more. It just doesn't fit what I knew of you in the past. But I'm proud of you, Franny. You've done great for yourself."

Franny busted out laughing. "Yeah, kind of a contrast isn't it. But that Franny has mellowed a bit. And besides, I would never take him home with me. He belongs here on the base, not at home with Darcie and my daughter. They deserve better than that two bit crazy cowboy."

"Here, here!" Steve called out, as he clanged his bottle up against Franny's. "Spoken like a true Charlie Company veteran and responsible Dad."

As the first of September approached, Steve went to see Col. Fontaine regarding a seven day furlough home before they shipped over to Korea.

Col. Fontaine listened carefully to everything Steve told him. "I'm so sorry, Steve I just can't do it. My orders are very strict on that matter. No one leaves unless there is a documented family emergency. I know how badly every man in this unit wants to see their loved ones before they leave, and that includes me. Martha wants to kick my butt since I can't come home. I'm going to miss the birth of my grandchild. Nevertheless, she understands military protocol. Besides, I need you here. We need to hone these men to a razor sharp edge. We need to be the best, maybe even better than we were back in Normandy. This is not going to be a cake walk. From what I'm hearing, this war is going to be as brutal as Bastogne or worse. These guys need your guidance, Steve. We just have to suck it up, I guess. You me, all of us."

Nodding his head, Steve understood the Colonel's dilemma. "Alright sir, I'll hang tough and get through this just like everyone else. But to be honest sir, these guys are good and they are ready to go. They'll make us all proud. You can count on that."

Col. Fontaine stood up to shake Steve's hand. "Hearing that from you makes me feel very confident. I'm so glad to have guys like you, Franny, Harry and Shrider covering my butt. By the way, how's that knee doing? I haven't heard anything from our First Sergeant about you lately."

"It's a lot better, sir. That week of light duty made a big difference, and I've been careful since then. I'm ready to go, sir." Steve shook hands with Col. Fontaine before leaving the office. He was happy he didn't have to mislead the Colonel. His knee actually was doing great. He just hoped it would continue to heal. Walking back to their orderly room, Steve knew Karen would be upset when she found out he couldn't come home. But there was simply nothing he could do.

On September 3rd, Col. Fontaine called the battalion together for a major formation. "Gentlemen, your days of training are over. We have been activated. I cannot tell you where we are headed first. But you all know Korea is the end game. We've done all we can to get you men ready. Now it's up to you to do your best for your country. Get your gear packed, letters written and be ready to roll out tomorrow morning at 0630. We'll leave by train right from the base. Try getting some sleep and be ready in the morning. Company commanders and platoon sergeants, meet me at my headquarters in thirty minutes.

When everyone was assembled in the meeting room Col. Fontaine walked in. "I'm not going to sugarcoat this one bit, men. Korea is a disaster, and we may not be able to save it. The war may be over before we even get there. MacArthur only had four divisions on occupation status in Japan. Most of them were undermanned, poorly equipped, and well out of shape to handle the rigors of combat. They were mostly garrison troops. Nevertheless, they are being thrown into the mix to help slow the advancing North Koreans. If we get there in time, we may be one of the few well trained, well equipped regiments in country. Now I'm telling you this in confidence so you are aware of the situation before we land on Korean soil. Do not repeat this information to your men. We need them at the top of their form if we do get into combat. That's all I have for now. I'll see you in the morning as we load up."

That evening the five platoon sergeants sat around the orderly room discussing the Colonel's comments. "This just scares the hell out of me," Sanchez stated boldly. "My men are ready to be sure. But at least when we dropped into Europe we had a game plan. Sure, we got dropped all over creation, but the plan remained intact. This just sounds like a death sentence to me. I'm worried about my men. I don't want them slaughtered by the damn North Koreans."

After finishing a cup of coffee, Sgt. Shrider looked at Sanchez. "I know what you mean. Beuzeville and Sainte Mere-Eglise had to be held. We all knew that, no matter the cost. And we did it. But this is a disaster. Does anyone have any sort of a plan to win this or are we just going to be cannon fodder so the big wigs can say, 'well we tried,' before the North Koreans polish us off."

Harry looked up at Eddie, "Hell, we made our own plans most the time in Europe. It was like we had guidelines, and we just went from there. I kind of think this might be the same if we do a combat jump. But if we are just thrown into the mix with poorly trained infantry, our men will be less than useful. I wish we could get some top of the line Intel as to what the situation is right now. What do you think, Steve?"

Looking at the other men Steve shook his head. "I have to agree. I'm very concerned. I spoke with Capt. Fargo this afternoon. He made it sound like we may be sacrificial lambs to do just what Eddie said. Cover the retreating butts of the Korean elite and American civilians. I don't want to be tossed into that role. It would be a waste of a lot of good men. I'm holding out hope that someone puts together a plan before we get there. MacArthur has to have some sort of idea what it will take to either win this war, or send the bastards back across the 38th parallel and hold them there. I guess we won't know until we get there."

After polishing off more coffee, the worried leaders retired for the night. None of them found any solace in the discussion that had just taken place. They all agreed on one thing. They had taken a bunch of poorly trained paratroopers and turned them into tough combat soldiers. It would be a shame to see them sacrificed for nothing.

The following morning under a hot Georgia sun the men waited in line to load aboard the train. After the officers were satisfied, the men filed into the waiting train as their names were checked off a manifest. This process reminded Steve of their trip from Camp Toccoa in Georgia to the waiting troop transports in New York, as they headed over to England in World War Two. He didn't look forward to the long cross country train ride, although it would give him plenty of time to write letters home. Once they sailed from California, he had no idea when there would be any type of mail exchange.

After double checking their lists, all the officers and NCO'S climbed aboard. Once the doors were sealed, the engineer throttled up the engines, heading the train on a westerly course. It would be one straight shot across the lower tier states, directly to San Diego. Sanchez was excited about their route. The train would pass just about a mile from where he grew up in New Mexico. It would be like old times seeing the dessert country where he played and rode horses as a youngster. He remembered how often he would sit up on the small rise near his home watching the great steam engines rolling across the very same tracks this train would be using. He dreamed of all the wonderful places the iron horse could take him someday in the future. Never had he imagined it would be taking him off to war again. Yet, it would be good to see his homeland once more before he left for war. It gave him a sense of comfort that the spirits of his family would be with him.

Eddie Shrider peered out the window at kids playing in a shallow river as the train rolled across a large wooden trestle. He thought back to his days as a child growing up along Lake Huron in Alpena, Michigan. He and his brothers loved swimming in the cold water during the long lazy summers, but now, he was the only one left. His older brother Karl was killed on Okinawa in 1945. His younger brother Ben was swept overboard off a tug boat on Lake Michigan, his body never recovered. That had been real tough on his mom and dad. His parents were happy when he returned home, and even though he had moved to Philadelphia to work in sports broadcasting, they knew that at least their surviving son would be safe from any major catastrophes. Now their hearts were broken at seeing him going off to war again. They just didn't understand it.

Franny made several attempts to write Darcie as the train rolled along, but he just couldn't seem to find the right words. He knew his folks would take good care of her and their daughter if anything happened to him. After all, his father was quite the philanthropist, and he didn't just sit on the Doogan fortune. His favorite charities were always well taken care of. Franny had to chuckle. He often wondered if the people receiving those generous checks knew how much of the money came from illegal liquor sales and gambling during prohibition. Grandfather Doogan had supplied liquor to some of the biggest gangsters in the country. There were rumors he had even supplied booze to Al Capone for quite some time. But all the fanfare surrounding the Doogan's hadn't been for Franny. He was happier in the army, and loved just being one of the guys. The thought of sitting on a corporate board wearing a stiff suit and tie every day was definitely not his thing.

Steve just let his mind wander back home to Glendale. He missed his family very much, and it hurt to think that Karen was going to have to endure all the pains of being a war-wife. Not knowing from day to day whether her husband was alive or missing, while having to take care of the children and the house. Her job as bookkeeper for the family business was a big job as well, but she had written that now it would be an escape for her. He knew Karen's mother and all of his family would give her plenty of support and help when it was needed. Gradually, Steve's eyes became heavy as he leaned back in his seat, and in short order he was sound asleep. Dreams of Karen and the children filled his sub-conscious, helping him to sleep rather soundly.

Likewise, Harry sat beside Steve, sound asleep. The gentle rolling of the passenger car made it quite easy to let their cares and worries drift away for a short period of time, though the idea of spending so much time on a troop transport at sea was not a fond memory for any of the veterans. At least this time, they wouldn't have to worry about being sunk by German U-Boats. Still, keeping discipline and order among so many tightly wound men would not be an easy assignment. All they could hope for were calm seas and light winds so an epidemic of sea sickness would not overcome the men.

CHAPTER 5
THE HOME FRONT

Alex and Mike were managing the farms affairs well, although they missed Steve's ability to coordinate several large projects at one time. The young men they hired throughout the year were more than adequate to keep the farm running effectively. Although planting season was late, it appeared Kenrude Farms was going to have a bumper crop of corn and more than enough fresh hay to feed their livestock throughout the winter months.

Once again Nancy worried about her eldest son as he prepared to enter another war. However, this time she had four grandchildren and two daughter-in-law's close by to help keep her mind occupied with more pleasant affairs. She was also happy to have Christine home for the summer months. She was a big help in the garden and loved to watch over her nieces and nephews whenever she had the opportunity.

In late August, Marylyn Jensen did come to stay a week with Karen, and always enjoyed being around Alex and Nancy. They treated her as if she were one of their daughter-in-law's. Marylyn also enjoyed having Glenda and Christine to spend time with. It was like having three sisters she never had growing up. Within just a couple days, it felt like a ton of weight had been removed from her shoulders. Several evenings Karen and Marylyn walked down to the lake just to be alone to discuss their hopes and fears. Although both women had experienced wartime before, this was totally different. Now they had children to worry about, and homes to take care of. Everything at home was much more complicated and worrisome, and this war appeared to be more political, and the politicians at times gave little regard for the men they sent into combat.

Mike was upset with the little respect that most Glendale citizens had for the war in Korea. You could strike up a conversation about the war at the feed mill or coffee shop, but for the most part no one seemed to care. This was not some major threat like World War Two, where our very survival as a nation was on the line. After all, how bad could it be? President Truman was simply calling this conflict a police action. It appeared he had basically handed responsibility for the conflict over to our great war hero, Gen. Douglas MacArthur. Most people Mike spoke to felt the same. Once our troops landed, the North Koreans would run back across the 38th parallel in full retreat within a week. They all felt this insignificant police action would be over within a month, and our troops would be home before Christmas.

Early one morning Mike drove to the feed mill to pick up supplies for the farm. Entering the mill, Mike observed the manager, Charlie McGrath, restocking shelves behind the counter. "What's up Charlie? Don't you have any hired help to stock shelves anymore?"

With a laugh Charlie called out, "Well, Michael Kenrude! How the hell are you? Give me a second to climb down from this ladder and I'll help you out."

"No hurry, Charlie I've got time," Mike responded, as he looked over an auction bill that was lying on the counter.

Moments later Charlie folded up the ladder before approaching the counter. "I see you noticed the Merriman auction bill. Think you guys are going to go after their land?"

Mike shook his head. "No, we've got plenty to handle right now. Especially with Steve gone. It's just not the right timing for us to do any expansions."

"Makes sense to me, Mike," Charlie exclaimed. "Oh, and by the way, I do have help. They're all out back in the storage shed rearranging fertilizer bags. I have some more coming in tomorrow." Mike laughed as Charlie imitated his guys struggling with all those heavy bags.

"So what can I do for you today, Young Master Kenrude?"

Mike handed Charlie a list of things he needed. "Now Charlie, I have a few other errands so you don't have to rush with that. Your guys can stack it on a pallet by the dock and I can pick it up later."

"Okay, that would be great. Yeah, it'll probably take them another half hour to finish up back there. I have one small order in front of yours, but I can have this ready to go in about an hour. Does that work for you, Mike?"

"Sounds great, Charlie. I'll head on over to the hardware store and get that project started," Mike replied with a smile.

As he turned to leave, Grant Bainsworth came walking through the door. "Well, Mike Kenrude. It's been a long time since I've seen you. How have you been?"

Mike never liked Grant in high school, and hadn't been impressed by him getting a phony deferment so he wouldn't have to serve in World War Two.

"I'm fine Grant, how's your Dad's business going?"

Laughing Grant shook his head. "Actually, we're partners now, so it's my business too. Having that fancy college degree has paid off, as I have found ways to get some lucrative government contracts."

"That's great. But I need to get going. I have a lot of things to do this morning," Mike replied as he turned to walk around Grant.

"Yeah, I'm sure your workload has increased since your older brother decided to go off to be a big war hero one more time," Grant stated sarcastically.

Mike stopped instantly. "Steve didn't have much choice in the matter. The Pentagon called him back as training new paratroopers became a huge priority before sending them off to Korea."

"Maybe so, but I'm sure he didn't put up much of a fuss. After all, playing war games seems to come natural to you Kenrude's. By the way, are you ever going to finish high school or are you always going to be just another drop out," Bainsworth queried as he snickered.

"Not that it's any of your business, but I did receive my diploma while I was in the army. It may not say Glendale on it, but it's as good as anything around here," Mike responded angrily.

Nodding his head, Bainsworth stepped in front of Mike. "You know, that was some real crap you played on everyone around here when you ran off to join the army. You should have been more respectable to your parents and friends. There were kids in school that were depending on you to help with class projects and the science fair. You just left everyone hanging. Then you come home and nearly steal the Miller place so you and your wife can live off the farm everyone else built while you were playing soldier. You're quite the act, Kenrude. None of the girls from Glendale were good enough for you. You had to—"

Before Bainsworth could say another word Mike pushed him back against the door. "You can say whatever you want about me. I don't give a damn. But don't you ever talk about my wife. Got it?"

"Wow Kenrude, seems you still have that magic temper. Maybe you should be over in Korea teaching those little snot nosed slant eyes how to behave themselves, seems like you have a lot of pent up anger left over from the last war," Bainsworth replied pushing Mike back a few steps.

Mike took a deep breathe, trying not to lose his temper.

"What's the matter, Kenrude? Couldn't live up to your brother's claim to fame in the war, huh? Now he's off living the good life playing soldier, while you're stuck at home babysitting all his ventures."

Charlie McGrath came rushing over toward the two men. "Bainsworth, that'll be about enough. If you've got business here, let's take care of it and you can be on your way. Otherwise cut the crap and move on."

"Quiet old man. Kenrude and I still have problems we need to work out here. Besides, he hasn't got the balls or the smarts his big brother does. He's been a wannabe from the first time I met him."

Before Bainsworth could say another word, Mike grabbed him by the shirt and shoved him against the wall. "Yeah, I still have some anger left in me alright. But not for the war or anything else. What irks me is the way you prance around this town like you own it. You got a phony deferment to stay out of the war—not because you were needed in your father's machine shop, but because you're a damn coward. You wouldn't have lasted five minute in combat. I saw guys like you piss their pants and run, tails between their legs, when the going got rough. I saw men die because punks like you froze when it came time to fight, too scared to do their jobs. Yeah, Steve is headed off to Korea alright, and I would go too if I could. And do you know why?" Bainsworth didn't answer. He just looked at Mike with wide eyes.

"Answer me, you bastard. Do you know why?" Mike asked again, as he tightened his grip on Bainsworth's jacket.

"I don't know. I don't know and I don't care. Let go of me," Bainsworth yelled.

Mike let go of Bainsworth while backing away. "You answered me when you said you didn't know. You see, even little yellow cowards like you deserve to have your freedom. Gutless wonders like you depend on real patriots to make sure you can live the good life and get your college education. You have no idea how many good men I watched bleed and die. They never complained, they never bad mouthed their country. They just did their jobs and gave it all they had. And yeah, I'd do it all over again, just like my big brother, because our president has promised to help a suffering people remain free. But you wouldn't understand what it's like to help anyone. You're nothing but a selfish, low life bottom feeder and you always have been. Oh yeah, that's right, I also remember what you did to Connie Elsworth. She deserved better from you. She deserved to be treated with respect. She was a good person! "

After taking a deep breath, Mike looked Grant straight in the eye. "You know, if you had any class or decency you'd go out of your way to show appreciation to all the guys from Glendale that served to keep your sorry ass free. But you're just not capable of doing anything like that, are you? I feel sorry for you, Bainsworth, I truly do."

As Mike started to leave, a chorus of cheers and applause rang out from the front of the store. Turning, Mike observed Mr. McGrath's entire crew applauding while shouting their approval as several of them walked over to shake Mike's hand. Totally embarrassed, Bainsworth ducked out the door and quickly headed toward his car.

All the way home, Mike questioned his behavior. There was no doubt that everyone in Glendale would know about the incident in less than twenty-four hours. He was sure Glenda and his parents would never approve of his public display of anger. But inside he was laughing. He knew if Bainsworth had accosted his brother in the same way, Steve would have done much more than push him up against the wall and read him the riot act. Grant would have been lucky to escape with a few broken bones. Steve had always disliked and mistrusted the Bainsworth's and never apologized for his feelings to anyone.

After church the following Sunday, Alex and Nancy decided to have coffee with Karen and her mother at Gloria's Coffee Shop. Entering the cafe they were greeted by many of their friends. After they were seated, several ladies from the Glendale Women's Group approached Nancy.

"So nice to see all of you, we haven't seen you here in the coffee shop for some time." Mrs. Shilling exclaimed with a broad smile. "Is there a special occasion we don't know about?"

Nancy shook her head, knowing Ethel Shilling was the biggest gossip in town. "No special occasion. We just thought coffee and a pastry sounded good this morning."

"Yes, Gloria does make the best pastry in a hundred miles," Mrs. Shilling exclaimed, smiling over at Gloria who was watching the conversation from behind the counter.

Turning back toward the table, Ethel Shilling looked down at Karen. "Well honey, we have missed you and Glenda at the Red Cross meetings the past few weeks. Is there some type of conflict with our meeting time?"

Karen drew in a deep breath. "No ma'am, that's not the issue. Glenda and I just feel the meetings aren't taking into concern our troops who are going to war in Korea. Yes, I am prejudiced about it, since Steve and his best friend Harry were called back up. But remember, during World War Two we wrapped bandages and made up boxes for the troops. Now, we sit around and talk about the blood drive, and make up collection boxes to help fund our local activities, but nothing to support our troops. All of those other things are important, I know, but it seems we're just spinning our wheels and not addressing the fact that our country is at war."

There was no doubt that both Mrs. Shilling and Charlene Waters took offense.

"This is not a war that needs our assistance, Karen. Our boys will have it wrapped up in a couple months and this entire mess will be forgotten. We may not even lose a single soldier in this police action, so why should we be rolling bandages?" Charlene Waters rebutted Karen's comments coldly, with a smirk on her face.

Slowly Alex stood up, staring at the two women. "Now, I don't mean to be offensive or rude on this pleasant Sunday morning, but everyone in Glendale needs to open their eyes. This is not going to be a walk in the park over in Korea. We have communist China and Russia to worry about and rest assured, they're not going to sit back and let us walk into Korea and do whatever we choose to do. No, this is going to be a bloody affair. Men will be injured, and others will die, just like the last war. It's time we stop kidding ourselves. Mr. Truman and General MacArthur have gotten us involved in a war we may not be able to win. Our son is busy preparing paratroopers to enter the war. He writes to us every week explaining how ill prepared our Army is. He's damned concerned. We need to hope those veterans that have been recalled can straighten things out before we end up sending green kids into combat that haven't got a chance. If they can't get things turned around, there will be bloodshed and plenty of it. Wrapping bandages might not be a bad idea."

Several people in the cafe applauded when Alex finished speaking.

"And I suppose you also approve of your other son roughing up the Bainsworth boy over at the feed mill the other day?" Mrs. Shilling demanded angrily.

"Actually, I don't approve, Ethel. But then again, if what Michael told me is true, and I'm inclined to believe it is, the Bainsworth boy bit off more than he could chew. He never liked Mike back in school, and apparently still has a burr under his saddle for him today. I can assure you my son will avoid that young man in the future. But if pushed, neither Mike nor Steve will ever back away. I can damn well guarantee you that," Alex responded in a stern manner.

Looking flustered, both women nodded before quickly walking out of the cafe.

"Nancy shook her head. "My Alex, always spit and polish on a Sunday morning." Everyone around their table broke out laughing as Alex sat down, feeling his face turning a bit red.

After taking a swallow of coffee, Alex looked directly at his wife. "Those two old hens had it coming, sweetheart, plain and simple. Be honest, can you tell me they didn't?"

With a large smile, Nancy took her husband's hand. "Of course they had it coming, dear. I was very proud of you. Thank you for being honest and forthright with them."

"I probably wouldn't have been quite so easy on them had I responded," Janet Donnelly remarked angrily. "The nerve! They just want to start problems, and I have been sick of their gossip and antics for some time."

Leaving the café, Alex and Nancy strolled slowly toward their car. Several couples from the coffee shop followed close behind. "Alex, wait up. So you believe Korea is going to be a real bloody affair?" Stuart Kensman, an attorney in Glendale inquired.

"Yeah, I sure do, Stu. So does Steve and many of the guys he's working with. Steve is almost more concerned now than he was before jumping into Normandy. He says the troops we have today don't appear to be up to the job. Not because they aren't good men, they're just green and need more training time. They're hoping to get them ready before they ship out. He also says many of the weapons they have are in bad shape, and some are even missing parts. How the hell do you fight a war like that?" Alex responded, shaking his head.

Stuart and his wife stood quiet for a moment as Mary Kensman placed her arm around Karen.

"What the hell, Alex? Why aren't we getting that kind of information out of Washington? What the hell is going on? They make it all sound like a Sunday picnic. Do you really think we're in over our heads?" Stuart asked, appearing nervous as he looked at his concerned wife.

"Yes, I do," Alex replied. "I think we all better get serious and start preparing for the worst. I don't think anyone has a clue of what's to come."

Dr. Lindblatt, Glendale's newest physician, stood by listening intently. "Well, I'm sorry to tell you Alex, you're simply wrong. If Doug MacArthur thinks we have everything under control, who are we to question him? After all, he bailed us out of the Pacific when everything was all but lost, and taught those Japs a lesson. For God's sake, the man is a hero! He knows more about war than all the politicians in Washington combined. If he says we can win this war, I sure as hell believe him. Shame on you for questioning the man's abilities and judgments. I'm sorry, but that's almost un-American as I see it!"

Alex shook his head. "No one is questioning the abilities of General MacArthur, Doc. The problem is he's not getting the straight story from Washington. I don't think he understands what a mess our stateside army is in. Besides, he spends so much time in Japan dealing with the occupation and problems with Formosa and China, he just can't give the war all the attention it requires. Besides, the man has to know China is playing us like a fool."

Dr. Lindblatt shook his head. "No, you're wrong. MacArthur knows the score. He knows exactly what kind of shape we're in, over there and over here. The man's a five star General. I'm telling you we all need to get behind the man and operate like we did during World War Two. It's the only way we can win this war and bring our boys, like your son, back home safe and sound."

Alex was beginning to get somewhat angry. After taking a deep breath he looked back towards the Doctor. "No one is saying we aren't backing the war or General MacArthur. For God's sake, Steve is on the way over there right now. I'm just saying that Washington has changed since 1945, and I think everyone knows that. Truman is not Roosevelt, and he doesn't have the smart war leaders around him that Franklin did. You can believe what you want, but there is a different wind blowing from the east. I think we need to question a few things before we jump in with both feet. That's my opinion folks. I guess you can take it or leave it. But now, Nancy and I need to get moving. We can take up this discussion another time."

Nancy, Karen and Janet quickly began walking toward their car, with Alex following a few feet behind. Once they were settled inside and he started the car, Nancy let out a major sigh. "Well, that was rather uncomfortable for a Sunday morning. I'm not sure I appreciate having that type of conversation when it's our son's life that's at risk."

Karen reached forward from the back seat, placing her hand on Nancy's shoulder. "I know how you feel, but Alex is right. Things are different this time. We have Steve's letters to prove it. The rest of Glendale will find out in good time. For now, all we can do is pray everything turns out alright."

Nancy turned to smile at her daughter-in-law. "Of course, honey. You're right. We will get through this just like we did the last war. We are a strong family and we know the power of prayer."

Similar discussions took place in Glendale over the next several weeks as depressing war dispatches concerning the military situation in Korea filled the daily news. No one wanted to admit the United States could be on the losing end of a war with Korea. Nor did anyone in Glendale understand that a different war of sorts was brewing in their community, and that the Bainsworth's would be right in the center of the battle.

CHAPTER 6
JOURNEY TO JAPAN

A misty dawn broke over the California coast, as the slow moving train rumbled onto the pier aside the troop transport Warren Randolph. The sleepy men peered out the windows at large formations of soldiers standing at attention near the ship. The gang plank leading to the main deck of the ship was already crowded with men in olive drab, carrying duffel bags over their shoulders. To the veterans, it was an eerie reminder of their prior departures from New York and New Jersey less than a decade ago. In a way, it was almost as if time had stood still.

Steve felt a chill race up his spine as he remembered that terrible trip across the rough, wolf-pack infested North Atlantic. Although this trip would not be as harrowing, it would still be filled with hard work and training exercises to keep the men occupied.

Harry stood up, stretching before slapping Steve on the back of the head. "Well, Stevie boy, here we are. I never thought I would set foot on board one of those damn transports ever again. Man, this is just such a nightmare. What I wouldn't give to be having a cup of coffee with Marylyn right now. Damn, I really miss that woman. I wonder what she's doing right now."

Steve smiled at his old friend. "I know the feeling, Harry. I miss Karen so much its driving me crazy. She has her hands full with the business books and the kids. It just doesn't seem fair, no matter what we might think about the whole thing. But here we are, and there isn't a thing we can do about it. I just want to get over there, get it done, and get back as soon as possible."

Sgt. Doogan came into their car at the tail end of the conversation. "Let's do it then. Grab your belongings men. First two cars are already getting off. Let's get moving. Platoon sergeants, have your men assemble on the south side of the train. Duffel bags will be brought up by trucks. When your men have their bags move on to the gang plank. Capt. Fargo will meet you on deck directing you to your quarters."

Just as the rear door of the car was unsealed, Harry called out, "Alright, you heard the man. Let's go, fall out! Move it men, we haven't got all damn day, we have a war waiting for us."

Quickly, the men from Alpha Company began moving as they were directed. When the company was fully assembled, a captain and three military police officers arrived to take muster. By the time they were finished, two trucks arrived filled with duffel bags. Platoon sergeants along with military police watched intently to make sure each man returned to the formation after collecting their belongings. The Army was making sure no one went AWOL. After a second roll call was completed to assure everyone was present, Alpha Company was directed toward the gang plank. Steve followed the last man from first platoon on to the ship. Approaching the main deck he observed Capt. Fargo and Col. Fontaine looking over a clipboard with a naval Commander. "Kenrude, follow Shrider into compartment twenty. We'll berth all of Alpha Company together regardless of what this screwed up directive states." Col. Fontaine called out as he shook hands with Steve.

Entering compartment twenty, Steve appointed his men to take the bunks along the back wall. Harry stopped by Steve, as he ordered his men to follow first platoon filling every empty bunk.

"We got to keep these boys busy, Steve. If we don't, they'll be one miserable bunch by the time we reach Japan, and discipline will go all to hell," Harry said, shaking his head.

Hearing Harry's concerns, Franny stopped by his two friends in the middle of the compartment. "You got that right, Harry. These guys are not as disciplined as we were back in '43. They're going to have a struggle with all this sea time. We best come up with a plan and do it quick."

Eddie Shrider now joined the veteran group. "Any plans for a stop in Hawaii for a quick shore leave, or maybe even the Philippines? It would be nice to let them blow off some steam."

"Not from what I'm hearing," Franny answered, as he looked about the busy compartment. "The Army doesn't want to take a chance on guys going AWOL, or having to round up a bunch of drunks when it's time to sail. Nope, we're heading straight across the Pacific from what I heard."

Minutes later, Capt. Fargo joined the circle of platoon sergeants. Sgt. Sanchez quickly repeated Eddie's question.

"Damn, that would be nice, Sanchez. But the orders state we go straight across without stopping. The only time we'll slow down at all is when we refuel at sea four days from now. Col. Fontaine has a pretty good list of activities put together for the men to follow along the way. It should keep them fairly busy. We don't want them sitting around with too much empty time on their hands. Every evening I'll give each of you a list of activities for your platoons for the next day. You can add anything you want if you have any special ideas. Just keep them busy," Capt. Fargo explained with a slight smile before he left the compartment.

Before anyone could say another word, an announcement came over the loud speaker, "Now hear this. We sail in thirty minutes. All hands man your sailing stations. The gang plank has been pulled."

Steve called out, "Everyone, let me have your attention. If you want to watch the ship sail, head on up to the main deck and grab a piece of railing.

Chow will be served about forty-five minutes after we sail. They'll have an announcement over the loud speakers when it's our turn, so pay attention. After chow all platoons will have a gear lay out inspection. So get back in here as soon as you can so we can get moving with it. Now you can head top side and watch us sail if you want to, and say goodbye to the States. You may not see the good old United States again for quite a while."

As the five platoon sergeants joined the men along the rail, Harry looked at Steve. "Boy, if this isn't just too familiar. I feel for these guys. But it's a hell of a lot warmer than our last departure."

Steve nodded in agreement. "Yeah that's a fact. At least this tub is a lot nicer than that scow we sailed on last time, too. Man that ship stunk all the time. I didn't think I would ever get that smell out of my head. Maybe the food will be better, too. It sure couldn't be much worse."

Harry laughed as he placed his hand on Steve's shoulder. "Yup. I remember, all you wanted was a steak and a baked potato, a salad if it was available, real coffee, and all of it served by a waitress wearing lipstick with a bow in her hair. How's that for remembering our trip back from England."

Steve laughed as he shook his head. Damn, I almost forgot about that. Yeah, I had my sights set pretty high alright. To be honest, I got that meal I dreamed about. Not the waitress though. Karen is a far better upgrade in that category."

Harry looked at Steve. "I don't know, buddy boy. That waitress in Des Moines during our New Years Eve party in 1946 kind of fit that bill. What the hell was her name, Bubbles Malloy, or some damn thing. Hey Franny, what was the name of that waitress in Des Moines who had the hots for Brandt during the New Year's Eve Party? And did you ever get your shots?"

Franny shook his head for a moment as he looked over the side of the ship. "Man I should just come over there and slap you for that comment. I stayed away from her like the plague. She was something else. I tried my damnedest to bail Brandt out of that mess but he just kept sliding right back into it. You would think he hadn't learned a thing from us over in Europe. Yeah, I remember her name. She called herself Bambi Delight. And Brandt picked up way too much on the delight aspect I think. I thought sure as hell he was going to ask her to get married right there in the middle of that ballroom. If it hadn't been for Marylyn. Damn crazy Brandt!"

Harry laughed even louder. "Yeah, Bambi Delight! How the hell could I forget? Marylyn was about ready to claw her eyes out the way she hung on my shoulder for a while. Where the hell did that hotel ever find her? You would have thought we were having a bachelor party, not a New Year's Eve celebration that was respectable with wives and girlfriends. Bambi Delight. Yeah, what a night!"

Steve laughed the more he thought about it. "Yeah Brandt had it bad for her alright. I remember him looking up at me saying, she's a swell girl Kenrude. I think my mom would like her. Karen wanted me to lock Brandt in his room until morning. Crazy, damn that was absolutely crazy."

Harry laughed some more as he pushed Steve. "And you blamed me for hiring her!" Franny and Steve laughed all the more as they enjoyed reminiscing about New Year's Eve, 1946.

Finally the ship shuddered, as two tug boats began pushing it from its berth. Slowly the vessel turned sideways, giving the men a great view of San Diego.

"It would have been nice to check out that city for a few days. I might not have made my way back if I had the chance to think about it though." Franny exclaimed, as he pretended to be placing a glass down on a bar. Wiping his mouth with the back of his hand he added. "A good bourbon would have been nice."

"Do you always drink alone? What kind of manners do you have, Doogan?" Harry inquired as he gave Franny a shove. "Who knows, you might have run into Bambi Delight in one of those bars."

Steve laughed as he watched his two friends antagonize each other. If he had to sail off to war, it was good to be going with such good friends. After a few moments Steve looked over at Sanchez. "You've been pretty quiet, Israel. Anything you want to talk about?"

"No, not really, Steve. It just still feels like a bad dream. Like I'll wake up any time now and be back home. I'm sure not looking forward to ducking machine gun fire again. I guess maybe I'm a bit homesick already. We know what's ahead, but these guys don't have a clue. The poor bastards are green as green can be. I'm scared for them, Steve. Scared for all of us really."

Steve was quiet for a moment as he contemplated everything Sanchez had said. "I know what you mean. My guts have been churning since we left Benning. I think the closer we get to Japan the worse it's going to be. But we need to do our jobs and help these guys get through it. It's all we can do."

"Yeah, I know all that, and I sure as hell will give it my best. But I think this war is going to be very different than fighting the Krauts. In a way they were a lot like us. For the most part they were just doing what their country asked them to do. Sure there were some fanatics, but the rest of them were guys that you might meet in any town in the United States on a Saturday night. But these North Koreans are all fanatics. No doubt we'll even run into those fanatical Chinese soldiers hidden in the North Korean ranks. I'm thinking this is going to be brutal all the way around," Sanchez replied quietly.

Finally, the ship began moving forward under its own power, as Steve listened to the concerns of his comrades. It was nearly impossible to argue with anything Sanchez had said. Regrettably, all the brass Steve had spoken with at Benning had the same sickening feelings.

Steve patted Sanchez on the back as he straightened up from the rail. "I guess I don't have any words of wisdom, Israel. We all share the same fears one way or the other. Hopefully everything works out in the end."

Sanchez nodded his head in agreement as he smiled at Steve. "Thanks for the visit, Kenrude. It's nice to know I'm not the only one feeling like this. Don't worry, I'm with you for the long run."

As the ship began to pick up speed, Steve walked off toward the stern. In a few minutes Harry was at his side. "Where you going, Steve, is there anything wrong?" Harry inquired as he studied Steve's face.

"No, I'm okay. I just wanted to walk a bit. I wanted to watch the U.S. fade away as we sail west. I know it will be sometime before we set foot on her soil again. I tell you, Harry, after this war, I'm going to go home and be the best husband and father I can be. I'm never going to take one thing for granted ever again. All I want is my family, friends and the farm, all tied up in one neat package. Screw the world and all its damn problems and wars!"

"Amen to that, Steve. Amen to that," Harry replied, placing his hand on Steve's shoulder.

The two men stood by the rail watching the coastline slowly fade into the morning mist. "There she goes, Harry. No Statue of Liberty for us this time. She was one pretty lady, though. I thought about her a lot while we were over there. Someday I'm going to take Karen and the kids to see her. They need to learn how important she was to so many young men during the war. I think we should have a statue like that on both coasts."

As the coast slowly disappeared into the thickening fog, Harry patted Steve on the shoulder. "So right you are, good buddy, so right you are."

Capt. Fargo's training list was quite extensive. Each day began with a serious round of calisthenics, followed by a long run around the upper deck of the ship, weather permitting. If the decks were wet, the men would run the stairs and ladders of the ship repeatedly, from the engine room to the upper decks, until they were completely drenched with sweat from head to toe.

After breakfast and throughout the day there were classes in parachute maintenance, hand to hand combat, and weapons care and cleaning specific to the harsh Korean weather. Captain Fargo made up enemy aircraft and tank recognition charts for the men to study. Col. Fontaine was a pure master at keeping his men's minds and bodies occupied. Of course, there was also time for additional calisthenics and running to keep them in shape.

After the third day at sea, many of the men from Alpha Company started to protest their rigorous training schedule. They saw a lot of other men on board lounging in the sun, sleeping or playing deck games. The more they complained, the more Capt. Fargo made them run. Finally the men decided there was no way to fight city hall because Capt. Fargo held all the cards.

On the fifth day of the voyage, Private John Warner from Sgt. Shrider's third platoon went missing during morning roll call. After a routine search of all berthing compartments, the MP's failed to find him. The ship was locked down as Marine's from the ships security detachment, along with Army MP's kept the men in their quarters. An aggressive search of the vessel was carried out by officers and platoon sergeants. By midday it was evident that the man was definitely not on the ship. Painstakingly, officers began interviewing everyone in Alpha Company regarding the last time they had seen or spoken with Warner since evening roll call.

As the interviews were taking place, machinists in the engine room began having problems with one of the huge turbine fans required to cool the ship's engineering equipment. Removing part of the duct work, they found a bayonet partially covered with blood jamming the turbine. Immediately, they notified the Skipper of their find.

The investigation process changed from random interrogations, to having each man display his field equipment. After verifying each man had his assigned bayonet, Sgt. Shrider and Harry discovered that Warner's bayonet was missing from his gear. It had obviously been taken by the perpetrator to replace the one used in the assault or possible murder.

As darkness settled over the vast Pacific, the fate of Private Warner remained a mystery. It was evident that someone had either killed or seriously wounded Warner, and disposed of his body.

Col. Fontaine rubbed his jaw as he paced the corridor outside compartment twenty. "Damn it, Fargo, you know as well as I do there's a man inside who knows exactly what happened to Warner. And sure as I'm standing here, I know there are other men who know, but are afraid to talk for some reason, or just won't because of some misguided concept of all for one and one for all. We need to find the man we can quickly break and get to the bottom of this in a hurry."

Captain Fargo looked over at Sgt. Shrider. "Come on Eddie. You must have some idea who had it in for Warner enough to do him in. Somewhere along the line you must have heard something."

Sgt. Shrider looked back at the Captain. "Warner was not always the most squared away troop in the platoon. But nobody seemed to mind him. It was like he was everybody's little brother. They all seemed to look out for him and help in any way they could. I mean, I was a bit worried about how he was going to handle combat. But I figured he would either sink or swim. And Captain, you know in Normandy, there were guys you never thought anyone could count on that became the very best soldiers."

Capt. Fargo nodded his head. "That's a fact, Eddie."

"Damn it guys. We're not solving this thing. There has to be something we're overlooking."

Marine Lieutenant Oblander who was standing nearby approached Col. Fontaine. "We're as stumped as you are, Colonel. We have interviewed every damn trooper you have, some of them twice, but we've got zilch. Their code of honor is remarkable, but we've got to find the weak link"

Steve looked at Col. Fontaine. "Maybe a gambling debt gone bad, or someone saw something he shouldn't have?"

"Like what though, Kenrude? What did he see that could have gotten him killed on this scow? Why didn't the perpetrator just wait until we got into combat and shoot the S.O.B. in the back?" Col. Fontaine asked in an irritated tone of voice.

"I'm not sure, Colonel. Maybe he saw a crime committed off base. A robbery, an assault, a murder, maybe a rape, then he gets on board and tells the guy, 'I know what you did and I'm going to tell the brass.' Just a thought Colonel, remember what happened in Austria after the war when those two guys from Dog Company were observed raping that Kraut General's wife. Before the witness could snitch out the two guys that committed the rape, they had hung him down by the lake. Luckily they had the noose wrong and he survived to tell the story," Steve reminded his frustrated commander.

"Yeah, I see where you're coming from, Kenrude. It's a long shot, but hell we don't have anything else," Col. Fontaine replied, as he continued slowly pacing down the hot corridor.

A Marine corporal standing nearby spoke up. "Sir, second night out we were told about a little scuffle going on between some guys in storage compartment eighteen. When we arrived, there was no one inside, but the hatch was left partly open, so we knew someone had been in there since our last security round. It's in our nightly report, Colonel."

"Yeah, Yeah. I did see that. If that's the case, we definitely know more than one trooper knows about this. Alright here's what we do. Each one of you Platoon Sergeants jot down a list of those men in your platoons you feel might crack if taken away from their safe zone and give them the third degree. I want this started now," Colonel Fontaine replied as he struck the bulkhead with his fist.

As soon as the lists were compiled, Col. Fontaine told the MP's to start with fifth platoon and work their way to the first. He instructed Lt. Oblander to conduct the interrogations since he was a Marine and had no connection to the Army.

As Private Andrew Tormay from third platoon was brought in, the lieutenant quickly observed his nervousness.

"Something bothering you, Tormay?" Lt. Oblander inquired.

"No, sir. I, I just don't know why I'm here again. I told you everything I knew when you talked to me this morning. What's going on?" Tormay responded as sweat began to run down his face.

Going right to the point, Lt. Oblander, slammed his fist on the table separating the two men, yelling, "Where the hell is Private Warner? You best help yourself out right now and tell us what's going on, or I damn well guarantee you'll be on the first ship back from Japan headed to Leavenworth for a long stay! I'm not playing games, Tormay. I got you and you know it!"

As Tormay rose from his chair he screamed out, "Go to hell! I didn't do anything wrong. I have rights. I want to see a JAG attorney. I want to speak to the Colonel right now!"

"Sit down, Private!" Oblander yelled, placing his hand on the butt of his service weapon. "If I can't get you to talk one way I sure as hell will do it another. Do I make myself clear?"

"Alright! Alright! I'm screwed either damn way, Lieutenant. If I tell you what I know the guys in the unit will kill me. If I keep my mouth shut, I'll end up just like Warner. I'm just plain fucked, sir," Tormay yelled out as he began to cry and pound his fists into the table.

Lt. Oblander drew a deep breath as he sat down. "Go ahead Tormay, tell us what you know. We'll keep you segregated on board. When we get to Japan we'll have you shipped back state side. I guarantee your safety. Just tell us what you know, it will make you feel better in the end."

Nodding his head slightly, Tormay looked directly at the Lieutenant. "It was two days before we shipped out, me and a couple of other guys went to town with the soul intention of getting drunk and laid before we shipped out. Warner kind of tagged along. You know he was kind of quiet and different. So when we were half drunk we started looking for some women to hustle. Warner backed out and disappeared. Later that night, I suppose around two in the morning, we started making our way back to camp. We ran across Warner, sir. He was shaking bad and looked pale as hell, like he'd seen a ghost. I asked him what was wrong and he wouldn't say. He just said, 'get me back to base' over and over." Tormay sat back in his chair shaking his head as his hands trembled.

"Go on, Tormay. What happened next?" Lt. Oblander directed the troubled soldier.

"Well, the next morning Warner was still acting stupid at breakfast. He said he was going to go AWOL. I told him he was crazy. I explained this was during a time of war and he could be shot for desertion. He motioned for me to follow him over toward the motor pool. Once we were alone he told me he witnessed one of our men slit the throat of a young girl. He said the man made him help pry up a man hole cover then drop her body inside. Warner told me the man threatened to kill him if he ever said a word. It was driving him insane. He told me he either had to kill the son-of a-bitch or turn him in. That's all I know. I guess he went after the killer and wound up dead himself. Warner was losing it, he didn't know how to handle the situation or who to talk to. The poor S.O.B."

Lt. Oblander looked down at Tormay. "I think you better finish telling us the rest of the story. If Warner confided all this to you, he told you who the killer was. Give me the rest, Tormay."

After a deep sigh Tormay looked up at Lt. Oblander. "You promise to get me back to the states ASAP after we get to Japan? This guy has friends. If they find out who snitched him out they'll kill me sure as shit, and they'll make it brutal. You got to promise to help me."

Lt. Oblander nodded his head. "You're as good as on the transport back right now, son."

Tormay sat silently for a moment then nodded. "Alright, it's Rausch from first squad, sir."

Lt. Oblander spun around facing his security detachment. "Go get the bastard."

Several minutes later they returned with Rausch in handcuffs. He looked calm with a slight smile on his face. Col. Fontaine entered the room just as Rausch sat down. Standing beside Lt. Oblander for a moment he looked coldly at the accused soldier. "Do you know why you're here, Rausch?" Col. Fontaine inquired.

After looking at everyone in the room Rausch spit on the floor. He smiled at Lt. Oblander for a second before turning to Col. Fontaine. Spitting on the floor once more he nodded his head. "Some ignorant bastard blamed me for Warner's disappearance. Well, you got the wrong man."

Angrily, Lt. Oblander slammed his fist on the steel table. "Should we ask the young girl you threw down a man hole back in Georgia if you're the right man, you son-of-a-bitch?"

Rausch was clearly taken back. He turned ashen gray as he began to breathe heavily. "What the hell are you talking about? I didn't—"

Before he could finish, Col. Fontaine stepped forward. "Right now we're having the ship radio back to the states. We're going to contact the local authorities and have them check a certain man hole to see if there is a body inside it. What do you think they're going to find down there?"

Rausch looked at the Colonel angrily. "The little bitch played me. She told me she was nineteen. Turns out she was fourteen and pregnant. Yeah, and I was the father. I was banging her for several months. When I told her to get lost she told me she was going to contact my superior officer and make me pay. The bitch had no right to threaten me like that. I just lost it with her, it was all her fault."

"The same way you lost it with Warner? Where did you dispose of him?" Col. Fontaine yelled.

"Damn him!" Rausch yelled as he kicked the heavy table. "I told him to keep his damn mouth shut and everything would be alright. So he comes to me and tells me to meet him near the winch on the rear of the ship at midnight. He tells me to either fess up or he will go to the Colonel. And the bastard had the balls to point his bayonet at me. I took that damn thing and jammed it in his chest three times so fast he couldn't react. I pitched his body overboard. Figured the props would shred him just fine for shark food. I sprayed down the deck real quick with a water hose that was nearby, and tossed the bayonet down one of the air intakes. I never figured it would be found that quickly. All the bastard had to do was keep his mouth shut. He probably would have been killed in combat anyway, he was a worthless soldier and a fuck up. We were better off without him."

Slowly Rausch began hanging his head. "I guess I really fucked up. I don't know what to say. What will happen to me now, sir? I would rather die in combat then die in prison."

Col. Fontaine shook his head. "You will be charged with one count of murder under military law. After your trial you'll be sent back to Georgia to stand trial for the murder of the girl. As to where you do your time, I really don't give a damn. There's no place rotten enough for a sick bastard like you, Rausch. I'm just glad to be rid of the likes of you. These men around you are brave patriots. They don't deserve to have a piece of crap like you in their midst."

The Marine security team took Rausch from the room, placing him in the brig until the ship arrived in Japan where he would await a military trial.

"Do you want us to search for anyone else who knew about the crimes and refused to come forward?" Lt. Oblander inquired of Col. Fontaine.

"No! Hell no! Whoever those men are, they will have to live with it the rest of their lives as it is. One dead paratrooper and one in the stockade for life is enough for this cruise. Let's just try and finish this damn trip without any other major problems. I guess I better go write the Warner's a letter. What the hell do I tell those poor people?" the Colonel muttered, walking from the room.

Word spread quickly throughout Alpha Company along with the rest of the ship. Some of the men who were friends of Rausch got treated somewhat badly for the next few days, although no one attempted to hurt them or get retribution.

The ship chaplain held a small service for Warner on the rear deck, near the spot he was murdered. After a mock burial, the ceremonial flag was folded by the honor guard to be sent home to his family along with the letter from Col. Fontaine.

The following day Col. Fontaine handed out rigorous new training schedules for the last few days of their voyage. He wanted the men to keep focused on their mission while putting the murder of Warner behind them.

The original plan had been to dock the Warren Randolph in Tokyo Bay, then transport the men cross country by train. However, the brass felt the delay in getting the men prepared for battle after the long cruise was unacceptable. At the last minute it was decided to dock the transport on the west side of Japan at the ancient seaport of Moji, just a short distance north of Hakata.

As heavy fog covered the coastline of Japan, the Warren Randolph slowly and inconspicuously glided into the Moji harbor. The air was filled with whistles and fog horns as several naval ships, cargo vessels and tug boats cautiously moved about the small harbor. Two Naval tugs guided the Warren Randolph into the narrow berth where several trains were already parked on the pier, waiting to carry the newly arrived soldiers to their base.

The airborne soldiers of the third battalion were ordered to disembark first. Capt. Fargo led Alpha Company down the gangway walking toward the first train, where they tossed their duffel bags on an open box car directly behind the coaches. Loading the train went like clockwork, as everyone was happy to be back on dry land once more, even if it brought them closer to combat.

After Steve finished taking a head count he sat down next to Harry. "Welcome to Japan, old friend. When we left Germany I never thought I would see this corner of the world."

"Yeah, I have been thinking the same thing. Whoever thought we would see Japan in a totally different war, where we're actually allies with them," Harry responded, shaking his head.

An MP standing nearby overheard the men talking. "Where you guys from? You sound like Midwesterners."

Steve smiled, "Glendale, Minnesota."

"Clearview, Iowa," Harry called out as he shook hands with the Military Police Officer.

"Hey great. I'm from St. Paul, Minnesota. I haven't met too many guys from our part of the country since I've been here. Believe me, you'll like Minnesota and Iowa better than this place. Sorry to say I'm not impressed with Japan."

With a jerk the train began rolling off the pier. It rolled through an industrial area that was still partially in shambles from American air raids during the war. Nevertheless, it was clear enough to see a new more modern city beginning to rise from the ashes of defeat. As the train rolled on, Steve and Harry enjoyed swapping stories about home with the young MP who was clearly homesick.

There was little to see along the way, as dense clouds of fog rolled back and forth from the sea. Steve recalled stories he had heard from several B-29 pilots about the fog causing them to miss their targets in Japan on a daily basis. Now he could totally understand their dilemma. There were times he could not see more than ten yards from the train. He began wondering if they were going to be able to get practice jumps in with the incessant fog. There was little doubt in his mind that the men definitely needed some jumps if they were going to be ready for combat when they were called up. The long cross country train and ship rides could easily have dulled their senses.

Neither Capt. Fargo nor Col. Fontaine informed anyone where they were headed or how long the train ride was going to be. However, Steve knew before leaving Fort Benning that they would end up somewhere on the southwest side of the island. He had studied an army map of Japan in Capt. Fargo's office. He observed a large military base circled near the city of Hakata. The city lay just about a hundred miles across the Korean Straights, from the Korean Peninsula. It made perfect sense to base rapid response airborne units near a city just a hundred miles from the war zone. If an emergency jump had to be made to aid the beleaguered South Korean forces, this would be the perfect place to launch from. About an hour later the troop train slowed to a crawl as it entered what appeared to be a rather large city. The train slowly rolled along the fog shrouded coast before turning inland on a spur track.

Steve turned toward Harry who was still half asleep. "Wake up buddy boy. I think we are approaching our destination."

"Oh yeah!" Harry exclaimed as he stretched. "Just where the hell are we, anyway?"

"I'm not sure yet as I don't read fluent Japanese, but I think the sign said something like Hakata. But we appear to be continuing on through it," Steve responded, as he peered out the rain soaked window.

"Goodie for you, Stevie boy. You finally passed your tenth grade geography class," Harry called out, slapping Steve on top of the head.

Moving inland, the fog dissipated, allowing the men a chance to see some very ornate Japanese gardens and houses that lined the railroad tracks exiting the city. After a few minutes more, the train turned off the spur line rolling through a large fence. A sign read, "Caution, Now Entering Camp Wood, United States Government Property."

As the train came to a stop, Col. Fontaine's voice came over the speakers. "Gentlemen, we have reached our final destination just outside the city of Hakata. The base is still undergoing some major reconstruction work, but the area we will occupy is pretty much finished. As your car unloads, we will do another roll call before loading on to trucks. Once we arrive at our barracks, all platoon leaders meet with your company commanders immediately."

Before the MP's unsealed the doors, the men watched as Private Tormay was taken from the train to a waiting staff car where two officers awaited him. After it departed, Private Alvin Rausch departed the train in handcuffs and leg irons. He was escorted to a three-quarter ton truck where several armed MP's patiently stood guard. Once the truck disappeared onto the base, several more MP's quickly unsealed the car doors allowing the men to exit the stuffy confines, and breathe in the cool humid air of southwest Japan.

With roll call completed, trucks hauled the men just a few miles to an area filled with newly refurbished brick barracks. They were long single story buildings with metal roofs.

After depositing their gear, Alpha Company squad leaders assembled around Capt. Fargo outside the orderly room. "Welcome to Japan, men. We have lots of work to do in a short period of time. We're not sure when MacArthur is going to call us up, but we expect it to be soon the way things are going with the war. Starting tomorrow and every day after, we'll run at 0500, breakfast will be at 0630. Training will commence at 0800, and end when we decide to call it a day. Our other meals will be served either in the field or here in the mess hall, depending on where we are and what we have going on. We are working on a schedule for jumps but it's not complete yet. There will be no passes to town, at least for a while.

Relations between the Japanese people and Americans are still on the mend. MacArthur doesn't want any drunken G.I.'s gumming up the works.

We are working on activities to keep the men occupied. Are there any questions?"

Sgt. Shrider raised his hand. "Captain, is it for certain that we'll be used as airborne units and not just ground troops to fill holes in the line?"

"That's a good question, Shrider. To be honest, no one really seems to know exactly what is happening day to day over there. Everything is fluid. We expect to be used as airborne, but things can change in an instant. We will do what we need to do and we will do it well, because we are airborne. Are there any other questions?"

First Sgt. Doogan raised his hand. "Captain, Korea is pretty mountainous. None of us, even the veterans, have ever jumped into that type of terrain. Will we get any practice with mountain landings before we are forced to actually do it?"

Captain Fargo's faced tightened as he stared back at Franny. "I'm sorry Sergeant, but that just won't happen. I checked into that issue myself on the way here. The brass feels if it comes to that we'll just have to improvise and do our best. I know that answer isn't what anybody wants to hear, but that's it, Sergeant."

Franny shook his head in disbelief. "Sir, do you know how many casualties we could take in that type of landing? We could be rendered ineffective as a fighting force before we ever see combat. That would be just plain suicide and put our entire operation in jeopardy."

"I know that, Doogan, and understand your point completely. You're preaching to the choir here. We all had to overcome fierce obstacles when we landed in Normandy. This will not be any different. We will have to learn as we go." Captain Fargo responded in a stern but reassuring tone.

After the briefing, they returned to their men to update them on the latest information and prepare them for the following day.

After the evening meal, Steve lay on his bunk and began to write letters home. He removed the photograph of Karen from his writing pack. He missed her so much. It seemed like an eternity had passed since he kissed her good bye. He wondered how she was doing and how she was handling their separation. Karen was always such a trooper when it came to their relationship. She could deal with just about any crisis while hiding her fears. However, now she had two kids to care for, while being mother, father and business agent for the farm. Slowly, he ran his fingers across Karen's smile as he tried hard to remember what it was like to kiss her. For a moment it seemed as though he could smell her favorite perfume. Slowly, he began placing his feelings and misgivings about their mission on paper. While he didn't want to scare Karen, he felt it important that she be aware of the way things were going. He felt as if he needed to prepare her for the worst possible outcome.

Finishing his letters, Steve walked over to the barracks of the Second Platoon to see Harry. Finding him sound asleep, Steve quietly walked over to the orderly room to see if Franny was still at work. Steve found him sitting outside the office wiping, down his Thompson.

"You still look naked without that damn B.A.R.?" Steve called out with a smile.

"Damn, Stevie boy, I still feel naked without that beautiful piece of machinery. It almost felt like a part of me by the time that war was over. I actually wish I had ole Betsy back again," Franny replied, adding more oil to his rag.

Sitting down beside Franny, Steve looked up at the darkening sky. "We've been here before, old buddy. Just like this. No idea of what we're getting into or who will be coming back. It shouldn't be this way, Franny. I mean, what the hell? How many times can you put yourself on the line before your luck runs out? Sometimes when we were in France and Belgium I felt like my ticket would be punched, and it would all be over with, but then everything worked out. I think about guys like McBride and Eddington. What great soldiers they were. How full of life one minute and dead the next. Damn war. Seems like it just takes and takes and now we're going to see it all over again. I don't know that I'm ready for it, Franny!"

Placing his Thompson down on the bench, Franny looked over at Steve. "I've thought about the same thing, Stevie boy. Sure I stayed in, knowing I could end up in another war. That's the way it goes. But damn, not this soon. I still hurt inside from so many different things. Now, here we are again, and we just need to do our jobs. We need to do them well, because we got green kids that won't make it back without us. I know we were green once, too, but these guys are just, well, unprepared is the word I would use. During World War Two we all wanted to kick either Hitler or Tojo in the ass for what they were up to. I mean we were ready, green or not. These kids don't understand why they are even here or what this damn war is all about. Actually, I'm not sure myself at times. Everyone is on the run over there, and we're supposed to go in there and do what? Hold the line? Slow down the withdrawal? Or just be sacrificial lambs? I don't know, Steve. It all sounds a bit crazy to me. Sounds like Market Garden all over again, one big nasty cluster."

Steve nodded in agreement. "Well Franny, I came here to check out my feelings, and you confirmed I'm not just a chicken shit, so thanks. In a way, I'm really glad to hear you express the same thoughts that have been going through my head the last few days." After a few moment of silence, Steve stood up. "Well, I'm going to try and get some sleep. I have a feeling it will be a trying day tomorrow. Good night old buddy, sleep well."

Franny nodded as he picked up his weapon. "Good night Steve, get some rest."

The following day started with a two mile run before breakfast, followed by a field pack march to the rifle range. After qualifying with their weapons, they had three hours of obstacle course, then hand to hand combat to round out the afternoon. A longer return march kept the men going well into dusk. Steve was extremely happy with the day, as there were no drop outs from his platoon.

Capt. Fargo called all his lieutenants and platoon sergeants together for a meeting around twenty-two hundred. "I know you're all tired so I'll make this quick. Our time table for entering Korea has been moved up. I don't know the exact date, but I can tell you we need to be ready on a moment's notice. Tomorrow we'll make a jump at 1000hrs. This is not a big base so we'll need to fly out over the ocean for the planes to get organized. Then we'll fly back inland toward the jump sight. We'll make one jump a day for the next three days. The last one will be a night jump. So, first thing in the morning get your men squared away so we can be at the airfield no later than 0830."

As the men walked toward the barracks, Harry looked over at Steve. "I'd give you a penny for your thoughts, but I have a hunch they're the same as mine. We're heading to war like a runaway freight train and there's nothing we can do to stop it."

Steve shook his head. "No Harry, not quite the same. It's like a runaway train heading down hill at full speed, with a bad wheel. Everyone knows that wheel is going to come off sooner or later, causing a crash. But everyone wants old engine thirty-seven to be on time so they just ignore the problem. More sooner than later, old thirty-seven is going to come apart at the seams, scattering cargo across the landscape. Then everyone will be pointing fingers, and yelling, 'See I told you so.' And guess who we are."

Harry nodded in agreement. "We're the damn cargo, like it or not"

"Got that right, Jensen," Eddie Shrider chimed in as he walked up beside Harry. "We're the cargo. Just dump us out and hope we can figure this fucking war out, damn the casualties." Not another word was spoken by the veterans as they walked back toward their barracks.

The following morning the sergeants did their jobs well, having everyone ready to depart for the airfield at 0745, despite all the complaints.

Along with several new C-47 Skytrains, Steve observed quite a few older C-46's and one C-119 Flying Boxcar lining the airstrip. Capt. Fargo directed his men toward the C-46's. Although they were not a bad plane, they seemed to be a bit more bouncy in rough weather. Despite their large cumbersome packs, with a little help from ground crews, boarding went as smooth as could be expected.

At 0950 planes began rolling down the runway. The first platoon's C-46 was fifth in line to take off. After climbing to an altitude of about 500 feet, the pilot banked hard toward the left. In just a few minutes they were above the crystal blue waters of the ocean below. Looking out the window across the plane, Steve could see several other planes circling to join the air convoy. After circling twice over the water, their pilot came on the intercom.

"Alright, we are starting our run, it should take us about ten minutes. Listen to the jump master and you should all get out of here in good shape, happy landings, gentlemen."

From somewhere in the plane a soldier yelled, "Wanna take my damn place, fly boy?"

Everyone had to laugh, including Steve. They all knew the pilot had no idea what it was like to hit the ground doing close to twenty miles an hour while carrying such a huge load. The jump alone could kill you before the enemy ever fired a shot.

Moments later the jump master called out, "Stand up, hook up." Everyone promptly stood up, hooking their static lines to the steel cable. They then began checking the man in front of them to assure everything was right with their gear. As the green light came on, the first man by the door bailed out before the jump master could even call out 'go.' Steve jumped half way through his platoon.

Although the air was heavy with moisture, the sky was a clear radiant blue. Steve's chute immediately popped open with a sharp snap. After adjusting his risers he took a few seconds to look around. The ocean to his left was a turquoise blue and crystal clear. Lush green fields separated by rows of large trees dotted the country side. It was not much different than jumping in the United States or Holland. Moments later Steve made a near perfect landing, although his right knee hurt somewhat. After dropping his chute he began assembling his men. Once everyone was accounted for, he marched them down a small field road toward the company assembly area.

The third and fifth platoons were already assembled, while Harry and Wentworth were coming with their platoons from the north, just a short distance away. Capt. Fargo was pleased with the speed in which everyone assembled and reported in. He was even more pleased to hear there were no major injuries.

After a meal of C-Rations, the men worked through several training problems designed to emulate real issues they might incur once they landed in Korea. Several tanks from the base joined the training, giving the men a more realistic workout.

The following day dawned dreary with moderately overcast skies and occasional light drizzle. As the men prepared to load onto the transport, Sgt. Kilburn approached Steve. "Sarg, I have a man in first squad upset by the weather. He doesn't want to jump. I've tried everything, but I can't get him to leave the truck. I think you better talk with him."

Steve followed Kilburn over to a deuce and a half, where the young soldier was sitting. "What's your name, soldier?" Steve inquired.

"Hector. Hector Gomez, Sergeant," the man replied in a shaky voice.

"Alright, Hector. What seems to be the problem?" Steve asked, as rain dripped from his helmet.

"I'm scared. I don't want to jump in weather like this. I'm afraid to die, sir. My mother, she wouldn't have a man in the family to take care of her. My father died last year in a car accident. I can't leave my mother alone."

Steve nodded his head. "Well Hector, no one is going to die today or tomorrow. This weather is no big deal. I've jumped in far worse. You need to jump today—you have to, son. If you don't, I can damn well guarantee that Col. Fontaine will file court martial papers on you. What do you think your mother would rather have? A son who was brave enough to jump regardless of the weather, or a son who was put in the brig for failing to do his job. You need to think about that real quick."

"I don't want to jump, but I sure as hell don't want to end up in the brig. Alright Sarg, you convinced me. I'll just keep praying."

Steve patted the man on the arm, as Sgt. Kilburn started to help Hector with his gear.

Before Steve walked off he called out, "Gomez! That praying thing—it's not a bad deal, keep it up! God is always listening. He never turns his back on airborne soldiers, since we're always close to heaven."

Hector looked back with a big smile as he made the sign of the cross and took off to catch up with his squad.

Meanwhile, Sgt. Kilburn had a question. "Do you think Col. Fontaine would really have thrown Gomez in the brig for failing to jump?"

"Hell no, the Colonel wouldn't do that on his worst day. It was clear that Gomez was far more interested in his mother than anything else, so I just played on his emotions." Steve explained his strategy as he slapped his first squad sergeant on the back of his helmet. "Keep that in mind for the future."

"I'll need to remember that routine for sure. It worked far better than anything else I tried," Kilburn called out with a laugh.

As the planes once again circled above the straits, the water below was totally different than it was yesterday. The crystal blue mirror had disappeared, replaced by a wild and churning greenish-gray cauldron. With the heavy overcast skies, it took several more circles over the frothing ocean before everyone was set. Finally the planes picked up speed in route to their drop zones. Steve could not help think about Archie back in Normandy. He had predicted his own death. Steve hoped giving Gomez that pep talk wouldn't backfire on him. But every man was going to be needed when they went into Korea, he couldn't afford to allow one man to effect the morale of his whole platoon.

The plane was seriously bouncing as they approached their drop zone. Several men got sick, vomiting on the floor and their equipment. The air in the plane was immediately fouled with the odor of high grade aviation fuel and vomit, so no one wasted any time bailing out of the aircraft when the welcoming green light came on.

The cold wet rain slapping Steve in the face was a refreshing relief. There was no time to look around today as everything below was shrouded in a rolling mist. Every paratrooper must have his wits about him to avoid a dangerous landing. Steve landed safely in a large puddle in the middle of a small field. After dropping his chute he blew on a whistle before yelling out, "First platoon over here." Today the men assembled at a much slower rate, as they were scattered over a larger area. Two men were stuck in trees and required assistance to get down. One of them was Gomez. As Steve approached the tree, Gomez waved at him. "Not quite on the ground yet Sergeant."

"Close enough, Gomez. Close enough," Steve called back with a broad smile on his face.

Once again, Capt. Fargo was impressed with his men. Although there were a few minor injuries, they each came through the jump intact. Unfortunately, that good luck would not hold up for the night jump. Once again a light drizzle was falling as the huge transports rolled down the runway carrying their cargo of paratroopers. Steve became uncomfortable as the plane continued circling over the dark murky water below. Through the window across the plane, Steve could see the dancing blue flames emanating from the exhaust ports of another plane, which appeared to be uncomfortably close.

"Let's go, let's go!" Steve kept muttering to himself. The last thing he wanted to do was crash over the ocean. No one would survive ditching out in these deep cold, shark infested waters at night.

Moments later, he settled down a bit as the pilot announced they were on the way in. He kept a continuous eye on the window though, still worried the neighboring plane would strike them. However, Steve was watching the wrong aircraft.

Suddenly, their plane was shaken by a large explosion. Burning debris fell past the window looking like large fire flies in a dark sky. The shriek of a falling plane roared through the cabin. Seconds later the pilot came on the intercom. "Our rudder is damaged. You all need to jump now so we can lighten our load. We just came over land. Good luck, get out now!"

As the jump master opened the door, everyone hastily bailed out of the damaged aircraft. Leaving the plane, Steve could see the lights of Hakata, off toward the north. It was actually a very interesting sight.

To the east he could see what he figured were lights from the military bases. Below him everything was still shrouded in darkness. Finally Steve observed headlights from several moving vehicles directly below him. They were moving north and south. That had to be the coastal highway. Reaching for his risers Steve directed his chute to carry him east away from the busy road. Approaching the ground it was evident that many other troopers had chosen this same area for their landing. Parachutes and back packs littered the ground as men moved about.

Shortly after he landed, Sgt. Whitebear from third squad ran up to him. "Sarg, I have all of my squad and most of second squad assembled near the tree line to your left. Some men are still wandering in from all around the area. Sgt. Hagen is back near that warehouse type building looking for our guys."

"Great, good job Whitebear. Let's see if the whistle will help." Blowing a long blast on his whistle, Steve followed Whitebear toward the assembled men.

Minutes later Sgt. Hagen and Sgt. Kilburn arrived with a large group of men. "All of fourth and first squads are accounted for, Sarg. Martinez is coming with what should be the rest of second squad in a few minutes. Some of the men landed way to the north and one was tangled up in a tree," Sgt. Hagen reported, as he did another quick head count to assure he was accurate.

About five minutes later, Sgt. Martinez arrived with four men, making up the balance of second squad. "That should be everyone, Sarg," Martinez explained, as he quickly removed his parachute harness.

Facing his platoon, Steve inquired. "Are there any injuries I need to know about? We may have quite a hike ahead of us." No one said a word. "Fantastic! Good job men. I think our best bet is to parallel the road to the north. It should take us back to the base. It may not be the shortest route, but it sure as hell beats wandering around out there in the dark, battling obstacles we don't know about. Those of you who dropped your packs, go retrieve them. We leave nothing behind but the chutes."

Everyone appeared to agree with Steve's assessment as they began readying their equipment for the long march back.

"Kilburn, lead on. The rest of you follow through by squads. Let's go," Steve called out as he loosened his helmet. He knew damn well it was going to be a long hike for his men with full field packs. But it would be unwise to let all the equipment stay in the field so far from base.

The tough looking paratroopers laden down with heavy packs and weapons drew strange and nervous looks from Japanese civilians they incurred along the road. Some civilians slowed their vehicles to a crawl before yelling what Steve thought were insults, before racing away into the darkness. Nearly forty-five minutes into their walk, two Jeeps and a staff car pulled up along the column. A young Major stepped from the staff car while a young MP climbed from the lead Jeep. "Who is in charge here?" the Major called out.

Steve walked forward, removing his helmet. "I'm Sgt. Kenrude, First Platoon, A-Company Third Battalion, sir."

"Any casualties we need to be aware of Sergeant?" The major looked nervous as he asked the question.

"No sir. We are one hundred percent in good shape. We have all of our equipment minus the chutes. It would have been impossible to carry them back with us," Steve explained.

"Understood. That was a good decision, Sergeant. We'll send a truck out to pick them up before the Japanese civilians cut them up," he responded, waving one of the MP's forward.

"Radio back to base and get some trucks out here to get those chutes picked up pronto. And get some vehicles for these men."

"Already done, sir, trucks are on the way," the MP replied with a smile on his face.

Seeming a bit irritated by the MP's cocky response, the Major looked back over at Steve. "Did you see anyone else out there?"

"Negative. I think everyone else either landed farther inland, or out there in the ocean. If they hit the water they were doomed. They would have sunk like a rock."

"Are you telling me none of you had proper safety gear to complete this mission, Sergeant?"

Shaking his head, Steve drew in a deep breath. "Sir, we learned at Normandy that those damn vests were worthless. With the weight of the gear we carry, they could never keep us afloat, even for a second. All they were was something to make us feel good and get in our way. When we were asked if we wanted them, all the veterans rejected the idea right from the get go," Steve explained, clarifying the situation for the major, who seemed too young to have seen action in Europe during the war, and likely knew very little about airborne operations.

"Oh, well then I guess that is that. You men can drop your packs and wait here for the trucks. We'll move on looking for any survivors or lost souls," the major called out, waving the MP's back to their Jeeps. Seconds later they sped off toward the south in a hurry.

"Alright men, drop your packs and have a seat. Smoke if you want to, just don't wander off anywhere," Steve instructed his men as he laid his weapon and pack on the ground. Sitting down on the cool grass he couldn't help but wonder how many men might have perished tonight. It was terrible to think of the young men who would have to die even before they entered combat. Training was important, but pushing the envelope always seemed to end up in tragedy. About forty minutes later, a large convoy of trucks rolled to a stop near the men. Steve walked to the lead Jeep. "We're ready to go any time you are, Corporal."

"Great, Sarg. Have your men load up. Use as many trucks as you need. Whatever I have left we will use to pick up chutes or other survivors."

"How many more survived the crash?" Steve inquired of the young corporal.

"Well, right now I don't know. We were just told to pick up you guys and then meet the major down the road. I don't have any specifics at this time," the young corporal responded.

Nodding his head in understanding, Steve turned toward his men. "Alright load up. Fill them up but no need to cram them tight. We can use as many as we need."

Arriving back at base, Steve had his platoon leaders complete a head count. Knowing everyone was accounted for, he dismissed his men for the night. After stowing his gear, he went outside and sat down on a small bench beside the door of the barracks. There was no way he could sleep until he found out who was involved in the crash and how many men might have been killed. Nearly an hour later more trucks filled with paratroopers began arriving in the compound. Steve walked over to see who was returning. Instantly, he saw Harry climbing down from one of the trucks. "Glad to see you back, Harry," Steve called out, helping him with his pack. "You guys alright?"

"Yeah, we're fine. I'm not sure yet whose plane that was," Harry responded.

Minutes later Franny came walking over to his friends. "Good to see you guys. All your men make it back?"

"Yeah, both our platoons are accounted for. How did the other guys make out?" Harry inquired.

"Shrider and Wentworth are both fine. They should be arriving soon. They were way off course," Franny explained, in an angry tone of voice.

"Well, that just leaves Sanchez," Steve said quietly.

"No. I think Sanchez was calling in fifth platoon to our north. I know I heard his voice. I'm thinking the planes were from another company, Steve," Harry explained, as he turned to watch more trucks arrive.

As the men watched the trucks pull in, Capt. Fargo walked over. "Good to see you men. I was worried about you, Kenrude. I heard your plane was hit. The flight crew made it back alright, but they feared some of your men might have hit the water. How did that turn out?"

"No sir, we all landed on dry ground. Everyone is accounted for and in the barracks," Steve informed his worried Captain.

"Good, good. Glad to hear that. I'll inform Col. Fontaine. He's been plenty worried. However, it looks like Charlie Company took the losses tonight. I'm not sure yet, but the way it looks they might have lost nearly a full platoon. I do know all the men from one of the planes involved bailed out on time. Their flight crew was also able to clear the wreck before it went down. I guess we'll have to wait until morning to get the extent of the bad news. Get some rest men." With that, Capt. Fargo walked off toward headquarters, looking like a tired and defeated man.

Everyone was happy to see Israel Sanchez climb down from a truck that arrived about ten minutes later. After hearing everyone was accounted for from his platoon, the men slowly strolled back to their barracks for the night.

At morning formation, a grim Col. Fontaine addressed his men. "I have some bad news this morning as you might guess. There is never an easy way to hand out this kind of information. As you are all aware of what occurred last night, what I'm about to say will not be a great surprise. Charlie Company lost nearly all of second platoon. Most of them were lost in the ocean. We have Navy personnel dragging the area looking for bodies as I speak. Some of the men had their chutes catch fire as they bailed out. So, of course, they fell to their deaths. Unless we find someone who wandered away from the scene, it looks like we lost thirty-five good men last night. Once we've recovered everyone, there will be a service here in the compound. I'll let you know when that will be. I have spoken to the Pentagon regarding our losses. They're sending some new paratroopers that were training in the Philippines to bring Charlie Company back to combat strength. That's all I have for now. Get some breakfast and let's try putting this behind us. We still need to be ready to shove off at a moment's notice. One more thing, when we get to Korea, the South Korean Army will be known as ROK troops. We will refer to the enemy as DPRK, which stands for Democratic People's Republic of Korea. Keep that in mind so we always know who you're referring to. Last thing we want to do is kill our allies and piss off the South Koreans."

The replacements arrived two days later by aircraft. It was decided to build one new platoon around the thirty-five replacements, as those men were already used to operating as a team under harsh conditions. Since all the men were already well trained and combat ready, the transition was seamless.

On the 15th of September, Gen. MacArthur took a major risk landing troops on the shores near Inchon. His intention was to land at the rear of the North Korean forces and cut their supply lines, thus forcing them to break off their southern attack. That same day orders arrived, activating the 187th for combat. However, this time they weren't going to jump into combat. They were going to fly to Korea and land at Kimpo Airfield to join forces already on the ground. New forces were desperately needed to strengthen American lines and plug holes caused by massive casualties and retreating forces.

Steve remembered Franny's words from just a few weeks earlier, *'Everyone is on the run over there and we're supposed to go in there and do what? Hold the line? Slow down the withdrawal or just be sacrificial lambs.'* Suddenly it appeared to Steve they were going to be exactly that—the sacrificial lambs, allowing tired forces a chance to disengage and complete their withdrawal. This wasn't what good airborne forces were to be used for. How could the top brass just write off so many highly trained good men when they may be needed down the road for more serious action.

Sand tables were quickly prepared, allowing the men to acquaint themselves with the topography they would be fighting in when they landed in Korea. Each company was assigned a sector they would be responsible to hold.

Col. Fontaine remained an observer, as he turned the intense training over to each of his company commanders. This ensured each company could ask pertinent questions regarding their mission, while receiving answers directly from their localized commanders. In a way, this was D-Day in Normandy all over again. Capt. Fargo was nervous about his green untested paratroopers. Although he had worked hard preparing them for combat, he fully realized most of them wouldn't have a clue what to do when they hit the ground. He realized their main mission would be to hold off North Korea troops attacking toward the south. But how large a force would they be up against? Would there be tanks to contend with? Would his paratroopers receive adequate artillery support to bolster their mission? Yes, this was Normandy all over again in many respects, too many questions with not enough answers from the top planners. Although this time they had one huge advantage. This attack would take place at dawn instead of in the dead of night. Col. Fontaine was proud of his men and his leaders. He felt sorry for the retreads from World War Two he was sending back into hell. But without them, these young paratroopers would be nothing more than cannon fodder. They needed every piece of luck possible to survive.

Late on September 19th, the men were informed they would be leaving early the following morning. Although everyone knew it was coming, Steve felt a knot in his stomach he could not untie. It made him nauseous. All of his memories from Europe flowed back into his mind like a ruptured damn. He remembered the dead, the cries of the wounded, and the constant smell of decaying flesh. Faces of the men he lost in battle paraded through his soul in an endless circle. They were all so young, yet each of them looked old beyond their years. Those hollow eyes and bearded faces streaked with mud, grime and blood sent shivers down Steve's back. He knew in just twenty-four hours he would be seeing new faces join that sad and endless parade of death he had come to live with. Sitting on his bunk that last evening of peace, the words he wanted so desperately to write to Karen and his family would not come. Never had he been at such a loss for words for the people he loved so much, and may never see again.

Quietly Harry approached Steve's bunk. "Having a hard time writing home, Stevie boy?"

"Yeah. I just can't think of what to write. I know what's in my head and my heart but I just can't put it into words. I just feel sick," Steve replied, looking over at his best friend and confidant.

"That's why I came over here. I had the same problem. It's funny in a way. We've been here before, yet it's like it's all brand new somehow. I feel mixed up. I just want to go home and forget all about what's coming our way. I don't want to see the bodies and the blood. I don't want to hear another kid like Danny Garnet calling for his mother before he died, or see another Oscar Joblanski have his leg ripped off. I'm not ready for that," Harry explained nearly inaudibly.

Drawing in a deep breath Steve looked at his best friend. "If I have to do this, I'm glad I have you with me. I wish we would be fighting side by side like we did in Europe. I always trusted your judgment and knew you had my back. This time we'll be on the same battlefield, but having different challenges to deal with. I'll miss you, Harry. Take care of yourself out there."

"Yeah. You too Stevie boy, no more theatrics. Just do your job. Somehow, I think we used up most of our nine lives last time around. There may not be many more we can hope for," Harry replied, as he stood up. "I guess I better find the words I need to write Marylyn. She is one special lady. It's bullshit doing this to her, it's just not right."

Steve forced a smile as he nodded his head. "Yeah, I know it. Sleep well and give my best to Marylyn."

Harry patted Steve on the shoulder before walking slowly from the barracks.

Dawn came way too early the morning of the twentieth. The sound of grunting trucks broke the morning calm around 0400. After a quick breakfast, the men began assembling with their equipment, ready to board the waiting transports. As they were checked off, each man climbed aboard, taking a place on the wooden benches without saying a word.

As their trucks pulled up next to the massive air transports, pilots and ground crews busied themselves making last minute checks. After everyone was loaded, the pilots spun over their huge engines, creating a tremendous roar while filling the air with clouds of oily smoke and dust. In a few minutes, the engines settled down to a methodical pulse, as the pilots raced them up and down, gradually bringing them up to proper operating temperature.

Then somewhere out on that vast airfield, an officer signaled his Jeep driver to lead the first aircraft onto the taxiway rolling steadily toward the runways. One by one, the huge C-118's took to the air through the morning mist. Today they assembled over land before beginning their run over the Straits of Korea toward the dreadful war that awaited them.

Steve looked around the plane. Most of the men sat quietly looking straight ahead. He knew each man was praying in his own way, just hoping to survive this war. Outside the thin skinned aluminum walls of the planes, the sky was a brilliant blue with just a few small cirrus clouds to the north. It appeared this would be a smooth ride with excellent weather all the way to Kimpo Airfield. That didn't ease Steve's mind a whole lot. Because clear skies meant enemy anti-aircraft batteries would also have a good view of the approaching airborne armada. Hopefully, the America fighters they were promised were already in action, striking at enemy anti-aircraft batteries, trying to put them out of commission before they could do any damage to the massive airborne armada.

However, that was not the case. As they approached the Korean coast line, heavy anti-aircraft fire filled the sky with large black puffs of smoke and deadly steel. Before any serious damage was inflicted upon the slow moving transports, the entire flight turned back out to sea. They paralleled the coast line for nearly a half hour before turning west back toward the coast line. This time there was much lighter enemy fire from smaller caliber weapons. The pilots raced on through the flak without using evasive tactics as they headed straight in to their assigned landing fields. The die was now cast. Every enemy soldier in the surrounding hills knew reinforcements were on the way. Steve was sure they pretty much knew which airfields the Americans would use to deliver troops, in order to bolster their collapsing front. That meant the fight would be on the minute they touched down. In broad daylight this could be a blood bath of major proportions.

Seconds later Steve's thoughts were affirmed by their pilot as he came on the intercom. "Alright men, listen up. Kimpo Airfield is under attack as I speak. When we hit the ground you need to get off this aircraft in record time so we can get back in the air. General MacArthur doesn't want to have these birds burning on the tarmac. We won't throttle down much so watch out for our propellers when you leave the door. We're on the way down now, we should hit the runway in about five minutes." Tension levels inside the plane built dramatically after the pilot quit speaking.

The soldier next to Steve quickly inquired. "Sarg, tell me what to do when we leave the plane, anyway? Where do we go? We'll be in the damn open like sitting ducks. What do we do?"

Steve looked at the nervous soldier. "Get off and run to the edge of the runway then hit the dirt. Be ready to fire back at the enemy. But for God's sake, don't shoot when our planes are rolling by. We don't want to shoot down one of our own aircraft. Understood?"

"Yeah Sarg, I got it. I won't let you down," the young soldier replied as he adjusted his helmet again and took a deep breathe.

Answering that question immediately brought Steve right to the place he needed to be mentally in order to lead his men into combat. He instantly knew that Sgt. Kenrude of 1944 was fully back into his system, ready to take charge and get the job done, but he knew a quick prayer wouldn't hurt one bit.

Suddenly the tires screeched as they slammed down against the tarmac. Looking about the plane, Steve called out. "Lock and load gentlemen. You've just touched down in Korea and the greeting committee is already showing their bad attitudes. Let's show the bastards what we're made of."

As the C-118 came to a stop on a concrete pad, the cargo master swung open the large door. Before he could tell the men to disembark, a bullet struck him in the head. He spun around before falling to the concrete below. Several more rounds struck the aircraft, punching holes in the aluminum skin while additional rounds ricocheted of the runway.

"Move, get off this damn plane! Move, damn it, move!" Steve yelled, as the men rushed by him.

Exiting the aircraft, Steve observed one of his men lying several feet away with a bullet wound to his lower leg. Grabbing him by the belt, Steve pulled him back to his feet. "You either get moving son, or you die right here, it's your choice! Do you hear me, damn it?"

"Yeah, yeah, I hear you Sarg. But damn it hurts." The soldier yelled above the clamor as he hobbled forward beside Steve.

"Believe me, the next one won't hurt at all because the angels will be there to lift you up. You best begin to think if you ever want to get the hell out of here alive!" Steve screamed at the whining soldier as he pulled him along. After making their way to an earthen embankment at the edge of the runway, Steve pushed the man to the ground, yelling, "Medic! I need a medic over here!"

As their plane roared back down the runway, Steve took a good look around. Everywhere he looked was the burned out wreckage of aircraft and trucks. Much of the runway and the adjacent parking areas were pock marked with holes from artillery and mortar strikes. Not one building remained intact. Fires still blazed in one C-118 and two large structures. Even the huge concrete maintenance building behind them was severely damaged. It reminded Steve of the destruction he had witnessed in Europe on so many occasions.

Up and down the line of Alpha Company, medics worked diligently tending to the wounded. Steve peered at the body of their jump master lying on the runway. He couldn't stay there if other aircraft were going to land once they cleared out the enemy snipers, so someone had to move him.

Dinsmore, Steve's radio man, charged forward calling, "Sarg, Capt. Fargo on the line for you."

Grabbing the handset, Steve reported in. "Captain, we're behind the earthen embankment about a hundred yards from the damaged maintenance hangar. So far, it looks like I have one dead and at least a few injured.

What's our next move?"

"Kenrude, you need to cross that damn runway and take out that small hill to your left. That's where most of the sniper fire is coming from. I'll have mortars on the way in about a minute. As soon as they hit, you move. Don't wait for anything."

"Got it, we'll be ready." Steve took out his binoculars to scan the area. There was a small depression just in front of the hill. That would be as good a place as any to start the war from. He quickly passed word down the line so all his men knew what they were about to do.

But now it was waiting time. Bullets whizzed overhead as an occasional enemy mortar slammed into the airfield. For the moment, no more planes were attempting to land. They circled overhead waiting for the fire to be suppressed. How long could a minute be? Steve kept looking at his watch, where each second ticked by slower than the one preceding it.

Finally, the shrill scream of mortars filled the air, followed by explosions on and around the hill as they prepared to begin their assault. In mere seconds the little knoll occupied by the enemy disappeared in a cloud of smoke and dust. Now it was time for the new paratroopers to engage with the enemy. It was time to see just what his men had learned throughout all their training. But worst of all, now was the time for men to be killed. Not unlike Normandy, each man would have to work through their fears while meeting the enemy head on. There would be no second chances. Each man either fought with every ounce of energy in his body, or he would die where he lay. There was no easy way to jump into combat for the first time, and the North Koreans were not handing out free passes today.

Steve looked left, then right. Raising his arm he gave out a mighty scream. "Move out!"

Without hesitation, his men charged forward, pouring fire toward the dug-in enemy. As his men raced forward, Steve turned back toward the runway in the hope of getting the jump master off the runway before any pilots attempted to land. Grabbing the stricken world war two veteran by the belt, Steve dragged his lifeless body toward a concrete aircraft revetment. After taking a deep breath, he again raced across the wide open runway to join his platoon to lead them into combat.

CHAPTER 7
AUTUMN ARRIVES IN MINNESOTA

Vibrant shades of red, orange and yellow leaves all covered in dew glistened in the morning sun, while busy squirrels scampered about, hauling loads of fallen acorns back to their nests. On the edge of the woods, a mother deer and her two fawns also fed on the plentiful acorns, attempting to put on weight for the coming winter. Light wisps of steam rose into the early morning sky from the many lakes and ponds surrounding Glendale. Fall had once again arrived in Minnesota.

The Kenrude men had been working for several hours before the sun began burning off the light fog that shrouded the farm. After a hearty breakfast, and plenty of hot coffee, Alex planned to start chopping corn in three of their fields. His hired men were already in the machine shed hooking up the baler so they could bale the last of the alfalfa which had been cut earlier in the week. Since the forecast called for rain over the next few days, Alex wanted the baling completed before his beautiful crop became soaked and would be ruined.

Nancy hurried breakfast, since Alex was chomping at the bit to get going. She missed getting help from Christine who had returned to nursing school in Minneapolis at the beginning of September. Just as they sat down to eat, Mike and Glenda drove in the yard. Alex jumped up from the table, grabbing his hat off the counter.

"Wait just a minute, Mr. Kenrude," Nancy called out. "I worked hard getting this breakfast ready so you will sit down and eat. They are more than welcome to have coffee and a roll with us. Now plant it, buster."

Alex laughed, looking at his determined wife. "Buster? Where the heck did that come from?"

Nancy had to laugh. "I don't know I guess I picked it up from Christine when she was home. She was always calling Mike that, it must have rubbed off."

As Mike and Glenda came through the door, Alex returned to his meal. "Grab a cup of coffee and a roll. Your Mom made a huge batch of them this morning."

Mike followed his father's instruction instantly. He was never one to turn down any type of sweets.

Glenda smiled at Mike as she poured a cup of coffee before pulling up a chair at the table.

"Have you heard how your mom is doing with Matthew on her little excursion?" Nancy inquired of Glenda.

"Yes, Mom called last night actually, and said everything is going fine. She was really surprised as how well Mathew had been on the drive to St. Cloud. She said her new neighbor's kids are having a great time with him, and vice versa, so it looks like it all worked out. She is so glad she moved up here to Minnesota to be near us, and she really likes working at the College in St. Cloud. I think Dad would have liked Minnesota also. It's a shame he died so young." After taking a drink of coffee she continued, "So, I know you've been busy, but have you decided what you're going to make for the fall festival yet?"

"Oh I don't know, Glenda. I just can't make up my mind. Maybe just some jam. Honey are you busy today, would you like to help me out?" Nancy inquired, anxiously hoping her daughter-in-law would agree.

"That's actually why I came along with Mike. I was hoping I could talk you into making something today. I always learn so much when I work with you," Glenda responded with a smile.

The two women began planning their projects as Mike and Alex drank down the last of their coffee.

"Well, we're off. We'll be back about noon if that works for you, honey," Alex inquired as he adjusted his hat.

"That's fine, Alex. Take care out there in the fields, you two. Say hello to Karen for me. Tell her to drop by if she's not too busy today. Let her know Glenda and I are going to make preserves," Nancy responded before turning back to Glenda.

Karen had just finished getting Tommy and Abigail bathed and dressed for the day when Alex and Mike drove into the yard.

Walking up on the porch Alex called in through the screen door. "Anyone home in there?"

"Yeah, come on in, Dad," Karen called out as she walked into the kitchen with several wet towels.

The two children scrambled past her calling out, "Grandpa, Grandpa!"

Alex knelt down to give his grandchildren a bit hug. "You guys seem to get bigger every day. Pretty soon you'll be too big to hug."

Abigail looked at Alex for a moment before asking, "How big is that before we can't be hugged? I don't ever want to get that big, Grandpa. Can't I stay small?"

Alex laughed squeezing Abigail tightly. "You'll never get too big to be hugged, sweetheart."

Standing up, Alex looked at Karen. He informed her of Nancy and Glenda's plans before asking, "Is there anything you need, or is there anything that needs repair around the place?"

"No Dad, everything is as good as it can be. Oh, I received a letter from Steven just yesterday. He said they had a bad accident while doing a night jump, and a bunch of men were killed. He also says he figured they would be in Korea by the time I received the letter. So, I guess we can assume he is in the thick of it by now." She looked over her shoulder to see where the children had gone.

When she observed them in the living room with Mike, she continued. "Dad, it scares me worse than in World War Two. He needs to come home to watch his beautiful children grow up. It scares me that Abigail doesn't mention him much anymore. She just says 'Daddy had to go away. I don't think he loves us anymore.' I've told her over and over that their Daddy loves them very much and wants to come home, but she just seems to have made up her mind."

"Honey, she's just three years old. There's no way she can understand the concept of war. Just keep doing what you're doing and she'll be fine," Alex encouraged Karen with a smile.

Seconds later, Mike came in the kitchen placing his arm around Karen, "Well, we need to get moving if we're going to get all that corn chopped today, so we'll see you later." After giving Karen a kiss on the cheek he walked toward the door. Alex gave his grandchildren another big hug before following Mike out to the truck.

The general attitude in Glendale regarding the war had taken a rather sharp turn. Most people now understood this was no laughing matter, and that the cost was going to be way too high.

Phil Stenous, son of the dentist in Glendale was home on leave after being severely wounded several months earlier. Any chance he got, he informed folks about the desperate battle being waged. He explained why the survival of South Korea looked pretty bleak, even with the help of American forces. His prediction was that Korea would fall to the communists by Christmas.

Fourteen men from the Glendale area had now left for military service. Twelve had been drafted into the Army, while one enlisted in the Navy and one in the Air Force. There were no large groups of men waiting to enlist as there was during World War Two. One of the draftees was Ralph Brickman, son of the local minister. Although Minister Brickman fought desperately to keep his son from being drafted, it was no use. After all attempts failed, he worked tirelessly to convince the draft board that Ralph was a conscientious objector.

They gave Ralph one option. Report for duty or go to jail for refusing to be inducted. After returning from his last meeting with the draft board, Ralph told his father he was ready to go and do his part. The discussion became heated when Ralph told his father he would never be able to live with himself if he chose to be a conscientious objector. He explained how much he admired the men who fought in World War Two. Now it was his chance to answer the call to duty, and he would have nothing to do with options he considered cowardly.

Minister Brickman, angered by the decision, demanded Ralph move in with his grandparents until he left. Although Ralph's mother Ida did her best to restore order in the family, her husband would have nothing to do with her requests for peace and understanding. The day Ralph left for basic training, his father refused to see him off. The rift in the family regarding the war was compounded when Ida chose to move out of the house. She told everyone her husband had lost his way, becoming an angry, bitter man who hated his country and disowned his only son. Many people in the community were upset with Minister Brickman's actions, and the attendance at Sunday services fell dramatically.

A month after Ralph departed, the church elders called for a special meeting to discuss what the congregation should do to bring peace back to their church. In a nearly unanimous vote, the congregation chose to ask Minister Brickman to leave the church.

Without argument, he packed up and moved to St. Paul with his brother. About a week later, Ida left town without offering a clue as to where she was headed.

The church elders chose a young Glendale man who had just completed seminary school in Illinois. Andrew Moore, along with his young wife Genève, gladly accepted the challenge of healing the wounds and bringing life back to the Glendale Community Church.

However, a more serious event rocked the once quiet community that fall. Early one Thursday morning, the badly beaten body of Grant Bainsworth was found hanging from one of the large corn bins behind the feed mill. Sheriff Waylon 'Bull' Richards along with two of his deputies spent several hours photographing and collecting evidence around the crime scene. When they completed their work at the scene, the body was sent to a crime lab in Minneapolis for an autopsy. Grant's father, Herman Bainsworth, quickly established a two thousand dollar reward for providing information leading to the apprehension of whoever was responsible for the murder of his son.

The problem was, most Glendale residents had little time for Grant or most of his family. Although the elder Bainsworths used their wealth to enhance many civic projects, they also used their influence and money to get what they wanted, even when it hurt other citizens. Understandably so, the list of people Sheriff Richards had to question was not only quite extensive, but rather belligerent.

The following Monday as Alex worked to replace the water pump on his largest tractor, Sheriff Richards drove in the yard.

"Need a hand there, Alex?" He called out from the patrol car as he rolled to a stop by the machine shop.

"Well, hello Bull! What brings you out to this part of the county so early in the morning? I figured you'd have your hands plumb full with that Bainsworth mess. I'd imagine Herman and his cantankerous wife are breathing down your neck every waking hour." Alex responded while wiping antifreeze from his hands.

"Come on Alex, you know me well enough. Neither the Bainsworth family nor anyone else is going to influence me on this investigation, or anything else. I've been Sheriff a long time and you're damn well aware of how I run my department."

Alex smiled, seeing how easily he ruffled the sheriff's feathers. He knew very well that Bull was not a big fan of the Bainsworth family either. "Yeah, I know you run one heck of a taught ship, Bull. I just had to give you a little crap this morning. Would you like to come in the house so we can talk over some hot coffee?"

"No, Alex that probably would not be a good idea this time. What I need to talk to you about might just anger your lovely wife a bit, and I don't want to upset Nancy."

Looking puzzled, Alex walked over to the patrol car. "What would you have to say that could irritate Nancy?"

Taking a deep breath, Sheriff Richards looked sternly at Alex. "Mike was in town early last Thursday delivering a load of corn to Charlie McGrath at the feed mill. Charlie said he saw Mike pull up but it took him a while to come inside. He said when Mike came into the office it was evident he was upset, plus he had blood on his right hand. What can you tell me about this, Alex?"

"Now wait just a dog gone minute, Bull. You and I have been friends since we were kids. Our boys went to school together, played sports together and served in the war. You know damn well Mike had nothing to do with the death of Grant Bainsworth," Alex replied angrily, pounding his right index finger into the Sheriff's chest.

"Look Alex, I don't want to believe Mike could have anything to do with this either. But everyone knows there's been bad blood between those boys all the way back to grade school. Remember there was that shoving match between them at the feed mill after Mike returned home. That got pretty ugly after Bainsworth made some comments regarding Mike's wife.

And Bainsworth made it clear to several people that he never forgot the incident, and swore someday he would settle the score. Now, I know Mike did everything he could to avoid that damn hot head, but Mike has been known to lose his temper a few times in the past as well. So, what do you know, Alex?" Sheriff Richards demanded of Alex as they stood looking eye to eye.

Nearly shaking with anger, Alex stared hard at his friend Bull for several moments. "Part of me wants to just plain knock you on your ass, Waylon. It angers me something fierce that you could feel my boy might be guilty of murdering someone. Sure, I know he killed during the war. So did your boys, damn it. But that was different. He never killed anyone in cold blood. He just did his job, same as all our men. I can't believe what you're insinuating here."

Bull shook his head before looking back at Alex. "Look Alex, I told you I don't want to believe Mike had anything to do with this, and I sure as hell don't want to lose our friendship, either. But a man is dead and I have a job to do. I need to talk with everyone I think might be able to lead me in the right direction on this investigation. I also need to talk to anyone who had a problem with Bainsworth, and as you know, that's a lot of damn people. But that's just the way it works, Alex."

Slowly, Alex turned, walking back toward the tractor. After placing his rag on the tool box he turned to face the Sheriff, who followed just a short distance behind.

"When Mike came back from town, he complained about the hitch on the truck and what a rough time he had unhooking the trailer on the incline near the scale. He had a small rag wrapped around his hand as his knuckles were still bleeding. He said when he finally was able to pull the trailer tongue free, he slammed his knuckles into the lower framework we added to support that massive hitch. Nancy cleaned up his hand and bandaged his knuckles. I never questioned his explanation at all since that hitch has been a problem in the past with a heavy trailer hooked up. I've been meaning to do some remodeling on it, but I just haven't had the time." Alex explained in a solemn tone.

Bull was quiet for a moment as he mulled over Alex's explanation. "Did he say anything about seeing Bainsworth or anyone else while he was there?"

"Yeah, he said he saw Frank Mullins over by the warehouse throwing fertilizer sacks on a truck. Mike said, he never talked to him they just waved. Why don't you talk to Mullins? Maybe he can shed some light on the issue" Alex growled.

"I did talk to Frank for quite some time. He never mentioned seeing Mike throughout our entire conversation," Bull countered, scratching his head. "I guess I need to talk with Mike. Can you tell me where he is this morning?" The sheriff inquired very officially.

Nodding his head, Alex replied. "He was going to fix the pump in his basement first thing this morning. Then he was going to head over to Steve's place to start picking corn in the south field."

"Alright, I saw a tractor and corn picker in the field when I drove by there. Guess I'll head over and speak with him. Just one more thing, Alex, what time did Mike get back here?" Bull inquired.

"That's easy, Bull. I was just going to listen to the six-thirty national news out of Minneapolis. I wanted to hear what was going on in Korea when Mike came in dripping blood on Nancy's clean floor. Can I come along while you talk with Mike?" Alex asked respectfully.

"No Alex. I'm sorry, but I need to speak with Mike alone," Bull replied, before climbing back in his car and pulled away.

Mike was just swinging the tractor around near the county highway as the Sheriff drove down into the shallow ditch. Mike turned off the tractor as Bull approached him from the road.

"Hi, Sheriff. What can I do for you? I sure as hell couldn't have been speeding with this worn out old International," Mike called out, jumping down from the tractor.

"No you weren't speeding. I don't think we'll ever put speed limits on field work," Bull said laughingly. "But I need to talk to you about something more serious, Mike. You need to tell me everything you can about last Thursday morning while you were in town."

Mike nodded his head. "Yeah, I was expecting you or someone else would be talking to me sooner or later. Everyone knows Grant and I never saw eye to eye on anything. I've heard he had been going around town telling people he wanted to settle a score with me since we had our little shoving match in the feed mill office when I first came home." Mike leaned back against the patrol car as he wiped sweat from his forehead. "Well, I pulled up to the feed mill around five-thirty I'd say. There was a wagon on the scale already, so I couldn't pull up on the level platform. Charlie told me the night before to just drop our trailer if someone else parked on the scale during the night, that he would call us when it was empty. I was parked on that incline just before the scale with my wheels turned somewhat. But that damn hitch on the truck is just not right for such a heavy trailer. The tongue has a tendency to run up hill making it super tough at times to get it to slide free. So I yanked on it with all my might and it finally popped lose." Mike held up his hand in order to show Sheriff Richards his smashed knuckles. "I slammed my hand into that heavy frame work we built to support the hitch. I swore like a son-of-a-bitch and ended up wrapping my hand in a rag that was lying on the seat of the truck."

"Then what did you do?" the Sheriff inquired as he looked intently at Mike.

"I threw a block of wood under the back wheel of the trailer so it wouldn't roll. It would have been the left side. I saw there was a light on in the office so I walked in to tell Charlie the wagon behind the scale was ours.

We chatted a minute then I left. I wasn't in the mood to talk since my hand hurt and I was still a bit angry about that stubborn hitch," Mike responded.

"Did you see anyone else around the mill?" Bull inquired, studying Mike's facial expressions.

After thinking about it for a second, Mike answered, "Oh yeah. When I went toward the office I saw Frank Mullins throwing fertilizer on to a flat-bed truck over by the new warehouse. I didn't talk to him. We just waved. Figured I'd say something when I came back out, but he wasn't there when I walked back out to the truck. He would have been the only other person I saw besides Charlie."

Sheriff Richards looked closely at Mike. "Son, I have questioned Frank at length. He says he never saw anyone in the yard behind the mill Thursday morning. Can you explain that?"

"Well, like I said we never spoke. We just waved at one another, maybe he just forgot. But he sure as hell must have heard me swearing out there. I really yelled. I was so pissed off when I smashed my hand, I swore a blue streak," Mike replied nearly laughing. "You know Sheriff, if you look at the back of the truck there still has to be blood on the frame where I hit my hand."

"Where is the truck right now, Mike?" Bull inquired.

"It's parked over at my place. I used it late last night to haul hay back to the steers in the west pasture. Drive me over there and we can take a look."

Parking the patrol car in Mike's driveway, the two men walked up to the truck. Mike pointed to the blood on the frame. "Right there, Sheriff. There's my blood. There might be blood on the trailer tongue too. We can go over to Dad's and take a look if you like?"

"No that's fine, Mike. Your story seems to add up, except for the deal with Mullins. We need to figure that out yet before I can clear your name totally. But leave that to me. My suggestion to you is to avoid all the Bainsworths and keep your mouth shut about this entire investigation. If someone does get in your face, don't lose your cool. Got that, Mike?" Bull explained in a very stern voice.

"Yeah I do, Sheriff. Look, I admit I never liked Grant. Not one bit. He was always a jerk. Most of all, it really upset me the way he treated Connie Ellsworth back in high school. It was plain pathetic. She was a neat girl. I always liked her," Mike explained shaking his head.

"Mike, tell me more about that. Ellsworth, I mean. I was on the Minneapolis Police Department at the time and I don't remember much about it," Bull asked, as he folded his large arms across his chest.

"Connie was probably the prettiest girl in our class. And she was sweet as pie to boot," Mike smiled as he remembered her. "Well, every guy in school wanted to date her, me included. But she had her eye set on bigger things. She was always teasing Grant and Stan Cochran. Stan's dad was an attorney in town back then. So like I said, she was after guys with big bucks. Sadly to say she wound up pregnant just as we started our junior year. She told everyone that Grant was the father. He denied it, and pointed fingers at every guy who ever gave her a second look. Worse, the bastard called her a slut and a whore right to her face in front of several kids in the gym. She broke down crying. The more she cried the more he poured it on about her being poor white trash that would never amount to anything. I had been playing basketball when this all took place. I walked over, pushing Grant out of the way. Then I took Connie by the arm and walked her out of the gym. As we walked off he yelled out, 'Yup, Kenrude is the father. He's taking his little bitch away to wipe her nose.' She quit school the next day. Over the next few weeks, signs started showing up in her front yard calling her all kinds of despicable things. Grant would laugh about it in school. He never denied putting the signs there when he was accused. He would just say, 'No little tramp is going to ruin the name of a Bainsworth in this town.' Eventually the Ellsworth's moved to Mankato. Rumor had it Grant's dad helped pay for the move just to get Connie out of town. She committed suicide about six months after she had the baby. What a damn shame!"

Bull nodded in agreement. "Did this Cochran boy say much about the entire situation?"

Mike thought a few seconds. "Well, like most of us he was really angry about the way Grant treated Connie, but I don't recall him saying much. You could tell he was hurt by what happened though. He liked Connie. I mean, he really liked that girl a lot. And he treated her right. I don't think he dated another girl the rest of our junior year. Of course about that time I ran off to join the Army and didn't graduate, so I don't know what happened in our senior year."

"Where is he today, Mike?" Bull inquired as he took a notebook and pen from his pocket.

"I don't know, Sheriff. I haven't heard a word about him from the time I enlisted. Actually, most of the kids I went to high school with treat me like a lower class citizen since I didn't graduate with them. But who gives a shit, I got my GED in the service anyway," Mike replied with a smile.

As Sheriff Richards returned Mike to the tractor he said. "You know Mike, I didn't think this interview would go so smooth. I expected you to be cockier and much more of a smart ass. You really have grown up. Thanks for all the information. I'll stay in touch."

That evening as Mike and Glenda had dinner with his folks, he explained everything that happened with the Sheriff. Nancy was actually surprised Mike kept his cool during the entire interview.

Alex then explained how angry he became with his old friend out by the barn that morning. He finished by saying, "Someday I'll have to apologize to Bull. He was just doing his job, I guess. He's a damn good Sheriff."

Several weeks later Sheriff Richards once again drove into the Kenrude farm. This time Alex and Mike were rebuilding a small gas engine they used to operate a water pump.

"Is that thing ever going to run again?" Bull asked, as he walked into the machine shed.

"Only if this kid of mine can find the new bearings we bought last week," Alex replied as he gave Mike a small slap on the shoulder.

"Well, I have some news for you," Bull announced, as he sat down on a bale of hay. "We arrested Frank Mullins late last night for the murder of Grant Bainsworth. We probably wouldn't have figured it out but for the information you gave me, Mike."

"Me? What the hell did I say to help you out?" Mike inquired, tossing a brown paper bag containing the missing bearings toward his father.

"I questioned Mullins several more times about that morning. He swore he never saw you unhooking the trailer, and never heard you yell. The third time he said he kind of remembered hearing two men arguing. And that one of the men could have been you. I asked him why he didn't check it out since it was five thirty in the morning. He said he didn't want to get involved. I asked him if he was positive it was you. He said he couldn't be sure. I asked him what Bainsworth would have been doing at the feed mill that hour of the morning. Of course he didn't have an answer. Well, after doing some digging, we found out Mullins is actually Stan Cochran's real father. A young lady Mullins got pregnant gave up the baby for adoption to the Cochran family before leaving town, and they never told Stan he was adopted. Mullins knew, so he always kept an eye on Stan from a distance. He lost contact with Stan when he joined the Navy during the war."

Bull got up and stretched, then continued his story while Alex and Mike looked on. "Well, this past summer Stan returned to visit his aunt and uncle, the Burning's. While he was here, he ran into Bainsworth down by the lake. He jumped all over Bainsworth for what he did to the Ellsworth girl. As things would have it, Bainsworth knew that Cochran was adopted. He told Stan his real father was Frank Mullins and that he was a bum and a drunk just like his real old man. Later that night Stan ran down

Mullins asking him if it was true. Mullins ended up telling him the whole story. Stan left town the next day angrier than hell. I guess I can't blame him, that must have hurt something awful. Mullins was just as angry with Bainsworth for telling Stan the truth. Several times over the rest of the summer the two exchanged words. Stan told me that Mullins called him Wednesday night saying he needed help; that he had done something real bad. Stan jumped in his car and drove all night from Moorhead to see what had happened. Mullins told Stan that Bainsworth Land Holdings had just purchased the apartment building he lived in. Unfortunately, Bainsworth ran into Mullins over at the Starlight Club Wednesday night where both men were pretty juiced. Bainsworth told Mullins he was being evicted because he was nothing but a low life drunk and they didn't want his kind living in their building. When Bainsworth went to leave, Mullins followed him to the parking lot where he beat him to a pulp. Then he tied him up and hid him behind the fertilizer warehouse until he could figure out what to do next. He said when Bainsworth came to, they argued until nearly dawn. He told Stan that when he heard you drive in he got nervous. He was afraid Bainsworth would start yelling. So Mullins hit him with a wrench and hanged him before heading out on his route delivering fertilizer."

Alex whistled at that news and Mike looked on with his mouth hanging open in surprise. The Sheriff sat down heavily on the hay bale to finish his story.

"When I tracked down Stan he sang like a bird. Says he was dumbfounded that Mullins would hang Bainsworth. He never felt Mullins had it in him to commit such an act of violence. But Stan Cochran was really scared. He's a legal assistant in a big law firm over in Moorhead. He wanted no part in keeping what he knew from Mullins under wraps, as he could lose his job if he were involved in the murder or withheld evidence. He told me everything," Bull explained as he shook his head. "Quite the mess, but the case is closed, and there's no question one way or the other as to how it all went down," the Sheriff concluded.

Mike shook his head. "Wow, that's some story. I'm glad you were able to figure it out and close the case. Thank you. What a shame it all turned out the way it did. So many lives ruined."

"Well, that's the way it usually ends up, Mike. Frank Mullins will most likely get a life sentence for what he did." After a moment of silence, Sheriff Richards stood up and smiled as he shook hands with the two men. As Mike and his dad returned to their work on the pump, Sheriff Richards drove slowly away from the farm.

With all the excitement from the past summer, most Glendale residents were more than ready to have the quiet of a long winter settle in. The war continued to be front page news as battle lines rolled up and down the Korean Peninsula, with no clear victory in sight. Many more men were drafted into the service as President Truman continued increasing the U.S. military presence in the conflict. In October, the first two casualties of the war returned home to Glendale. First came the body of Johnny Kimbal, who was killed during the Inchon landings, then Eddie Stalwert arrived a week later, after having both his legs blown off by an artillery explosion. They were sad reminders that this war would have the same horrible costs as World War Two. The Kenrude's prayed fervently every day for Steve's safe return.

CHAPTER 8
PARATROOPERS JOIN THE BATTLE

Steve raced through the blinding dust as mortars screamed overhead. After what felt like an eternity, the depression was finally directly in front of him. With a loud thud, he dropped into the safety of the position next to Sgt. Kilburn. Fire from the enemy snipers dropped considerably as American mortars continued pounding their positions. Looking to his right, Steve observed Sgt. Martinez kneeling beside his squad. Waving his arm Steve called out, "Martinez, over here!"

Dashing across the depression Martinez dropped to his knees aside Sgt. Kilburn, just as Whitebear and Hagen arrived.

"Alright, we start the war here, gentlemen. Martinez and Kilburn, take your squads around the north side of that damn hill when the mortars stop. Hagen, you go around the south side. Whitebear, you and I will take your squad right up the front to clean out anyone left in fox holes. And tell your men to be very careful not to shoot each other as you get around the back side of the hill. You guys got that?"

They all nodded in agreement as they charged back to their squads. Now Steve would be able to see what his men had learned in training. He would be able to determine if they were truly up to the rigors of combat. He knew he had good squad leaders; now it was a matter of the men following their instructions while under hostile fire.

After the last mortar landed, the three squads began moving out to circle the hill as they were instructed. Steve nodded at Whitebear, "Let's go, son." Third squad charged forward, taking some light fire as they began their climb. Shots rang out all across the hill as his men confronted the DPRK troops still dug in.

As Steve ran around several small bushes, he observed two enemy soldiers digging out from a caved in position. One of the men observed Steve at exactly the same time. As he reached for his weapon, Steve fired two short blasts from his Thompson. Both men fell silent.

He looked over the two dead men for a moment. "No, not this time, buddy boy. Not this time," he muttered as he continued climbing the hill.

Minutes later the men reached the summit of the hill. Steve motioned for them to continue down the back side as he observed his other three squads cleaning up several DPRK men who were attempting to flee the area.

When the fighting ceased, the four squads joined together. Steve called out, "Casualty reports!"

Incredibly, everyone survived their first battle in Korea. Although it was just a small fight, Steve was proud of the way they operated. He now knew his men were a cohesive team he could rely on in the future. Needless to say, he had no idea what the future held for these young warriors.

Motioning for his radio man, Private Dinsmore, Steve called out, "Get me Capt. Fargo."

Seconds later Dinsmore handed him the handset, "Capt. Fargo, Sarg."

Steve took the handset as he peered into the bright blue sky. "Captain, we have the hill secured. No casualties. What next?"

"Good job, Kenrude. Bring your men back toward the burned out hanger. We'll start from there," Capt. Fargo happily replied.

As Steve brought first platoon back across the runway, Harry and their happy first Sergeant, Franny, walked over to shake hands with him.

"That looked good, Stevie boy. So all the men did well?" Harry inquired.

"Yeah, everyone did their job. No one appeared to hesitate to pull the trigger. I think we did well training them," Steve replied with a smile.

As the men assembled to hear from Col. Fontaine, C-118's were once again landing to drop the balance of their battalion. "Alright, listen up." Col Fontaine called out to the troops from atop several pallets. "We're going to march south to a town named Suwon, once everyone is on the ground. It's about a five mile hike. No doubt we'll have to deal with DPRK snipers and stragglers all the way so keep your eyes and ears open.

Our mission is to clear the Cumpo Peninsula of all enemy activity. I understand they have a large build-up of troops in the area so it will not be an easy task by any means. We'll have air and artillery support. There's a small stock pile of equipment beside the hanger. Grab all the extra ammo, grenades or other equipment you think might come in handy. We should be ready to move out in about an hour, so take a moment to grab some chow."

Harry handed Steve six extra magazines for his Thompson. "Sanchez and I already raided the pile. Do you want any extra grenades? I have a few more than I really want to carry."

Taking the magazines, Steve questioned his friend. "Man, what is it with you and grenades. Back in France I swear you were laying them things like a chicken lays eggs. You never seemed to run out and your uniform bulged from every seam, you were carrying so many. Sure, give me a couple more."

"Hey, so I like blowing things up. What's wrong with that?" Harry laughed, as he passed several grenades to his friend. "Try it more often, Stevie boy. You might get to like it."

Steve encouraged his men to break open a few more ration crates and stuff them into their packs. He knew there would be a time they would come in handy. It was clear to first platoon that this five mile walk could take some time and be dangerous, depending on how much the enemy attempted to react.

About an hour later the long line of paratroopers, along with two companies of regular infantry, containing one heavy weapons platoon and one South Korean company began the long walk to Suwon.

Luckily there was very little trouble along the way. Several DPRK soldiers charged the column with fixed bayonets but were killed before they were able to make contact. Three American soldiers were wounded by snipers, but thankfully, none of the injuries were life threatening. They passed never ending columns of civilians pulling carts, or directing hay wagons pulled by nervous horses the rest of the day. The disorderly evacuation of uncooperative peasants jammed roads, slowing the progress of the troops considerably. They were clearly terrified by the fierce looking soldiers and clunking tanks, but kept heading south, evacuating the peninsula as fighting intensified. Most of the people appeared to be older farm type individuals, usually with a few cows or goats. Some young families were mixed into the pathetic procession. Their young children would run among the GI's holding out their hands hoping to receive gifts of chocolate. Most often their little begging acts were successful as the soldiers loved playing with the children. It seemed strange to Steve that these small children could already be immune to the roar of jet fighters, exploding artillery and strange soldiers speaking different languages. Yet nothing seemed to bother them. They were dissimilar from the kids they had encountered in World War Two.

In Europe the kids were usually displaced victims often without parents. They were usually dirty and boisterous, just seeking something to eat. In time most would be reunited with their families then return to their rebuilt homes and cities and live a comfortable life. But these little urchins probably had no idea what running water or electricity even was. Most of them had never ridden in a motorized vehicle or gone to school. Many of them would never travel more than a few miles from their homes throughout their entire lifetime. Yet, they appeared to be happy playing with a stick and a pet goat. It was quite a clash of cultures for the average American soldier.

Continually, fighter aircraft roared overhead attacking enemy positions all along the front. Explosions shook the ground as their heavy ordnance struck home. Large clouds of smoke rose from the hillsides as American artillery zeroed in on enemy troop concentrations and weapons emplacements in rear areas.

During their journey they passed through what had been several small hamlets. Now, all that remained was the charred remnants of homes and small market places. Here and there lay the bloating remains of horses, cows and pigs. Most of the men covered their noses as they passed through. The horrific odor was enough to make the toughest man get sick. Steve wondered how many hundreds of years these small hamlets must have existed before being decimated by this war most rural Koreans didn't even understand. It was ancient civilization meeting twentieth century warfare. Steve was sure not one of these villagers could comprehend the meaning of this war, or the sheer brutality and destructiveness of the North Korean forces who claimed to be their friends.

They arrived at Suwon just as night fell across the battered Cumpo Peninsula. The companies were set up in a defensive perimeter in case large groups of DPRK troops attempted to over run their position. Everyone busied themselves digging fox holes while fortifying them with logs or other heavy debris they could find nearby. Capt. Fargo and Sergeant Doogan made a thorough inspection tour of the whole perimeter to assure every inch was defensible. Second platoon was held in reserve in case a segment of the Alpha Company perimeter needed reinforcement during the long night. That gave Harry time to meet with Steve and Wentworth to assist in setting up the perimeter.

"I think we're in for a long one tonight, Steve. I have a feeling those bastards are going to probe all night. They'll want to see what we're made of and see if they can spook the new kids in town. I don't like this one bit," Harry said quietly as the men ate a meal near Steve's fox hole.

"Yeah, I agree a hundred percent. Man, what I wouldn't give right now to be sitting down to a hot meal with Karen and the kids. We don't belong here, Harry. We've had our war. You have no idea what it was like to fire my Thompson today and kill a couple of guys. It just—well it's just not what I want to be doing all over again, the killing and dying. It was bad."

"Yeah, I've thought of that, too. About what it'll be like the first time I have to shoot again. And I know it's coming, either tonight or tomorrow. I'm trying to psych myself up for it," Harry replied, as he peered out into the eerie darkness.

"Don't bother trying to prepare yourself, Harry. You'll get in that position and you'll just pull the damn trigger. You'll do what you know you have to do. That's what I did this morning. It was like, instantly all the reflexes were back," Steve explained, as he studied the worried face of his best friend.

"Yeah, I guess," Harry said, with a slight smile. "I think I'll go check on my boys."

After Harry walked off, Steve made another round of the first platoon sector, ensuring everything was ready, and that the men were remaining vigilant.

He ended up stopping by a foxhole in fourth squad being manned by a soldier with a Browning automatic rifle. Steve knelt down. "How are you doing, Fulbright? See anything out there, yet?"

"I'm alright, Sarg. A bit tense but other than that I'm good. There's a lot of noise out there, but I can't see a single thing. Sometimes it feels like the bastards are just a few yards away. But we ran a wire with tin cans tied to it between a couple stakes about twenty yards out. So far, no one has made them rattle, so I guess it's my imagination playing tricks on me."

"Yeah, darkness can be your worst enemy at times. It's unnerving as hell. Hang in there Fulbright, and keep that B.A.R. ready to go," Steve directed as he began to move on.

Moments later, the tin cans rattled, sending a shiver up Steve's neck. Dropping to the ground Steve called out. "That's not your imagination Fulbright. Let them come to us. Just hold your fire."

Aiming his Thompson in the direction of the noise, Steve took a long breath. Seconds later, all hell broke loose as dark shapes appeared from the darkness, running straight toward the area secured by fourth and first squads. Steve opened up with his Thompson, cutting down several figures immediately. Fulbright, using his deadly B.A.R, ripped into the advancing figures. Several of them dropped before the balance of the attackers withdrew into the darkness once more. Moments later, everything was quiet except for a few moans coming from outside the perimeter.

Somewhere out in the darkness, a voice called out in Korean. You could hear the anguish in his voice. He called out several more times before he began to sob.

Hagen came down the line checking on his men. He lay down next to Steve. "Wow, that was something," he whispered. "Do you think they're going to come again, Sergeant?"

"Oh yeah, no doubt. It's just a matter of when and where," Steve replied, as his heart raced uncontrollably.

The injured man called out again, screaming in pain. Seconds later a single gunshot was heard, followed by the sound of someone running away from the perimeter.

"Well, I guess that was easier than bringing up a medic," Hagen whispered to Steve before checking on the rest of his squad.

About twenty minutes later, fourth and fifth platoons were hit by an assault of larger proportions. They breached the perimeter between fifth platoon and Baker Company, only to be met by Harry and two of his squads, who came up from the reserve. The fighting was intense but brief as the attackers ran into a solid wall of fire.

About an hour later, Charlie Company was hit even harder. The heavy weapons unit that accompanied the paratroopers continuously dropped mortars into the attacking hoards, while using their fifty caliber machine guns to halt the advance.

Nearly twenty more attacks of varying size struck the perimeter during the night. As dawn broke, it was evident that the enemy had taken the most casualties. Bodies lined the perimeter in every direction. Surprisingly, American casualties had been very light, with ten dead and twenty men suffering various types of injuries.

Two supply trucks came lumbering down the road from Kimpo at about 0900. They delivered ammunition, medical supplies and food. Medics filled the empty trucks with wounded men requiring advanced medical treatment. After the trucks departed, Col. Fontaine organized third battalion to begin a sweep to the northwest, aiming for the Han River. Along with second battalion on their right, they were hoping to squeeze the DPRK troops into a pocket with the sea on their right and the river to their backs.

Unfortunately, American intelligence did not include the fact that there were nearly 3,000 men belonging to the 107th Security Regiment of the DPRK Army on the peninsula. Once battle was engaged, the fighting was tough and bloody. These battle hardened soldiers were not about to be pushed around by the green American forces. All too often, it appeared the DPRK forces were falling back in strength toward the river, only to set up an ambush hoping to catch large segments of American forces off guard as they charged forward.

On the third day of the campaign, Harry's second platoon was directed to clear a small hamlet that appeared to be abandoned. Moving in teams, third squad cautiously moved to the edge of the hamlet. Harry slowly scanned the quiet little village with his binoculars. There was not a single sign of movement anywhere. Not a dog, not a human, nor were there any birds chirping in the area. It reminded him of the silence around the concentration camp they discovered in the last days of the war in Europe. Something was not right and he could feel it in his bones. His first squad leader, Mike Harrison, dropped down beside him. "What's the plan, Sarg?"

"I don't know yet, Harrison. I don't like what I'm seeing. It's just too damn quiet. Do you hear anything besides that light breeze?" Harry asked.

"No, nothing. That means the civilians and the DPRK have both moved out. We can clear the place in minutes and move on out," Harrison stated boldly. "I'll take first squad up to that barn. After we clear it, the rest of the platoon can follow us."

"Hold on, Harrison. I give the orders here, not you. You stay put while I move over to fourth squad's position to have a look. Do you understand me?" Harry barked at his impatient squad leader, who he was beginning to mistrust more and more.

"Yeah sure, but don't take too long. My men are getting anxious," the young squad leader replied indignantly.

Angrily, Harry turned back toward him. "You got some place you're supposed to be, Harrison? What, you got a dinner date in Seoul tonight with some hot hooker? Don't be a damn fool. We ain't getting anyone killed because you're in such a damn hurry. Now stay put—and that's an order!"

As Harry moved over toward fourth squad, Harrison dropped down by his B.A.R. Operator.

"What's going on, Sarg? When are we moving into the hamlet?" Pvt. Scanlon inquired.

"I don't know and neither does that crusty old World War Two veteran. If you ask me, he's plenty scared and just doesn't want to make a move until

MacArthur himself tells him it's safe to go. I sure wish we had a real leader," Harrison replied angrily to his anxious heavy weapons man.

Scanlon was quiet for a moment before he spoke again. "Sarg, why don't we take about half the squad and rush up to the barn like you said. When we get there we signal the rest of the men to follow. We can clear the hamlet before the idiot can ever come up with a plan. You can be the hero, Harrison."

"Yeah I could show him, alright. I could tell Fargo that Jensen's all washed up and needs to be replaced. After my move, Fargo just might make me platoon leader. Let's do it." Harrison agreed.

Quickly he informed his men about the plan. Taking six men with him they raced for the barn.

"What the hell?" Harry called out as he observed half of his first squad running toward the hamlet. "I'll kill that son of a bitch Harrison myself if the North Koreans don't do it first. Wiley, get your squad ready to give support fire. That hamlet's occupied. I saw movement in that little greenish shack near the church."

Seconds later, the balance of first squad, minus Corporal Quibbley, raced toward the barn as Harrison waved them forward. Quibbley directed the men to stay put, but they refused to listen.

Fire erupted from nearly every building as the six men ran toward the hamlet. Four of them fell instantly. The other two were able to crawl back to their positions near Cpl. Quibbley. Third and Fourth squads returned fire as Harry ran head long toward the barn firing his Thompson. Dropping down into an irrigation ditch, he motioned for the men near the barn to fall back. Regrettably, a Russian made DPRK tank began rumbling down the side of a hill about a half mile away.

"Oh shit! Come on, fall back. Tank, tank," Harry screamed, as he pointed down the road.

Harrison yelled out. "Stay where you are. Our chances are better here than crossing that open ground."

Regardless of Harrison's order, two of his men turned away from the barn, and began running back toward the ditch where Harry was blasting away at several DPRK soldiers who were attempting to sneak up on the men from the village.

Once he knocked them down Harry called out again. "Come on, damn it. Fall back!"

Before they could move, an explosion tore the barn apart. Harry watched in alarm as the other four men were thrown through the air. Grabbing his binoculars he observed three of them moving, but there was no way for him to get to them. Harrison stood up, grabbing Scanlon by the arm. They hobbled to the ditch by the grace of God without getting hit. Scanlon was badly injured, while Harrison had minor cuts. The third injured man finally regained his feet, only to be torn apart by a second shell from the approaching tank.

"Everyone low crawl back to your positions by second squad, move. I'll keep you covered." Harry screamed above the rage of battle.

"No, you go Sarg. I'll stay. I ain't going to make it anyway," Scanlon barked at Harry as he repositioned himself to begin firing.

"Scanlon! That was an order. You go with Harrison. He'll get you back to second squad. Now go," Harry yelled angrily.

Harrison and the others took off without another word, leaving Harry and Scanlon in the ditch.

"Now it's you and me, Sarg. And I can't go. I'm finished." Reaching into his shirt he handed Harry a letter. "It's to my mom and dad. I didn't get a chance to finish it last night. Finish it for me Sarg. Send it to them. Tell them I did my best for everyone back home. Let them know I'll always love them." Crying, Scanlon looked intently a Harry. "Now get the hell out of here before I shoot you myself! Get out of here, go damn it! Please do this one thing for me, Sarg."

Outraged at what happened, Harry attempted to grab Scanlon to drag him back to safety.

"Damn it, Sarg. I told you to go. Now get the hell out of here and let me do what I need to do. Please, Sarg. Don't die over me. Those men need you. Go and save as many as you can."

After throwing down his Thompson and every magazine of ammunition he had, Harry took a deep breath. "Here kid. Use them as best you can. We'll try to lay down covering fire for you."

Half smiling, Scanlon picked up the Thompson. "Fire power, that's just what the doctor ordered. Thanks Sarg. Now go. Please go before you can't."

Nodding his head, Harry bailed out of the irrigation ditch as Scanlon began hammering away at a large group of North Koreans charging toward their position. On the way back, Harry grabbed an M-1 Carbine and several clips of ammunition from one of his men that had been killed while charging toward the barn. Bullets whizzed over his head while another round from the tank exploded about ten yards behind him. With all his might Harry threw himself behind a rock pile near second squad.

"What do we do now?" Sgt. Umberto asked, as he crawled up to Harry.

"We retreat. Start falling back to the high ground we crossed on the way here. Try and hang together." Harry informed his second squad leader as he waved at third and fourth squads to fall back. Harry watched Scanlon as he hammered away at the wall of approaching DPRK soldiers. He knew it was just a matter of time until he either ran out of ammunition or was killed. As Harry began falling back, he heard another shell from the tank explode. Dropping to his knees, he scanned the trench with his binoculars looking for Scanlon. The shell had landed right behind this brave, badly injured man. The fight was over. Shaking his head Harry raced back toward the high ground to join his men.

He had barely taken cover when two American fighter planes streaked overhead firing rockets and cannons at the exposed North Korean's. A third jet took out the Russian made tank with a rocket, striking it directly in front of the turret. The iron monster erupted into a tremendous ball of flame. No crew members could have ever escaped the raging inferno.

Harry sat quietly for a moment contemplating the loss of nearly an entire squad because of a foolhardy decision. The rest of his shattered platoon sat quietly as they awaited orders from their leader.

Slowly, Harry stood up. "Harrison, get your butt over here."

Very slowly Harrison stood up, looking at Harry not sure what to expect.

"I said come here!" Harry yelled, as he turned to face his first squad leader.

Harrison walked over as Sgt. Umberto followed close behind. "Look, Sarg—"

"Shut up!" Harry barked. "Take his side arm, Mr. Umberto. He'll be in your custody until we return to the company."

Next, Harry removed his bayonet from its scabbard. He commenced cutting the sergeant stripes from Harrison's uniform. "You're no longer a sergeant, and you're no longer a squad leader. I'm placing you under arrest for failure to follow orders, leading to the unnecessary deaths of nearly an entire squad."

Walking over to Sgt. Wiley, Harry yelled. "Divide second squad and first squad survivors between you and Phillips. Sgt. Umberto will have his hands busy the rest of the way back. Can you do that?"

"Good as done, Sarg," Wiley stated soberly as he double timed back toward the nervous squads.

Scanning the smoldering battlefield with his binoculars, Harry looked at all the American bodies lying near the hamlet. Turning toward Harrison, he said coldly. "I should just put a bullet right through your brain, but I don't want to cheat the hangman, you sorry son-of-a-bitch."

After glaring at Harrison for a few more second, Harry called out, "Sgt. Wiley, send out a couple men to walk point and let's get moving. Phillips, have part of your squad cover our rear until we meet up with friendly forces. Mr. Umberto, if Harrison should try to run, go ahead and shoot the bastard. We'll just save them the cost of a military tribunal and a new rope."

About a half hour later they ran into Wentworth and fourth platoon patrolling out ahead of A-Company.

Wentworth walked directly up to Harry. "Heard you ran into some trouble out there, how many did you lose?"

"Eight damn good men, all because of Harrison's failure to follow my orders. Damn it, Bob. I knew that place was occupied. All he had to do was stay put. We could have called in air power and wiped that place right off the face of the earth with no one getting hurt. I busted that bastard and put him under arrest. I hope that SOB loves hard labor, because he's going to get a life time of it," Harry responded furiously.

Wentworth shook his head. "Man, that's tough, Jenson. Come on. Let's get you back to the company."

Both platoons headed south for nearly twenty minutes before reaching A-Company lines.

Harry immediately explained the situation in detail to Capt. Fargo, while Steve and Franny listened.

After hearing everything, Capt. Fargo looked over at Franny. "Go get Harrison and bring him to me. Treat him like a prisoner not a U.S. soldier. Jenson, you did fine work saving what you did. I'll fill your squad with regular infantry for now. Once we fall back from this operation we'll get new airborne reserves to replace your losses. Who are you going to put in charge of first squad?"

"Quibbley, sir. He stayed put and tried to keep order among the men as Harrison ordered them forward. He'll do a good job," Harry informed Capt. Fargo.

"Sounds like a wise choice. Alright, I'll take care of things from here, Jenson. Get me some completed reports as quickly as you can. I'll try getting Harrison out of here by chopper before night fall. I don't want his attitude rubbing off on anyone else."

Several minutes later, Franny, along with two of his men, delivered Harrison to Capt. Fargo. "Son, if I had my way I'd put you up against a wall and have a firing squad finish this mess right here, right now, but the military won't allow me to do that. So I'm calling for a chopper to take you back to Pusan. There is no doubt that you will be tried on numerous charges. Thankfully, that's up to an attorney to decide. May God have mercy on your soul. Doogan, get him out of here!"

As Franny took him by the arm, Harrison spun around facing Capt. Fargo. "Don't you want to hear my side of the story? Don't I get a chance to explain what happened?"

Capt. Fargo approached the pleading soldier. "No, you don't son. In my book you're guilty as charged. If you can't understand why, just try and remember the names of the men you got killed. Have you given them any thought at all, Harrison? You should have to write their families explaining why their sons and husbands are dead. You should tell their children just why Daddy isn't coming home, and why they will never sit on his lap again! Doogan, get him out of here before I shoot the bastard!"

Franny pulled Harrison away from the Captain, leading him back to a truck they were using as a brig until he could be transferred.

About 1400, a chopper along with several MP's arrived. After retrieving all the paper work from Capt. Fargo, they handcuffed Harrison and placed him in the chopper.

Sanchez and Steve stood a ways off from the chopper, watching as it left for the rear. "I think Harry showed good restraint. I might have shot the bastard right there," Sanchez said, shielding his eyes from the blowing dust.

"No you wouldn't have, Sanchez. You sure as hell would have knocked him on his ass and busted him down, same as Harry. But you would never have taken justice into your own hands. That's just not you, Sanchez," Steve assured his fellow platoon leader, as he turned away from the spinning blades.

Second platoon was put in the reserve position for a few days, so Harry would have time to familiarize the replacements into what their roll would be for the near future. They all appeared to be solid soldiers, which made Harry feel comfortable. Sgt. Quibbley took to his new role as squad leader as if he had been in charge all along. In no time, second platoon was once again ready to take its place back in the company, right where Harry wanted to be.

Heavy fighting erupted all along the line held by the 187th, as they continued clearing the Cumpo Peninsula. Although the fighting was somewhat similar to the land battles that raged across the European Continent during World War Two, there were some differences. At no time during the previous war did German infantry attack in screaming waves at night, attempting to break through defensive lines with sheer force. It was nothing for American forces to kill a hundred or more well-armed DPRK forces in a single bloody assault on a small segment of the perimeter, every single night. They would come out of the dark screaming and wailing like crazed wild men, firing their weapons, throwing grenades or swinging swords and bayonets, ready to slash anyone attempting to stop them. All too often, some of the first attackers breached forward positions, forcing defenders into fierce hand to hand combat. If possible, they would drag an injured American soldier away into the darkness. After the attack ceased, you could hear the man screaming and pleading as ruthless DPRK soldier tortured and hacked the man to pieces, all the while laughing ghoulishly.

These nightly incursions wore on the men's nerves tremendously. It was imperative that each Company Commander rotate platoons forward in order to give the men a chance to regroup, and keep their wits about them. However, as time went on, the American troops began constructing booby traps and fake forward positions, drawing the enemy away from their real positions, thus allowing the men to have more advantage over the attacking hordes. After an incredibly tough day on

September 27th, Capt. Fargo assigned first platoon to man the forward positions. The weather was horrible and visibility was hampered by low hanging clouds dropping copious amounts of wind swept, bone chilling rain. By nightfall, most of the men were already shivering under their ponchos, with no relief in sight. Making matters worse, the men had little or no time to prepare booby traps or obstacles, as dusk came early due to the low dark clouds. Throughout the early evening hours, Harry and several volunteers from second platoon worked diligently, delivering ammunition and grenades to every man in the line. They all knew that nights like this just emboldened NPRK troops to attack with renewed ferocity.

Up until midnight, there were several smaller probing raids, followed by a half hour long mortar attack. Between attacks, the blood curdling screams and cries for help in perfect English tortured every man.

Each squad leader continually checked their men to make sure none of them had been hauled away. At 0115, the sound of hundreds of running feet could be heard rushing toward first platoon. Steve quickly called in mortar fire, as machine guns and B.A.R.S. opened the American attack. Seconds later, the few mines the platoon had been able to plant, exploded. Screams of the injured DPRK men filled the air. Then, out of the darkness came the on rushing assault. Every weapon on the line began firing into the human wave attack. Regardless of the intense fire, some of the attackers were able to breach the perimeter. Two North Korean soldiers charged directly toward Steve's position. With a quick blast from his Thompson, both men tumbled to the ground. A third attacker jumped over them to be cut down by a shot from Sgt. Whitebear. From Steve's right, several more attackers rushed into the perimeter, one of them waving a large sword. Before Sgt. Whitebear could fire, the soldier knocked him over while raising his sword. Nevertheless, Whitebear managed to roll to his side just as the sword hit the ground.

With a ferocious kick, Whitebear struck the man in the knee. The soldier gave out a shrill scream as he lost his balance, falling to the ground next to the agile third squad leader. Without hesitation, Whitebear grabbed the sword, driving it through the man's body and straight into the ground. The second attacker lunged at Steve with a bayonet, but failed to see the tree stump separating them. As the soldier spun to the ground, Steve emptied the balance of his magazine into him. Another North Korean came over the top of the first three men that had been killed in the attack. Before Steve could reload, the soldier ran straight into him holding a bayonet in his right hand. Dropping his Thompson, Steve grabbed the man's right hand as they plummeted to the earth. The bayonet spun free from the soldier's grip, landing several feet away.

For several seconds the two men rolled back and forth, attempting to gain dominance as the North Korean kept reaching for his weapon. With all his might Steve swung with his left arm striking the soldier in the jaw. The man groaned as Steve heard bones being fractured. Bleeding profusely from the mouth, the soldier again scrambled for his weapon before attempting to regain his feet. Free from his attacker, Steve pulled the .45 automatic from his holster, firing three shots point blank into the soldier's chest. For a mere second, the man staggered from side to side before falling to his knees. He reached out his left hand toward Steve as if asking for help. After another raspy breath the dying man fell forward. After giving his assailant one more glance, Steve grabbed his Thompson, swiftly slamming in a fresh magazine. The attack appeared to be leveling off as he took up his former position. Quickly gazing over toward third squad, he observed Whitebear firing at several attackers still trying to breach the perimeter. Behind him lay two more bodies that Steve hadn't observed earlier.

Whitebear was the consummate warrior, born from his heritage as an Ogallala Sioux. It was because of his toughness, agility and lack of fear, that Steve had picked the usually mild mannered Native American to be a squad leader. Tonight, Whitebear had proven Steve right. The surviving North Koreans had barely withdrawn into the darkness before screams and calls for help in English broke the eerie silence. Immediately, Steve checked his squads. Fourth squad reported one man dead and several wounded. Second and third squads reported only minor injuries.

Regrettably, first squad reported several minor injuries with one man missing.

Slowly, Steve scanned the field in front of first squad with his binoculars. What appeared to be the body of an American soldier was tangled in the wire about ten yards in front of their position. As dawn broke, Steve took two volunteers out toward the wire to retrieve their comrade. Their task was hampered by all the dead bodies they had to walk over before reaching the wire. The body of the young American hung lifelessly as the men worked diligently to untwist him from the stiff wire.

Apparently, North Koreans pulled him from his position, hoping to torture him. Mercifully, the solid wall of lead had saved the soldier from such an agony. His body was riddled and torn by countless bullets.

There was little doubt that the man had been struck repeatedly by both enemy and friendly fire. After finally cutting away the heavy wire, Steve's volunteers carried their comrade back to first platoon.

Immediately Steve sent runners to his other squads, informing them the screaming was only a ruse, and not to react in any way. As a welcome sun cleared the eastern horizon, quiet settled over the battle field.

The surviving DPRK forces continued fleeing northward, as American jets pounded them whenever possible with rockets and cannon fire.

Two large bucket loaders from an engineer company came forward to bury the dead DPRK soldiers, abandoned by their own. One operator dug several huge pits, while the second operator filled them with bodies. Several men from Alpha Company became ill as they watched the huge machines drive over bodies as they rolled the stiff corpses along the ground.

Martinez stood beside Steve watching the grotesque operation. I heard about human wave attacks in the Pacific during the war. I never thought I would see it firsthand. What a waste of good infantry.

Then to be buried in a pit like that makes you sick. But I guess they can't expect much better of a burial when they put so little value on human life to begin with. I wonder if anyone really cares. Hell, it would be impossible to dig individual graves for all of them."

"Yeah I understand what you're saying, Martinez. But just remember each one of those men is someone's son, brother or husband. Their families will forever wonder what happened to the beloved soldier they sent off to war. They'll never have the peace of knowing where or how they died, or where their grave is. Can you imagine how they'd feel if they knew their loved ones were being torn apart by those machines? Put your mother into that situation, Martinez. Give that some thought," Steve explained to his squad sergeant before walking off to make his morning report to Capt. Fargo.

Col. Fontaine rotated his men after that night's actions. The reserves now took point so Steve's tired men could get a breather from heavy combat. Moving forward up the Cumpo Peninsula became more of a mop up operation, as the fighting strength of the DPRK forces had been spent. Some small pockets of resistance held out, refusing to give ground until their last man was dead. Col. Fontaine continued putting air power and artillery to good use in order to save American lives. As third battalion approached the Han River, evidence of America's destructive air power was everywhere. Burning tanks, trucks and Russian jeeps lined the roads, while smashed artillery pieces and mobile rocket launchers littered adjacent fields. Personal equipment and weapons lay discarded on the shore by the river, deposited by terrified soldiers attempting to swim for their lives. Odds were, not many men could have completed the swim across the cold fast moving river. Yet, there was no way to know how many failed to make it across. Because several miles to the west, the mighty Han flowed into the Yellow Sea, which would have swept away the bodies of those that failed to complete the treacherous swim.

Scanning the distant shore with binoculars, all Steve could see were about five bodies and several more burned out trucks. It was not to be known until much later that the 187th Airborne wiped out nearly three battalions of the 107th North Korean Defense Regiment. About three hundred survivors escaped during the night by small watercraft from the town of Tonglin, to a small island just off the west coast. Civilian informants stated that some DPRK forces remained in Tonglin, hoping to escape at nightfall. Quickly, South Korean defense forces backed by the187th, moved forward turning west along the river road to clean out any remaining forces in Tonglin.

The DPRK forces fought ferociously as South Korean troops began moving on the town. With their backs to the ocean and no chance for escape, they were not going to go easily. After an hour of getting nowhere, Capt. Fargo radioed Steve.

"Kenrude, take your platoon to the south of that damn town and cut them off. I'll have Jensen create an attack from the east with Sanchez and Wentworth in reserve. Jump off will be at 1600."

Sgt. Kilburn led first platoon toward the south as mortar and artillery blasted the town into rubble. However, the World War Two veterans were not to be surprised, they knew what was about to happen. The enemy would hunker down until the barrage lifted, then occupy the ruins which made for good defensive positions, and would have to be dug out like rats. Two South Korean platoons joined Steve on the South. A Sgt. Kimm was in command of both platoons. He was a capable man with good soldiers. However his top command left much to be desired. Steve met with Kimm to explain how he wanted the attack to proceed once the barrage lifted. Nodding in agreement, Kimm sent runners out to his platoons. Exactly at 1600 the barrage lifted. First platoon along with South Korean forces began a sprint to the edge of town occupying damaged buildings and piles of rubble. Thus they were able to fire upon the enemy as they emerged from their shelters. The battle was brisk, as second platoon along with two platoons of South Koreans came in from the east. Both allied teams formed a solid wall within just a few minutes. Slowly the North Koreans were driven from their defensive positions as third and fifth platoon men filled in the gaps, increasing the pressure on the bedraggled DPRK soldiers. By 2000 hours, fighting came to an end with only four enemy soldiers surrendering. Quickly, word came in that patrols operating west of the city were receiving sniper fire from the surrounding hills. Col. Fontaine did not want to see his precious paratroopers engaged in a protracted battle for the hills if he could avoid it, so he ordered combat to end for the night.

In the morning, heavy artillery and air assaults tore into every inch of the hills. Col. Fontaine wanted every enemy emplacement destroyed before committing his ground forces. After nearly a two hour barrage, Col. Fontaine committed one battalion of his South Korean forces and one battalion of airborne troops to take the hills. After mopping up some light resistance in the surrounding foothills, his battle hardened forces drove nonstop to the summit without further opposition. All they found on the way up were smashed Russian equipment and the remains of about a hundred enemy soldiers.

The campaign for the Cumpo Peninsula was finally complete. It had been a tough fight all the way, as DPRK soldiers proved to be a tough effective combat force, fighting brutally for every yard of territory. Descending the hills Steve was happy this phase of the war was over. His men had done a marvelous job all the way. He now started seeing them in the same light as the men he fought with in Europe. It was a good feeling to know all that hard training paid off. While fighting raged throughout the Cumpo Peninsula, Gen. MacArthur succeeded in a major gamble. Picking one of the worst beaches in the world for amphibious operations, he landed thousands of men near Inchon. They immediately drove inland, chasing DPRK forces north. It began to look as if the war in Korea might not take as long to win as many had earlier expected.

After bringing up fresh South Korean and America forces to hold the line along the front, tired forces in the Cumpo area were moved south to take a short rest. On October 2nd, airborne forces were delivered to the shattered Kimpo Airfield, where they occupied the nearly intact military dependent housing complex. Although the men were in much need of rest, there was also much work to be completed. Every weapon was broken down and inspected for wear or damage. Replacements for dead or wounded members soon arrived to fill the ranks. Steve found his new combat veterans acting much the same as their World War Two counter parts had done regarding green replacements. They shied away from the new men, refusing to share their experiences or explain effective combat procedures they had learned. In order to bring cohesiveness back into the ranks, Col. Fontaine set up simulated war games in and around Kimpo. Platoons took turns assaulting damaged buildings where mock enemy forces were dug in. Long foot patrols were set up, where they had to recognize hazards while dealing with well-coordinated simulated sniper attacks. Col Fontaine made sure his company commanders made the training as realistic as possible. He used umpires to evaluate who was dead and wounded during each exercise. This allowed new troops to become acquainted with air lifting wounded soldiers from the field of combat. Air lifts were all new to combat soldiers. But many would soon learn the huge green helicopters increased their survivability if they were wounded. Midway through the month, Col. Fontaine became increasingly happy with the operations of his men. That became very important as plans were being set in motion to send the 187th back into combat again.

CHAPTER 9
MODERN AIRBORNE COMBAT

October 18th, the 187th was ordered back into combat. They were to prepare for a new type of drop never performed in the history of airborne operations. The drop would be made on the Sukchon-Sanchow line, in order to stop thousands of fleeing enemy forces from reaching sanctuary in the north.

This drop would be different in many ways. Not only would the new C-119 aircraft—nicknamed the 'flying box car'—drop paratroopers, but 73 of these highly technical aircraft from the 314th Troop Carrier Squadron would drop 105mm howitzers, 90mm towed anti-tank guns, plus the trucks and Jeeps required to move them into battle, along with ammunition and crews. Included in the operation were forty C-47's from the 21st Troop Carrier Squadron. I-Corp planned to put 1,479 paratroopers on the ground along with 74 tons of equipment on a drop zone labeled, 'William,' just south of Sukchon. Planes began landing on the refurbished runways beginning on the 18th, giving ground crews a chance to check over the massive transports before sending them off on their new airborne mission.

Many paratroopers were apprehensive as to whether such heavy equipment as the large trucks and artillery could survive the dangerous drop. Nevertheless, they all knew without it, the success of their mission would be in doubt. D-Day was set for October 20th at 0400.

The night of the 19th, Col. Fontaine set up company briefing sessions in a hanger. He explained all the whys and wherefores of their mission. Using a large map of Korea someone had painted on a sheet of plywood, the Colonel was able to describe how the battlefield was going to be laid out once they arrived. Everyone knew fighting a tough enemy was one thing, but fighting an enemy desperate to survive at any cost was going to be a far tougher assignment.

A cool breeze blew across the Korean Peninsula as men of the 187th began streaming on to the runways around two in the morning. Large cargo bundles filled with everything from ammunition, first aid supplies and rations were to be loaded on each aircraft, and boarding was going to take extra time. Once the paratroopers finally boarded, they found it nearly impossible to move about with their large packs. Seating was another problem. Since cargo bags were piled haphazardly, many seats along the outer walls were not accessible. Many men just dropped down on top of bags in the aisle. This made for problems when it came time to jump. The men on the bags ended up requiring assistance from their comrades to stand up, so they could hook their parachutes to the static line overhead. Comfortable or not, on cue, the pilots began maneuvering their huge transports onto the taxiway in preparation for takeoff. One by one, the lumbering aircraft sped down the runway reaching for the predawn sky.

Steve sat across the plane from Eddie Shrider who appeared to be asleep. Eddie had been a very confident soldier back in Europe. Steve liked him from the first time they met. Now he had proved to be a very efficient platoon leader, always looking out for the welfare of his men. Looking about the darkened aircraft, Steve understood there were men who were totally scared. Some would be praying while others might even be crying. Everyone dealt differently with those last few minutes before combat. Looking down at his watch he observed they were less than five minutes from their drop zone. Taking a deep breath, he closed his eyes for a moment as he thought about Karen and the kids back in Glendale. It made his stomach hurt. He just wanted to get back home and live out his life in peace. Opening his eyes, Steve felt a twinge of pain shoot through his right knee. He prayed silently, asking God to help him survive this battle and to give him the wisdom he needed to lead his men properly, and bring them all back home again. He prayed faithfully, even while he knew it was an impossible request. Some would die, that was just a fact of war. All he could do was give each man the best possible chance of survival, and he hoped he had done enough. He was jolted back to reality as the jump master called them to action.

"Stand up, hook up!"

Eddie Shrider stood up next to Steve, snapping his parachute cable onto the static line. Yelling above the roaring engines and rushing wind from the open door he called out. "Well, here we go once again, Steve. At least we don't have flak to worry about. Sounds like a level field down there, too."

Steve smiled, "Yeah that helps a lot, Eddie, see you on the ground."

As the green light came on, two aircrew members tossed out several bags before the jump master began calling out, "Go! Go! Let's go men!"

Steve led his platoon out the door with Sgt. Shrider's men directly behind. After a sharp tug, Steve's chute deployed properly. It was still too dark to see the ground accurately below. He could make out shadows but that was about it. The sky around Steve was literally filled with paratroopers and cargo bags racing each other to drop zone William.

Moments later Steve was able to figure out the terrain below him. It appeared to be a wide open agricultural field of some sort. His hope now was that retreating enemy soldiers had not planted landmines in it on their way north. Seconds later Steve's feet touched down on the field. Dropping to his knees, he quickly unhooked his harness as the heavy equipment bags began crashing around him. Jogging toward the north he began calling out. "Alpha Company first platoon, fall in with me!"

To his left he could hear Harry calling out for second platoon. It was nice to know his best friend had made the jump alright.

Within minutes his squad sergeants were assembling their men. With everyone accounted for, Steve led them foreword to the Alpha Company assembly point, where a small dirt road crossed the north-south railroad tracks.

Arriving, Steve walked up to Capt. Fargo. "First platoon intact ready to move out, sir."

"Good, that's good. We're just waiting on Wentworth and we'll be set," Capt. Fargo replied as he watched fourth platoon approaching from a short distance away.

As Capt. Fargo assembled his platoon leaders, the sound of engines could be heard as artillery crews began firing up their trucks. The jump had been a masterpiece of operations with few injuries, and everything delivered within the drop zones. The paratroopers began engaging DPRK forces almost immediately as sporadic small arms fire erupted across the valley.

"Alright, our mission is to close down this rail line for right now, and hook up with forces moving down the north-south Sukchon-Pyongyang Road. Shrider, Kenrude, Jensen, you all move east, dispersing your men along this dirt road until you meet up with forces covering the main highway. Wentworth and Sanchez, spread your men west along the road until you meet up with Charlie Company. Make sure you know your targets before shooting. Remember we have men picking up artillery and cargo bags out there," Capt. Fargo advised his anxious men.

Without hesitation, the platoon leaders carried out their assignments. Once everything was set along the dirt road, Steve made his way over toward second platoon looking for Harry.

He found him hunkered down in a newly constructed trench with his radio man and Sgt. Wiley from fourth squad.

"Harry, how the hell are you doing?" Steve whispered, as he dropped down beside him.

"Hey, Stevie boy. I'm good. The jump went well. I had one guy knocked a bit silly by one of those damn bags, but he's fine. How about you?" Harry replied smiling.

"We're all good. No injuries. Where do you think the bastards are? Just seems way too quiet if this is supposed to be the escape route for thousands of fleeing enemy troops." Steve said to Harry as he scanned the area south of them with his binoculars.

Nodding his head in agreement, Harry looked over at Steve. "My guess is they hunkered down when they heard the planes and all the commotion on the ground. Whoever was here, headed north lickety-split, whoever is south of here dug in for the night. I would guess we'll start dealing with them in the morning. By that time the artillery guys should have those guns in place, ready to repel anything coming our way."

Placing his binoculars back in the case, Steve was quiet for a moment. "Yeah, you're probably right. Well, I'm heading back toward Whitebear. I really trust his night abilities." Slapping Harry on the arm, Steve took off to join his third squad.

He found Whitebear scanning the dark field with his binoculars. "Seeing anything out there?" Steve asked, as he sat down in the deep trench, removing his helmet.

"No, not anymore. When we first got in position I watched a few of our guys pick up the last of the equipment bags. Since then it's been all quiet. The shooting we heard earlier quit too. So I guess we just wait for the bastards to come."

After chatting with Whitebear a few minutes more, Steve checked in with the rest of his squad leaders, ending up with Kilburn, who was lined up closest to the rail line.

Dawn came late as the sky was heavily overcast. A slight drizzle began to fall as the wind kicked up the loose parachutes littering the field. After talking with Kilburn for a while, Steve worked his way back to Alpha Company Command Post, about fifty yards to the west of the rail line.

He found Capt. Fargo scanning his map in a hastily dug pit. "Ah, Kenrude. What are you seeing out there?"

"Nothing sir. Just billowing parachutes from the wind. Other than that everything has been quiet. What are our orders once daylight comes in?"

"I received orders about a half hour ago." Covering Steve and himself with a poncho, Capt. Fargo turned on his red flashlight to illuminate the map better.

"At 0830, we're to move north toward Opari where we'll meet up with the British 27th Commonwealth. Rumor has it—and that's the best way I can put it—there's a large contingent of enemy forces occupying a line between Opari and Yongyu. Our objective will be to clear out Opari before taking Hill 287. Col. Fontaine is ordering some artillery support to move forward with us. Probably a 105 and a couple of 90mm's for close in support. You and Sanchez will lead the way. Jensen and Wentworth will follow with Shrider in reserve. Baker Company will be on our east side, Dog Company will take the west. I'll send runners to our other platoons. You'll coordinate with Sanchez for an 0830 start."

After taking another longer look at the map, Steve saluted the Captain. "I'm on it, sir."

After conferring with Sanchez, Steve gathered up his squad leaders. He gave them the lowdown on the operation, appointing Kilburn to take point for their platoon when they moved out.

Exactly at 0830, both Fifth and First Platoons left their positions along the dirt road heading north. The drizzle became more of a light rain as the men proceeded towards Opari. Off to the west it appeared Charlie Company was meeting some heavy resistance. But from the railroad to the north-south highway, everything was still quiet.

Hill 287 was becoming more prominent in the distance as they moved forward. Steve knew full well whoever occupied the summit controlled whatever happened on the ground approaching Opari.

There had to be mortar and artillery pieces zeroed in on every approach. If the American artillery following along couldn't suppress enemy fire, this could turn into a bloodbath before they ever arrived at Opari. Steve thought about the bloody battles for Monte Casino and Mount Suribachi during World War Two. He hoped today would be different.

Corporal Dinsmore came running forward holding out the handset. "It's the old man, Sarg."

Steve knelt down. "Go ahead Captain, this is Kenrude."

"Already spoke to Sanchez. Hold your position. Artillery and aircraft going to strike target."

After replying, Steve ordered his men to dig small slit trenches for cover while they awaited further orders to move out. He wanted to keep them as safe as possible if the enemy began firing on their position.

Several American and British fighter bombers soared overhead dropping their ordnance on the hills, before turning back to attack with rockets and cannon fire. Three American artillery pieces began firing at targets called in by a small Cessna spotter aircraft flying above Opari. It was encouraging to see large secondary explosions sending tons of rock and debris into the air. The bombardment was clearly reducing the risk for the advancing ground troops.

After nearly an hour, Steve and Sanchez received orders from Capt. Fargo, directing them to continue their attack toward Opari.

The town appeared to be pretty much intact, although artillery and air strikes had done some damage. Black smoke rose from several fires in burning buildings near the center of town.

Kilburn led first platoon up to a stone wall about twenty yards from the first buildings. Arriving at the wall, Sanchez spread out 5th Platoon to the left. Wentworth and Harry closed up quickly, lining up behind the lead platoons. After scanning the town once more, Steve placed his binoculars back in the case and took a deep breath. Raising his right hand in the air, he motioned for his men to attack. After jumping over the wall, the men raced in double time the last twenty yards, taking cover along the buildings. Steve directed Kilburn and Martinez to take their squads up the main road, as Whitebear and Hagen worked their way up a nearby alley. Sanchez deployed his platoon up additional routes leading into the town.

It was slow going as each building needed to be cleared. It reminded Steve of the many towns they encountered while fighting in Normandy and Holland. Suddenly, several surviving artillery pieces on Hill 287 began dropping rounds into Opari. Everyone scattered for cover as shrapnel and deadly debris of all types screamed through the air.

Steve took cover along with Whitebear in a small house near the end of the first block. From there Steve could see down the next alley toward the town square. There was a tank with its treads blown off parked just inside the square. The turret appeared to be intact, and a Russian machine gun still rested in its cradle. That was going to be a problem if they continued up the alley, unless they could take it out during this artillery barrage.

Steve called Sgt. Hagen over. "Where's your bazooka man?"

"Across the street in that garage type building," Hagen responded, as chunks of concrete came crashing down on both men.

"Go get him right now," Steve ordered Hagen, as he wiped concrete dust from his face. Moments later, the bazooka man and his loader came running up to Steve in a swirl of dust.

Pointing toward the alley, Steve explained to the crew. "There's a Russian tank parked just inside the square at the end of the alley. Right now they're buttoned up because of the artillery barrage. The treads are gone so they can't move, but the turret looks intact. You need to slip down that alley and finish that damn thing off. Hagen, supply them with a B.A.R. and rifle team! Now get going before this barrage ends."

Immediately, the men took off running across the street toward the open alley. Things went well at first, until the hatch on the turret opened. Seeing the four Americans in the alley, the DPRK soldier spun the machine gun around, preparing to fire in their direction. The four men took cover just as rounds began to fly. Swinging his heavy weapon out from behind a power pole, Brimly, the B.A.R. man, fired several rounds at the turret. However, the tank gunner didn't appear to be influenced by the short volley of fire at all. Swiftly, the bazooka operator rolled out into the alley pointing his weapon at the tank. Unfortunately he never got his round off, as the machine gunner ripped him apart. Now the bazooka lay useless in the alley with three more men pinned down.

"Dinsmore!" Steve called out to his radio man. "Where the hell are you?"

"Right here, Sarg," Dinsmore replied, from under a table to his left.

Smiling, Steve motioned for the radio. Using the small map of Opari he was carrying, he spoke with the artillery spotter, giving him the best coordinates possible as to where the tank stood. Seconds later the 105 began lobbing rounds in the direction of the city square, but none of them hit the tank. Steve attempted to redirect fire to no avail.

Encouragingly, the falling artillery rounds made the gunner nervous. Letting go of his machine gun, he slid partially back into the turret, holding the hatch close to his head.

With the machine gun threat temporarily neutralized, the bazooka loader and a rifleman dashed out into the alley, scooping up the bazooka. They ran headlong toward the tank, with Brimly following on their heels. Just as the tank gunner noticed them, the bazooka team fell to their knees. It was going to be a race to the death to see who could shoot first and accurately.

The North Korean threw the hatch cover back, swiveling the machine gun toward the bazooka crew. Steve held his breath as he watched the back-up team fumbling with the heavy weapon.

An instant later a blast from the rear of the bazooka told Steve the rocket was on its way toward the tank. The round hit perfectly into the body of the tank, close to where the upper tread should have been. Flame rushed up from the open turret after Brimly fired a long blast from his B.A.R. toward the desperate gunner. Seconds later, an internal explosion tore through the helpless tank, sending a column of fire and debris up from the open turret. Instead of retreating back toward the platoon, the three men continued toward the city square. Standing at the end of the alley, they peered to the right and left before quickly ducking back into a damaged building.

Steve and Sgt. Hagen watched intently as the rifleman loaded another round into the bazooka, with direction from the gunner. Lying down, the gunner worked his way back to the corner of the building, dragging the bazooka beside him. Once stabilized, he pulled the bazooka up to his firing position. With this shot he wasted no time. Taking quick aim he fired the deadly projectile. Hearing the explosion, Steve watched as the men high tailed it back down the alley toward his position. When they returned, Steve thanked them for a job well done before asking about their second target. Still out of breath, the loader stated there had been an armored personnel carrier, with four heavy machine guns on top, parked about ten yards from the burning tank. It was now out of commission.

As the artillery barrage lifted, Steve directed his men to move back out. Knowing the alley was a safe route toward the town square, both 3rd and 4th squads moved up quickly, checking buildings as they progressed.

Heavy fighting was taking place to Steve's left as Sanchez's Fifth Platoon and Wentworth's Fourth Platoon battled their way into town in the face of heavy resistance. The square was filled with burned out vehicles and bodies, both military and civilian. Quickly, Steve's First Platoon with Harry's Second Platoon as back up, attempted to gain control of the town square with moderate resistance from roof tops and windows. Harry ran up beside Steve near the entrance to what had been some sort of church.

"Hey, buddy boy. What are your plans once we get this square under control?" Harry inquired, as small debris from the structure rained down on them.

"Well, I was going to keep heading north, but it sounds like Wentworth and Sanchez are bogged down. I think we should come up from behind the enemy positions and bail out our men. What do you think?" Steve suggested, knowing full well Harry was going to agree with him.

"Yup! Sounds like a plan. We'll move down that road by the white building. You can move down that side road. We should be able to break the bottle neck in no time," Harry rejoined, waving for his first squad leader to follow him.

With the square now under control, Steve took his platoon toward the side road, leaving no one to cover his rear, since Sgt. Shrider's Third Platoon was now moving in to town.

Sniper fire continued to be a problem as the men moved up the wide street. It took a huge amount of time for teams to clear out sniper nests before they could continue forward. Several buildings had been booby-trapped with hand grenades and mines, slowing progress to a crawl. Fortunately, none of the well placed booby-traps caused Steve's men any casualties. They had learned well to be aware of such obstacles and how to disarm them safely.

Finally, First Platoon came upon entrenched DPRK soldiers firing toward Fourth and Fifth Platoons. The defenders were stunned and confused when they realized they were caught between two American forces. Some of them attempted to run, while others just turned in place, returning fire before they were cut down in their exposed positions.

Brimly wasted no time charging forward with his B.A.R. Enemy soldier's collapsed en masse as he raked their positions with deadly fire. Four DPRK soldiers dashed into an abandoned store. Steve grabbed two men from first squad to give chase. In short order Steve cut down one man with his Thompson as he tried to run up the stairs toward the second floor. Another was killed attempting to run back toward the Americans, with a bayonet in hand. The other two disappeared into the cellar below. Private Lester removed two grenades from his web gear. Pulling the pin on the first grenade, he carefully tossed it into the cellar. After it exploded, he charged down the stairs firing his carbine. Stopping at the bottom, he tossed the second grenade around the corner. Once the smoke and dust dissipated, Lester and Steve entered the basement finding the last two dead on the floor. Returning to the street, Steve and his second squad linked up with Wentworth's men coming in from the southeast.

With forces now combined, the men drove north, linking up with Harry's Second Platoon as they were clearing out the last defenders blocking Sanchez's forward movement. With the south half of the town under their control, the men from Alpha Company turned their attention north. As dusk began to settle in, the final resistance inside Opari was eliminated. It had been a tough day of fighting, with plenty of casualties to prove it. Between all the platoons, twenty-seven men were killed with another fifteen seriously wounded. No one counted the DPRK deaths, but it was evident their toll was much higher.

The men set up a perimeter on the north edge of Opari with Hill 287 still waiting for them tomorrow. Capt. Fargo set up a Command Post in what had been a small grocery shop several blocks from the perimeter. Around 1830 Steve walked up to the Captain. "Sir, we have something we need to show you. I think you might want to come with me right away."

"What is it Kenrude? Would you like Lt. Rather follow you instead?" The tired Captain inquired with a frown on his face.

"No sir, I think you might want to see this for yourself," Steve insisted.

After grabbing his helmet, Capt. Fargo and his aide followed Steve up toward the perimeter where his tired men were eating rations while keeping watch.

Entering what was left of an apartment type building, Steve led the Captain into a small room filled with radio equipment. Kneeling down beside the bodies, Steve pointed to the uniform.

"Those are Communist Chinese uniforms, Captain. Not North Korean."

Kneeling down beside Steve, Capt. Fargo took out a pocket knife to remove patches from the uniforms. After studying the situation for a moment, he stood up, handing the patches to Lt. Rather. He walked over to a table in the center of the room covered in maps, code books and identification papers. "Man, this just doesn't look good at all. Did you see anything like this today during the fighting?" Capt. Fargo inquired, as he glanced over the documents.

"No sir. Although we know most of their equipment comes from China, all the patches and medals I saw today were North Korean. I called Sgt. Jenson over here to take a look at this also. Before heading back to his platoon, he stated he'd never seen anything like this either," Steve explained, as he flipped through one of the code books.

"Very good, Kenrude, I'm glad you came to get me. I'll send these patches back to headquarters as well as these documents. I heard China sent about 20,000 troops across the Yalu River, but I didn't think we had any this far over. If their backing the DPRK in this battle, we may be in for a butt kicking. Headquarters needs to see this stuff, pronto," Captain Fargo explained before retreating back to his Command Post.

After checking his defensive line one more time, Steve walked over to check on Franny who was checking the perimeter to his right.

Walking into a small house where Franny was inspecting a machine gun emplacement, Steve looked at his tired friend. "Tough day, First Sergeant?"

"Yeah, plenty tough! I tell you Steve, these DPRK men fight harder than the damn Krauts did. They just don't care if they die. At least most of the German's wanted to get back to the Fatherland to settle down, drink beer and raise a family. Not this bunch. I saw several suicide attacks today, by small groups that were being overwhelmed by our guys. They just don't quit. That takes a toll on our men. It kind of spooks them to a point, and me. I talked to guys who were in the Pacific during the war and they said the same thing. After a massive banzai charge, some of our men lost it mentally and never recovered. Say, I hear you found some Communist Chinese guys. Is that a fact?"

Sitting down across the table from Franny, Steve took a deep breath. "Yeah, we found two guys in Chinese Army uniforms in a radio center. We found personal papers and what appeared to be code books and maps. Capt. Fargo's sending it all back to headquarters for evaluation. He's worried Chinese forces may sneak into this battle without our knowledge. That would be bad news, Franny."

"Yeah I hear you buddy. That could doom us all in a quick way. I don't know if the politicians back in Washington have any idea on how to operate this damn war, or what could possibly happen to all of us now that China's jumped in. We're all kind of just hanging out here waiting to be kicked in the ass by China or Washington. Not the way a war should be fought," Franny replied, while tossing a candy bar wrapper angrily on the floor.

Nodding his head in agreement, Steve looked up at the ceiling. "Well, I just hope we all survive this thing. Twenty-seven dead today was a kick in the ass. We should have just wiped this place off the face of the earth. We have the power to do it, what the hell is wrong upstairs? Who's in control of this war? We sure don't have the leaders like we did back in Europe. Don't get me wrong, Fargo and Fontaine are good, they get it. But they take orders from people upstairs who are more worried about who gets elected next year than what's happening on the battlefield."

"Yeah, Stevie boy, that's a mouthful alright. Just keep your ass down and don't take chances. No heroics this time around," Franny replied with a smile.

"Heroics! When the hell was I ever heroic? We all did what we had to do, Franny. You, me, Harry—we're all cut from the same cloth. We just do what we have to do. Plain and simple." Steve responded as he stood up. "Well, I'm heading back to my boys. It's going to be a long night I'm afraid."

Steve slept very little that night as he continually walked among his men. They needed to know he was out in the cold and wet, same as them. As before, English speaking North Koreans taunted the young Americans all night long. But now the paratroopers were battle hardened and never fell for their games. In fact, most of the time, some of the more smart ass troopers would yell back insults just to keep the dialog going. Not amazingly, most of the American taunts were on the down and dirty side, frequently involving the wives and mothers of the enemy soldiers. Steve had to laugh because it was easy to hear anger in the North Korean voices over the vile sexual comments his men were making. As Steve's father always reminded him, 'All is fair in love and war.'

As dawn broke over the Korean Peninsula, Hill 287 loomed larger than it had the day before. Steve was never involved in taking major hills while in Europe. He hoped his men had learned enough by now to get the job done without major losses. The plan was to start with an artillery barrage and air assaults at first light to soften up enemy positions, or maybe drive DPRK forces from the hill completely.

At 0700, the first shells of a tremendous barrage exploded into the south face of the hill. Spotters walked rounds up and down the side several times before slamming them into the summit. When the barrage lifted, allied aircraft hammered the hill with bombs, rockets and cannon fire for nearly another half hour. With air power circling overhead, Alpha Company, supported by Baker Company on the left and Dog Company on the right moved forward toward the hill. A small amount of mortar fire continued raining down around the advancing forces until they reached the foothills. Then it became a test of wills, taking out the stubborn remnants that refused to leave their positions. It didn't take long for Fourth and Third Platoons to find access trails up the sides of the hill. Sanchez fed his platoon up behind Wentworth's Fourth platoon as they were making good progress. Harry ran into booby traps and land mines slowing his drive. Finding no real paths up the hill in his sector, Steve's First Platoon had to battle their way up rough terrain one foot at a time. After an hour of battling their way up, it became evident that the enemy fighters were not going to be kicked off this high ground without a solid fight. Sgt. Shrider's platoon made good progress clearing enemy positions on their way toward the summit. Echo Company was repositioned to bolster the attack, by attempting to drive up the east side of the prominence. They also ran into stubborn resistance. Finding a small dugout, Steve grabbed Dinsmore, pulling him into it beside him.

Taking the handset he called Capt. Fargo. "Foxtrot, Foxtrot this is Oscar King do you copy."

A moment later he had a reply. "Oscar King, read you loud and clear. What's your position?"

"Foxtrot, we're about two hundred yards up south face, meeting strong resistance from fortified positions. Can you give us mortars?

"Affirmative. Give coordinates," Capt. Fargo instantly replied.

After studying the map carefully for several minutes, Steve radioed back the coordinates. Only moments later, a concentrated barrage of mortar rounds began falling exactly where Steve requested them. The hill above First Platoon quickly became obscured by dust and smoke as the hill shook violently from the continual pounding. When the barrage lifted, Steve yelled out, "Let's go!" First and Third Platoons, who were stopped during the mortar barrage, charged up the hill with renewed vigor, overpowering stunned enemy troops where ever they presented themselves.

As Steve and Dinsmore passed what remained of a machine gun nest, two DPRK soldiers came out from the cave where they had sought refuge. Steve dropped to his knees, firing several short bursts from his Thompson. Both men rolled down the hill as a third man emerged from the cave, firing his automatic weapon. Two rounds smashed the radio on Dinsmore's back before Steve could finally take him out.

Sgt. Whitebear jumped into the cave opening, firing with his Thompson until his magazine was empty. Pulling a grenade from his belt he tossed it into the hole. The blast was followed by a larger explosion as stored ammunition detonated deeper underground.

Scanning the hill with his binoculars, Steve was pleased at the progress his platoon was making. However, it hurt him as he passed the bodies of men he recognized from his command. These last two days of fighting had cost Alpha Company a lot of good men, and the battle was far from over. About fifty yards from the summit, his men came across a large bunker made of stone and concrete, which had been partially blasted away by the artillery barrage. Apparently the bunker was built deep into the hill with a series of connected spider holes covering the surrounding area.

One by one, the men reduced the spider holes, but not without cost. As Sgt. Whitebear dropped a grenade into one hole, a DPRK soldier jumped clear from another less than ten feet away. Before anybody could react, he fired three rounds into Whitebear's back. Although seriously wounded, the very capable Native American spun around, killing his assassin before dropping to the ground himself. Angered by the loss of their beloved leader, several men from third squad rushed the bunker, engaging the last survivors in brutal hand to hand combat.

Just before nightfall, men from Alpha and Echo Companies were occupying the summit of Hill 287 and the surrounding smaller hillocks. Soldiers from Baker and Dog Companies were finishing off enemy survivors who chose to use escape routes through some of the smaller hillocks on the north side. In one larger bunker located near the top, they found an ample supply of 120mm mortar shells stacked neatly,

ready for firing. Thankfully the tube had been irreparably damaged by either a bomb or artillery shell. Had they been able to use that weapon, losses would have been catastrophic for both companies.

Col. Fontaine arranged Third Battalion into a defensive perimeter on the hills in case the North Koreans counter-attacked during the night. Before dark covered the hills, helicopters flew many missions, evacuating wounded and dead soldiers. Steve had one of the returning helicopters already set to bring fresh ammunition and rations, also bring him a new radio in case trouble arose during the night. Men who were able, cleaned out foxholes or trenches dug by DPRK soldiers for their own use. It sure beat digging new holes from scratch.

Wanting Dinsmore close by with the radio, Steve worked diligently cleaning out a nice size hole that would fit them perfectly. Dinsmore found several pieces of wood to make a small roof over part of their hole so they could keep somewhat dry as light rain began to fall. With October drawing to a close, the nights were becoming very cold. Hoping to get some sleep, Steve pulled his poncho and a warm pair of gloves from his pack. He hunkered down under the makeshift roof beside Dinsmore. Covering up with his poncho, he quickly fell asleep.

The sound of a far off explosion awoke him about 0600. Crawling out of their hole, Steve scanned the surrounding area with binoculars, searching for any signs of enemy activity. Seeing everything was quiet, he dropped back under the roof to close his eyes for a few more precious minutes.

"All quiet, Sarg?" Dinsmore inquired, as he laced up his boots.

"Yeah. Everything looks good. This would be a good time to break open some rations if you're hungry, it's hard to tell what's going to happen in the next hour or so. Stay here with the radio. I'm going to roust out the rest of the platoon and give them the same heads up. I'll be back shortly."

Intentionally, Steve stopped at third squad last. After finding Cpl. Trost, Steve promoted him to Squad Leader. Trost was a tall Texan with a comical attitude, but he never had a problem getting his hands dirty. In many ways, Trost reminded him of Wade Rollins, another young man from Texas who was killed early during World War Two. Returning to his hole, Steve quickly chowed down on some cold rations as he awaited orders for today's action.

And he didn't have long to wait, as Capt. Fargo called all of Alpha company. "This is Foxtrot for the entire den. At 0730 evacuate premises. Destroy all enemy munitions. Assemble north of town no later than 0815."

After receiving those orders, men from Alpha and Echo Companies finished assembling all known enemy mortar rounds, machine gun ammunition and captured weaponry into the large bunker. Once Steve was assured the cleanup was finished, several charges were placed among the huge piles. With all American forces off the hill, two men from Echo Company detonated the explosives. A sheet of flame roared from the bunker, sending rocks and debris nearly a hundred feet in the air.

As Alpha Company assembled, Capt. Fargo assessed the casualties they had taken over the past two days of combat. It was evident that every platoon needed to be brought back up to strength before moving on. Reviewing Capt. Fargo's request for replacements, Col. Fontaine ordered Fox Company to be brought up from the rear. They had been held in reserve since operations began. Three of their platoons were integrated into the other companies to bring them back up to combat strength. The balance of Fox Company was still going to be held in reserve.

After re-supply, the battalion was ready to resume combat operations. They joined Fourth and Fifth Battalions, who were already on the move.

Charlie and Dog Companies were in the vanguard moving toward Yongyu, where a heavy concentration of DPRK soldiers had stopped the allied advance cold. Fighting was brutal as Allied forces attempted to clear out the many small hills and wooded areas along their avenues of approach.

Col. Fontaine once again ordered Alpha and Echo Companies to assault several hills about eight miles south of Sukchon. These hills had the highest ground commanding the area around Yongyu. If they could be taken, American artillery and mortars could dig in on the summits giving ground forces a much needed punch. Approaches to the hills were covered with woods and several small orchards.

Echo Company moved to the east of the orchards, beginning their battle in several small foothills. Alpha Company took the task of cleaning out the wooded area before beginning their ascent. Charlie Company was thrown into the battle as both Alpha and Echo Companies bogged down under heavy resistance. Marine fighter bombers continually strafed enemy positions near the trails with cannon and machine gun fire, but it did not appear to be having much effect on the well dug in and fortified enemy forces.

Late in the morning, Harry saw an opening develop along the border between his platoon and Steve's fourth squad. He radioed Steve immediately. "Oscar King, Oscar King, this is Butcher Blue, do you copy?"

Hearing Harry on the radio, Steve quickly grabbed the hand set from Dinsmore. "Gotcha Butcher Blue, What do you need?"

"Oscar, there is a hole in the DPRK line west of your fourth squad. Can you move anyone over to help me take advantage? I'm preparing two squads now with Sgt. Umberto in the lead," Harry explained.

Steve quickly assigned Sgt. Martinez to pull one of his squads out of action and prepare them to move west to the hole in the defensive line.

As the men started moving, Steve grabbed the hand set. "Butcher Blue,

I have one squad in route. They will meet at far end of fourth squad, ready to break through."

"Copy that Oscar. Umberto is there now waiting for your team. He will attack on my command. Inform your fourth squad to be ready to move fast."

Steve rushed over to Sgt. Hagen, explaining what was about to happen. When the joint platoon charged forward into the gap, Hagen ordered his men to follow. Seeing the stunned DPRK forces reeling from the unexpected attack, Harry called Capt. Fargo.

"Have enemy on the run—Sector 56. Can we get mortars right now above them in Sectors 57 and 58? Send us part of Fox Company if you can. We can make this happen."

Response from the Captain came in the form of mortars slamming into the hill, exactly where Harry requested them. The DPRK defenders were now caught in a trap. They couldn't move up because of the mortars, and they couldn't move down because of the aggressive Americans. Screaming jets pounded the hillside with continual cannon fire taking out large numbers of defenders.

Directly above Alpha Company, a group of about thirty enemy soldiers decided to charge down the hill into the approaching paratroopers. Rushing down the hill with knives and bayonets, they ran into men from first and third squads that refused to give up the ground they had gained. They stood firm, holding their positions while firing into the screaming horde. Steve joined his men, jumping up onto a rocky outcropping, firing his Thompson at the enemy until he ran out of ammunition. By the time he reloaded, the charge was over. Looking back at his stunned men, he yelled. "Go! Go! Keep it going, damn it! Don't stop now, we got the bastards on the run!"

By this time, Harry had called for a cease fire with the mortars. Men from Fox Company were flowing up the hill, sweeping what remained of an entrenched enemy swiftly to the side.

Following his men forward, Steve had to shoot several wounded DPRK men who refused to put their weapons down. He could not allow these soldiers to snipe at his men as they moved up.

Just short of the summit, Capt. Passton of Echo Company radioed that his men were bogged down on the east side by heavy machine gun fire, about a hundred yards from the summit. Harry took an assembly of his men and Fox Company paratroopers and punched through to the summit. Hand to hand combat broke out as DPRK soldiers fled, leaving their weapons behind. As more Fox Company men poured forward, resistance faded, allowing them to begin taking out the machine gun nests that were hampering Echo Company. As Harry began working his way down the east slope, a Communist Chinese soldier jumped from a slit trench with a grenade in his left hand and a bayonet in his right.

Attempting to avoid the bayonet, Harry fell to the ground on his butt, letting go a quick burst of fire from his Thompson. Although it did not kill the soldier, it struck his left wrist causing the grenade to roll down the hill towards another machine gun pit. Before Harry could stop sliding down hill, the wounded soldier came after him, slamming the bayonet into the ground just short of Harry's shoulder. The wounded soldier reacted quickly, thrusting it once again toward Harry's chest. In utter desperation, Harry swung the stock of his Thompson like a club, striking the soldier in the head, sending him rolling off to the side. As the injured man fell to the ground, Harry pulled his side arm from its holster. In quick succession he fired two rounds into the man's head.

Harry lay back on the hill for just a moment to catch his breath. Standing up, he scooped up his Thompson which was now inoperable, clogged with dirt and grass.

A Lieutenant from Fox Company stopped by. "Sergeant, are you alright?"

"Yeah, I'm fine. He's not though," Harry replied, pointing toward the dead Chinese soldier.

"I was right over there, but I couldn't get a clear shot at the bastard. I was afraid I might hit you instead. Nice job the way you finished him off," the Lieutenant explained. "That's the first Communist Chinese I've seen so far. I'm guessing there will be more."

Harry nodded as he patted the Lieutenant on the shoulder. "Nice to know you were looking out for me. Much appreciated." The two men stood where they were as they observed their men destroying the last of the machine guns pits that had pinned down Echo Company.

About fifteen minutes later most of the fire ended around the hill. In the distance, trucks towing 105mm artillery were already approaching from Opari.

Returning to the summit, Harry sat down on the edge of a gun pit where he could take his weapon apart. Steve joined him for a minute before preparing his men to move on.

"Having problems with that delicate piece of machinery Harry?"

"It just doesn't work when it's full of sand, mud and God only knows whatever else. I let the damn thing slide down the hill over there to deal with a belligerent son-of-a-bitch. Now it's plugged up like Granny's sewer," Harry replied shaking his head.

Laughing, Steve slapped his buddy on the helmet. "You'll get her working old pal."

After organizing the men, they began working their way down into the foothills. Resistance was light as most of the DPRK forces still living had transferred to the next hill about a half mile away. American and British aircraft were already pummeling the prominence with everything they had. A sudden whoosh had Steve and his men stop in their tracks. One of the jets had just dropped a napalm canister on the south face of the next hill. Hot roiling flames spread across the surface, as thick acrid smoke rose skyward. Moments later another canister dropped from the belly of a Marine fighter. It tumbled through the air until it crashed into the ground near the summit. With his binoculars, Steve could see several men running from gun pits with their clothing on fire, although they did not run far before collapsing. The sight was gruesome.

Closing in on the second hill, it was evident the enemy had taken tremendous losses, as resistance was light. After killing several snipers in the wooded valley, the men began a slow methodical advance up the second hill. An awful stench filled the air as they approached the area burned clear by the napalm. It was a combination of diesel fuel and burned flesh. All around them lay bodies of DPRK soldiers who attempted to flee the fighting on the first hill. As they climbed, seeking refuge from attacking paratroopers, they were burned to death by napalm. Their bodies lay in grotesque formations, most of them burned clear to the bones on their arms and legs. In areas closest to the impact zone, severed and shredded body parts littered the ground. Although most of the men had become hardened toward the harshness of war, many still became sick from the putrid odor. Even Steve, who had seen so many people burned to death in Europe, had a hard time with what he was observing. Although it made him sick, he knew it was important to his men that he show a strong appearance and not waver.

By now, many of the DPRK forces that fled or went underground during the air assault had returned to their weapon positions near the summit. Some began rolling live grenades down the hill toward the advancing paratroopers, while others took over unmanned machine gun emplacements. Once again the paratroopers went back to gaining ground one foot at a time. It was hard bloody fighting, often turning into hand to hand combat in order to clear out gun pits. As dusk began to settle in, the tired paratroopers finally reached the summit. They now held all the high ground overlooking Sukchon and Yongyu. The men were delighted to see artillery units already in place on the first hill they captured.

Directed by forward observers in the valley and a circling Cessna, artillery was assisting ground troops battling their way toward Yongyu. Understanding full well that North Korean leaders would attempt to retake the high ground to defend Sukchon, Capt. Fargo carefully posted his men in strategic positions to defend the perimeter overnight. He knew it could be a long brutal twelve hours until dawn, but it had to be held.

DPRK soldiers attacked in small and large groups all night long. Steve was extremely happy the Captain ordered two mortar units to hump their equipment to the summit before darkness set in. They were instrumental in helping turn back every raid but one. Shortly before 0200, twenty DPRK soldiers moved quietly up the west slope. They attacked with bayonets and swords, breaching the perimeter. The dark was pierced by blood curdling screams from attackers, as they hacked paratroopers to death with heavy swords. With so many soldiers from both sides scrambling about, it was nearly impossible at times to know who was who. As Steve ran toward the attack, he observed a man coming over the summit decapitating a paratrooper with his sword. Raising his Thompson, he fired a short blast into the soldier which normally would stop anyone. Nevertheless, the man continued in Steve's direction, yelling as if possessed, while swinging his deadly sword. Steve fired a long blast into the man, emptying his magazine. Almost as if in slow motion, the soldier's legs buckled as he fought to regain his balance. With one final scream, he made a last ditch effort, stumbling forward about three feet, where he finally crumpled to the ground.

Slamming another magazine into his weapon, Steve rushed toward the battle which was now dying out. The carnage was incredible. Men he knew so well lay in foxholes with their severed heads beside them. Others lay near their pits with all their internal organs hanging out. One man was lying dead as he still clutched his severed arm. It was sickening!

Yes, this was war, but to see his men butchered in this fashion infuriated him. He knew until this war was over, he would never give another North Korean or Chinese Communist the benefit of the doubt, no matter the situation. After resetting the perimeter, Steve began walking back toward the Command Post they had established on the summit.

Franny met him half way there. "That was brutal, Steve. I ain't ever seen anything like that in my life and don't want to ever again."

Steve stopped to take a deep breath. "Franny, I emptied an entire magazine from this thing into one of those bastards, and he kept coming. What the hell was that all about? Even with a blast of pure adrenaline, you could never survive that."

Franny nodded his head. "I spoke with a guy the other day from Fox Company. He said while they were in reserve they were told these clowns get pumped up on heroin or opium, to the point where there bodies don't react the way a normal person does to pain or bullets. Their bodies just continue until they bleed out, I guess. Most of the time, they only pump up on that stuff when they're going to do a suicide charge like they did tonight. It gives them plenty of courage and they don't mind dying. Scares the hell out of me to be honest."

"Yeah, I think it scares a lot of men, Franny. You just can't react normally to a deal like that, especially when the bastard's won't go down. Man, I still can't believe that," Steve responded as the two men continued walking slowly toward the command post.

After making another round of the perimeter at 0400, Steve laid down in the CP. He pulled a half-finished letter to Karen from his pack. After thinking for a minute he started to write.

'Oct. 23 about 0420. Today was...'

After closing his eyes for a moment, he folded the letter up, placing it back in his pack. There was no way he could write to his beautiful wife what he wanted to tell her, after what he had gone through today. He couldn't write about love, family and coming home, after experiencing the carnage he had witnessed. He felt sick, tired and old. There was absolutely no reason for anyone who fought in World War Two to be here. This was rapidly becoming sheer torture. Pulling his poncho over his cold body, Steve closed his eyes, hoping sleep would quickly overtake him. But that was not going to be the case. Several minutes later, a large explosion shook the surrounding area. Steve jumped to his feet, grabbing his Thompson on the way out of the CP. He could see smoke rising against the starry sky above the north end of the hill. That was Shrider's perimeter. Joining every extra man who was near the north slope, Steve observed Shrider speaking with one of his Squad leaders. Once the conversation was finished, Steve walked over.

"You alright, Eddie?"

"Yeah, sure am, Steve. We're still not sure what the hell blew up. The explosion was well below our perimeter, but it was huge. I saw flame nearly fifty feet in the air. I'm thinking the bastards had a huge cache of explosives down there that they knew was impossible to move, so they decided to set it off so we couldn't get to it. I really don't know what else it could have been. There hasn't been any follow up attack, and we were ready for it, let me tell you."

Steve gave Eddie a slap on the back as he turned back toward his own perimeter. After looking things over, he jumped in a hole with Sgt. Hagen.

"What was all the fireworks about, Sarg? Scared the hell out of me," Hagen inquired, with a half-smile on his weary, unshaven face.

"Shrider thinks maybe they blew an ammo cache. They didn't follow up with an attack, so it's anyone's guess, but he may be right, let's hope he is." Steve informed his fourth squad leader.

After a moment of silence, Hagen looked over at Steve. "I really miss Whitebear. He was the best. He always seemed like he knew what to do in any case. Nights like this were his specialty. Maybe because he was Native American, or maybe he just had a sixth sense that allowed him to sense trouble in the dark. If I had to be with anyone on a night like this, I wanted it to be Whitebear."

Nodding in agreement, Steve smiled at Hagen. "Yeah, I liked the guy to. He would have made a great officer. You could trust him to a fault. And you're right, he did have a sixth sense about him. I think Trost will do alright, but he has big shoes to fill. Believe me I can tell you for fact, you very seldom get more than one guy like that in any war. Heroes from birth. Yup, that's what they are. Heroes from birth."

The two men sat quietly for some time before Steve slipped out of the foxhole on his way to join Kilburn and first squad. He found Kilburn and Martinez sharing a freshly dug hole at the intersection of their squads.

"Hey Sarg," Martinez said quietly, as Steve knelt down beside the hole. "What's next for us tomorrow?"

"Right now can't say. I'm guessing we strike out toward Sukchon, but that's just my opinion. I would think there is enough pressure on Yongyu that we're not needed there anymore. But we'll have to wait until the old man contacts us in the morning," Steve responded, looking down at his watch.

"Do you think Trost will do alright, Sarg? He hasn't had much leadership training. I sure hate for him to get his guys messed up," Kilburn stated in a matter of fact tone.

Steve liked Kilburn a lot, but didn't appreciate him questioning the decision to make Trost a Squad Leader.

"I think Trost will do well. He handled that attack tonight like a pro. He was comforting a few of his guys when you could tell it was bothering him a whole lot. Believe me, if I see a problem, I'll yank him. Capt. Fargo agreed with my choice, so for all intent and purpose it stays as it is," Steve explained in a stern voice.

Kilburn realized he had stepped on Steve's toes in a big way. "Look Sarg, I wasn't questioning your decision. I just never got along with Trost very well. He seems a bit arrogant to me. That's all I was getting at. I'll work with him, like I do everyone else. There's no problem here, Sarg."

Preparing to leave Steve looked at Kilburn, "Arrogance? You think Trost is arrogant? How does he measure up to MacArthur when it comes to arrogance? When you've figured that out give me a holler. I'd really like to hear your arguments on that matter."

After Steve was out of hearing range, Martinez busted out laughing. "If you were a pilot you would be going down in flames right now Kilburn. He just totally burned your tail feathers right off your sorry ass. Yeah, I have some reservations about Trost just like you. But he hasn't done a damn thing so far that makes me mistrust him. You better stop at the next five and dime we pass and get the Sarg. some good cigars to make up for that head up your ass display."

Nodding his head with a sheepish grin, Kilburn looked at Martinez. "And I suppose I'll be hearing about this for a while."

As Martinez scanned the hill below with his binoculars he said quietly. "Well now, is the Pope Catholic, Kilburn?"

At first light, a wave of helicopters began landing on the summit. The first units removed dead and wounded while dropping off artillery and mortar crews. The second wave dropped off mortar tubes and ammunition. The last two choppers brought in 105mm artillery pieces that were hanging by cables from the bottom of their aircraft. It was evident that Col. Fontaine planned to use this hill to his best advantage after figuring in the cost to capture it. After coming down from the hill, Alpha and Echo Companies assembled in the valley below. The remaining platoons in Fox Company were once again used to fill in for losses.

Once the men were rearmed, they were directed to join the battle for

Yongyu. Headquarters had underestimated the amount of North Koreans defending the town. It was turning into a battle of inches.

About mid-morning, a sizable force of about 500 DPRK soldiers counter attacked against the 187th, attempting to fight their way out of Yongyu. At the same time, in a coordinated attack, about 300 DPRK soldiers hit the right flank of the paratrooper's formation, attempting to force an American withdrawal.

Alpha company was caught right at the intersection of the formation where the front line tied into the right flank. They were hit incredibly hard. Shocked by the potent assault, both Fifth and Fourth Platoons gave ground in the first few minutes of the attack. Capt. Fargo attempted to bolster the line by sending in Sgt. Shrider's Third Platoon, who he held in reserve. Little by little the men began pushing back against the sustained assault. Steve and Harry had been assigned to cover the flank with Echo Company. When Fifth and Fourth platoons fell back, it allowed DPRK forces to break through their formation. Steve pulled Trost's third squad out of the line to contend with the infiltrators. Small battles took place as the determined enemy was not going to be deterred easily. Concerned about being struck from behind, Wentworth turned his fourth squad around to help wipe out the rear guard threat. At times, there was so much fighting going on it was impossible to tell where the main combat lines were.

Trost and his B.A.R. man Blanchette, chased down three of the attackers heading straight for Capt. Fargo's rolling headquarters. The attackers dove into a small gully where they opened fire on the advancing paratroopers. Trost sought cover behind a large boulder, as his B.A.R. man made for a stand of trees. It quickly became a stand off as neither side had the power to overwhelm the other. Angered by the situation, Trost threw a grenade which went over the DPRK positions. As it exploded, he made a charge forward, spraying the gully with his Thompson and wounding two of the infiltrators. The third man returned fire, striking Trost several times in the chest. Blanchette ran from his cover, diving into the gully about ten yards from the North Koreans. Racing forward he fired on the three men until they were all dead. Leaping from the gully he ran over to Trost, his chest was totally covered in blood. Kneeling down beside the squad leader, it was evident he was dead. Finding no pulse, Blanchette ran back to the main battle, reporting to Steve what had taken place. Immediately, Steve assigned Blanchette as leader of third squad. Steve would work out the B.A.R. assignment later when time permitted.

As the battle raged, Steve and Harry worked together, desperately moving men around in order to close holes created by casualties. Although the enemy was also taking losses, it was evident they were not going to back down. As Steve was making another adjustment late in the morning, he was thrown to the ground by an exploding mortar round. Looking up, he observed two DPRK soldiers racing through the line toward Capt. Fargo's command center. Grasping his Thompson, he fired a short burst until the weapon solidly jammed. One attacker fell, while the other kept running straight toward him, with a fixed bayonet. Tossing his Thompson to the ground, Steve began reaching for his side arm, but realized he would never get it out in time. Hoping to gauge his actions properly, he jumped to his right at the last minute, grabbing hold of the man's ankle and twisting with all his strength. The soldier landed face first on the ground as his rifle flew several feet in front of him. Losing no time, Steve sprang to his feet drawing his bayonet. Lunging forward, he landed solidly on the soldiers back. Raising his right arm, he plunged the blade into the man's throat. Instantly, he could feel life drain from the body below him. Standing up, Steve rolled the soldier over to make sure he was dead. Looking at the corpse for a moment, Steve felt some compassion, knowing the man must have had a family somewhere that would now mourn his death. But at the same time, he was the enemy, a man responsible for the death of young American soldiers. Turning to walk away, he looked back at the still corpse one more time before uttering, "That's for Whitebear and Trost, asshole. They didn't deserve to die!" After clearing the dirt from his weapon, Steve returned to the battle without giving a thought to what had just happened.

About 1300, the British 27th Commonwealth Brigade arrived, throwing their weight against the North Korean onslaught. Mercifully, the battle began to turn in favor of the allies. Instead of holding the line, they were now moving forward, covering five to ten yards at a time. All around them lay bodies of dead and wounded DPRK soldiers. Steve accompanied Kilburn's first squad as they overran a mortar pit. One of the loaders jumped from the pit holding a Russian made rifle. Before he could fire, Kilburn shot him square between the eyes. The rest of first squad surrounded the pit, shooting until all movement stopped. After taking a moment to survey the scene, Kilburn yelled. "Let's keep going and kill some more of these bastards."

Although Steve understood Kilburn's comment, he felt a bit sick to his stomach. Just a short time ago he called a dead man an asshole, without giving it a second thought. Now listening to Kilburn, he wondered what this war was doing to them mentally. Yes, they had to kill the enemy, but were they beginning to revel in the moment? Or, were they just beginning to voice their disgust with the brutality of this new brutal concept of war? In all the months he served in Europe, he had never witnessed such savage, brutal combat where the enemy appeared to favor death over life. It was maddening and somehow it appeared sanity was becoming a rare commodity in this war.

By late afternoon the battle subsided. Just a few sporadic shots echoed in the valley from time to time, although evidence of death was everywhere. Bodies stacked upon bodies, wounded men screaming in pain with no one available to treat them. Right or wrong, many paratroopers felt it more merciful to just silence them. Yongyu was now in allied hands, battered and broken as it was. Every civilian had evacuated the town days ago, with whatever they could carry in carts or on their backs. They knew full well the extent of what was coming down upon their village. As Alpha Company took time to eat and rest, Steve, Harry and Franny walked through the small town. It reminded them of Europe in many ways. Craters in the middle of once nice cobblestone roads, many buildings completely blown away, others were just burned-out shells, as fire had eaten everything else away.

Franny walked away from his friends, picking up a small rag doll lying near a damaged wooden hand cart. "I wonder if the little girl who owned this made it out alive, or where she is today? The way these people live, it might have been the only toy she had. What a damn shame. What a disgusting shame!" Placing it carefully on top of the wooden cart, Franny added. "Maybe when they come back she'll remember where she lost it."

Steve had to smile at the tenderness a child could bring to a warriors heart. Who knows, maybe Franny was right. Maybe she will come back, finding her precious doll perched on the wheel of the wagon where Franny so gently placed it. It was a nice dream to hold on to for today.

By dusk, a safe perimeter had been created around Yongyu, comprised of both American and British soldiers. Alpha Company was assigned to patrol south of the city, checking for enemy activity that might be building in nearby valleys.

After completing their assigned mission, Steve directed First Platoon back to Yongyu over a different route. Sgt. Martinez and second squad walked point with Steve and Dinsmore directly behind them. Suddenly Martinez directed his squad to spread out in battle formation. Everyone else knelt down, preparing for a fight.

Martinez signaled Steve forward. "Sarg, there's a baby crying somewhere up ahead. We also heard people moving through the underbrush. Don't know if it's civilians or the enemy screwing with us." After Martinez drew a small sketch in the dirt as to where he felt the sounds were coming from, Steve made a decision.

"Alright. Martinez keep your men where they are. Blanchette and Kilburn, make a skirmish line flanking second squad. Hagen, bring your squad with me. Moving slowly into a large overgrown orchard, Brimly took point with his B.A.R. The crying appeared to be coming from their right, and was getting louder. When Brimly knelt down, Steve crawled up to him. "What do you see, Brimly?" Steve whispered, as he peered into the blackness.

"It looks like some type of structure right beyond this last row of trees. I can't make it out totally. But I know there are at least two people moving around out there. One was carrying some type of rifle. That's all I can tell you unless I crawl up to the end of the tree line to get a better look," Brimly replied, as he continued gazing into the dark.

Wanting to keep Brimly ready with his B.A.R, Steve called up another man from the squad to crawl forward. A southern boy named Scott came forward after volunteering for the job.

"I used to help my Papa hunt at night, Sarg. I can crawl within five yards of a wild boar without it knowing I'm there."

Steve had to smile. "We're not hunting boars, but I think you're the man for the job."

After Steve explained what he wanted, Scott crawled off, and was unbelievably quiet through the underbrush. Returning about ten minutes later, he sat down between Steve and Martinez. "Four men and one woman from what I can see. I can't tell if there is anyone in the building. I think it was an old storage barn. The back half has collapsed. Brimly is right. One man is armed for sure. Looks like an old hunting rifle, probably a 30.06. Nothing automatic that I could see. I think the baby is just inside the barn in what appears to be an old apple crate. They're nervous. I think they're waiting for someone. The old guy keeps pacing and grumbling."

Nodding his head, Steve turned to Martinez. I'll take Brimly and Scott. We'll approach very cautiously. Have the rest of the men ready to attack if things go sideways."

"Sarg, hold on! Two soldiers just arrived. I think they're North Koreans," Brimly whispered, as he pointed through the brush where the old man stood.

This time Steve crawled forward with Scott to investigate, with Brimly right on their heels with his B.A.R. ready to fire.

Scott pointed toward three North Korean soldiers that were now exiting from inside the barn. They appeared to be very anxious. The two new men stood silently to the right of Steve's patrol. The lead soldier from the barn argued with the old man for several minutes before drawing his weapon. After several more words he shot him point blank in the chest.

"That's it. Brimly take out the guys to our right. Scott we get the others. Go!" Steve directed as he jumped to his feet.

Brimly rolled out of the underbrush, firing his deadly weapon at the men to his right. Steve shot one of the soldiers near the barn, attempting to escape. Scott shot the lead soldier in the shoulder, and killed his accomplice. The old man carrying the rifle began swinging it down in preparation to fire, just as Scott killed him with a shot to the head.

The woman screamed as the other two men with her fell to their knees with their hands up.

Scott unarmed the wounded soldier before pushing him to the ground. Several more men from Martinez' squad rushed forward, converging on the barn. When Steve knew everything was clear, he approached one of the kneeling men. "Do either of you speak English?"

Both men looked up, appearing to be very scared and confused.

Steve looked at the woman who had retrieved the baby from the apple crate. "Do you speak English?"

She began rattling on in Korean about something nobody could understand.

Finally the wounded soldier spoke up. “I speak English.”

Steve walked over to him pulling the man to his feet. “So tell me. What’s going on here?”

“The old man has not paid his monthly allotment to us. We warned him last week but he refused to pay. Now we were going to take it from him.” The soldier explained in broken English.

Before Steve could say anything, one of the kneeling men called out, “Lie!”

Martinez pulled the man to his feet giving him a good shake. “So, you do speak English.”

Shaking with fear, the man nodded his head. “Just a little. But I tell you, he lies.” In broken English he continued. “They wanted to sell the baby and turn my niece into a whore for the troops. We tried to escape, but with all the fighting we decided to stay here. We should have kept going.”

“He lies! The soldier called out. He is a North Korean officer. He kept them here until we returned. The other man is just a farmer.”

“Search him!” Steve instructed Martinez and Scott. Just as the two men prepared to search the man, the woman turned and began running toward the barn. Two squad members stopped her from entering. Pointing toward the door she began to cry.

“Check in there damn it, be damn careful!” Steve ordered the two men.

Finishing the search, Martinez handed Steve a North Korean Military Identification book and a pay voucher. His men also brought out a Chinese made military rifle, and a North Korean uniform.

Steve shook his head. “So that answers everything. Martinez, tie those guys up. We’ll take them back with us. Scott, you help the lady with her baby and things.”

Just as Scott approached the woman, she pulled a knife. Backing away quickly he tried to assure her he was only going to help her and meant no harm. As he took a step toward her, she tossed the baby into the air directly toward him. As Scott dove to catch the infant before it hit the ground, the woman pulled a Russian made automatic pistol from her jacket. Just as quickly, the wounded officer jumped forward, pushing Steve backward while attempting to grab his Thompson. Martinez fired quickly at the woman, striking her in the chest. Sgt. Hagen, who came forward with the rest of the platoon, fired on the officer, killing him instantly.

The other soldier dropped to the ground covering his head yelling uncontrollably. Martinez pulled him back to his feet, slapping him in the face to shut him up.

When everything was quiet, Scott stood up, holding the crying baby. "Its fine I think, Sarg."

"Tie both of those men up. I couldn't care less if that guys a farmer. Tie them up and tie them good. We'll let headquarters sort this mess out!"

After using water from his canteen to wash up the baby, Martinez made a rough diaper from part of the blanket the baby was wrapped in. After handing off his machine gun to Scott, he picked up the baby. "She looks bad, Sarg. I think the poor kid is really sick, she's got one hell of a temperature."

Angry over everything that happened, Steve had Kilburn lead the way back toward Yongyu. Arriving at headquarters, Steve informed Capt. Fargo about what had taken place. After turning the baby over to a South Korean Officer, Steve led his men to their encampment sight. It had been a long day and he was dead tired. The next morning, Col. Fontaine arrived by helicopter. Climbing up on the back of a Jeep he gathered the men around him. "I could never be more proud of you men as I am right now.

"You have demonstrated to the world what well trained paratroopers can accomplish. During the last few days of fighting you have destroyed the 239th North Korean Regiment. We have taken over 300 prisoners and we estimate you killed nearly 1,000 combatants as well as destroying tons of Russian and Chinese equipment. It appears, between the 187th Airborne, regular U.S. ground forces, our British allies, and combined air power; we have killed in excess of 6,000 North Koreans during this major battle. Yes, we have taken casualties. But our numbers are small in comparison to the damage we inflicted on the enemy. Thankfully, many of our wounded will live to fight another day, due to our mobile airlift. I can tell you General MacArthur is proud as hell of you men. I-Corp informed me they plan to put the 187th in for a Presidential Citation. I strongly concurred. Congratulations men, you deserve it. And for some real good news, we're being pulled out of action for a while. I'm told were heading south to rest up, re-equip and have some well-earned R and R. Job well done, men."

No one was happier than Steve to be leaving the battle for a rest. He knew his men were just as tired and mentally worn out as he was. They had worked hard and fought hard. His plan was to let his men recuperate for a few days before calling them together to make assignment changes. Hagen was going home due to a hardship in the family, and Martinez had been accepted into Officer Candidate School. It would be tough to fill in behind such good combat leaders, but he now had great, battle hardened, well qualified candidates to choose from.

Steve never finished that letter to Karen he had been carrying in his pack. Somehow, all the words he wrote seemed inappropriate after what they had been through. So he took out a new sheet of paper and placed it on his desk. He looked at the blank page for some time before he began to write. The easiest part was the salutation. "To my beautiful wife."

Several days after arriving at the rest area, Steve was summoned to headquarter by Col. Fontaine. Arriving at the orderly office, the Colonel shook his hand. "Kenrude, I have been proud of you since we first met. Your instincts always carry the day for you. Allied leaders are so happy they're busting their seams over what you did. The baby you found was the daughter of a high ranking government official here in the south. She was kidnapped and being held for ransom. The soldier you captured spilled his guts on the entire operation. The other man you brought in was in fact a farmer. He and his wife had been taken hostage to care for the baby. His wife tried to run away with the child a few days ago and was killed. The woman you killed was a Communist Chinese Operative. Job well done, Kenrude."

"Thank you sir. My men did a great job. Everything happened so fast they didn't have time to think it over. They just reacted. I have a great platoon, sir," Steve explained with a smile.

On his way back to camp, Steve felt proud of what they had accomplished. In the middle of this massive war they had returned a kidnapped baby to her parents, and left a rag doll in place for a young girl to discover. He wondered if she ever came back looking for it. Of course he would never know. But in his heart he wanted to believe that this very night she was cuddled up in her straw bed next to her long lost best friend, having sweet dreams in a brutal country torn by a war she could never understand.

CHAPTER 10
PROBLEMS IN GLENDALE

It seemed as if summer had just begun when the first hints of frost appeared in the early part of September. Alex stood by the kitchen window having a cup of coffee while Nancy finished preparing their breakfast.

"You know it feels like summers go by faster every year the older we get. Years ago when the kids were small, it was like we had all the time in the world to watch them run and play. Now we barely get seeds in the ground and it's time to harvest again. Where does the time go, Nancy?"

Looking up from the stove his wife smiled sweetly. "Why Mr. Kenrude, are you feeling old all of a sudden? Do I need to chase you around the house to make you feel young again?"

Alex laughed, "Sorry honey, but at my age I don't think I could run around the house. You probably would catch me before I got off the porch."

Placing a plate of bacon on the table, Nancy called out to her husband, "Well, if you're still able to hobble over to the table in your old age, breakfast is served."

Sitting down they both had to laugh. After a few minutes, Nancy inquired. "What do you have on the agenda for today? Remember Michael has a dentist appointment first thing this morning so he won't be around for a while. Can you wait for him?"

"Yup, I remembered that. I think I'm going to have Jake and Sam finish picking corn over on the north plot, and have Frank help me with that corn grinder we're rebuilding. We need it up and running as soon as possible. We also need to fix that hoist in the barn so we can get the rest of the hay up in the loft. So there's plenty to do until Mike gets back. Then, maybe we can fire up the other corn picker and start over by Karen's place."

"Good Lord Almighty, Alex. Rome wasn't built in a day and you have enough work planned today for about ten men. Just get done what you can. Tomorrow is another day. And a few minutes ago you were feeling all old and decrepit. Now you're talking like a thirty year old. Actually, I kind of like it Mr. Kenrude,"Nancy replied with a wink.

After another cup of coffee, Alex kissed Nancy on the nose before heading out to the barn. His lead worker Frank was already working on the grinder. "I think I found the problem, Alex. It looks like the bearing turned on the pulley shaft. We'll have to take the shaft into Bratton's Machine Shop to get it fixed. We also have a cracked gear. That part we'll have to order. But the machine is definitely worth fixing, so it's no big deal. Give me about ten minutes and I'll have it completely apart."

Alex nodded in agreement as he checked out the cracked gear. "I wonder what made that thing go? Still, this thing has a lot of hours on it, so I guess anything is possible."

Frank smiled as he finished tearing everything down. "Well, those are the only two problems I can see. Do you want me to take them into town or do you want to go?"

"No, no. You go, Frank. I think I'll see if I can figure out what's wrong with the hay hoist. Something must be jammed somewhere," Alex responded, as he smiled at Frank.

"Now don't you go crawling around up in the loft, Alex. Mike will be here in about forty-five minutes and I should be back in a little over an hour. So don't get nuts while I'm gone," Frank admonished Alex very sternly.

Once Frank drove off, Alex began checking over the electrical box near the door. When he determined everything was fine there, he walked over to the hoist to check the connections. After several minutes of inspecting the wiring, he screwed the cover back on the hoist. He then walked over to the rope that controlled the hoist once it was in the air. Everything appeared to be loose and free. Scratching his head, he turned on the hoist raising it from the floor. He swung it over to pick up six bails that were neatly stacked on the floor. Once the hoist was clamped, he tried to raise the load. Just like the other day, the hoist came about four feet off the floor before jamming.

The only thing Alex could think of next, was that the pulley system up in the loft area was broken or falling apart. He peered up at the pulleys for a moment before heading toward the barn door. Looking at his watch, Alex mumbled, "That damn thing. Well, Mike will be home in about an hour, so he can look at it."

Shaking his head, he took one more look at the lift before leaving the barn. He was halfway to the house when he decided to go back to the barn. Taking the controls, he moved the load down to the floor then back up again. The next time he moved the hoist he looked toward the loft to see if he could figure out what was wrong. Sure enough, one of the pulleys was twisting when there was a load in the lift. That meant the collar holding it in place had to be broken.

Searching a parts cabinet, Alex found a new pulley assembly ready to install. Grabbing several wrenches and a crow bar, he climbed the ladder to the hay loft. Standing on the loft floor, the pulley was still way out of reach. Methodically arranging several hay bales, Alex climbed up directly below the damaged pulley. After removing the bolts holding the pulley assembly in place, he found the large pin it rotated on would not slide out of the rafters. Following several unsuccessful swings with a hammer to dislodge the pin, Alex realized it was going to take a bit more muscle. Picking up the crow bar, he repositioned himself on the bales in order to get better leverage for prying against the rafter. Just as he began to push the pry bar, several strands of twine snapped from the bales beneath his feet.

Feeling the bales beginning to come apart underneath him, Alex made a desperate attempt to throw himself sideways, back toward the loft floor. Nevertheless, the entire pile of bales shifted when he began transferring his weight. Seconds later, he slid from the hay loft along with several bales of hay. He let out a scream as he reached for the lift rope that dangled mere inches from his face. Unable to grab it, Alex fell backwards toward the floor below. Although partially landing on several broken bales, he struck the bale lift with his left side and head. Pain tore through his body as his arm fell uselessly to his side. He struggled frantically for several seconds to pick himself up to no avail. Each massive breath he took caused him excruciating pain. With his right hand he rubbed his right eye as it seemed to be clouded. No matter what he did, slowly his right eye went dark. Alex peered up toward the ceiling with his left eye as tears ran down his cheeks. He wanted to see Nancy once more before he died, but no matter how hard he tried, he couldn't call for help.

Laying his head back down on the hay he could sense it was wet. Alex knew he was losing blood from the back of his head, but to what extent he couldn't be sure. After one more unsuccessful attempt to call for help, he began to lose consciousness. This is what death felt like, he thought. He would now slowly drift away until he awoke in heaven, he hoped. As his jaw trembled he whispered, "I'm so sorry, Nancy. I'm so sorry. I never meant for it to end this way. I'll always love you."

Returning from the dentist, Mike walked into his parent's house. Nancy was sitting by the kitchen table mending a pair of Alex's coveralls. "Well, how did it go with the new dentist?" she asked, expecting Mike to complain as he'd always hated going to the dentist.

Pouring himself a cup of coffee, Mike shook his head. "I don't think any dentist is very gentle these days. He just ground down the tooth a little bit but it felt like he was using one of the grinders we have out in the shed. Man, I thought he was going to end up right down on my jaw bone."

Laughing, Nancy looked up at her youngest son. "You might have been a brave soldier, and you are one heck of a worker, but you have never tolerated the dentist well, Michael. I remember when I used to take the three of you for your summer check-ups. You would always try and find a way to disappear or hide behind that big couch in the waiting room. Bravery was not your best suit when it came to dealing with a dentist." Standing up to fill her coffee cup she kissed her son on the cheek. "My poor baby." She added with a laugh.

Mike glanced out the side window. "So, what's that father of mine up to? Did he leave any instructions as to where he wanted to meet me?"

Feeling a bit concerned, Nancy looked over toward the barn. "He and Frank were going to finish tearing down the corn grinder this morning. I saw Frank take off with some parts about a half hour ago but I haven't seen your father. He must either be in the barn or he might have taken the other tractor over to Karen's place. But I don't think I heard it drive out of the yard. That's strange."

Finishing his coffee, Mike kissed his mother on the forehead. "Well, I'll hunt him down and we can get to work. Dad kind of wanted to pick corn in the field over by Karen's like you said. If he isn't over there, I'll get the tractor started and we can get to work. We'll be back around noon for lunch if that works for you."

"That's fine, Mike. I'm just going to heat up that beef roast we had last night. We can make sandwiches and a salad," Nancy explained, as Mike turned to head out the door.

"Sounds good, Mom. See you in a couple of hours," he added, as he walked out onto the porch.

Half way across the yard, Mike's favorite dog, Champ ran up with a stick. "You want to fetch, old boy," Mike said with a laugh, as he watched Champ jump around waiting for him to toss the stick.

After teasing Champ a few times, Mike gave the stick a good toss and it landed right near the barn door. Champ ran toward the stick, but suddenly stopped. Slowly approaching the barn door he began to yelp. "What's the matter Champ, losing your eye sight? It's right behind you," Mike called out to the visibly upset animal.

Seconds later, Champ was clawing at the door as he looked back toward Mike, yelping all the louder. Puzzled by the dogs behavior, Mike walked over to the barn. "What's the matter, boy, something in there that shouldn't be? Alright, boy. Let's have a look."

Opening the barn door, Mike yelled, "Son-of-a-bitch!" He ran head long toward Alex, calling out, "Dad! Dad! Are you alright?" Looking down at his father, Mike knew Alex was anything but alright. Fearing the worst, he began checking Alex's vital signs. Realizing he was still alive, he made a beeline for the house where he found his mother on the phone talking to a friend of hers. Mike pulled the receiver from her hand as he said, "Go to Dad in the barn! I'll call for help. Go!"

Redialing the phone, Mike called the emergency number. "This is Mike Kenrude. My father has been seriously injured out in our barn. We need an ambulance and a doctor if you can send one out here. He's hurt real bad. He needs help fast, he's barely breathing." The dispatcher informed him she would send the ambulance out immediately.

Hanging up the phone, he realized his mother had not left the kitchen and had heard everything he said. She was standing near the sink with her hand over her mouth as tears rolled down her face.

"Is he going to die, Michael? Am I going to lose my Alex?"

"I don't know, Mom." Grabbing a blanket from the porch, Mike looked at his mother. "Come on Mom, you need to help me. We need to keep him warm so he doesn't go into shock."

Nearing the barn door, Nancy came to a stop. "Michael, I'm scared. I can't go in there. I can't."

Without saying a word, Mike took hold of his mother's arm, forcibly pulling her into the barn. Placing the blanket over Alex, Mike once again checked his vital signs.

"Is he alive?" Nancy inquired, as she shook nearly uncontrollably.

"Yeah, but just barely, he's lost a lot of blood, Mom." Mike replied, as he shook his head. "He should have waited for me."

Nancy knelt down beside her husband as tears streamed down her cheeks. "I told you to be careful, Alex. What did you do? Can you hear me, Alex I love you." She took hold of her husband's right hand, massaging it slightly. "Oh Alex, what did you go and do? Michael, we need to do something. We can't leave him like this." As she reached out to grab him, Mike pulled her away.

"Mom, we can't move him. We don't know how bad he's hurt. We could do more harm than good if we try to move him."

"No. I want him in the house. If you won't help me I'll do it by myself. He needs to be in the house, Michael." His mother screamed, beating her son in the chest with her fists. "He just needs to be in the house. I don't want him dying out here like this. No! Not like this." With that, Nancy collapsed into her son's arms weeping uncontrollably. Mike had never seen his mother like this, and was not sure how to console her. After all, his folks were nearly inseparable.

Mike turned his head as he heard footsteps entering the barn. It was Karen, carrying the farms financial books. "I heard the screaming out in the yard. What's going—" she stopped in mid-sentence when she saw Alex lying on the hay. "Is he—"

"He's alive. Karen. The ambulance is on the way. I wish they would get here," Mike said.

In the distance, the distinctive wail of the Glendale ambulance siren could be heard as it closed in on the Kenrude farm. Minutes later, the white and red Cadillac pulled up outside the barn. Two attendants, along with the new young emergency doctor ran toward the barn. Karen took Nancy back to the house so they could call Christine and Mike's wife, Glenda.

After checking Alex, Doctor Faust looked at Mike. "He's not good. Not good at all. We'll take him to the hospital in Glendale and do what we can do for him. If he survives the night, we'll see what we can do about getting him to the University of Minnesota. He's lost a lot of blood."

Doctor Faust, along with the attendants and Mike, got a back board under Alex. Being careful not to move his head too much, Doctor Faust cautiously applied a compress against the huge gash on the back of his head. With that finished, they rolled the gurney out to the ambulance. Minutes later, with the siren screaming, the ambulance departed for Glendale at top speed.

Mike ran to the house where he found Nancy seated by the kitchen table looking ashen gray. Karen was just hanging up the phone. "Glenda will meet us at the hospital. I tried calling Christine, but didn't get any answer. I'm guessing she's either in school or working one of those intern sessions in the hospital. We can try her later."

Mike took his mother by the arm, leading her out to Karen's car. All the while she kept mumbling. "What am I going to do without Alex? If he dies I want to die too, Michael."

Arriving at the hospital, Karen checked with one of the emergency nurses to see what was happening with Alex. Mike sat with his mother, holding her tight and attempting to reassure her that Alex would be alright. Just as the nurse arrived to speak with them, Glenda came charging into the emergency ward. She grabbed hold of Karen whispering. "Tell me he's still alive!"

Karen nodded her head as she gently stroked Glenda's back. "So far. So far."

The nurse looked over the assembled family. "I'm so sorry this accident happened. Alex is in the x-ray department right now. They'll get x-rays from the top of his head to the bottoms of his feet. So that will take a while. We know he's lost a lot of blood from the severe gash on the back of his head. Dr. Faust believes he has a punctured left lung, along with several broken ribs. But for now I can't tell you any more than that. After the x-rays are read, we should know a lot more. Dr. Faust has already notified the University Hospital about Alex, and requested he be moved there in the morning. They're making all the arrangements as we speak. I will be back to talk to you when we know more."

Mike stood up quickly. "Nurse, has he regained consciousness at all?"

Shaking her head the nurse replied. "No, and that's a major concern. I'm not going to lie to you about that. We know he has some degree of head injury, and likely his back as well. Right now we just don't know to what extent. That is another reason he'll be transferred to the University."

As the nurse left, Nancy grabbed Mike. "My God, what if he's paralyzed forever. Oh Michael, what are we going to do?" Nancy ripped lose from Mike's arms as she began running toward the x-ray department. "I have to see him, Michael. I have to see him. Oh God, Michael I want to be with him. He'll come back if he knows I'm there. He's all alone, Michael! He needs me!" Nancy yelled out as she fought desperately to break loose from Mike's powerful grip.

Both Karen and Glenda helped Mike bring her back to the waiting area. Every few minutes Nancy said, "Listen, it's Alex. He's calling for me. I need to go to him." Karen and Mike kept her seated, although she continually pleaded for them to let her go.

A short time later, Minister Moore walked into the hospital. Kneeling down beside Nancy, he forced a reassuring smile. "I was informed about Alex's accident by the Sheriff. How is he doing?" After Mike finished explaining everything they had been told, the Minister looked up at Nancy.

"You have a strong faith, Mrs. Kenrude. You know God is looking out for your husband. All we can do now is pray. God will always do what is best. Your faith brought both your son's home from World War Two, and God is now watching over Steven again. He knows both you and Alex are righteous people. Pray with me now, Nancy. Let's all pray for Alex."

When they were finished praying, the young Minister stood up. Taking Mike by the arm, they walked slowly down the corridor away from the family. If there is anything Gene've and I can do to help out just let us know. We'll pull the entire congregation together to help in any way we can."

Mike nodded his head. "Thank you, Reverend. We just don't know anything right now. This is so damn hard. I don't know what would become of Mother if Dad didn't make it. But I will keep in touch."

"We need to trust in God, Michael. Keep your faith." Laying his hands upon Mike's head, the Minister said a short blessing before leaving.

After several more attempts, Karen finally was able to reach Christine in her dorm room. She was already at the University doing an internship, so she would be there to meet them the following day when they arrived.

Janet Donnelly took care of all four grandchildren so Karen, Mike and Glenda could stay at the hospital with Nancy. It was a long night for the Kenrude family, as Alex's condition appeared to change hourly. At one point, Dr. Faust informed them that Alex had broken his left shoulder, collar bone, and six ribs. One vertebra was cracked and two others were moved out of place. Making matters worse, he had a punctured left lung and appeared to have some internal hemorrhaging. He would need surgery when he arrived at the University. Nevertheless, Dr. Faust was still unsure about the condition of the spinal cord, or exactly why Alex had not regained consciousness. He considered Alex to be in very critical condition.

The following morning, nurses prepared Alex for the long ambulance drive to St. Paul. Mike and Glenda followed along in their car, while Karen drove Nancy home, so she could freshen up and pack clothing for the stay in St. Paul. Arriving at the University, Alex was taken to their intensive care unit where he was prepared for emergency surgery. Christine met Mike and Glenda for a tearful meeting in the waiting area. When Karen and Nancy arrived at the University, Nancy's entire demeanor had changed. She walked up to her children, taking them by the hand. "Your father is going to be alright. He may not make a hundred percent recovery, but he'll come back to us. I have prayed harder than I can ever remember over the last twenty-four hours. And I know God is not going to let Alex die. Now, no one must write to Steve about this until we know what's going to happen. That young man has his hands full leading men in combat. We can't put this on his mind. Karen, can you do that?"

Nodding her head, she looked at Nancy. "I couldn't agree more. Steven would do anything he could to come home right away, but if he wasn't allowed to leave, he would be distracted and he could get himself or his men killed. No, as terrible as it sounds, we will just have to wait. Steven may be angry, but in the long run he'll understand."

By late afternoon, Alex was out of surgery. The surgeon who performed the operation came out and spoke talked to the family. "We found several internal injuries. First we removed his spleen, then we repaired an injury to his liver. An orthopedic doctor set his shoulder and collar bone. We placed a new type of patch on his lung. In twenty-four hours we'll try to re-inflate it. We're pretty confident that will work well. Later tonight, we'll take Alex down to x-ray to determine whether or not his spinal cord is intact, and to see if he has any major head injuries. Our equipment is more advanced than the standard x-ray set up the hospital at Glendale has, so hopefully if there is more to find, we'll be able to see it. In a couple days, an orthopedic surgeon will operate to repair any damage to his back that can possibly be fixed. Of course, all that depends on how Alex responds to treatment, and what we find with the new tests. I can assure you we will do all we can for him."

Mike stood up slowly. After pacing the waiting room for a moment he inquired. "What's your best prognosis?"

Shaking his head, the surgeon replied. "Right now Mr. Kenrude. I can't really say for sure. There are too many unknowns and variables. Frankly, it's a miracle he's alive after an accident like that."

The following morning the family met with Alex's primary physician, Dr. Parsa. After everyone was seated, Dr. Parsa began placing x-rays on the light box. "Alright, we shall start here. Based on all the x-rays we took, we know that Alex's spinal cord is intact. However, it took quite a shock and there is considerable swelling. He may have some paralysis when he comes to. But with therapy he should recover nicely. However, his head is a different situation." Pointing toward a head x-ray, Dr. Parsa continued. "Alex has a severe concussion, but there does not appear to be any bleeding on the brain. However, sometimes x-rays don't show us everything inside the head. Right now, we don't really understand why Alex is still in a coma. It could be caused by shock, loss of blood, or the tremendous jolt his entire system took when he landed. We just can't be sure. There is nothing we can do medically to bring him out of it. When his body is ready, he will return. But when that might be we can't tell."

Nancy cried as she listened intently to everything Dr. Parsa described. After composing herself she inquired, "Will he be back to normal? I mean will he be able to function around the farm? Will he be able to do everything he did in the past?"

Shaking his head, Dr. Parsa looked downward. "Surely you understand that Alex is not a young man. We won't know fully how he's going to be able to function until he comes to, and we can get him on his feet. And get all the swelling taken care of. Like I said, odds are he will need some back surgery as well. It's just a waiting game now, Mrs. Kenrude."

After the Doctor left, Mike and Glenda went outside to get some fresh air. After they had walked for about fifteen minutes, Glenda pulled Mike over toward a short stone wall. After they were seated she looked at her worried husband. "Tell me what's on your mind, Michael."

Smiling back toward his wife, Mike took a deep breath. "I've always known the day would come when Dad wouldn't be able to function around the farm. Of course I never expected anything like this. So, if he can no longer work, or if his brain or body is impaired, everything will be up to me until Steve gets home. It will mean hiring another hand. But honey, I don't think we can afford that. Maybe a part timer, but full time, I don't think so. And if Mom can't manage Dad out there, we might have to think about moving them to town. But that would kill them both. What the hell are we going to do?"

Glenda fully understood Mike's concerns. "I've thought many times about what would happen someday if they had to leave the farm. I always shoved it to the back of my mind and refused to think about it, assuming we had many years before it would come up. Maybe we could have them live with us. Or we could rent out our house and move in with them. The kids love them terribly, so that wouldn't be a problem. But Michael, I think that would be a better idea than moving them into Glendale, where they wouldn't be in the country and around the animals."

Mike sat quietly for a moment. "Glenda, that is the most unselfish thing I've ever heard. It would mean more work for you, but Mom would help all she could. And it would give Dad some piece of mind. Thank you, honey." After hugging Glenda, Mike continued. "Maybe we're putting the cart before the horse though. Dad might come out of this just fine. Who knows? But at least we have a workable plan if worse comes to worse." Returning to the waiting area, Glenda took Karen aside to inform her of their plans. Not surprisingly, Glenda discovered Karen was already thinking along the same lines, and she knew Steve would never allow them to move away from their beloved farm.

As Alex remained in a coma, Mike and Glenda chased back and forth to Glendale several times over the next week, checking on their children and their farm operations. Frank took it upon himself to hire a part time hand to fill in for Mike, since there was still plenty of work to do before the snow flew.

Driving into the yard, Mike observed the double doors open to the barn. Walking inside he observed the crew unloading a wagon full of straw into the hay loft. Jake turned to Mike.

"How's your pa? We decided to finish up what he started so we could get both wagons emptied. He knew what he was doing alright. Damn, he should have just waited for one of us."

Mike shook hands with the men before explaining what was happening with his father. He thanked them for finishing the project Alex had started. When he finished talking to the crew, Frank walked him back outside toward his car. "The corn grinder is up and running. We still have some corn to pick over by Karen's, but we should wrap that up by Monday. The Ford tractor has a carburetor problem, but I'll get a kit for it next time we run into town. Oh, and the new International tractor your pa ordered will be here next Tuesday. We're still going to keep it, aren't we?"

"Yeah, nothing changes, Frank. If Dad can't run the operation anymore, Steve and I will take over the reins. We're still going to be Kenrude Farm's, Incorporated, no matter what. One more thing Frank, I'm glad you hired Gilly. He was going to be my choice if push came to shove. Go ahead and work him as you see fit. While I'm gone, you continue making all the decisions. I'll pay you accordingly," Mike explained to their trusted and efficient lead worker.

Smiling Frank shook hands with Mike. "Don't worry about a thing. Just take care of your folks. You know you can always count on me."

That being said, Frank walked back into the barn. After a few moments of thinking over everything Frank had told him, Mike walked into the house where Glenda was already sorting through the mail.

After retrieving all the important items Karen needed to keep their farm running, they drove over to Janet Donnelly's home to visit the children.

Janet was anxious to hear firsthand news about Alex. She also thought their plan to take care of Alex and Nancy was a great idea and offered to help any way she could. After putting the children to bed, Mike and Glenda drove to their home to get some rest before heading back down to St. Paul later the next day.

Early in the morning, Mike and Frank drove to town to pick up equipment and pay a few bills. As Mike walked into the feed mill everything came to a stop. Charlie McGrath, Sheriff Richards and several other men surrounded him, asking question upon question. It was like that everywhere he went that morning. It was gratifying to know how much his folks were loved in Glendale.

Waking back toward the feed mill, Mike passed C.J. Portman's, the biggest clothing store in Glendale. Just as he approached the door, Wauneta Bainsworth exited the shop.

"Well Mr. Kenrude, I was hoping I wouldn't run into you or any of your family," she said coldly.

Without saying a word, Mike sidestepped her as he continued on his way.

"That's right Kenrude. Slither away and go hide in your hole," she yelled, for everyone to hear.

Mike spun around instantly, never wanting this discussion, but unwilling to walk away from it if she was going to make a scene.

"Look Wauneta, whatever your problem is, it isn't with me. Stan Mullins admitted to killing Grant. It's over. If you can't accept the facts, that's too damn bad. Just leave me alone."

Smiling, Wauneta replied. "Yes, I heard your dear old daddy may not make it. What a shame. Maybe it's payback for all the problems you caused my brother. Maybe it would have been best if you had never come back from the war, you and that self-righteous make-believe war hero brother of yours. Who the hell do you people think you are?"

Mike was just about to unload on her when Bull Richards walked up behind him. "Mike, why don't you take a walk. You don't need to answer to her in any way shape or form. Just walk away, son."

Mike glared at Wauneta for a moment before walking back to the feed mill where Frank was waiting for him.

Sheriff Richards glared at Wauneta for several moments before addressing her. "Woman, I don't know why you moved back here to Glendale. You were better off in Chicago. You knew damn well what kind of jerk your brother was, and how your daddy and grandmother always paid off everyone necessary to keep him out of trouble. So why don't you pack up and head back to all your high and mighty Chicago elites and leave Glendale alone. In fact, the entire county would be better off without you causing problems wherever you show up."

"To tell you the truth, Sheriff, I don't have much time for this piss ant one horse town, or you, and least of all the Kenrude's. And I wouldn't be here if my aunt hadn't asked me to come and settle up some of my grandma's business ventures. Actually, I can't wait to get back to Chicago. But that Mike Kenrude makes me angry. Who the hell does he think he is? Do you know he thought he was too good for me in high school? Think of that, Sheriff! A Kenrude better than a Bainsworth! Not in this world. He treated me like crap and I always vowed that someday I would get even. I thought we finally had him when Grant was killed. Well his day will still come,

Sheriff. I'll still get my pound of flesh from that bastard. I want to see him squirm like the worm he is!"

Bull looked down at the sidewalk for a moment then back up at Wauneta. "Let me tell you something, Miss Bainsworth. I'm the law here in Kandiyohi County, and I just heard you threaten that young man. Be assured if anything happens to him, I'll be looking for you first thing."

"Go ahead, Sheriff. As far as I'm concerned, you and this whole damn town can kiss my royal ass." After spitting on the sidewalk she charged over to her Cadillac and drove off.

Bull stood on the sidewalk a few moments contemplating the conversation. Somehow he knew he hadn't heard the last of Wauneta Bainsworth, and it bothered him very much.

Later that evening after seeing the children again, Mike and Glenda returned to the University Hospital. Although Mike dreaded going back, the farther he was from Wauneta Bainsworth the better he felt. He knew she was pure evil and would never go down without a serious fight.

Two days later, Alex began mumbling and stirring in his bed. Dr. Parsa kept a close eye on him, hoping he was finally coming around. Finally about midnight, Alex opened his eyes slightly, attempting to focus on all the faces above him. With half a smile he reached for Nancy's hand. "That's the face I was searching for. Although you're still pretty as an angel, I knew if I found you I wasn't dead." Everyone laughed with excitement as Alex was able to talk and move his right arm, although it wasn't perfect.

Nancy wept for joy as she clutched her husband's hand. "Oh Alex, where have you been? I've missed you so much, where have you been? And what were you doing in that loft?"

Seconds later, tears were running down Alex's cheeks as he trembled. "I'm sorry, honey. I just wanted to feel worthwhile. Lately I feel like I'm getting old and ready to be turned out to pasture I tried to call for you, but I couldn't talk. I didn't want to die alone in that barn."

"Hush now," Nancy stated boldly. "We'll have no talk of death now. We weren't ready for that, and neither was God. You have lots to do on this earth yet, Mr. Kenrude."

Doctor Parsa finally stepped forward. After introducing himself to Alex, he began asking him questions as to how the accident came about. Although the last few seconds were kind of fuzzy, Doctor Parsa was extremely happy with the recollections Alex was able to articulate, as well as his memory in general.

Taking a deep breath, Alex looked up at Dr. Parsa. "Before I passed out, my right eye went dark. Now it's fuzzy and grainy. Will I see properly again?"

Dr. Parsa nodded his head. You had a severe concussion, Alex. You are not totally out of the woods with that issue yet. But yes, I believe in a few weeks your eyesight will return to normal."

Alex smiled broadly after receiving the good news. Over the next few days, the hospital staff began working with Alex, despite his broken bones. His right leg worked just fine, but his left leg gave him some problems. However his natural strength and determination took control, and he was not about to be denied returning to normal.

One week after regaining consciousness, Alex was on his way home. They decided not to operate on his back, but he would require much therapy at the Glendale Hospital, and lots of tender loving care at home. Nancy assured Dr. Parsa there would be no lack of that.

His second night home, Alex used a cane to make his way to the front porch. With a little help from his wife, he sat down in his favorite wooden chair. He took in a long deep breath. "Ah. Fresh hay and the feeling of frost in the air. That's what makes life so precious, sweetheart."

Nancy sat down across from him admiring her strong husband. "What was it like being in a coma? Did you know we were there?" She inquired almost nervously.

"Kind of like having your brain locked in a jar," Alex replied. "There were times I could hear you and the kids. I swear I could. But I couldn't answer. I couldn't move. I kept screaming it in my head, 'Nancy I'm right here.' But you never answered. It was the strangest damn thing!"

Tears rolled down Nancy's face as she forced a smile. "Well, I'm here now, Alex. And I'm not going anywhere without you."

Smiling Alex took his wife's hand. "It's good to be back, honey. It's good to be alive."

With everything pretty much back to normal, Mike dug back into work that needed to be finished before winter arrived. On a warmer than average December morning, Mike took Gilly into town to help load sixty sacks of feed concentrate at the grain mill. Once that project was completed, Gilly walked over to the drugstore to pick up a prescription. Mike had a cup of coffee with Charlie McGrath and several other farmers.

When Gilly returned, Mike asked if there was a problem. Shaking his head, he replied. "No, I guess I'll have to go back to the doctor for some more tests. The pharmacist gave me a note. That's all."

Smiling, Mike slapped Gilly on the back. "Hey, you're young. Can't be anything to serious."

Gilly half smiled. "Naw, I'll be fine, I guess." After saying good bye to Charlie, the two men drove back to the farm.

The next day as a cold winter wind blew, Mike drove the new tractor down toward the lower meadow to make sure the water trough had been emptied before it froze solid, damaging the tank. Finding the tank and equipment already prepared for the winter, Mike picked up the float, tossing it onto the tractor. He looked down at Champ, who had followed the tractor out to the field, then up at a flock of ducks preparing to land in the slough. "Yeah, winter isn't far away old friend." Champ began yelping and barking as he watched the ducks disappear behind the tall weeds on the knoll to their left. Mike laughed as he watched Champ spin in circles as if saying, 'Come on, come we have to go after them.' Mike peered down at his watch. "Well, I guess we have a little bit of time. Let's go take a look."

Picking up a stick, Mike tossed it in the direction of the slough for Champ to fetch. Instead of returning it, he ran up on top of the knoll where he sat down to watch the ducks. Arriving on top of the knoll, Mike knelt down beside Champ, just as another flock of Mallards arrived from the north. Champ looked up at Mike and began to bark and whine. "You want to hunt them, don't you boy? Yeah, you remember coming out here with Steve and me when you were just a year old. We got some ducks that day, yeah that was fun."

Standing up, Champ licked Mike's face as his tail wagged furiously.

Mike rubbed Champ's head. "Well, old boy, we're not hunting today, but if you want to have some fun go ahead." Releasing Champs collar, Mike gave him a light swat on the rump. Instantly Champ charged down the hill, barking and jumping over clumps of weeds until he arrived at the edge of the water. After growling for a second at the ducks, he charged head long into the slough.

The air was filled with the squawks of terrified ducks as they splashed their wings in distress. Within seconds, every duck in the slough became airborne while circling overhead. Mike laughed as he watched Champ swim around in circles in search of just one duck to grab hold of, but there wasn't one left to be seen anywhere. Minutes later, Champ charged back up the knoll making two complete laps around Mike before coming to a stop. As Mike went to stand up, Champ shook all the cold water from his coat.

"Hey, what the heck was that all about?" Mike declared as he wiped the cold water from his face. Champ lay down by Mike's feet as they watched the ducks take back control of their home for the night. Gazing off toward the west, Mike could see the sun beginning to set behind some light clouds. Clapping his hands, Mike called out to Champ. "Come on boy. Time to head home. Dinner will be on the table real soon."

As they began heading back toward the tractor, something made Mike stop and look toward the grove of trees about fifty yards east of the slough. He had played in the familiar grove his entire childhood and knew every tree and rock. Some people still insisted the grove was haunted, as several Indian warriors were hung there in the 1880's by drunken settlers. Legend had it those Sioux Warriors still haunted the area, seeking to extract their revenge on unsuspecting white folks who dared to enter the area at night. Mike and Steve had spent countless hours sitting on that knoll when they were young, attempting to taunt the Indians to come out and chase them. One night they even armed themselves with sling-shots and searched the dreaded grove, but came up empty. Mike had to smile a bit when he remembered how fast they ran home after a huge owl hooted and flew directly in front of them. They didn't go near the grove the rest of that summer.

But tonight something wasn't right, he could sense it. After taking one more look around, he began walking toward the tractor. After about ten yards, Mike froze in his tracks as the hair stood up on the back of his neck. His attention was drawn back toward the grove for some unknown reason. Just in front of him, Champ stood facing the grove as he growled viciously, showing his sharp canines. Mike knelt down beside Champ, putting his mouth close to the dog's ear. "What is it boy? What's out there?" Mike noticed his companion was shaking and very nervous about whatever was out there. He had raised Champ since he was a pup, and trusted the dog's instincts one hundred percent.

As the sun began dipping below the horizon, Mike felt a sense of urgency over take his soul. Whatever was out there wasn't good, but Mike still felt he had to check it out. Standing up, he looked down at Champ, who was ready to attack. Releasing his collar, Mike yelled out, "Come on boy, let's go get it."

Champ took off like a rocket, barking up a storm. Suddenly, a shot rang out from the grove. Champ yelped in pain as the bullet tore into his firm body. Filled with rage, Mike ran toward his friend before something struck him, sending him into a spiral before he fell to the ground. Instinctively, Mike placed his hand inside his jacket. Removing it, he found it covered in blood, he knew he had been shot. Lying in pain and totally defenseless, Mike glared out at the grove, hoping to see some sort of movement, but it was getting too dark. Mustering every ounce of energy inside him, Mike struggled to regain his feet, attempting to stumble toward the tractor. His head was spinning as he gasped for air, but he knew he couldn't stop. Whoever was stalking him was still out there, he could feel the person's eyes burning into him.

Arriving at the tractor, Mike leaned against the tire for a moment as he collected his thoughts. For the first time since March of 1945 in Germany, he was on the receiving end of enemy fire, but this time there was nothing to fire back with, and he felt totally helpless. Grabbing hold of the tractor, Mike began climbing up toward the seat, but he knew he wasn't going to make it. He observed the muzzle flash of a rifle in the grove, seconds before another bullet struck his side, knocking him back to the ground. Totally exhausted and in tremendous pain, Mike laid next to the tractor. He feared whoever was out there in the woods would be there shortly to put a bullet in his brain.

Desperately, Mike pulled himself along the ground, hoping to take cover near the brush pile on the far side of the field road. It seemed to take hours to make the short journey across the rugged ground as sweat poured down his face. Reaching the brush pile, he found a small opening where he could crawl in for protection. Lying next to him was a branch about five feet long and one inch in diameter. Taking the pocket knife from his jacket, Mike quickly carved a point on one end to create a nice spear. There was no way he was going to go down without some type of fight. The problem was, it was becoming totally dark, and the thick cloud cover reduced any chance of using star light to recognize a moving adversary approaching his position.

However, with a weapon in his hands, he prepared mentally for the coming life and death struggle. Just beyond the tractor he could hear noise in the tall dry grass coming toward him. Despite the pain in his shoulder he picked up his spear and a good size rock, hoping to hit his opponent in the chest or face, giving him a chance to draw first blood. His heart pounded and sweat ran like rivers down his face as he prepared for battle, knowing he was the ultimate prey.

Moments later, Champ dragged his wounded body around the back of the tractor whimpering as he crawled. Mike felt incredibly bad for his friend, but was afraid to give away his position. But that didn't matter. Champ knew exactly where his wounded Master was, and crawled right up to him. It was easy to see the bullet had struck Champ high up on the back, severing his spinal cord, causing him to lose the use of his rear legs. There was little doubt his loyal friend was dying, but there was nothing he could do for him. It was obvious Champ just didn't want to die alone out there in the dark. Mike cradled Champ in his left arm holding his head against his chest. Slowly Champ raised his head, licking Mike one more time on the face before taking his last breath. As tears rolled down his face Mike rose up to his knees and yelled, "Come on asshole! Bring it on. You want a fight, you got one. Here I am you son-of- a-bitch, here I am. Let's finish this!" Minutes passed like hours, but nobody appeared.

Mike strained his hearing, hoping to catch any sounds of approaching life. However, all he could hear was the creaking branches of the dry trees behind him. Sitting back down on the ground, Mike was positive his assassin was still out there, but was waiting until total darkness to finish him off. Petting Champs head, tears once more came to his eyes. What had been a few fun-filled moments by the slough had instantly turned deadly. As night fell over the field, Mike began sharpening several smaller sticks, and placing them in the ground outside the brush pile with the points facing toward the open field. This was going to be the Alamo, his last stand, as he was positive someone was going to come and finish him off before morning. However, the loss of blood was beginning to take its toll. He felt weak, as dizziness began blurring his eye sight. What was that sound? Mike peered out in the blackness looking for any signs of German tanks. He could hear the unmistakable sound of their clanking treads.

Suddenly, Lieutenant Stabbler knelt down beside him on his right, as Private Mulligan, the crazy Kentuckian knelt down on his left, winking at Mike. "Where the hell have you been, Lieutenant. I've been covering this area all by myself for a while now."

Smiling, Lt. Stabbler patted Mike on the back. "We've had your back all the while, Kenrude. There was a small German patrol back there we had to clean up first. The rest of the platoon is on the way. Give me the low down on your situation."

Mike nodded his head as he smiled at the capable Lieutenant. Pointing toward the tractor, Mike began. "That tank has had it, the crew is dead. Looks like an eighty-eight took it out. There appears to be a platoon of Krauts back in that wooded area about a hundred yards or so to the east. They have been sniping at me for quite a while. I've heard tanks in the last few minutes, but I haven't seen any yet. What's your plan sir?"

Lt. Stabbler looked over at Pvt. Mulligan. "How's your ammunition holding out Mully?"

Mulligan smiled broadly, "I'm good sir. I reloaded before we left the trucks."

"Good, that's good, how about you Kenrude, you good with ammo?" The Lieutenant inquired as he slammed a new magazine into his Thompson.

Picking up his spear Mike replied, "I'm good sir, fully loaded."

Pvt. Mulligan leaned closer to Lt. Stabbler. "We better figure something out quick, sir. I think they're getting closer. I can hear the grass crunch."

Lt. Stabbler nodded in agreement. "Let's wait a few more minutes until they get closer to the tank. Then we'll rush out at them and get them by surprise. What do you think, Kenrude?"

With a smile on his face Mike responded, "I like it sir. They'll never see us coming." Sweat poured down Mike's face as he readjusted his helmet, preparing for combat.

"Sir, I think they have their bayonets fixed. We better move quickly or we're dead," Mulligan explained as he quietly slid the lethal bayonet onto his carbine.

Lt. Stabbler nodded in agreement. "Alright wait, wait for my command. Here we go. Now. now!" The Lieutenant screamed as he fired a long blast from his Thompson.

Mike charged forward over the brush pile, attempting to avoid the sharpened sticks he had placed in the ground. He smiled as he saw bodies falling to the ground as Mulligan picked them off one by one. Letting out a loud scream, Mike charged out into the battle as fast as he could go with his injuries, preparing to attack the enemy that awaited him. The battle field was alive with screams and moans as the balance of Lt. Stabbler's platoon joined in the bloody, ferocious attack.

About five-thirty, the phone rang in Nancy's kitchen, it was Glenda. "Mom, have you seen Michael around there? He said he would be home by five. I have dinner ready and two hungry kids but no husband."

Placing her hand over the receiver, Nancy asked Alex where the guys were working. "Hell, Frank asked me if he could send the guys home at four-thirty since there really wasn't much they could do as it was getting dark. I told him that was fine. I don't know where Mike was, I didn't see him," Alex replied calmly.

Putting the phone back to her ear, Nancy said, "Honey, right now we don't know where Michael is. I'll call Frank and see what he knows then call you back right away."

After several attempts, Nancy finally got through. "Frank, this is Nancy. Do you know where Mike was when you left? We just don't know where he is?"

"I sure don't, Mrs. Kenrude. I saw him drive the new tractor out on the meadow road about three-thirty. I don't know where he was going. We have everything cleaned up out there in both pastures for the winter. He talked about taking Champ out there to do some duck hunting one day. Maybe he took his shotgun with him to check for ducks in the slough. Don't worry Nancy, I'll come back with Sam or Gilly and see if we can find him."

Hanging up the phone, Nancy felt a bit relieved for a moment. Then nervously she turned toward Alex, asking, "Is Mike's shotgun in the gun cabinet?"

Alex walked into the entry way to take a look. "Yeah it's here, why what's up?"

Nancy turned toward the kitchen window, placing her hands over her face. Instantly, she knew that something bad had happened to her youngest son. But where? The farm had grown so much it was hard to say where he could have driven with the tractor. As she watched the final rays of the sun drop below the horizon, a terrible feeling gripped her soul. Spinning around she looked at her husband. "Alex, what has happened to our boy?"

Alex shook his head as he gazed at his worried wife. "I know Mike can take care of himself, but something is wrong here, Alex." He stepped forward, taking Nancy into his arms.

As Glenda fed her two hungry children, Matthew looked up at her. "When is Dad coming home? He always eats dinner with us."

Glenda ran her hands across her son's bushy hair and forced a smile. "Any time now, Matthew. Your dad had some things to take care of, so he's a little late tonight."

As Matthew returned to his plate, Glenda peered out the kitchen window. This was not like Mike at all. He was rarely late for dinner, and always enjoyed joking with the children as they all ate together. He always called it his unwinding time. Staring into the darkness, Glenda knew something bad had happened to her husband, as tonight the dark fields surrounding their house took on a menacing appearance that haunted her soul.

CHAPTER 11
THE 187TH GOES INTO RESERVE

Following a long drive south, the 187th finally arrived at their rest camp. There wasn't much for frills, as Army engineers had just finished building the base. With Communist Chinese forces pushing hard against Allied lines, it was impossible to say how long the men would be in reserve. Reinforcements were tough to come by, as every available man was being sent to the front in order to stem the tide of the Chinese onslaught. The few reinforcements who arrived were a mixture of new men and more veteran's from World War Two, who volunteered for combat. It was good to have well-trained men falling into their ranks. Steve took advantage of the situation, grabbing two veterans to replace Martinez and Hagen.

Devin Kraus, a former 82nd man who came into World War Two about three months before the war ended, was given fourth squad. Arnie Stebbins, a 101st man who fought at Bastogne before being wounded and discharged, was given second quad. Steve remembered him slightly from the rest camp in France before they were sent up to Bastogne. Stebbins had been a hell of an athlete in the camp, playing every sport like a pro.

Several days after Stebbins arrived, Steve and Harry sat with him in the mess hall during dinner. "So, what made you decide to reenlist, Stebbins?

Why would you want to get back into this shit when you were torn up so bad last time?" Harry inquired.

"Well, things didn't work out well when I got out of the hospital. When I got home to Detroit, I found out my girlfriend was banging my best friend, who was refused by the military because of his eye sight. Then my old boss wouldn't take me back as the war contracts were finished. He didn't need the help anymore. So then I got a job assembling Chevrolet's. It was a good job with good benefits, but I really missed my girl, despite her whoring around. We tried to make it work, but she didn't want to live with a car assembler the rest of her life. After about eighteen months, she moved out. Well I just kept building Chevy's and playing baseball for an amateur team. It was alright for a while, but I felt like my life was spinning out of control, and I needed to do something worthwhile. When this war broke out I figured what the hell, I might as well come back. But the bastards turned me down because of my old war injuries. Needless to say as things heated up they came crawling to me. So here I am wiser and smarter, I think. At least I hope I am!"

Steve laughed, although he felt sorry for Arnie. "Man, that's quite the story. I'm sorry things didn't work out better. You sure as hell deserved better than you got."

"Yeah, maybe I did, Sarg. I don't really think about it that much. There were some guys who came back to Detroit who were all messed up. One guy I went to high school with was in the Navy. He had two ships sunk out from under him. One night he watched about ten guys get sucked under by sharks as they waited to be rescued. He couldn't deal with it according to his sister. One night he took his dads shotgun and blew half his head off. Another guy who lived a few blocks away from me had been a devout Catholic all his life. He wanted to be a priest. He ended up in the Marines fighting through Iwo Jima and Okinawa. During the battle for Okinawa he was assigned a squad. During a battle they were cut off by the Japs and tried to fight their way out of it. He watched two of his men get decapitated and another blown to bits in a foxhole right next to him. Only he and one other man made it back. About six months after he came home he parked his car near a railroad crossing. Just as the train came, he drove onto the tracks. No, I think I was better off than some of the guys. That damn war took a bad toll on a lot of good men."

Steve looked over toward Harry. "Yeah, we had a buddy named Larry Woodward who committed suicide in 1947. He fought with us from Normandy. We found him and Franny near a busted up glider after D-Day. We took them into our unit and kept them throughout the rest of the war. Larry was a great all around soldier. Always ready to jump in and totally fearless. Hard to say what takes a man to that breaking point, but I guess we'll never know."

Harry nodded his head in agreement. "Yeah I was stunned when I heard Larry took his life. I never expected anything like that from him. It was kind of funny. After I told Marylyn what he did, she wouldn't let me out of her sight for a minute for nearly two weeks. She checked up on me when I was in the garage or working in the basement. We finally had to have a long talk, but she was scared for a long time. She didn't deserve that."

"Yeah, Karen was a bit nervous after we received the call about Larry, too. But she got over it in a week or so. That damn war was tough on everyone. People back home really never understood that guys came back different than when they left. Odds are we'll have the same thing happening after this one."

After looking over the two men Steve stood up. "It's been a long day and I still have a few reports to fill out. I'm going to head back to the orderly room and get them done."

Walking toward the office, Harry looked at Steve. "Did it ever cross your mind, Steve?"

"Did what ever cross my mind? Are you talking about suicide?" Steve inquired.

"Yeah, I never thought about it, but a guy I grew up with shot himself when he came home. He was pretty messed up from a Jap POW camp. They went through a lot of torture and hell," Harry explained.

"No, I never thought about it. I got depressed sometimes when I thought about the men we knew who were killed. But to be honest, after Marjory killed herself in London, I decided that was never a route I would take. It left me angry inside, still does. Then I felt the same way all over again when I heard about Larry. So no, I never gave it a thought. Besides, like you and Marylyn, I had Karen to talk with," Steve explained with a smile.

On Sunday, Steve made another pleasant surprise. Leaving the chapel after services, he observed Father O'Heally, the Catholic Chaplin, walking toward the chapel for Catholic services. Smiling, Steve approached the happy go lucky Irish priest. "Long time since we last talked, Father."

"Well son, by your age I would have to say it must have been in Europe somewhere," Father O'Heally replied, as the two men shook hands.

"Yes. It was, June 5, 1944, in Newbury, England. I couldn't sleep, so I went for a walk. I ran into you near the airfield as crews were servicing the C-47's," Steve explained.

"Ah yes. So you were one of the troubled souls I spoke with before the invasion jump. There were a lot of troubled men that night. I suppose some of them never came back. You know, I felt somewhat guilty about all of that. Here you men were out there searching for answers and I had none—simply because there just weren't any. All I could do was try to give comfort and some sort of hope that everything would turn out alright. Yet, I knew in my heart that for many it would not turn out alright. Some would die, others would be captured, and still others would just simply vanish forever. How do you attempt to deal with the stark realities? Perhaps it was best I never took names of those I counseled. Being able to find out who died and who didn't might have been heart breaking for me. But, then I see you made it. Did you make it all the way through the war unscathed?"

Shaking his head, Steve explained about the night he was so severely injured at Sainte-Mere-Eglise.

"And yet here you are again. I take it you were called up, and did not volunteer," Fr. O'Heally added, looking into Steve's eyes.

"You're right, Father. I really didn't want to come back. I have a family and heavy responsibilities back home. But the government wouldn't give me a break. So here I am once again, fighting another war and watching more good men die," Steve responded somewhat bitterly.

Looking sympathetically toward Steve, Fr. O'Heally led him over to a bench beside the chapel. "Son, no one understands why God permits war. After all, one of his commandments is even 'thou shall not kill.' And we kill by the thousands during war. We kill the enemy so we may live, vindicated by our cause. We kill the innocent and the refugees by accident as they just happen to be in the way. It's a lose-lose situation all the way around. And caught in the middle we have men like you who are forced to make those horrible decisions. And that is why the military gives rank to trustworthy and honest men, so we can prevent some of the tragedies that happen in war. Then we all must do the best we can. Do you understand, Sergeant?"

After a moment of thought, Steve nodded. "Yes, I do understand. But it seems each time I kill, another part of me dies, too. You don't know what that feels like, Father."

"On the contrary, Sergeant. I do, actually. As ground forces were rushing into Bastogne to break the siege, I was with Patton's Third Army. One evening while traveling between commands, my driver and I became hopelessly lost in a snow storm. We thought we would certainly freeze to death. But then by the grace of God, or so I think, we saw a light coming from a still intact farm house. When we knocked on the door the light was extinguished. After knocking a second time, a farmer with a pitch fork came up behind us. Once we explained who we were, and why we were there he dropped the fork and allowed us in. The house was wonderfully warm. He and his wife and two daughters were in the process of making their evening meal and of course, they asked us to join them. I warned them about covering their windows so no one could see the light, as it might bring danger upon them. Sure enough, about half an hour later, three half-frozen Germans kicked in the door. One of them was a Gestapo man. He spoke adequate English. I tried to explain that the people were just giving us shelter from the storm and had no ties to the American Army. I told him they would give them shelter also, as they were good God fearing people. He would hear nothing of it. He ordered his men to tie us up, as well as the farmer and his family. He told them they would be transferred to a stockade in the morning where they would be tried and executed for giving aid and comfort to the enemy. I pleaded with him to no avail.

"As the night went on, his two bodyguards began to get restless. I saw them looking over the girls and the farmer's wife. When one of the men pulled the wife from her chair, the Gestapo man asked what he was going to do with her. The soldier basically told him he was going to rape her as she was no better than a common whore to begin with, and he should pick a girl and join in. The Gestapo man laughed and nodded in agreement. The soldier took her into a bedroom where he raped and beat her. I still hear her screams today. When he returned, the two soldiers looked over the girls, deciding which one they were going to take. I pleaded with the Gestapo man to stop them. He looked at me and asked? 'Would you also like a turn with them? You can of course, no one will judge you. In fact I think you should, as you men of the cloth think you're so much better than all the rest of us. Maybe we can soil your almighty soul and prove you are as human as the rest of us.'

"He walked over to me, cutting the ropes that bound me to the chair.

Holding his Lugar loosely in his hand he yelled out, 'Padre, take your choice, or I will decide which one you get.'

"I yelled back, 'I'll take you.' Before he knew what was happening I pulled the gun from his hand and shot him right in the chest. Without even thinking, I shot the other two animals before they could reach their weapons. Just that fast, three human beings lay dead on the floor of that house—at my hand. I still question if there was a better way. But I couldn't see any other way to save those girls and their folks.

"After the war I returned to my parish work in Cincinnati. Each day I struggled with those feelings. When I preached brotherly love and forgiveness, I questioned whether or not I was a hypocrite. I counseled for several years in order to put it all in perspective. So you see Sergeant, I do understand your feelings. That is why I volunteered to come to Korea. I felt it was my duty to come here, and do good works in order to cleanse my soul. Granted, Bishop Brooks was dead set against me returning to war. But in the end, he allowed me a leave my parish for a second time, to tend to my soldierly flock."

Steve was quiet for a few moments before responding. "Father, for what it's worth, you did the right thing that night. Like me, you were faced with a life and death situation. When it was all said and done, those murderous bastards would have killed that family, along with you and your driver since you had been witness to war crimes. You had no choice if you wanted to survive, and save five more innocent lives. Believe me, God won't punish you for your actions that night."

Father O'Heally took a deep breath. "My son, it has actually been a pleasure speaking with you. For the first time in a long while, I feel some liberation from my guilt. Well now, I must go and prepare for mass. I have a large flock that needs my attention this blessed morning."

Standing up, the two men shook hands. "I look forward to talking with you again, Father."

"As I do as well, Sergeant. Now you must also go and attend to your own flock. Although slightly different, we both will be doing the same thing, getting those men ready to face their fears in this most horrible war," the kindly priest instructed, before saying a short blessing.

Steve smiled while nodding in agreement as the padre walked quietly toward the chapel. Walking away Steve felt uplifted somehow. The conversation had truly inspired him. He felt somewhat at peace, just as he had back in 1944 at Newbury, England. Somehow, Fr. O'Heally always had a way of making sense of a world gone mad, and this morning was no different.

That evening at mail call, Steve received letters from Karen and his mother, both explaining everything that happened to his father. At first he was angry that nobody had contacted him right away. He would have loved to be by his father's side, supporting him however he could. Nevertheless, he understood his mother's explanation as to why they didn't contact him. Feeling relieved that his father was going to be alright, Steve wrote Karen and his mother long letters.

On December 18th, division commanders held a large meeting near Pusan at which upcoming airborne operations were discussed. Most of the officers and some of the non-commissioned officers attended the three day affair. Capt. Fargo and Sgt. Doogan were encouraged to attend by Col. Fontaine. As attendees were leaving the conference center at the end of the first day, a large truck exploded in a nearby parking lot. Shrapnel spread out for nearly fifty yards in every direction. Capt. Fargo sustained severe injuries. He was given emergency treatment in Korea before being sent to the Navy Hospital at Sasebo, Japan. Franny helped for hours getting men to the aid station, or performing first aid on those who did not need immediate care. Later that evening, Franny had several small pieces of shrapnel removed from his left thigh.

Col. Fontaine was extremely lucky. He had walked back into the building just before the explosion. The next day, two Communist Chinese subversives were arrested near the conference center with sniper rifles, as they prepared to shoot high level American representatives attending the meeting. Both men were executed as spies by the South Korean government.

Arriving back at the rest camp, Col. Fontaine immediately assigned Capt. Jim McGlynn from Battalion Operations to lead Alpha Company. The Captain was an 82nd Airborne man in World War Two. He enjoyed having veteran staff at his side, so he was excited Sgt. Doogan was the company First Sergeant. As usual, Franny gave Capt. McGlynn every reason why he could appoint someone else. He said he would be glad to take over a platoon. Nevertheless, Capt. McGlynn's decision stood. He wanted a man with combat experience and a man that had been around the military for a while. As Franny had been full time Army before the war broke out, he was exactly what the Captain was looking for.

Harry and Steve were delighted to keep Franny as their First Sergeant. They knew he was a no nonsense type of guy, who always looked out for his men. When observing problems, Franny would fight tooth and nail against the Officer Corp until he determined every deficiency had been corrected. Besides, Franny already had the undying loyalty of the five platoon leaders, and was well known to the men of Alpha Company, In turn, Franny asked the new captain if he could expedite paper work he had submitted for posthumous Bronze Stars for Jimmy Whitebear and Kelly Trost for their bravery under fire, before being killed in combat. Capt. McGlynn signed off on them immediately.

With every vacancy filled, Alpha Company once again led the way in Third Battalion. The entire battalion was like a tightly wound spring, ready to be set lose upon the enemy.

Nevertheless, as in all wars things change rapidly. On December 21st, the first and second platoons were removed from Alpha Company for a special mission. Franny protested to everyone who would listen. Taking on two new platoons from Japan that had never seen combat was going to put Alpha Company at risk. Nevertheless, the orders stood, to his great dismay.

Steve and Harry's platoons were transferred south to Pusan where they were secluded from the rest of the combat forces. The following day, Col. Fontaine led his two platoon sergeants into a large conference room containing no windows. In the middle of the room were three tripods holding maps that were covered by white sheets. An armed Military Police Officer stood behind each tripod.

As the side door opened, one of the MP's yelled out, "Attention!"

Swiftly, a Brigadier General, a Colonel and two Captains entered the room. It was silent for several moments as the Colonel handed the General several files.

The General looked over Steve and Harry for several seconds before speaking. "I'm General Booth. Col. Fontaine here tells me you men are the most capable platoon leaders in all of Korea. Well, you damn well better be, because you and your men are going on a mission that will take every ounce of courage and guts you can muster. Any screw ups, and none of you will be coming back. Turning toward the tripods, he called out, "Take the covers off."

Quickly, the MP's removed the coverings from the large situation maps.

Walking over to the first map, the General came to a stop, "Gentlemen, this is Operation Piggyback. It was designed by Capt. Corker from my staff. We have thoroughly vetted the plan and agree it has good potential." Pointing to a spot on the map, he continued. "This is the town of Kwjang in Pyongan Pukdo Province. For all intents and purposes, it has no military value. However, on 25 December, North Korean General Hung Tenyu will be arriving there for a conference." The General proceeded to the second map, which contained an exploded view of the area. "Here is your challenge. On 24 December, you will parachute into this mountain valley at

0200. From there you will proceed to Kujang, and capture Gen. Tenyu. And I mean capture! Not kill!"

He walked over to the third map. Following a predetermined trail out of the valley with his finger, he continued. "This is your escape route. You will be picked up no later than 1800, 25 December, at the top of this ridge. We will supply ample air cover to get you and your men out. Anyone not there at pick up time will be left behind. It's a tight time-line with no room for foul ups or rescheduling. Any questions?"

The men walked over to the maps, examining the terrain. "Sir, what's down in that valley? Is it all forest?" Steve inquired.

"The best Intel we have is that the valley is pure virgin forest," Colonel Manners responded.

Shaking his head, Harry looked over at the Colonel. "Whose dumb ass idea was this to begin with? We could take fifty percent casualties dropping into a forest at night, before we ever engage the enemy. Broken bones, concussions, severe cuts with loss of blood. What happens to those men when we go to evacuate?"

Looking angry, the General walked over to Harry. "If they're mobile, they can be rescued when we pick up your men and the General. If not, they're on their own. Sorry, but that's how it is."

"Like I asked, who in I-Corp came up with such a stupid operation? It's a suicide mission at best," Harry barked back at Gen. Booth.

"Not that it matters, Sergeant, but the idea came down from MacArthur's office. You men were chosen because we felt your experience would give us the best chance of pulling it off. If you want to back out, you are welcome to do so. However, you will be confined here at Pusan until after the mission is completed. You will then be discharged and sent home with a general discharge. Make your decision now, because your training starts when this meeting is over. Do I make myself clear?"

Steve walked over, placing a hand on his friends shoulder. "I say we go, Harry. The jump can't be much worse than Normandy."

Col. Fontaine stood next to Steve, nervously awaiting Harry's response.

Nodding his head, Harry looked at Steve. "I don't like it one bit, Stevie boy. But if you think it's doable, I'm not letting you do it alone. Let's get the men ready."

Smiling, Col. Fontaine patted Harry on the back. "Thanks Jensen. I owe you big time."

General Booth stood silent for a moment. "Alight it's done then. The Colonel will give you maps, coordinates and photos of Gen. Tenyu. Get your men ready as quickly as possible."

With that the officers exited the room while the MP's removed the maps and tripods.

Col. Fontaine walked his two Sergeants back toward their barracks. "I have to leave in about an hour. The battalion is undertaking a new operation in the next few days. I will miss you men. Be safe." After saluting his capable sergeants, the Colonel walked off to a waiting staff car.

The two platoons quickly began going over all the operational reports for operation Piggyback. Steve and Harry made sure the men memorized every detail of the bizarre operation.

Steve's platoon would be dropped just west of Kujang. Half the platoon would hold the drop zone, while the other half would proceed to capture the General. Harry's platoon would be cut in two as well. Half would land east of Kujang, to cut off any reinforcements that might attempt to foil their operation. The second group would be dropped on a hill top designated Lucky 7, to clear any trees or brush that might interfere with helicopter landings and create a perimeter. Steve's call sign would be Blue Fox, while Harry was Red Star. The pickup choppers were designated Sun Catcher.

The men practiced two night jump landings in a valley farther inland from Pusan. Several of the men were injured, but nothing that would keep them out of the mission. Steve and Harry timed their men while adding situations that may arise for discussion. On December 23rd they were as ready as any paratroopers could possibly be with just two days of preparation time.

At 1130 hours the men began boarding their transports at an airfield near Pusan. Col. Manners and Capt. Corker arrived with a young Lieutenant. "Kenrude, Jensen, this is Lieutenant Silverton. He will accompany you on this mission to make sure everything is handled properly. He is airborne qualified, so that will not be an issue," Col. Manners explained

Steve looked over at Harry for a moment. "Colonel, we don't need a baby sitter. We know what we have to do, and we're perfectly capable of carrying it out."

Col. Manners looked at the ground for a moment. "The General knew that would be your response. Nevertheless, the Lieutenant goes with you. No discussions regarding the matter. Capt. Corker has read him in on everything regarding the mission."

Steve was quiet a moment before responding. "Have you seen combat, Lieutenant?"

The Lieutenant glared at Steve. "As a matter of fact, no I haven't. But then, you were green yourself one day. And look at you now. Is there a problem, Sergeant?"

Harry was about a second away from knocking the Lieutenant flat on his ass when Steve stepped up to the cocky officer. "Listen really good sir. I won't have time to take you by the hand. When we hit the ground, its game on. My men know what to do and how to do it. Don't even attempt to counter my orders or redirect my soldiers in any other details than what the operational plan calls for. When the shooting starts, you'll have to fight just like the rest of my men. You screw up, you'll die out there with no one to hold your hand. And heaven help you if you get any of my men killed.

And lastly, if you can't keep up, we leave you where you're at. Do you understand me?"

Before the Lieutenant could speak, Col. Manners spoke up. "Look Sergeant, no need to get all melodramatic here. The Lieutenant will do just fine, he has been handpicked."

"Melodramatic? What kind of idiot are you, Colonel? This isn't going to be a walk in the park. Men are going to die out there tonight," Harry screamed at Col. Manners.

Shaking with anger from head to toe, Col. Manners stepped up to Harry. "If this mission were not so important, I would pull you out of it and have you held on charges!"

"You don't have the balls, Manners. I suspect you've never seen combat either. Want to come along?" Harry replied indignantly.

Swiftly the Colonel retired toward his staff car without saying another word.

Peering at his watch, Steve called out. "No more time to waste. Let's get rolling."

Minutes later the huge transports rumbled down the airstrip and out over the ocean before turning north. Steve glared across the aisle toward Lieutenant Silverton, who was attempting to strike up a conversation with the man next to him. He made Steve's insides crawl. His responses during their argument told Steve he wasn't combat ready. He hadn't even done a practice jump with them. Odds were he wouldn't even survive this mission. Several hours later the pilot called out. "Jump zone, ten minutes out."

Instantly, the jump master opened the door. "Stand up! Hook up! Good luck, gentlemen!"

Everyone stood quietly waiting for the green light to begin flashing above the door. As the light came on the jump master called out, "Let's go, men!"

Without hesitation, the men bailed out the door. Their green canopies snapped open as they came to the end of their static lines.

Like all the paratroopers, Steve peered toward the dark valley below. It was impossible to make out anything right now. But he knew any second he might have to adjust left or right to avoid a dangerous target below. Moments later, Steve crashed into some underbrush with a thud. All around him he could hear the sounds of men breaking tree branches before striking the ground. After dropping his chute, Steve held up a flashlight with a dull red cone on top of it. The men assembled around him in a matter of minutes. One by one his squad leaders checked in. Everyone was accounted for with no serious injuries.

Kneeling down, Steve took the radio handset from his new radio man, Cpl. Taggered. "Blue Fox calling Red Star, do you copy?"

Seconds later Harry responded. "This is Red Star, Blue Fox, on the ground here, one casualty, over."

Steve shook his head. "We are all good, Red Star. Moving out now."

Returning the handset to Taggered, Steve smiled. "Where I go, you go. Never stray from me."

"Sure thing, Sarg," the nervous corporal responded.

"Kraus, set your two squads up just like we discussed. Stebbins, you and your men follow me. Lt. Silverton, come along but be quiet."

The walk toward Kujang took about a half hour. Stopping just short of the town, Steve analyzed his map one more time. Looking to his left he could make out the small hostel where the General was supposed to be staying. But it all appeared to be way too quiet. Where were the sentries? Someone this important would have major security. Looking toward his right, even the small military barracks appeared to be abandoned. Not one military vehicle was parked near any of the buildings. Taking the radio handset he called Harry, "Red Star, this is Blue Fox, do you read."

"Go ahead Blue Fox," Harry whispered into the radio.

"Way too quiet here. No sentries anywhere. No activity by the barracks. Somethings not right," Steve explained to his partner.

"Blue Fox, we have company here. They haven't made us out yet, but it's a large group. We're holding our breath. Over." Harry nervously explained.

Lt. Silverton spoke up quickly when Steve was off the radio. "What are we waiting for, Sergeant? It's just what we wanted, total surprise. Let's go get the General. We need to move!"

Steve held the Lieutenant back. "Something isn't right here, sir. There should be sentries and nervous staff officers going crazy with a General sleeping in this small town. Do you see anyone?"

"That's just it. They're complacent, Sergeant. We need to move and we need to move now. We can't waste this opportunity. That's an order, Sergeant. Get moving," Lieutenant Silverton demanded as he glared at Steve.

This was December 24. He should be at home, sound asleep in bed with Karen, excited children anticipating Santa's visit, anxious to find the festively wrapped packages under a gorgeous Christmas tree. Instead, he was dealing with a whining inexperienced officer who was trying to get him killed in the middle of the winter in North Korea.

Before Steve could respond, all hell broke loose east of town. It was obvious the patrolling North Korean forces had detected Harry's men. But still, nothing moved in the town.

Steve was bewildered. Just as he was going to tell his men to retreat, Lt. Silverton charged forward toward the hostel. A machine gun in a house directly across the street from the hostel opened fire. Silverton was struck several times, he was dead before he hit the ground.

Moments later, fighting broke out back near their landing zone. Steve could make out the heavy rattle of a B.A.R blasting away at the enemy. Almost immediately, a tremendous volume of fire began pouring in Steve's direction from other buildings in the town. North Korean soldiers appeared from the sides of the hamlet, charging toward the trapped paratroopers. "Back away, back away!" Steve yelled at his men.

Moving into a slight depression, Steve ordered his men to form a quick perimeter. Grabbing his radio, Steve called, "Red Star this is Blue Fox. What's your situation?" There was no answer. Once again, Steve called, "Red Fox, what's your situation?" Nevertheless, there still was no response from Harry.

"Damn it," Steve called out. As snow began falling heavier over the dark Korean forest, the rage of battle began to die out. Only an occasional gunshot broke the eerie silence. Apparently, the soldiers near the hamlet were not sure of Steve's location, so they had ceased their attack.

Sgt. Stebbins crawled up to Steve. "Other than the guys at Lucky 7, we must be the only ones left alive. What do we do now, Sergeant? What the hell went wrong?"

Shaking his head, Steve looked over at the World War Two veteran. "There's got to be a traitor back at I-Corp. Someone tipped off the North Koreans. This was a damn set up from the beginning. Right now I'm not sure what's going on." After thinking for a moment, Steve continued, "I think we should back up and see if any of our guys are alive back there."

"Yeah, my thoughts exactly, Steve. I'll get the men ready to move out," Sgt. Stebbins responded as he slid down below the rim of the depression.

Being extremely cautious, Steve led his two remaining squads back to their landing zone. The forest floor was littered with the bodies of his men and many North Korean soldiers. After checking to see if any of his men were alive, it was evident that either private Dymetrie escaped the massacre, or he was taken prisoner. Steve felt sick. Never had he lost so many men at one time. As he began contemplating their next move, heavy fighting erupted up near Lucky 7.

The attack on their escape route only intensified Steve's belief about the presence of a traitor back in I-Corp, Private Krizek, who was just a few feet away grabbed Steve's arm. "Do you think we can get up there in time to help them, Sarg?"

"I doubt it, Krizek. By the time we work our way up that hill, it will be over. Besides, I'm guessing they'll have a rear guard just waiting for us to jump in," Steve explained.

Krizek was angry. Once more he insisted they had to make an attempt to save the men. Understanding the young man's feelings, Steve turned to him. "Sorry son, but there's just nothing we can do. My job right now is to keep you men alive and figure out how we get the hell out of here in one piece."

As Steve finished explaining the situation to Krizek, the sounds of combat up on the hill ended abruptly. Lucky 7 had been over run.

As an eerie silence settled over the valley, Sgt. Stebbins crawled back over to Steve. "What now, Steve. We really can't stay here, they'll find us sooner or later."

Fighting back tears, Steve took a deep breath. "There's a river about a mile to the west of us. Let's try to make our way there and hunker down for the day. We can get some rest and figure out what the hell we do next."

About an hour later, the small band of men reached the river. There was a major rock outcropping to their right, it would offer good cover for them while they slept. However, their luck was quickly running out. As dawn broke, a contingent of well over 150 North Korean soldiers moved in on their position from the north and east.

With only two squads, there was not much anyone could do to create a defensive perimeter against that large of a force. After setting each man where he wanted them, Steve thanked them for their bravery.

Now it was a waiting game with a very predictable outcome.

Regrettably, they didn't have to wait long before mortars began raining down on their small strong hold. After nearly a half hour of pounding, the overwhelming enemy force descended down upon them like a tidal wave.

Although, what remained of the two squads fought valiantly, they were no match for the massive force ripping into them.

Then, just as quickly as the attack began, it was over. Two North Koreans walked among the dead, firing bullets into the heads of soldiers they thought might be still alive.

A sickening peace settled over the river once more as the enemy force moved north, fading into the forest. Steve awoke with a terrible headache. His head and face were covered in blood. Attempting to stand, a tremendous pain shot up from his right leg. Looking down, he noticed a large piece of shrapnel from the mortars sticking out of his calf muscle. Sitting back down on a rock, he carefully began to pull the steel shard from his leg. Luckily, the piece must have been very hot when it entered his leg. Most of the veins had been cauterized so there was very little bleeding when he pulled it out. After applying sulfa and binding it with a battle compress, he attempted to stand once more. Although his leg hurt, the pain was manageable. He walked among the dead, taking a quick check to see if everyone was accounted for.

Sgt. Stebbins, his radio man Taggered, and Juarez were missing. To Steve that was a good sign. He knew if Stebbins had realized the end was near, he could have grabbed the radio man and hightailed it away from the fighting. It wasn't much, but still it was a glimmer of hope on a very dark Christmas Day.

Making his way down to the half frozen river, Steve washed the blood from his head and face. Although the cold water revived him, it also made the cut on his head begin to ache. Taking a look at his helmet for the first time, he was shocked. A piece of shrapnel had penetrated the steel shell and helmet liner before coming to a stop against his scalp. He figured the amount of blood on his face and uniform probably led the enemy to believe he was dead, and thus did not require a bullet to his brain. Climbing back up on the outcropping, he gently removed a helmet from one of his dead comrades. Standing among his dead heroes, he could not believe what he was seeing. His entire platoon was now wiped out. Worse yet, it appeared Harry and his men were also gone. It was heart breaking.

Steve sat down on the rocks, taking a drink from his canteen. What should he do now? Yelling for Arnie Stebbins or Taggered would just bring more enemy soldiers down upon him. The light snow shower soon turned into an all-out snow storm, as howling north winds churned the snow into near blizzard conditions. Placing the borrowed helmet on his head, Steve slid down from the rocks. After some thought, he began walking south, paralleling the river. He stayed just inside the tree line on the riverbank to avoid any prying eyes. As dark overtook the forest, Steve sat down on a log for a quick rest. He was cold, hungry and felt extremely weak from the loss of blood. Struggling back to his feet, he became dizzy and everything began to spin.

"No," he called out. "No, I won't quit! Damn you sons-a-bitches!" Collapsing in the snow, he looked out over the river. "Karen! Karen, I'm coming home for Christmas. Wait for me, I'll be there!" he screamed at the top of his lungs.

Getting back up on his knees, he began crawling forward, dragging his Thompson in the snow. Finding a fir tree that would give him some protection from the raging snow storm, he sat up against the trunk. Smiling, he held out his hand toward the river. "Karen. I knew you would find me. I knew you would bring me home for Christmas."

He had to laugh as he watched her slip and fall a couple of times, as she came across the river. "Where are the kids, sweetheart? Did you leave them with my folks? Did you come by yourself or is Mike here to help you?" Gazing through the heavy snow, he yelled, "No! Karen, come back. I'm right over here. Don't leave me."

Closing his eyes, Steve felt his body getting numb. Looking back across the river one more time he attempted to call out, "Merry Christmas, sweetheart."

Feeling someone touch his head, Steve pulled his pistol from its holster. A woman yelled as a man's voice began speaking swiftly in Korean. Steve couldn't understand what was happening, and slowly he slumped over into the snow.

Waking up, Steve began wiping his eyes. He looked about the small, warm log cabin he was sitting in.

A very skinny middle aged, one armed man was attempting to clean his head injury. Behind him was a small woman holding a baby. Cautiously, Steve lowered his weapon.

Speaking in Korean, the man pointed towards Steve's head holding a wet towel. Smiling slightly, Steve nodded his approval. Very carefully the man came forward. After cleaning the wound, he applied a dressing from an American Corpsman's medical satchel that lay on their table.

Backing away the man smiled as if to assure Steve he would be alright. Walking back to a cooking pot that hung over an open fire, the man withdrew what appeared to be some type of soup. He handed the bowl to Steve.

Looking at the bedraggled, skinny man, Steve handed the bowl back. "You eat. You eat," Steve repeated, as he made a motion like eating with the spoon. The man shook his head no, as he once again held out the bowl for Steve.

Although it was painful, Steve stood up from the blanket they had placed him on. Walking slowly over to a shabby table, he set the bowl down in front of the woman. He directed the young mother to eat the hot soup. Nervously, she looked over at her husband for his approval. After he nodded his head, she advanced toward the table.

Gently, Steve took the baby from her arms as he pointed to the bowl and smiled. The woman sat down and began consuming the thin soup, all the while keeping an eye on her baby in the arms of this strange man. She finished the soup as if she hadn't eaten in days. When the baby began to cry, Steve looked over at a small baby bottle that was sitting on a shelf near the fire. After testing the temperature of the liquid on his arm, he made a motion as if to feed the child.

The woman smiled and nodded, as Steve sat down across from her. He fed the beautiful child until the bottle was empty. After looking into the big brown eyes of the baby for several moments, he looked about the cabin.

"What, no Christmas tree? No gifts? How can that be? This is Christmas."

The bewildered couple looked at each other, not understanding what he was talking about.

"Well, we can fix that." Handing the baby back to her mother, Steve opened his pack. Taking out a pair of heavy duty G.I. issue thermal socks and a pocket knife, he handed them to the man. Returning to his pack, he removed a green scarf his mother had knitted for him when he was in Europe. He handed it to the woman, along with three cans of C-rations. "Merry Christmas. Merry Christmas to you both, you saved my life. Thank you."

Once again, the perplexed couple looked at this strange man they had let into their humble home. A man that had given them such precious gifts when he was clearly in desperate need himself. They spoke back and forth for several moments.

Once more Steve walked up to the woman, taking the baby from her arms. He sat down at the table kissing the infant. He began singing a lullaby that he had sung to his daughter when she was a baby. The small girl smiled widely at Steve, appearing to appreciate the soothing lyrics. After the baby fell asleep, Steve walked over to a handmade cradle sitting aside the couples bed. After he covered her with a well-worn blanket, Steve said softly, "Sleep well, beautiful child."

Smiling at the couple, he walked back to the blanket where he first had awakened. Lying down, he covered himself with his heavy field jacket.

Closing his eyes, he drifted off to sleep, feeling no fear from this poor bewildered couple.

With the stranger in their home sound asleep, the couple also prepared for bed. After extinguishing the small lantern that lit their home, peace settled over the warm tiny cabin.

As the first light of dawn shown through the cabin's frosty windows, Steve awoke. The woman was opening the two ration cans he had given her the night before. He inquired as to where her husband was. Understanding Steve's inquiry, she pointed to the fire that was just about burned out. Putting on his coat, Steve walked outside to help the one armed man bring in a supply of wood. Searching around the cabin, he found a large pile of split wood, but not her husband. Becoming nervous, Steve drew his side arm and slid the safety off.

In the distance, he could hear angry voices in a heated discussion. Walking cautiously toward the sounds he discovered two North Korean soldiers, beating the one armed man. Infuriated, Steve charged into the small clearing. Before either soldier could retrieve their weapons, Steve shot them dead.

Running over to the injured man, he helped him off the ground. "Are you alright?" Steve inquired, knowing the man could not understand him. Forcing a small smile, the thin man placed his hand on Steve's shoulder, nodding his head. They barely made several steps toward the cabin, when a Korean Lieutenant accompanied by three soldiers appeared out of the tree line.

The Lieutenant smiled brightly before speaking in near perfect English. "Well, it looks like we didn't get all of you last night, after all. And now, you have killed two of my men. So that makes you not only an armed insurgent behind enemy lines, but also a murderer. So, by rules of the Geneva Convention, I have the right to execute you on sight."

Waving his arm, his men began to raise their rifles. Before they could shoot, gunfire erupted from the bushes to Steve's right.

"Not today, you son-of-a-bitch," Harry yelled out, as he and several other men fired on the North Korean firing squad.

Spinning around, Steve observed Harry, Arnie Stebbins, Cpl. Taggered, and Privates Manuel Juarez, Sal Demytrie and Bill McCormack stepping clear of the bushes.

"You alright, Sarg," Stebbins inquired, as he examined the wound on Steve's head.

Before anyone could say another word, the small Korean woman came running from the cabin. She grabbed her husband and kissed his arm. Smiling, she looked up at Steve.

Motioning with his arm, Steve said to her, "Take him inside. Please go." Promptly the couple disappeared into their warm cabin.

Getting back to the question from Stebbins, Steve replied, "Yeah, I'm mostly good. How about you guys?"

Harry stepped forward to shake hands with his best friend. "Well, when you consider we lost nearly two complete platoons for nothing, how the hell are we supposed to be? McCormack and I crawled forward to see what was happening in the town when the shooting started. We began heading back, but were cut off by a large group of enemy troops. We retreated into the woods, and for some reason they didn't come after us. Guess they figured they could mop us up later. Damn Steve, there had to be over two hundred plus North Koreans in that attack. They over ran my team in minutes. Then they went around shooting each man in the head to make damn sure they were dead. We were staying just minutes ahead of those bastards for a while, before they turned and headed to the west. Later, we saw another group of about a hundred coming from the north. Then we heard the shooting. We ran into Stebbins, Taggered and Juarez, fighting their way out from the outcropping. We killed about twenty of them before it was time to get the hell out of there. After they left we returned. You were missing, but we found your helmet, so we knew you were alive somewhere. Then we ran into Demytrie this morning. I'm guessing we're all that's left. I don't think anyone survived that attack on Lucky 7. They were outnumbered by about twenty to one. We thought the bastards all headed to the north. Seeing these guys, I guess there are still a few around looking for survivors."

"Look, that couple has been good to me. If it wasn't for them, I would have died last night. We need to get these bodies away from their cabin. Can you help me drag them deeper into the forest before we go?" Steve asked of the small and very cold band of men.

After completing the grizzly mission, Harry had his men bring a large load of firewood into the couple's home. Finishing up, Steve returned to the cabin to fetch the rest of his equipment. He hugged the young woman and shook hands with her husband before walking over to the crib. He held the child for a moment before placing her back into her bed, on top of several hundred Korean Won he had taken off the dead soldiers. He knew when they found it they would be able to put it to very good use.

Returning to the men, Steve looked intently at Harry. "Where do we go from here? Our extraction was planned for no later than 1800 hours. Can we make it to Lucky 7 by that time?"

Harry studied his watch for a few moments. "Well, it's just about 1100 now. It was about a six hour trek from the village, and we are farther south than we planned. Plus, we now have strong enemy activity in the area, and we don't know what we're going to find up at Lucky 7. But, what other choice do we have? It's try it, give up and be murdered, or get taken prisoner and never be heard from again."

Sgt. Stebbins nodded his head in agreement. I think we go, Steve. How else are we going to get out of here? I have no desire to become a prisoner of these assholes."

Private Taggered walked up to Steve. "You're pretty dinged up, Sarg. What condition is that leg in? Think you can you make it?"

Smiling at his trusty radio man, Steve replied. "Just how long is that cable on the hand set?"

Harry slapped Steve on the back, as the weary soldiers shared a good laugh. "With that attitude we're in good shape. Let's get moving."

Following the way Harry and the men had trekked through the woods, they were making good time. On several occasions, they stopped just to listen to the sounds in the forest. It was 1730 as the men began their climb up the hill toward Lucky 7. Private Juarez was walking point. Suddenly, he stopped, and pointed toward three North Korean soldiers dug in on the hill just below the crest.

"I wonder how many more there are on the other side?" Harry whispered to Steve and Sgt. Stebbins.

"Want me to take McCormack and check it out?" Stebbins suggested.

"The problem is time, Arnie. It could take you nearly a half hour to work your way around. And that's if you don't run into problems. My guess is they left those guys behind with several rocket launchers to drop any choppers making an attempt to land. Let's take them out quietly," Steve explained, removing his bayonet from its sheath.

As they prepared to move, the sound of choppers could be heard in the distance. "Call them off, Steve. Call them off now!" Harry screamed as he raced up the hill toward Lucky 7, with McCormack and Stebbins close behind.

"Sun Catcher, this is Blue Fox. Break off, break off! Hot L.Z. Repeat break off!" Steve yelled into the radio.

The choppers began a sharp turn toward the east as Harry and his men attacked the enemy position. Several North Koreans from the far side of the hill came forward to join in the fight. Juarez threw himself to the ground, firing at the oncoming soldiers. One fell immediately while a second grabbed his leg tumbling forward. The third man was cut down by Demytrie as he jumped around the enemy dugout to help Juarez. Quickly Demytrie put two more bullets in to the wounded man before charging across the L.Z.

"All clear over here," he yelled back toward Harry as he waved his arm.

After killing the last enemy soldier in the pit with his bayonet, Harry yelled down toward Steve. "It's now or never brother, bring those birds in."

"Sun Catcher this is Blue Fox. L.Z. is clear. We'll only need one chopper for seven souls. Come on in, we got you covered," Steve yelled into his hand set.

"Blue Fox this is Sun Catcher, we copy and are in bound," the pilot responded calmly as he turned his chopper toward the hill top.

Seconds later, a large green helicopter hovered about three feet off the ground as the seven survivors piled on. Two fighter jets pounded enemy positions on the north side of the hill as a third fighter circled overhead. Steve looked across the chopper toward Harry. He had removed his helmet and closed his eyes, but his face reflected the pain that haunted his soul. The rest of the men sat quietly, deep in thought or saying prayers of thanks.

Rage filled Steve's heart as he thought about their men, now lying dead on the forest floor, covered in snow. What would ever happen to them? Who was the bastard that had given away their mission? Somehow, someday he would have to pay for this. Thankfully, Steve slowly dozed off as the chopper rocked him to sleep.

It didn't seem like much time had passed at all before the crew chief was waking the tired soldiers. "Taegu is dead ahead, gentlemen. We should be on the ground in about ten minutes. The brass is waiting to greet you."

The chopper gently came to rest on a remote section of the airfield. Dismounting the helicopter, the three MP's they saw before the mission came to greet them. The Sergeant looked over the men. "We'll take your weapons."

"Like hell you will, Sergeant. Get the hell out of my way and take me to General Booth. I'm personally going to kick that son-of-a-bitches ass," Harry screamed, while sticking his Thompson into the man's ribs.

Before the other MP's could lift their weapons, Steve leveled his Thompson. "You lose both ways here. Be stupid and you die. Right now I simply don't care, and neither does my buddy Sgt. Jensen here. You can either be collateral damage, or you can drop your weapons and take us to the General. Better decide real quick like so I don't have to make the decision for you."

Without saying another word they gently placed their weapons on the tarmac.

"Jensen, Kenrude. Lower your weapons," a familiar voice called out. Col. Fontaine came walking around the front of the chopper. As one of the MP's went to pick up his pistol, the Colonel added, "I suggest you leave it lay right where it is for your own safety, son. I cannot be responsible for Sgt. Jensen if you intentionally attempt to piss the man off."

Standing between the survivors and the MP's, Col. Fontaine took a deep breath. "It's over men. I-Corp is looking into it. It appears they found out after you were on the ground that someone had been leaking information to the North Koreans. And the worst part is, it appears no one in Japan ever authorized the mission, it was simply an idea. No one knew for sure if Gen. Tenyu was still going to be there or not, so the mission was never given any credence. You will never know just how horrible I feel about the loss of my men, and what you must have gone through to get out of there alive. I will be asking for a transfer back to the states. I don't feel I can command combat troops any longer after this. I have lost all faith in the mission and especially in I-Corp."

Steve and Harry approached their Colonel. "It wasn't your fault sir," Harry began. "If anyone would have stopped the mission it would have been you. But look, this war has a long way to go yet. Steve, myself and all the men of the battalion need to know we have good officers behind us. That leader is you, Colonel. You can't just leave us hang. We've been through too much already. This mess wasn't on you."

After Harry finished, Steve looked at his old friend and commander. "None of us truly want to be here, sir. But we have a mission to complete and it will be harder without you. You had our trust before and you have it now. Please reconsider your request."

Clearing his throat, and blinking his eyes rapidly, Col. Fontaine looked at the ground. "I am speechless. Never in a million years did I expect you men would want to keep me around after such a disaster. But if you really want me to stay, I'll scrap my request."

Sgt. Stebbins and the other men all joined in, asking him to stay. "Besides," Stebbins began, "Who else could have gotten us all the ice cream and booze we could consume when we were stationed in Austria at the end of the war. Only you could pull that off, sir."

All the veterans had to laugh. "Well, if that is your best criteria, Stebbins, it's hard to argue with perfection. Besides, I remember way too many of those morning headaches myself."

After a few more minutes of talking, Steve had to inquire, "Where is the General and his asshole assistant Col. Manners right now, sir?"

"The General has been recalled to Tokyo by MacArthur. Manners requested a transfer stateside. He got it without any problem, and he left this morning for California," the colonel explained.

"So, what was the reason these goons wanted our weapons when we arrived. Who did they think we were going to go after? Certainly not you, sir?" Harry questioned.

"No. It was leadership at I-Corp. They didn't want you taking out your frustrations on anyone when you returned. I knew how that would go over, especially with Jensen. That's why I drove out here to make sure things didn't get out of hand. Now, if you'll board those trucks, we'll take you over for medical checkups. Steve, I can see you need some attention. Then we'll get you showered, fresh clothes, a meal and a good night's sleep before flying you down to Pusan for debriefing over at I-Corp," Colonel Fontaine explained to his tired, dirty, angry men.

"And then?" Steve inquired.

"Either back to the Battalion after a few days rest, or we can have you train new troops down in Pusan if that fits you better. Your choice," the colonel responded.

Not surprisingly, all the men opted to return to the Battalion after a few days liberty in Pusan.

It was about 2330 when Steve finally got settled on his bunk. So many things had happened over the last forty-eight hours it was nearly impossible to remember it all. Looking about the warm, safe barracks, he thought about the young couple and their drafty log cabin. He had just eaten a fantastic meal of turkey and dressing. He wondered if the young couple were finishing the C-Rations the men left for them. It all seemed so unreal and unfair.

Most of all, he thought about his men still lying out in that cold, God-forsaken valley. How could anyone sell out his countrymen, allowing them to be slaughtered like that? Steve hoped whoever it was would meet his maker at the end of a long rope.

But, as always when he closed his eyes, his thoughts turned to Karen and their children. There was no way he could ever explain this situation to them. It would be impossible for them to even begin understanding what had happened. Welcome sleep finally overtook the skillful and weary warrior. What his dreams would be this night was anyone's guess. It was impossible for a person's mind to process what they each had gone through and witnessed in such short order.

CHAPTER 12
A RETURN TO ALPHA COMPANY

With fresh Communist Chinese troops entering the war on a daily basis, allied lines once again rolled south down the Korean Peninsula toward Seoul. By January of 1951, a fresh defensive line was created south of Seoul on a line between Wonju and Poyongtaek. It was imperative this line be held if there was any hope of saving South Korea.

As the line held, Gen. Ridgeway was able to bring reserves and rested men back to the skirmish line. After adjusting his line to meet new requirements, a January 21st date was set to begin an offensive that would drive the Communist Chinese back to the Han River. As the battle raged, Gen. Ridgeway kept the pressure on, allowing his forces to make considerable ground gains.

With the Communist Chinese falling steadily back, Operation Ripper was set to begin March 7th. When set in motion, the plan called for the liberation of Seoul once again. High Command felt taking the Chinese supply base at Chunchon was the secret to relieving the pressure on Seoul. They felt the only way to capture Chunchon quickly, was to drop allied paratroopers behind enemy lines.

Immediately, maps and sand tables were constructed to give the men of the 187th a good idea of what they were going to face when they hit the ground.

Franny was ecstatic to see his best two friends return to the Battalion. He knew they had survived the mission, but hadn't been sure they would end up back into third battalion. With so many losses incurred during the failed raid, Capt. McGlynn had to make some appointments to fill vacancies. Steve kept First Platoon, Harry kept Second, Shrider kept Third, Stebbins was given Fourth and Gus Rider was given Fifth. Gus Rider was new to Alpha Company. He had served with distinction in World War Two and Capt. McGlynn knew him well. Although Kraus was a good battle hardened veteran, McGlynn sent him over to Baker Company as they were short of experienced men for Platoon Sergeants.

Other than Dymetrie, Taggered and Juarez, First Platoon was a completely new team to Steve. On his first day he had Corporal Taggered promoted to Sergeant in charge of first squad, Manual Juarez took over second, Dymetrie took third, while Steve picked Sgt. Seaton for fourth squad. For a radio man, Steve chose Calvin Sweet, a smallish man who always seemed to be smiling.

Since there were many new members in the Battalion, every noncom and officer were excited and more than a bit relieved, that I-Corp's expectations for them when they hit the ground was realistic considering the circumstances, and not shooting for the moon. It would take time to acclimate the men to battle while creating tough, cohesive small combat units again.

With solid air support, third battalion should be able to take and hold Chunchon, forcing the Chinese to break and run without the use of a main highway. I-Corp was positive that by the time artillery and air strikes softened up the Chinese ranks, their discipline would dissolve creating opportunity for a major rout. Allied tanks and air power would then decimate the retreating forces, leaving only small mop up operations for their ground forces.

Planes, ammunition, mortars and artillery units were assembled near the airfield, just awaiting the order to load. Steve was happy to see the moral of Alpha Company so high. These men were ready for combat that would hopefully, bring this war to an end once and for all. March 22nd was chosen as D-Day for the airdrop. In many ways it was nice to know when you were heading back to war. The waiting game was always tough on everyone's nerves, whether you were a veteran or an untested replacement. As in World War Two, scuttlebutt and rumor mongering played havoc with everyone's nerves.

Just as the men of the 187th were reaching their fever pitch, combined units of a U.N. armored brigade slammed into Chunchon on March 19th, wreaking havoc on Chinese defenders. Allied leaders decided an airborne drop at this time would be uncalled for, as the front was totally fluid.

Since Seoul was again captured on March 14th, and with hope of a victory in sight, Gen. Ridgeway decided to widen Operation Ripper. He ordered an airborne operation scheduled for March 23rd using three thousand paratroopers and several units from the Second and Fourth Ranger Companies. The plan was to entrap fleeing Communist Chinese troops before they could escape and cross the Imjin River. There was no time to build new sand tables for this attack. Instead, men studied terrain maps to get an idea of what they would be looking at when they landed. Their main targets were the highways and railroad lines around the city of Munsan-ni.

At 0530 on March 23rd, Paratroopers and Rangers began assembling at the airfield. As pilots warmed their cold engines in the frosty morning, the thunderous roar made it nearly impossible to communicate. Ground crews scrambled about removing frost from windshields and wing, as trucks continued delivering paratroopers to their assigned aircraft. Large flood lights bathed the frigid flight line, as it was still hours away from sun up.

Jumping from his truck, Steve directed his men to begin loading. When they were started, he slowly walked around the massive C-119 transport as he contemplated their jump. After all he had been through on their failed raid into North Korea, he was anxious to get this jump over, and return to the reason the Americans came to Korea in the first place. Defeat the enemy, restore democracy, bring peace to the Peninsula and a suffering people, and then return home to his family forever more. Nevertheless, all too often it appeared that politicians in Washington and commanders at I-Corp had no idea how to obtain their illusive victory. The war just rolled up and down the Peninsula like a roller coaster. They would take a hill losing precious American lives, then give it back. It all made no sense to the average American G.I. in the field.

After putting on his toughest battle face, Steve began observing the final loading preparations. The men were complaining bitterly regarding bad food, snafus in every operation, short nights and cold weather. But that was music to Steve's ears. Quiet men are nervous men, and nervous men foul up in battle.

Steve walked up to Pvt. Ginsmore, one of the last to load. "Well Ginsmore, how are things going?"

Shaking his head in disgust, the man replied, "Not good Sergeant. The Plymouth is broke down again, my old lady wants me to send more money home, and my dad took me out of his will because I married the dame in the first place. Plus I'm tired of the same chow all the time and these new boots are killing my feet. Does it ever end?"

Smiling, Steve pushed a bit, testing the waters. "So Ginsmore, it sounds like you're not ready for this jump. Sounds like I better get you relieved."

"What the hell, Sarg? I'm as ready as any other man in this outfit. We need to go kick some Chinese butt and let them know what this battalion is made of. No sir. I'm not backing out on these guys," Ginsmore replied, with a sneer on his face.

That was all Steve needed to hear. His feelings were confirmed. First Platoon was ready.

Walking to the edge of the tarmac before loading, Steve threw a salute across the runway to Harry and Franny. After giving them a big wave he took his place in line to board the C-119.

Across the runway, Harry stood by the door of his aircraft, shouting out encouragement to each of his men as they boarded. Each man responded with a positive, but usually smart ass comment. Harry loved it more than he ever let on.

Last man to board before Harry, was going to be their First Sergeant. Walking up to Harry he held out his right hand. As the two friends shook hands Franny inquired. "Well Sarg. Have you got room for your First Sergeant on board?"

Smiling Harry responded. "Franny, you're always welcome no matter the circumstances. Just keep your mouth shut and allow me to operate my platoon as I see fit. Understood?"

Smacking Harry alongside his helmet, Franny replied. "I'm just a damn First Sergeant, Jensen. What the hell would I know about running a platoon? You know, I was going to climb aboard with Steve. But I knew he would do nothing but fill my ass with his philosophy on the jump the whole time. So, I decided to jump with you instead, like it or not."

As Franny climbed aboard, Harry laughed loudly. He knew Franny was right. Even though Steve acted calm as a cucumber, he would be nervous inside. And when he was nervous inside, his philosophical thoughts came to the forefront. There was nothing wrong with it, in fact Harry kind of liked it. It always gave him reasons to argue every point with his best friend, win or lose, which provided a good distraction.

Steve felt very confident as he looked about his aircraft before sitting down. Every man he looked at smiled while giving him a thumbs up signal.

After securing the door, the jump master sat down beside Steve. "Good to have you back with the company, Sergeant. Things just weren't the same around here without you and Jensen constantly picking on one another. Oh, and I heard you were jumping first today. Is that right?"

Steve nodded his head as he laughed. "That's correct. I want to be the first on the ground so I can have an extra minute to figure out what we're going to do once the men get down. As far as Jensen is concerned, that good old boy and I have been through a lot together. I don't think I would still be here without him. He's a special guy. But yeah, he can blatantly argue anything, just give him time and a topic."

Moments later, the massive aircraft began lumbering down the taxiway. It would be less then fifteen minutes before they took off. The pilots circled the airfield for several minutes, making sure each aircraft was in its proper position before heading north. Although most of the DPRK field equipment had been destroyed by allied bombing, a few anti-aircraft guns were still in action. Light flak pock marked the early morning sky, although it was well below the level of the air convoy.

The jump master rose to his feet when the red light on the intercom phone began to blink. "Making our final turn, Kenrude. Should be over the target in about ten minutes."

Nodding his head while adjusting his helmet, Steve took a deep breath and stood up. He looked over his men one more time. "Stand up, hook up, men! We're nearly there."

When the green light began blinking above the door, Steve bailed out into the cold crisp air. It was still exciting to Steve when he dove out into the clear blue sky. However, he also knew all too well, that some of the men that were still jumping out of the plane above him could be dead in a few hours. As always that bothered him, creating a nauseous feeling in his stomach. Even more so now after the losses sustained in the ill-fated Operation Piggyback. There was nothing he could do about it now but work to give each man the best chance at survival, and that was never easy.

Hitting the ground, Steve slid through the snow for several feet before coming to a stop. The snow was about eight inches deep. Though it was cold and wet, hopefully it had insulated the ground enough so his men could dig decent fox holes or slit trenches from which to fight.

All around him, men were beginning to land on the snow covered field. Alpha Company was on the far west end of the skirmish line. Off to the east, Steve watched as hundreds of parachutes came floating out of the early morning sky. It was quite impressive.

Blowing a whistle, Steve raised his right hand. "First platoon over here!"

Once the men were assembled, he began placing them along a line of defense that connected to second platoon. Each man immediately began digging into the hard ground to build himself some shelter before combat began.

Steve and Pvt. Sweet, his new radio man, worked together to dig a good sized hole in the half frozen ground, where the two men could have shelter from the onrushing enemy.

Once the hole was completed, Steve looked intently at Sweet. "As I told you in training, you never leave my side. Where I go, you go. No matter how bad it may get, never stand up and run. That radio could be all that stands between all of us surviving or being wiped out. Understood?"

Sweet nodded his head. "Yeah Sergeant, I got that. I had a long talk with Sgt. Taggered after you offered me the job. I'll do my best, you can count on it."

As the sun rose higher in the sky toward midday, the first waves of retreating enemy forces began to come in contact with the airborne blockade. Fighting erupted up and down the line, but no paratroopers gave an inch of ground.

Some of the retreating enemy fell back, in order to create a larger attacking force for their second attempt at punching through the defensive line. Their goal was to reach either the railroad trestle or the highway bridge spanning the Imjin River. Other than attempting to swim across the half frozen river, those were the only two safe routes home. Although many allied soldiers wanted to see the bridges blown, I-Corp simply would not allow it. They wanted them intact to facilitate a move north once the retreating DPRK forces were eliminated. I-Corp's goal was to retake Pyongyang with all due haste. On several occasions, Steve called in air strikes near their lines to prevent the attacking enemy force from rolling up their defenses, which would give them a clear avenue toward the bridges, as well as destruction of Second Platoon.

By late afternoon, DPRK forces on the north side of the bridges used the structures to attack the paratroopers from behind. Capt. McGlynn called desperately for air support to suppress the enemy troops, which were clearly attacking out in the open.

Repeatedly, Saber jets screamed low overhead, strafing the bridges with machine gun and cannon fire. American artillery began pounding enemy positions to the north, in an attempt to keep them off the bridges.

All the men in Alpha and Bravo companies were seriously distressed, as the high explosive shells roared over their emplacements. If just one fell short, it would mean the deaths of countless paratroopers.

As dusk began to settle in, a large contingent of DPRK soldiers launched a ferocious attack against First Platoon. The men fought back with every ounce of life left in their bodies. Saber's rolled in pummeling the attacking hordes, but still they came as if possessed.

Steve yelled at Sweet and the men closest to him, "Fall back to the river bank! Fall back! Hold that line. Don't let them get to the rail bridge."

Harry, fully aware of what was taking place to his right, grabbed his radio. "Franny, falling back along with First Platoon to the river bank. Position untenable. Can't hold. Need reinforcements!"

Franny looked seriously at Capt. McGlynn. "We could move men from

Fifth Platoon down to cover our right flank. If we don't, we lose the bridge and a ton of good men."

Nodding his head in agreement, he grabbed the radio, "River Command to Fifth Platoon. Send two squads to help Second Platoon. Immediately."

Gus Rider, who had very little action in his sector, sent his third and fourth squads to help cover. Thankfully, the river bank served better cover then their slit trenches, but it was the last line of defense. From here, there was no place else to go but over the cliff and into the river. They were clearly trapped.

Steve grabbed the radio hand set. "Turn this damn thing to the Air Force Frequency!" He screamed at Sweet above the tumult of battle.

When the channel was connected he told the spotter. "We've abandoned our position. We're on the river bank. Second Platoon has also fallen back. The entire area is open. Hit them hard or we're done." Looking over at Sweet, he called out. "Get me back on the net. I need to tell Jensen what's coming." But there was no reply. Screaming louder, Steve called out, "Damn it, Sweet, did you hear me? What the hell are you waiting for?"

Crawling up beside Sweet, Steve observed a bullet hole in his helmet. With no time to lose, Steve turned the radio to the company net. "Harry, air attack on the way. If you haven't moved all your men back, do it pronto."

Seconds later, Harry responded. "Done, done, done! Bring it on."

Steve took a kneeling position on the bank. He began hammering away at the onrushing enemy forces. To his left, Pvt. Curry was tossing hand grenades like a pro pitcher. Bodies were beginning to pile up just yards away from the river bank. Steve had just slammed in his last magazine when a call came over the radio from a Marine fighter jet. "Tallyho. Keep your heads down, gents."

From the north side of the bridge, three Saber jets came screaming above the river. Each of them dropped a napalm canister on the attacking hordes. Monstrous, angry black flames burst skyward, as a fourth jet strafed the area with very accurate cannon and machine gun fire. All four jets continued circling the battlefield, firing whenever they had a target to destroy.

Steve gently rolled Sweet on to his back. The bullet had gone straight through the young man's forehead. There was nothing that could be done for him.

Pvt. Curry stood by, watching, "He and his wife just had a baby girl last month. Damn Sarg, he never even got a chance to see her. That's all he talked about. He couldn't wait to get home. I know he started a letter to his wife last night. I think he put it in his jacket pocket. If it's there, could I finish it for him? I want to tell his wife what a good soldier he was. His daughter might like to read that someday so she'll know what her papa was all about."

Steve unsnapped Sweet's jacket pocket, removing what appeared to be a letter wrapped in plastic. Opening it, Steve read it to himself.

"Sweetheart, I hope you and little Flo are doing well. Can't wait until I come home, and we can be a family. That will be so nice. Got myself a new job yesterday. I'm the radio man for our platoon. I'll be with Sgt. Kenrude all the time when we're in battle. I know it will be a demanding job. But Kenrude is a good leader and I trust him a lot. Did my folks bring down that crib and chest of drawers? It should work out well in the nursery. We'll have many more babies, so it will get much more use before we're through with it. That's a promise, sweetheart. Tell your mom those socks she sent me are really warm. I wear them all the time. I could sell a case of them over here. Most of all, I love you with all my heart and can't wait to hold you in my arms again. Well, I need to go. Will finish later."

Refolding the letter, Steve placed it back into the addressed envelope. Standing up, he handed it to Pvt. Curry. "I think he would appreciate you finishing this for him. What a damn shame."

From time to time, there were errant shots fired by the men toward either real or imagined targets out in the dark battlefield. However, there were no further attacks. Franny took time to visit Steve and Harry to see how they had survived the intense battle. Arriving at First Platoon, he found Steve eating from a C-Ration can along with Pvts. Curry and Strongbear. "How you doing Steve? That was quite the afternoon. We never expected the attack to be that intense. We took a lot of casualties so far as I can tell. How many did you lose?"

Looking intently at his old friend, Steve shook his head. "Four, including my radio man. He was a real good kid. Strongbear has volunteered to take over the job, so I think I'm in good hands."

Strongbear laughed. "You are in the best of hands, Sarg. A Cherokee never lets his chief go down without a fight. Plus I speak fluent Cherokee and Navajo. Get me another code talker and we can kick some butt. I know a truck driver back in Pusan by the name of Runningelk. He speaks perfect Cherokee. We could make quite a pair, First Sergeant."

Franny smiled at the young Indian. "You just might just be on to something. Harry's radio man was wounded, so he's looking for a replacement also. Let me talk to the old man. He's talking about having replacements brought up before we move on. Maybe I can get this Runningelk to join up. Anyway, our plan is to sit right here tomorrow, until we can get supplies and reinforcements. You might want to dig in, just in case we get an attack from the north."

"I figured we would be here over night, Franny. I already told the guys to dig in. But we need ammunition pretty bad. I'm totally out for my Thompson, so I'm using Sweets carbine for the time being," Steve replied, holding up the rifle.

Setting down his heavy pack, Franny removed three magazines for a Thompson. "Here. I really stocked up before we left, and I didn't fire too much today because I was damn busy. Take these, I still have enough until tomorrow. Sounds like we'll get supplies sometime in the morning."

Steve slammed one of the magazines into his Thompson immediately. Cocking the weapon, he smiled at Franny. "I'm feeling better already. Now let the bastards come."

Laughing, Franny departed, heading back towards Alpha Company headquarters.

Throughout the night, DPRK soldiers on the north bank dropped mortars and fired machine guns across the river without much success, since the paratroopers were well dug in. Steve kept a good eye on the railroad trestle all night, just in case any DPRK soldiers attempted to hit them by surprise.

It wasn't until after the brilliant morning sun had burned off the fog that blanketed the battle zone, that the paratroopers were actually able to realize the level of carnage that had taken place the day before. Charred and dismembered bodies were scattered throughout the battle field in grotesque shapes. Smoldering bodies near their defensive perimeter were piled four high, and the intense odor was sickening.

Gazing over the incredible sight, Strongbear looked toward Steve. "I'm guessing this is what hell looks like. I never imagined until now just how ugly war can be. And to think I was part of it. I killed some of those men."

"Don't dwell on it, son. I've seen it before, and it never gets any easier. If you let it eat at you, your nerves will go all to hell. You won't be able to function or do your job, and you'll end up getting your own men killed. Just let it go," Steve counseled his young radio man.

As the paratroopers waited to be re-supplied, they loaded their dead into body bags so they could be taken back to Pusan. Approximately midday, a fleet of helicopters began descending on the road near C-Company. They carried ammunition, food, medical supplies, and most of all, replacement soldiers. Most of them were not airborne qualified, but for the time being it didn't matter. The next phase of this battle would be straight forward ground fighting. Throughout the balance of the day, choppers continued ferrying in supplies, artillery pieces and mortar teams to aid in the upcoming assault across the river. There was also one special delivery for Harry. His new radio man, Runningelk.

Near dark, the rumbling of tanks caught the attention of every man along the front. They came down the main highway, as well as straddling the railroad tracks. An unending procession of fuel and ammunition trucks lined the road for miles behind them.

Throughout the snowy evening, artillery and mortar crews worked diligently, setting up their weapons. All along the line, every man was advised that a massive artillery barrage would begin at 0600. Third Battalion's jump off time would be 0730 and there would be no delays.

Alpha and Bravo Companies would force their way over the rail trestle, while Charlie and Dog Companies advanced across the highway bridge with tank support. Easy Company would follow on the bridge in a reserve role. Air power was assigned to destroy any enemy attacks along the front that were threatening to slow their advance. Several British infantry companies were also on the way to help expand the bridgehead as soon as it was secure.

Exactly at 0600 hours, artillery and mortars began dropping their lethal shells among enemy positions on the north side of the river. Smoke and dust drifted off to the east, allowing the attacking paratroopers a clear view of what they were getting into once they started across. Shortly before 0730, Steve gave his last direction and pep talk to his nervous platoon before they attempted to cross the wide open railroad trestle.

Exactly at 0730, the barrage lifted. Sgt. Taggered jumped up to begin leading first squad from Steve's platoon forward onto the wide trestle, as C and D Companies began their charge across the highway bridge.

Steve was just beginning to direct third squad onto the trestle when enemy machine gun fire erupted on the north bank, cutting down two of his lead men. Everyone else on the trestle dropped down between the tracks to avoid getting hit. American mortar teams instantly roared to life, dropping rounds on the machine gun nests.

Steve raced out on to the trestle jumping over men as he went, with Strongbear following mere feet behind him. Reaching the front of the attacking first squad, he pulled his leading men to their feet by their arms. "Go! Go! What the hell are you waiting for? We'll all die out here if we don't keep moving!" Although his legs trembled and his heart was pounding, Steve ran full speed toward the north bank blazing away with his Thompson at enemy soldiers, who were rushing forward to cut off the assault.

Harry took over Steve's position on the south bank, pushing his men onto the trestle while yelling encouragement. Snipers, dug in on the north bank, took out several of the men, sending their lifeless bodies tumbling down into the cold rushing river below.

By the time Steve reached the north bank, a continual stream of hard charging infantry began setting up a bridgehead, throwing back every DPRK counter attack while taking out the entrenched snipers.

Over on the highway bridge, most of Charlie and Dog Companies were across in good shape. They were already expanding their position with help from their heavily armored vehicles. Easy Company was positioned halfway across the bridge, waiting to be placed on the line, or ready to reinforce another company in case of a major counter attack.

By the time Baker Company took to the rail bridge, all sniping had ceased. They raced across the trestle full speed to join the expanding bridge head, which was being reinforced by machine gun and mortar crews that were part of a heavy weapons team delivered the night before.

Watching a Soviet built T-34 tank exiting the city of Kaesong, Steve grabbed the radio handset from Strongbear, who was already pointing to the coordinates on the map Steve had laid out in front of them.

Keying the handset, Steve called for air support. "Top Cover, this is Alpha One. We have a tank in zone six heading south-west toward our position. Over."

Instantly, two fast diving British fighter planes came screaming from the east. They fired their rockets into the rumbling behemoth. The turret was tossed several feet into the air as a devastating explosion ripped the machine apart. Making a wide turn to the west, the fighters dropped back onto the battle field, paralleling the main highway. Releasing the balance of their rockets, two more large explosions shook the city. Swiftly, the fighters left the area, heading south to reload.

Reserve troops continued flowing across the two bridges, unhampered by enemy resistance. The bridge head continued to expand both east and west, until Baker and Charlie Company men were shaking hands. By dusk, nearly two thousand men and thirty tanks were occupying a solid bridgehead on the north bank of the Imjin River.

I-Corp was amazed at the success of the attack. As fewer and fewer enemy forces resisted, the decision was made to enlarge the bridgehead right away, before any organized resistance could take away the allied advantage. Every spare piece of equipment was rushed to the front.

Alpha and Bravo Companies were directed to attack to the west, along the Yellow Sea, and capture the city of HaeJu. They would then turn north to capture Sinchon, Arryong and Sariwon, with help from Charlie Company and British forces.

The following morning Col. Fontaine directed his men to begin their assault. They encountered very little resistance as they rolled northward. Reaching the outskirts of HaeJu, heavily armed DPRK forces dug in on the south side of the city blocked their advance.

Capt. McGlynn called in fire support from a cruiser and destroyer waiting off shore. Minutes later, a powerful barrage of five and ten inch naval shells pummeled the area. When the firing ended, Alpha Company proceeded to the west around the city, while Bravo Company proceeded to the east. A British unit coming up from the reserves entered the city on the main highway with armor support. Surviving DPRK forces fled the town, fleeing to the north in full retreat.

To the east, Allied forces were moving forward, rolling up stubborn resistance with air and armor support. I-Corp was delighted with the overall progress being made. Realizing Pyonyang, the prize of this offensive was becoming a reality, no request for equipment or troops was going to be denied by anyone.

After making a few line adjustments, Col. Fontaine received permission from I-Corp to restart his western offensive. Alpha and Baker Companies drove toward Changyon, which was west of the north-south road leading directly into Sinch'on. Charlie Company and two British companies fought up the main highway. Arriving at Changyon, Alpha Company accepted the surrender of a garrison of about one hundred DPRK soldiers. British forces occupied the area while American units proceeded to Songhwa, the most westerly coastal city.

Approaching Songhwa, a long line of refugees was once again moving south, creating traffic problems for the advancing troops. They carried what meager possessions they owned in carts or on horseback. Some of the people greeted the Americans with smiles, while others spat at them.

Steve's first squad was the lead unit to arrive at Songhwa. They were greeted by heavy machine gun and mortar fire. Two accompanying tanks opened fire on the dug in enemy, as British mortar teams set up their tubes to provide the infantry with close in support.

As the enemy positions were destroyed on the western side, the lead British tank rumbled into one of the cities side streets. Steve signaled his men to follow the smoke belching machine. Wally McGee, the first squad B.A.R. man jumped on the back of the tank. He began scanning rooftops for any signs of enemy activity as they rolled forward. A short way into the city, McGee began firing at a rooftop about fifty yards in front of their position. Two DPRK men fell from the roof to the street below. Seconds later, two more men appeared on the roof. One of them was holding a captured American bazooka. McGee and the tank machine gunner opened fire. One man fell backward onto the roof, while the other man spiraled to the ground, carrying the bazooka with him. More DPRK troops inside the building began firing from every possible window and doorway. Swiveling the turret slightly to the right, the tank commander fired a single round squarely into a second floor window. After debris settled from the explosion, Steve urged his men forward to clean out any remaining enemy forces. McGee made the job easier as he continued spraying the building anywhere he saw movement. Arriving at the north-west corner of the smoking building, Pvt. Donahue pitched a grenade into a first floor window as Strongbear kicked in a flimsy wooden door. Several DPRK soldiers lay dead on the floor. An injured man lying in a pool of blood called out in broken English, "Don't shoot."

Pointing to the stairway, Steve directed Donahue, Neederman and Savoy to check out the second floor. A minute late Neederman called out, "All clear up here, Sarg."

Steve knelt down by the injured man who was bleeding profusely from an abdominal wound. It was obvious the man was going to die, no matter what was done for him right now. He needed advanced medical care that was impossible to provide.

The dying man smiled up at Steve. He slowly placed his right hand on Steve's shoulder. "I taught at university in Seoul before war started," the man began in broken English as he fought to finish his words. "When the North came, they kidnapped my wife and children. They tell me fight for them or they kill my family. I have not seen them since." After gasping for air the man finished. "I am sure they have killed them by now. So I go and join them." Slowly the man's hand slipped from Steve's shoulder as his eyes slid shut.

Standing up, Steve retrieved his Thompson from the chair beside him. After looking at the dead man for several moments, Steve said quietly, "Alright. Let's move on."

"Are we just going to leave him there, Sarg?" Neederman inquired.

"Sorry Neederman. There's nothing we can do for him now. Yeah, it's a damn shame. But it is what it is. Come on. We need to get moving," Steve replied as he walked toward the door.

The tank and the rest of First Platoon had moved forward, and were in the process of meeting British ground forces advancing up the main road from the south. After several more minor skirmishes, Capt. McGlynn radioed Col. Fontaine that Songhwa was in Allied hands.

After reorganizing Alpha and Baker Companies on the north side of the town, Capt. McGlynn directed them to turn east, along with their British counterparts who were under direction of a Captain Montgomery. Their next objective was to be Sinch'on, however I-Corp informed them all enemy resistance in the city had dissipated and the local authorities had surrendered the town. Immediately, the combined forces turned their attention toward the city of Chaeryung. However, as the enemy appeared to be in full retreat now, I-Corp quickly decided to by-pass Chaeryung, and turn their complete attention on Sariwon, just a mere twenty-five miles from their prize of Pyongyang. They would allow reserve units and South Korean forces to clean out any stragglers that might still be hiding in or around Chaeryung.

I-Corp was sure that as they approached Pyongyang, North Korean defenses would stiffen. All available reserves were called foreword to assist in the upcoming battle.

Their prediction turned out to be accurate. As Allied forces arrived at the outskirts of Sariwon, heavy resistance brought their advance to a stop. DPRK forces were dug in around the city as artillery and T-34 tanks blocked the main highway. Heavy fighting broke out all along the Allied lines.

American and British artillery answered the Korean barrage with an incredible bombardment. British and American jets pummeled enemy fortifications for several hours before the Allied attack began pushing forward. The advancing forces found it incredible that anyone could have survived such an intense torrent of steel and explosives. Yet, many well-fortified positions remained intact, with enemy forces completely ready to fight to the death. It reminded many Pacific veterans of the battles on Iwo Jima and Okinawa. However, this time, Allied forces were able to overpower the resistance with fewer losses.

On the left flank, Alpha and Baker Companies were beginning to gain ground, forcing the enemy line to bend, but it did not break. Col. Fontaine immediately poured reinforcements of British and Canadian units into the battle. As a Canadian unit smashed into the center of the DPRK line it began to crumble. Every available man poured through the hole, attacking the defenders from behind. In short order, the defenders either gave up or were slaughtered in their emplacements.

After mop up operations were completed on the left flank, Col. Fontaine once again pulled his three toughest companies out of the line. He assigned Alpha, Baker and Charlie Companies, along with two British companies to seize the city of Namp'o, farther up the coast. I-Corp originally planned to bypass the city, allowing it to wither on the vine, as Allied forces under General MacArthur had done to the Japanese during the Pacific campaign. However, they had picked up rumors that DPRK forces were holding American POW's somewhere in the vicinity. It became imperative to take the area, lest the POW's be taken any farther north, never to be heard from again. As the striking force descended upon Namp'o, the defenders were caught totally by surprise. No matter how hard they attempted to get reorganized to challenge the advancing steam roller, the pressure was too great. Alpha Company, led by First Platoon, stormed onto the shipping pier as two destroyers off shore threw five inch explosive shells into the retreating DPRK lines. As First and Second Platoons held the south side of the bay, Third and Fourth platoons, along with help from Baker Company, broke the back of the resistance around the port area. Immediately, combat engineers who accompanied the assaulting forces, began clearing the wharf of enemy booby traps and mines. One of the engineers heard what appeared to be screams in English, coming from a small freighter tied up to the pier. Not sure what to make of it, they notified Sgt. Shrider, who's Third Platoon was providing security for the busy engineers.

Several engineers slowly began working their way onto the ship, checking for explosives. They were followed closely by Shrider's first and second squads. Moments later, the second squad leader ran back up to the main deck. Leaning over the rail he called down to his Sergeant and Capt. McGlynn, who had rushed to the dock when he was told of the situation.

"Sarg, you got to see this. We got POW's on board," Sgt. Wazniak called out.

"How many are in there?" Capt. McGlynn excitedly called back.

"A bunch, sir. I'm guessing around forty. Some are in pretty tough shape. We're going to need medics, along with food and water. I don't think they've eaten in days," Sgt. Wazniak explained from above.

"Are they all Americans?" Capt. McGlynn questioned, as he prepared to send a radio message back to Col. Fontaine in his headquarters van.

"Yes sir, every one of them," Wazniak responded.

Capt. McGlynn turned back toward his radio man, who was standing next to their Jeep. "Get everything you just heard back to the Colonel at once. Tell him we'll start working with what we have here, but they need to be evacuated from the front immediately. Get hold of Kenrude. See if he can't arrange help from Navy choppers to assist us." Grabbing Sgt. Shrider by the arm, the Captain continued. "Come on Eddie, we need to take a look at this for ourselves."

The two men started up the gangway, as medics who were in the area began hauling their meager equipment toward the ship.

Steve arrived on the dock, riding on the running board of an ambulance just as Capt. McGlynn, Sgt. Shrider, and Franny were walking back down the gangway. "I've contacted a destroyer off the coast. They radioed back that their carrier is quite a ways down south. They wouldn't get here to assist us with helicopter transport until sometime around noon tomorrow."

"Damn. That just won't do. These boys are in tough shape. I'll contact the Colonel and see what he and I-Corp can work out. You men stay lose. I'll be back shortly," Capt. McGlynn explained.

About a half hour later the Captain arrived back on the dock. "Alright, this is the plan. The Colonel has trucks and a few ambulances in route as we speak. Around 0700, we'll load the men onto the trucks, to transport them back to Pungsan. Choppers will pick them up and deliver them to the hospital at Pusan. Kenrude, you and your men will provide security for the convoy. I want men in the front and rear Jeeps with .50 calibers. I want the last deuce and a half loaded entirely with infantry. We'll have two armored half-tracks with infantry in the lead. You won't leave here until 0830 to make sure our aircraft won't make any identification mistakes in the dark. Are there any questions?" Hearing not a word, he turned toward Sgt. Shrider. "Your platoon will lock this wharf down tonight. No one comes on this damn pier without my authorization. Nothing is going to happen to those boys now. I have Sgt. Jensen setting a perimeter to the north where the pier area ends. Rotate your men as needed so everyone gets some sleep tonight."

During the night, several uncoordinated attacks were made by DPRK troops from the north. All of them easily repelled by British and Canadian forces who were well dug in and backed by tanks.

Just prior to 0700, medics and men from Third Platoon began escorting the sickly, half-starved POW's down the gang plank onto the awaiting transports. The worst cases were loaded into the ambulances or three-quarter-ton trucks so medics could look after them. The balance of the men were loaded into deuce and a half trucks loaded with blankets.

Steve walked among his men, making sure they all knew their jobs and were ready to go. The heavy weapons company provided additional machine guns along with several bazookas.

Exactly at 0830, the convoy carrying the POW's rolled off the pier heading south. Every man from first and second squads continually scanned the terrain watching for any threats. Steve was sure the convoy would arrive at Pungsan without any problems, as this area had already been cleared extremely well during their drive north. Of course, it was always possible for one or two survivors to make a desperate attack and gum up the works.

Arriving at Pungsan, the most critical patients were loaded onto choppers that were already waiting. As they took off heading south, several more choppers were arriving. Steve was delighted to see these men returned safely. He didn't even want to imagine the horrors they must have faced since being captured. Just as in World War Two, being captured was one of his biggest fears. Having your family notified that you were killed in action would at least give them some sort of closure. But never knowing what happened to their son or husband would be pure torture. He had always thought that if a moment came when he was going to be captured, he would shoot himself. That would be a tough decision, but it was more important to Steve that his family not have to wonder what happened to him for the rest of their lives. Steve remembered contemplating that decision in North Korea, before he was rescued by Harry and the five other survivors. It was something he never wanted to consider ever again.

Returning to Namp'o around 1600, Steve and Eddie Shrider checked in with Franny, who explained what their plan was for the next day.

At long last they were going to begin their push toward Pyongyang. It was the prize I-Corp had dreamed about when this offensive started. Over and above that, everyone in Third Battalion knew they would be going into reserve once they completed this costly but important operation.

Exactly at 0600 hours the following morning, allied artillery laid thousands of rounds of high explosives on several suspected DPRK positions. What remained of their reserve forces quickly vanished as they began fleeing north to avoid being killed by the bombardment, or taken prisoner once the Allied ground forces moved in.

Alpha and Baker Companies, backed by their trusty British and Canadian forces, began rolling up the coast toward Hamjong, about fifteen miles west of Pyongyang. Any DPRK forces who managed to escape and fall into the rear behind the swiftly moving machine were gladly mopped up by ROK units. For many DPRK men, the thought of being captured by ROK forces was a nightmare. They knew they would not be treated in accordance with the rules governing handling of POW's established by the Geneva Convention. Although it had been evident since the war began that DPRK forces mistreated and tortured POW's of every nation, most American soldiers and officers overlooked what many ROK troops did to the enemy they captured.

With Hamjong securely in Allied hands, the offensive turned east to slam the door shut on Pyonyang, now a mere fifteen miles away. With enemy forces fleeing north in a frenzy, there was no doubt those last miles toward their goal, would be covered in several hours.

Numerous Allied forces were already knocking on the door as they began their drive east. Col. Fontaine directed Alpha, Baker and Charlie Companies to divert their attention to the north in order to halt anymore fleeing DPRK forces, while assisting in the encirclement of the doomed city.

Steve assigned his third and fourth squads to clean out any enemy forces that may be holed up in a small assemblage of buildings on the northwest corner of the city. Demytrie's third squad immediately began taking heavy fire from one of the concrete buildings, resulting in the loss of two of his men. He ordered three of his men to fight their way up to a series of windows on the west side, then lob grenades into the structure. Four sharp explosions rocked the structure as the grenades exploded. Immediately, several men poured out of the building through a door on the south side. Pvt. Sharp attempted to stop their retreat, but was cut down before he could finish the task. Dymetrie observed Sharp attempting to crawl away from the building. Fearing other escapees might fire on the wounded man, Dymetrie ran full speed toward Sharp, scooping him up by the arm.

As he attempted to carry Sharp toward the rest of his squad for help, he felt a severe burning sensation in his right shoulder. Demytrie dropped to the ground as he was having difficulty breathing, as blood rolled down his arm and chest. No matter what he tried to do, his right arm would not respond. Hearing footsteps quickly approaching, Dymetrie rolled onto his side, firing his Thompson with his left hand. Although it felt cumbersome, his bullets struck home, killing the menacing soldier. Once again, Demytrie struggled to his feet, dropping his Thompson on the ground. With the only good hand he had left, he took hold of Sharp, and began pulling him forward. They barely made several steps before a bullet tore through Demytrie's right leg, shattering the bone. Anxiously, he looked back at his squad for help to no avail. His men, along with Sgt. Seaton's fourth squad, were seriously engaged in a running battle with about twenty-five DPRK soldiers, who had joined the battle from one of the other buildings.

Grabbing Sharp by the arm he yelled. "We need to crawl. We need to work together. My leg is gone, I can't stand up. Come on, you need to help!"

Seeing several Communist Chinese soldiers coming up behind him, he reached for Sharp's carbine. Regrettably, with just one usable arm, he was unable to get it into firing position. Within seconds the soldiers were upon them. One stabbed Sharp several times with his bayonet, while the second man fired a round into Demytrie's head. Before the North Koreans were able to make a dash for freedom, several men from fourth squad were able to cut them down.

Sgt. Seaton led the bloodied squads back to First Platoon, once their mission had been completed.

Seeing his squads approaching, Steve walked up to them. "What the hell happened?"

Sgt. Seaton explained the details at length, including how many enemy soldiers they had killed in the battle. Explaining how Demytrie died was the toughest part, knowing the relationship Steve had with the young Greek soldier.

Hearing the news, Steve tossed his helmet to the ground. He stood motionless with his hands on his hips for several moments. "What the hell Seaton? What the hell was that for? That kid proved in every way what kind of a good man and soldier he was. What was it all for? I'm just tired of this. I'm so damn tired," Steve yelled out before slowly walking away.

Strongbear picked up Steve's helmet, following just a few feet behind the tough Sergeant he had come to admire. Sgt. Taggered, who had been Steve's radio man until he was promoted, grabbed hold of him by the arm. "Are you alright, Sergeant?"

Slowly Steve turned to face his tough squad leader. After taking his helmet back from Strongbear, he gazed at his men for a moment in disbelief. He couldn't believe the emotional outburst he'd just had in front of them. Once again, he stood motionless for several seconds, not sure of what to say or do. Before speaking, he looked down at the ground to gather his thoughts.

"Alright everyone, we need to get ourselves back together and move on. This war isn't over yet. I'm sorry for my outburst, but every time I lose good men it hurts like hell. If anyone wants to transfer out of this platoon because you don't trust me, just say the word. There won't be any hard feelings.

Sgt. Taggered looked intently at Steve. "Hell no, Sergeant. There isn't a single man in this platoon that doesn't trust you. You had the right to blow of some steam for once. We do it all the time. You listen to what we have to say, then set our heads straight for a while, until we need it again. Demytrie died trying to save Sharp's life. It was because of you that he turned into such a good soldier. We were all wrong about him, but you saw his good side. You took an angry messed up kid and believed in him until he learned to believe in himself. You taught him how to be a man, Sarg. The kind of man willing to sacrifice himself for another. An honest to God hero. Now, as you said, we have a mission to complete, and we're ready to follow you wherever you take us. Sure, more of us may die, but it won't be your fault. So, what do you want us to do next, Sarg?"

Smiling at Taggered, Steve replied. "Alright then. I'm not going to appoint anyone to take over third squad. Taggered, you and Juarez divide third squad among the other squads. Once this operation is completed, we'll be going into reserve anyway. When we arrive back at Pusan we'll work out the details. Seaton, when we get back I want you to write up what you witnessed so we can get Demytrie the medal he deserves."

Sgt. Seaton nodded his head in agreement. "That won't be a problem, Sarg."

Taggered and Juarez went to work dividing up the balance of third squad to fill in the gaps throughout the rest of First Platoon as each squad had several casualties.

Strongbear stepped forward, handing Steve the handset. "Capt. McGlynn has been looking for you for several minutes. I told him you were tied up for a bit. He said to call back when you were free. He wants to know our position."

Nodding his head in acknowledgment, Steve called the Captain.

By nightfall, the encirclement of Pyongyang was completed. Charlie Company, along with two platoons of Canadian forces were currently holding hands with men from Easy Company, who arrived from the east. For the next two days, Allied forces cleaned out the final resistance inside the besieged city.

Very few enemy forces attempted breaking through the iron cordon, which was standing strong. I-Corp was extremely happy with the performance of the men under their command. It was a dream come true to have Pyonyang once more in their grasp. Nevertheless, many of the Allied troops who had taken part in this tremendous feat, were in serious need of rest and replenishment. They had all taken serious casualties from the beginning of the operation.

The problem in front of I-Corp now was deciding who should be relieved first and when. Luckily, the decision was made very easy for them. Headquarters in Tokyo demanded all airborne units be moved back to Pusan or Japan for immediate refit. It took I-Corp about a week to begin sending new or replacement soldiers back from the hospital to fill the ranks. Over the next twenty days, the 187th Airborne was completely detached and rotated back to Pusan.

The night before Alpha Company was to transfer out, Col. Fontaine had several men loading the last of their equipment onto cargo trucks. As they were doing so, an American three quarter ton truck entered the perimeter being driven by two men in ROK uniforms. Although their orders appeared to be proper, there was no way for the MP's to know they were North Koreans dressed in captured ROK uniforms.

As the vehicle neared the waiting convoy, one of the men detonated a large bomb located in the trucks cargo box. A sheet of flame and deadly shrapnel spread death and destruction in every direction. Several more explosions ripped through the compound as fuel tanks on the waiting vehicles ignited. Six men from Alpha Company were torn to shreds from the screaming hot steel. Doug Zombro and Conroy Dayton from Steve's platoon were working with the crew. Zombro was killed instantly as a wheel assembly crushed his chest. Dayton was hit in the back and head by a set of leaf springs from the rear of the exploding truck. He attempted to crawl away from the inferno without much success. Unable to move his legs and bleeding profusely from a serious head wound, he closed his eyes and prepared to die.

After Alpha Company was billeted, Steve walked over to the hospital to see if Dayton was still in country. Finding a lone nurse sitting at a desk, he approached her. "I am Sgt. Kenrude from Alpha Company, Third Battalion. I was wondering if you still have Pvt. Conroy Dayton here."

Without having to check her roster, she replied. "Yes we do. He's in very critical condition I'm afraid, and I'm not certain he'll be up to having any visitors. If you want to give me your name, I can tell him you stopped by."

Staring firmly at the nurse, Steve spoke his mind. "Look, the man was in my platoon and stepped up when I asked for volunteers for the task. Now, I want to see him and if you won't tell me where he is, I'll go walking through the hospital and find him myself."

The nurse nodded her head. "Look Sergeant, it's pretty grim. There was nothing we could really do for Pvt. Dayton. His spine was shattered and what was left of it was pushed off to the left, so a good part of his body is paralyzed. He has a large piece of his skull missing and there are pieces of bone and steel still lodged in his brain. The left side of his face was nearly torn away, his right arm barely functions, and most of his left hand is gone. We have him bandaged as best we can. If he would have been just a bit more stable he would have been flown to Japan this morning. We're hoping to get him there in the next couple of days. Lord only knows what will happen to this young man. Odds are he will die from a major infection or complications from his injuries. He refuses to talk with us. Usually, the only sounds we hear are screams of pain. So, if you still want to see him he is in ward three, second bed on your right. I just ask that you try not to upset him and get his blood pressure up."

Steve walked slowly down to ward three. Before entering, he stopped at the door to look at Dayton. All he could see of Dayton was part of his nose and mouth, his right eye and cheek. The rest of his head was bandaged. It was easy to tell that a large section of his skull was missing. As Steve neared his bed, Dayton turned his head slightly.

"What do you want, Kenrude?" he asked, with a very slurred speech. "If you want me for another work detail you'll have to check with the nurse. I think I'm booked up for the next few days. If you're here to ask if there is anything you can do for me, the answer is yes. Take out your side arm and put a bullet in my brain. Put me out of this misery."

Steve was quiet for a moment as he looked down at Dayton. "I can't do that for you. But—"

Before he could finish, Dayton cut him off. "You think I want to go home like this? It's not fair to my folks or to Mary. What the hell is she going to do with me? Put me in a freak show to make money? She has little Betty to worry about, and I don't ever want my daughter to see me this way. It would be better if they just had a grave to visit to remember me. So just end it, Sarg. Do one last good thing for me."

A lump stuck in Steve's throat as every word Dayton said whirled around in his head. "Look Dayton, we don't understand why God allows what he does. We don't have the answers. But I could never live with myself if I shot you. Maybe when they get you to Japan the doctors can figure something out to help you. You just need to pray and have faith."

As a tear rolled down Dayton's face, he looked up at the ceiling for a moment. "You talk about God and faith. Well, I guess all that Catholic upbringing didn't do much good, because I have no faith left, and I can't believe God let this happen to me. Tell me Sarg, where is God with all his mercy right now? Tell me, Sarg. Look, I heard the explosion and I tried to push Pvt. Meekam out of the way, and this is what I get in return? What the hell did I do to deserve this?"

Steve wished Fr. O'Heally were there to answer those questions, because he surely did not know what to say to the angry soldier. After a moment of silence, Steve took hold of Dayton's right hand. "I'm so sorry this happened to you, Dayton. You were a hell of a good soldier in every respect. If you need anything, please just let me know."

"I already asked and like a chicken shit you backed out. You really want to help, take out that side arm and shoot me, or else get the hell out of here now!" Dayton screamed.

Before Steve could say another word, the charge nurse came into the ward at a dead run. "Sergeant, it's time for you to leave. I warned you about upsetting this man. So please leave."

Two days later, the decision was made to attempt transferring Dayton to Japan. Surprisingly, everything went well until the second day after his arrival in Japan. At 0700 that morning, the charge nurse found Dayton dead with a pillow over his face. She immediately called the MP's and Dr. Martin Coltree.

Angered over what happened, Dr. Coltree demanded an investigation into Dayton's death. Major Fielding, a sharp and distinguished lawyer was dispatched to the hospital by I-Corp. The Major was baffled from the beginning, as there were only three other men in the ward with Dayton, and all of them were paraplegics. That narrowed down the suspect pool to 300 patients and fifty-two staff. On his third day in the hospital, he was walking through the fourth ward, which was closest to the intensive care unit, when Corporal Ed Price, who had served in Third Platoon of Alpha Company called him over.

"Major, are you still investigating the death of Pvt. Dayton?"

Nodding his head, the Major replied. "Yes I am. Do you have any information as to what might have happened?"

"Yes sir, I do." Cpl. Price began. "I went to see Dayton the day before he died, even though I didn't belong in that ward."

Before he could say another word, Major Fielding cut him off. "And he told you he wanted to die so you went and got a pillow and smothered him."

"That's it sir. I killed him. You can arrest me now and save the cost of a trial. I plead guilty, " Price boldly stated.

"Well, I'll be damned. I've now conducted twenty interviews, and everyone has pleaded guilty to the murder. What the hell am I supposed to think, Corporal?" Major Fielding sternly replied.

"Just keep going, sir. You only have 280 more guilty suspects to interview. You see, sir, none of us would want to go home in that condition, and he was getting worse. We all put the pillow over his head and suffocated him. You need to understand that every single one of us has seen men die. We heard their last wishes, we heard them cry out for their mothers or wives, and there was not a damn thing we could do for them. Nothing! You can be damn thankful you've never been at the sharp end of the spear and seen men torn apart like they were rag dolls. You've never seen a man disappear after a mortar round landed next to him, and all you have left are his boots and his feet. You can call it what you want, sir. Call it murder, mercy killing, whatever you choose. But in the end, I believe that God understands. He's the only judge those of us in this hospital have to fear. So Major, just do what you have to do, sir."

Without saying a word, Major Fielding turned to leave the ward. After he was gone, a round of applause went up for Cpl. Price.

The following morning the Major met with Dr. Coltree. "I understand how you feel, Doctor, but the case will never be solved. Everyone knows who did it, and no one knows who did it, and those facts will never change. What I have come to understand is that Dayton is better off today than he was before he died. You can put whatever you choose on the death certificate. My investigation will show that he died of natural causes and that the pillow was not a factor. Tell me, Doctor, what do you think will make his family feel better? After all, Dayton was not the only person suffering in his family."

After a moment of thought, Dr. Coltree nodded his head. "I think you have made a wise choice. I'll write up a new death certificate right away. Damn this war!"

After the Major closed his brief case, he walked toward the office door. Before leaving, he looked back at the doctor. "Besides Doctor, every one of these men can tell their maker when they arrive in heaven that they've already served their time in hell, and I agree."

It seemed like an eternity since the men had been in a rest camp. Food was plentiful, hot showers were a pleasure, and comfortable beds were fantastic. Although the creature comforts did much to relax the men, the trauma of what they had just been through would linger in their minds for a long time to come. The hospital and aid stations were full of men suffering from frost bite, trench foot, battle exhaustion and combat wounds. The physical injuries could be improved with medication and other treatments, but there would never be enough psychologists to deal with the mental issues.

Several men committed suicide during the first week they were in camp, including one man from Sgt. Shrider's third platoon. Col. Fontaine ordered each of his Officers and Sergeants to keep a close eye on their men, and report anything they felt might be a threat to the soldiers in their command. Steve almost had to laugh at the directive. Who among them was qualified to figure out what a man was thinking? Certainly Steve himself understood what it was like to come close to the breaking point, and in his mind every man in his platoon was at risk.

New arrivals flooded into camp from the United States nearly every day. Third Battalion was back to full strength quickly, but it would take more than just men to make the battalion battle ready. Most of the replacements had never seen combat, because many of them were right out of infantry training. Steve worked hard trying to get his men ready, but there was little he could do by himself. It would take a concerted effort by battalion leadership to solve this new dilemma.

CHAPTER 13
SHOWDOWN IN GLENDALE

Frank was usually leveled headed. He was not one to give into hinky feelings or believe in superstitions. However, today was different. After speaking with Nancy, there was a gnawing feeling of unease in the back of his mind that just wouldn't go away. In his gut, he felt something was terribly amiss. Frank picked up Gilly on the way to the farm, explaining what Nancy had told him.

"Push this damn thing, Frank. I got a real bad feeling about this. Things out at the Kenrude place just ain't been right since Alex got hurt. It feels like a dark cloud has descended over the farm ever since Steve went off to Korea. Can't explain it, but Alex's accident just set things in motion," Gilly explained, as he made the sign of the cross.

Frank had a tendency to agree, but didn't want to tell that to Gilly. Instead, he just pressed harder on the accelerator. Turning onto the main highway leading out toward the Kenrude farm, he finally responded to Gilly's remarks. "I've told you a thousand times, Gilly, I don't believe in all that hodgepodge, superstitious, star alignment crap. I usually think if something's going to happen, God must have a reason for it; good or bad, we just don't understand his reasoning. But this time I'm starting to believe you a bit and that scares the hell out of me!"

After a moment of silence, Gilly looked over at Frank. "Nothing good came out of Alex getting hurt, and nobody out there has been the same.

Sure, they were all worried if Alex would recover, and that's normal. But since then, everything out at that farm has had a strange aura about it. Can't really place my finger on it, but something bad is going on. And I for one sure don't like it. Say what you want Frank, but this is bad karma."

"Damn!" Frank called out. "That lazy no good Sheriff of ours, just picked the worst time to pull us over for speeding. I'll give that man a piece of my mind for sure this time! Frank jumped from the truck, as Sheriff Richards slowly crawled out of his cruiser, carrying a citation book in his right hand.

"Damn it Frank, do you have any idea how damn fast you were moving that piece of junk?" Bull called out angrily.

"Just hold on Sheriff, I've got a damn good reason. Nancy called and said Mike is missing, and they're really concerned about him. Last time I saw him was about three-thirty. I think something bad has happened to that boy," Frank explained in an agitated manner.

Throwing the citation book back in his car, Bull called out. "What the hell are we doing yelling at each other on the side of the road then? Get your ass back in that piece of scrap iron and follow me if you can. Otherwise, I'll meet you at the Kenrude place."

With the siren blaring and dirt flying from the rear tires, Sheriff Richards headed north, right down the middle of the highway. Frank and Gilly wheeled into the Kenrude farm mere moments behind the Sheriff. Nancy and Karen came running from the house as the cars stopped. Frank exited the truck, running up to Nancy. "Have you heard anything since you called me?"

"Nothing Frank. Not a word. Something terrible has happened to my boy, I just know it," Nancy responded, wiping her eyes with her apron.

"Like I said, I saw Mike driving down the back field road about three-thirty on the new tractor. I think we should look down there first," Frank explained to everyone in the yard.

Gilly had barely climbed back into the truck before Frank spun the old pickup around in the yard. Sheriff Richards followed Frank down the county highway leading to the field road.

Frank drove as fast as he could on the rutted trail, with Bull right behind. Arriving at a fork in the trail, Frank took the left road. Coming to the end of the trail, Frank and Gilly jumped out of the truck. After several minutes of looking around, Frank waved at Bull. "He's not here. Let's check the right fork." Quickly, they turned their vehicles around and headed back toward the north field road. As they neared the end of that trail they could see the tractor sitting near the water trough.

As the men exited their vehicles Bull called out, "My God, what the hell went on here?"

Quickly, Frank ran toward Mike who was lying just inches away from the body of Willy Gomez, as Bull ran for his first aid kit. After checking his pulse, Frank called out. "Mike's alive. Looks like he's been shot twice."

"That's more than I can say for Gomez. This spear has gone clean through him. Looks like he was hit at least twice before the last one got him," Gilly called out to Sheriff Richards.

Bull set Frank to work attempting to stop Mike's bleeding, while he called for an ambulance. When Bull was satisfied they'd done as much as they could for the moment, he stood up. "Let's load him in the back of the pickup. Gilly, get the blanket out of my trunk. Frank, you drive him carefully back to the edge of the field road and wait for the ambulance. After they have Mike headed to the hospital in the ambulance, drive over to the Kenrude farm and give the family a quick rundown on what happened out here. Whatever you do, don't take Mike to the farm in this condition. Do you understand? I'll call the hospital and have the ambulance meet you on the main highway."

"Yeah, Bull I understand. What are you going to do?" Frank inquired, as they began to lift Mike into the bed of the truck.

"After I call the ambulance I'm going to take a look around. It's supposed to rain tonight, and I don't want any evidence to be destroyed. We got to find out who is behind this," Bull explained as they gently laid Mike on a blanket from the patrol car. "Now don't bounce this truck like you did on the way out here. That could probably kill him."

As Frank gently turned around, Bull radioed again, checking on the ambulance and reiterating where to pick up Mike. After explaining the location again, Bull tossed the mic on the seat of his patrol car.

After watching Frank disappear down the road, Bull walked back to the body of Willy Gomez. Looking at the foot prints in the dirt, Bull shined his light toward the brush pile. "What in God's name!" he said aloud, as he observed the sharpened sticks still in the ground. Just as he was going to walk toward the brush pile, Deputy Stuart Johnson drove up in his patrol vehicle.

"Need some help, Bull?" he called out.

"Yeah, sure do. Hey, have you still got that handheld ship beacon in your trunk?" Bull inquired.

"Yup, and it's fully charged. We should get nearly eight hours out of it if need be," Johnson replied, as he jumped from his squad car.

As soon as Bull had the beacon turned on, they walked over to the brush pile where they observed the body of Mike's dog, Champ. Kneeling down he rolled the dog over to discover the bullet wound. Shining the light back and forth, he observed the wood shavings on the ground from the sticks and Mike's Spear.

"What went on here, Bull? And who is the dead guy by the tractor?" Johnson inquired.

Kneeling down, Bull looked over the scene. "That's Willy Gomez, Stu. It looks to me like Mike was hiding in this brush pile after he was hit. He set up a defensive perimeter as best he could, not knowing what to expect. When Gomez cleared the tractor, Mike must have charged out from his cover to attack. It was do or die and he was out gunned and he knew it, when he saw the .38 Gomez was carrying. He must have gone after Gomez like a bayonet charge, understanding he had one chance. Looks like Mike hit him twice, before he got in the killing strike."

Nodding his head in agreement, Deputy Johnson looked over the dead body. Picking up the pistol Stu opened the cylinder. "He got off two rounds. God knows where they went." After placing the weapon in an evidence bag, he looked at Bull. "Guess I didn't know him, Sheriff. Who was Willy Gomez?"

"Gomez has been the Bainsworth's hired man for several years. He's usually low key and very seldom speaks in public. So why the hell is he out here trying to kill Mike? This makes no sense." Standing up, Bull took a deep breath. "Come on, let's take a look around by the tractor."

"We got blood on the fender, Sheriff. It's smeared, like whoever was bleeding kinda slid along the side until they reached the back of the tractor. And look at Champ's paw prints and blood trail. I think he was hit somewhere else and pulled himself over here," the deputy reported.

"Yeah, I think you're right, Stu. Let's follow the blood trail and tracks, and see where it leads us," Bull directed as they began their slow walk.

After several minutes, the two men were standing where Mike was first shot. "We have lots of blood here, Stu. I think this is where he was hit first. The shooter had to be in those woods, watching every step he made," Bull explained, as he scanned the woods with his binoculars.

"Hey, there's a blood pool over here, too," Johnson called out as he followed Champs blood trail into the tall weeds. "The dog must have dropped here before dragging himself back to Mike."

"Yeah, that seems to make sense. Shine that light on the woods for a few minutes," Bull requested of his deputy. "Keep it on the woods, we're going for a walk, Stu," Bull instructed, as the two men pulled their side arms from their holsters.

Closing in on the woods, Bull pointed to a birch tree that had a nice crotch about five feet above the ground. "There, the birch tree. A perfect rest for a sniper. Let's be careful and see what we can find," Bull said quietly as they entered the dark woods.

Almost immediately, Deputy Johnson came across a new .22 shell casing lying directly below the tree. After sniffing the casing, Stu spoke, "It's fresh, Bull."

Carefully moving leaves, they found two more shiny .22 casings and several Kool Cigarette butts that had been crushed out very recently. "Well, the legend is that ghosts haunt these woods. But I doubt any of them smoke Kools and hunt with a .22 rifle," Bull said, as he continued looking around. "Stu, the tall grass is bent down heading back toward the west. Let's follow it." About twenty yards later, they were standing on another field road. As Deputy Johnson shined the light around, he immediately observed two unfired .22 rounds lying in the mud along side the road. Taking a closer view of the area, he observed tire tracks in the soft mud. Bull knelt down and began making a drawing of the tire imprint as his deputy held the light above him.

"Wait just a damn minute," Bull called out. "Hey Stu, remember me telling you about the strange new tires Jake Flood had on that new Cadillac he bought?"

"Yeah sure. Why? Does that tread match? Naw, I don't think Jake would do something like this. He's a great guy, the owner of the furniture store, why would he be involved in something like this?"

Bull smiled at his deputy. "You know, Stu, Jake may be the only person in Glendale with a shiny new Cadillac, but we have a visitor that drives one, too. I saw Wauneta Bainsworth get in a powder blue one on Main Street a while back. Let's bag all this evidence and get it back to the office. After we talk to the judge first thing in the morning and get a search warrant, we'll drive over to the Bainsworth house and see what we can find. I'll call in and have the ambulance come back out to pick up Gomez's body and have it delivered to Minneapolis for an autopsy when we get back to the car."

As they walked toward their cars, Bull remembered his conversation with Wauneta Bainsworth in town several months ago. After making several overt threats toward Mike, he had admonished her, saying that if anything happened to him, he would come looking for her. He found it hard to believe that she could have been stalking Mike. But then again, nothing the Bainsworth's ever did would surprise him. It had always seemed to him that all the Bainsworth family members were egocentrics, with a large nasty streak running right up their angry spines.

The following morning the two men finished up their reports, and put together all the evidence before Bull called Judge Wayne. After explaining everything that happened the night before, the Judge authorized a search warrant for the Bainsworth home and all their vehicles. After picking up the signed warrant, Bull had deputies Johnson and Cal Whitley meet him at the Bainsworth place. Bull parked his patrol car about a half block from the house as he waited for his men to arrive. He could see Wauneta's car parked near the front entrance. Several times she came out of the house with boxes, shoving them in the trunk. It was clear that she was either heading back to Illinois, or just plain running. Moments later, Cal and Stuart drove up behind Bull.

"Any update on Mike?" Stuart inquired, as he walked up to Bull.

"No, he's back in surgery. Hospital says he's in guarded condition. They are having more bleeding problems," he explained.

Bull recounted their investigation in the woods the night before to Cal, before explaining how they were going to handle this situation. With everyone ready to go, Bull led the deputies up into the Bainsworth driveway. The men cautiously walked up to the powder blue Cadillac. Cal pointed out the mud and grass still hanging from the undercarriage of the car, as Bull motioned toward an open pack of Kool cigarettes laying on the dash.

They also observed several more unfired .22 shells lying on the back floor. "She must have been nervous as hell as she was explaining to Gomez what she wanted him to do. I'm guessing somebody dumped the box of shells as they loaded the gun. In her desire to get away after Gomez was killed, she never cleaned up after herself," Bull mused, explaining his theory to his deputies as they continued walking around the car.

As they prepared to walk up to the door, Wauneta charged out of the house. "What the hell are you all doing here? This is private property, Sheriff. Bainsworth property. You have no right to be here, so I'll ask you nicely to leave. My attorney is already on the way over here. He'll toss your sorry butts off our property, so I suggest you get moving now before it gets ugly."

Bull looked at the screaming woman. "I saw ugly last night and it doesn't get much worse. You know Wauneta, our families go back a long way. In fact, they happened to be some of the first people to even settle in this area of Minnesota. I don't want any problems with you. Let's talk this out like old friends. No reason at all for this to get out of hand. Right now, with the evidence I have in my office, and what I see on and in your car, I'm sure we are in the right place. And there's no doubt in my mind that after we execute this search warrant, I am going to be arresting you for attempted murder, and conspiracy to commit murder on Michael Kenrude. And from what I can already see in your car, none of that is going to be hard to prove. So will you please open the trunk so we can take a look? "

Wauneta laughed as she paced back and forth on the top step of the front porch. "Kenrude shot! Whoo-ee! Let me give the shooter a check for five thousand dollars. What a hero he is! Let me know who it is when you find out. I'll even pay his damn bail."

As she finished speaking, her attorney Oswald Timer drove into the driveway, parking about twenty feet from Wauneta's car. Attempting to walk past the two officers, Bull grabbed him by the arm. "Timer you can do your job just fine from right here. I'm here to arrest Wauneta for the attempted murder of Mike Kenrude."

"Hey Sheriff, you said conspiracy. Who the hell did I conspire with? Tell me that," Wauneta yelled, as she paced back and forth.

"Your hired worker, Willy Gomez. We found him dead just a few feet away from Mike. He had a .38 pistol next to him, and we were able to trace his steps all the way back to the woods where the shots were fired from. And like I said, we have enough other evidence to tie you to the crime. So why don't you just come down here and surrender and save everyone a lot of trouble," Bull explained, knowing full well that was never going to happen.

Oswald looked up at Wauneta. "Honey, what have you done? Why don't you come down here and open the trunk as the Sheriff has requested. We can clear this up in just a few minutes."

Angrily, Wauneta stomped her foot on the step, "Look, you worthless piece of crap. Who the hell pays you? Who do you think made you a very wealthy man in this damn county? If it wasn't for the Bainsworth money, you would be cleaning toilets at some dung heap motel. You're supposed to be here to help me. Not assist the damn Sheriff! As far as Willy Gomez is concerned, he's a loser who should be deported. Grandmother hired the jerk, not me. So don't try and tie me to him! I'd have nothing to do with the likes of him, or his dirty little family."

Bull took a small step forward, "That's about enough, Wauneta. We're going to arrest you, it's just that plain and simple." As the three officers began walking forward, Wauneta pulled a .38 caliber pistol from her purse, before throwing the leather bag at Bull. The officers retreated several feet as they drew their weapons.

A shaken Oswald stepped forward with his hands in the air.

"Please, Honey put the gun down. You're just digging yourself a deeper hole here. You need help. I can take care of that for you and this all goes away. You don't want anyone to get hurt."

Wauneta laughed, "So you think I need help, Oswald? You think I'm sick or demented? Who died and left you as the last resident psychologist on earth? Whoo-ee! Is this situation getting out of control or what?" Continuing to laugh, she began swinging the gun from left to right as she yelled, "Who should I shoot next? Yeah, who's it going to be?" Swinging the pistol back to the right she shoved the barrel up under her jaw. "No one gives a damn about poor old Wauneta. No one cares one way or the other if I die, or what happened to my brother. We could own this town and send all you damn wannabes on your way. So why don't you just leave."

Slowly, Bull holstered his weapon. "Wauneta, that's not the answer, it doesn't accomplish anything. Put the gun down so we can talk about all of this."

Removing the gun from her jaw, she pointed it first at Oswald and then back at Bull, as tears streamed down her face. "Tell me, what have I got left? I'm a Bainsworth, and here I am with nothing to look forward to. This ugly little town took everything from me. Screw every one of you bastards. See you all in hell," she called out as she thrust the muzzle of her pistol tightly under her chin, pulling the trigger. Her body flew backwards into the front door of the house, spraying it red with her blood.

Oswald gasped as he fell to his knees covering his face with his hands. Bull walked slowly up the steps, removing the pistol from Wauneta's hand. After handing the weapon to Cal to be bagged as evidence, he knelt down beside her lifeless body. For a moment, he starred down at Wauneta, examining her empty emerald green eyes that would now stare for eternity into the crystal blue sky.

After standing up, Bull looked at Cal. "Call the ambulance, have them take her body to Minneapolis. Stu and I are going to walk over to the worker residence behind the house to speak with Mrs. Gomez."

As Bull and Officer Johnson approached the residence, Mrs. Gomez sat on a lawn chair aside of the door. "Is that bitch dead?" She asked the question of Bull, with an oddly calm demeanor.

Nodding his head, he replied, "Yes, she shot herself."

Almost smiling, Mrs. Gomez stated. "May her evil soul rest in hell. My husband is dead because of her, and my three children have no father. Now what am I supposed to do? Tell me, what am I supposed to do? Where do I go now, Sheriff?"

Bull was quiet for a moment before he spoke. "Can you tell us what happened last night?"

Mrs. Gomez stood up, pacing back and forth. "My husband was a good man, but he made a bad mistake. He knew a certain Mexican woman in Willmar that caught his attention. One night when he was supposed to be working, he drove to Willmar to see her where she worked, at the Blue Moon Bar. Wauneta was there with some friends. When Willy and this woman went into the back room, Wauneta followed them. She pushed the door open and found them doing things they should not have been doing. Willy attempted to keep her from telling me. She told him no one had to know about it if he did a big favor for her. When she told him what it was, he refused. She told him to either shoot Mr. Kenrude, or she would have him deported and he would never see me or the kids again. Then, over the next few weeks, the Willmar police stopped him several times when he went to the city to buy things for the Bainsworth's. Willy got scared. He tried to call it off, but Wauneta had her claws into him and would not let go, so he finally agreed. He and Wauneta left about 3:00pm. When I saw Wauneta return without him, I knew something had gone wrong. I asked her about it and she laughed, saying, 'Willy won't have to worry about being deported anymore.' That woman was pure evil, and I hate her with all my heart. So naturally I have been waiting for you, I knew you would be coming, Sheriff." Mrs. Gomez explained, as tears rolled down her face.

After listening to everything Mrs. Gomez said, they took her and the children to the Sheriff's office, so they could get her sworn statement.

After Bull was finished with Mrs. Gomez, he drove straight to the hospital. The Kenrude family sat painfully still in the hospital waiting room as doctors continued to work diligently to save Mike's life. Seeing Alex standing all alone near the water fountain, Bull walked up to his good friend. "How is Mike doing, Alex? Any word from the doctors, today?"

Alex stared at Bull for several seconds before shaking his head. "No, nothing really, Bull. There is more internal damage then they thought, and they are still having problems stopping the bleeding. What the hell was this all about, Bull? I don't get it."

Karen stood up, shaking with rage. "Does anyone in this Godforsaken town even give a damn about Michael Kenrude? Ever since he came home from the war, someone has been harassing him. I don't get it. What did he ever do to hurt anyone? When he was in high school, he was the kindest, gentlest boy I've ever known, just like Steve. Tell me Sheriff, what did he ever do wrong?"

Nancy flew out of her chair, taking hold of her daughter-in-law, who was just short of becoming hysterical. Karen sobbed, as Nancy sat her back down in a chair next to Alex. Starring intently at Bull, she inquired, "Do you even have any suspects? Or is this damn town just going to forget this ever happened? I want answers, Bull Richards. Who tried to kill my son?"

Bull took Nancy by the hand, helping her back into her chair. He then pulled another chair forward so he could be about in the middle of the family. After taking a deep breath, he began to explain the sordid details of his investigation, and the subsequent suicide of Wauneta.

As the room fell silent, Glenda, who hadn't uttered a sound since he'd arrived, stood up. "Bainsworths! I never grew up here, but I have heard so much about them and their underhanded schemes from so many people,

I've come to hate that name. Who do these people think they are? Why do they think they can kill my husband?"

Standing up, Bull walked over to Glenda. "Wauneta was the last of the kids from this generation, and I would say that Glendale's bad dealings with that family are over. I'm not sure we'll ever really know why the Bainsworth kids hated Michael so much. But they let their anger destroy any good thing they could have ever accomplished. It's a shame. Wealth can be a very bad thing at times, especially for those that have done nothing to earn it."

Glenda was just about to reply when the doctor entered the waiting room. Everyone held their breath as they looked intently toward the surgeon. Taking hold of Glenda's hands he began, "I'm sorry you've all had such a long wait for news. You have one tough husband, Mrs. Kenrude. Though it appears to run in the family. So, part of this you already know, but I'll back up so Sheriff's Richards can get the full story. One bullet entered his right shoulder, where it stuck his collarbone, before ricocheting into the deltoid muscle, where it exploded. The second bullet struck him in the lower right rib cage. It cracked a rib before bursting into pieces. All the pieces scattered around have been the source of the uncontrolled bleeding problems we've had. I am feeling more confident that we've found all the pieces, so there should be no more bleeding. Mike is resting comfortably. He's one lucky young man. However, he did lose a lot of blood so he's weak and his body has been through an ordeal. Give us another half hour or so and you should be able to see him for yourself.

The entire city of Glendale was shocked by Wauneta's malice toward Mike and her suicide. No one could understand how such terrible violence involving a Bainsworth could once again shake their innocent little town. It became evident that the Bainsworth family would no longer be tolerated by the community.

About two weeks after Mike was released from the hospital, he was helping Glenda remove dishes from the table after their evening meal when there was a knock on the door. For several moments Glenda stared at Oswald Timer, who reminded her of a scary undertaker. "What do you want, Timer? I would love to have Mike throw your sorry ass off our property. Can't you and your clients just leave us alone? The Bainsworth's have cost my family enough already?"

Understanding Glenda's rage, Oswald half bowed. "Please, Mrs. Kenrude. I will only take a few moments of your time. If you will just let me in to see your husband, we can take care of this quickly."

Begrudgingly, she pushed open the porch door, allowing Oswald to enter their home. They found Mike sitting at the table with a cup of coffee. Looking up at the Bainsworth's attorney, his blood began to boil. "What the hell do you want? Have you found some way to sue me over Wauneta's death or something? My Dad always called you a blood sucking leech that should never be trusted. So, just what is it you want?"

Glenda walked around the table, standing behind Mike and placing her hands on his shoulders, as Oswald stood silently, not knowing what to say after the serious tongue lashing he had just received. Regaining his composure, he opened his brief case removing an envelope. After staring at the couple for a moment he placed it on the table. "The Bainsworth family is very distraught and ashamed of Wauneta's horrendous actions. They realize they can never make things totally right ever again, so they have authorized me to deliver this envelope to you. Please open it."

Mike sat silently staring at the attorney. After a moment of silence Timer handed the envelope to Glenda. Opening the envelope she removed a check and gasped, "A hundred thousand dollars, oh my. Michael, I have never seen a check for so much money before." She handed the check to her husband, not sure what to think or do.

Mike looked the check over for a minute before handing it back to Timer. "Tell the Bainsworth family that no Kenrude can be purchased with their ill-gotten money. Then tell them to shove it up their ass. Now you can leave before I throw you out."

Feeling perplexed, Oswald looked down at the floor. "Mr. Kenrude, the Bainsworth family isn't trying to buy you. They know very well that could never happen. They truly are genuinely upset over both this matter and the way their son treated you when you returned from the army. This is the only way they know how to make amends with you and your family. You could use it for the farm, for your children's college education, or whatever else you feel is necessary."

Glenda looked intently at her husband. "I know I should be running around the house doing backflips, but I'm not comfortable with this, sweetheart. Something just stinks and I don't like it."

Smiling, Mike nodded his head in agreement. "Every time I hear the name Bainsworth, I know something is rotten, and I guess it will be that way forever. Take your check, put it back in the envelope and get the hell out of our home. And don't come back."

Oswald grabbed the check from Mike, tossing it into his brief case. "The family will not be happy about this, I can assure you."

Mike rose from his chair, escorting Oswald to the door. "You can leave now, and tell the Bainsworth's to leave us alone, now and forever. The best thing they could do for me and the town is to sell off their holdings, pack up and move back to somewhere they're appreciated. Now, get off my property, and God help you if you return."

Just about a week later, Oswald Timer closed his law office before moving to Boston where he joined his brother's law practice. It was not surprising to anyone in Glendale that the only attorney the Bainsworth's could find to handle their affairs after that was in Minneapolis. Every attorney for nearly sixty miles around refused to accept their accounts.

CHAPTER 14
THE TRIAL AT PUSAN

The men were not adjusting well to the quiet and boredom of the rest camp. Col. Fontaine spent hours attempting to find things to keep the men busy besides drill and ceremony. Baseball and football games let the men blow off steam, but all too often fights broke out between participants and fans, resulting in disciplinary measures and unnecessary injuries. As in World War Two, nightly movies were big draws. Everyone appeared a bit calmer after most movie nights.

The big question was, 'when are we going back to the front, and if we're not, how soon are we going to be sent state side?' Unfortunately, Col. Fontaine never had answers, but it wasn't for a lack of trying. He always did his best to question everyone from I-Corp that he thought might have some idea.

A month after arriving in camp, a strange delegation of officers and legal investigators arrived without notice. They immediately began rounding up officers from the Battalion as well as from I-Corp. Although everyone wondered what was going on, they didn't give it their full attention until attorneys from the Judge Advocate General's Corp rounded up Steve, Harry, Juarez, Stebbins, McCormack, Taggered, Capt. McGlynn and Col. Fontaine. New officers were placed in charge of Alpha Company and the Battalion on a temporary basis.

The eight men were transferred to a new brick compound near I-Corp. They were held in a large room for about half an hour, where they were told not to speak while three armed Military Police Officers enforced the rule. Finally two spit and polished JAG Officers entered the room. The taller of the two went right to work, setting up a tape recorder, note pads, and several file folders.

After watching the officer set up his material for a few moments, the second officer finally spoke. "My name is Captain McMurrey, my partner is Major Fielding. The Major also investigated the death of Private Dayton in Japan. We're here to investigate the attack on the town of Kujang, in North Korea. I will be prosecuting, and Major Fielding will be my assistant. As of this moment, none of you are being charged with any crimes. You are here as witnesses, unless something else should arise, causing us to feel you should be charged with war crimes. At that point you would be assigned your own JAG representative. You will be testifying in the trials of General Booth and Colonel Manners. We understand Lieutenant Silverton was killed in the raid. We will get into that as we move along. You will be held in private rooms so you cannot communicate with each other. You will be fed in your rooms and allowed to exercise in the evening by yourself. Any attempt to communicate with anyone else is punishable under the Uniform Code of Military Justice. You may write letters home, but you may not write anything regarding these procedures. Any attempts to interfere or create problems during this procedure will result in an automatic Court Martial. Have I made myself quite clear? Also, you will be called on for questioning whenever we feel it is necessary, and you may or may not be called upon to testify in court. With that being said, I want Sgt. Kenrude left with me, and Capt. McGlynn in the other room with Major Fielding. The rest of you will be taken to your rooms."

As the room emptied, Capt. McMurrey told Steve to take a seat. After looking through a file, the Captain continued. "So tell me Sergeant, what happened to Lt. Silverton?"

Steve shook his head for a moment before answering. "The man had no concept of combat. I'm not totally sure why he was there. I took a small group of men along with the Lieutenant to a small depression on the south side of town. It was obvious that Gen. Tenyu was not there. No sentries, no special coverage of any type. It was far too quiet. Lt. Silverton wanted to race in there like a fool. I told him it was a trap, but he wouldn't listen. He charged headlong toward the town and was cut down by withering fire. We returned fire as we began retreating back to the balance of our platoon. I heard fighting to the east, so I knew Sgt. Jensen—"

Steve was cut off mid-sentence by the Captain. "You can not testify as to what happened or did not happen to Jensen's men. You were not there, Sergeant. Stick to your operational movements only."

"Well, knowing we were going to be over run in short order, I attempted to figure a way out. Before I could do anything, the North Koreans wiped out most of the platoon. I gathered the men that were left and took cover in a rocky outcropping by a river. They eventually found us there. We put up a good fight considering we were far out numbered by about five to one. I was left for dead. Several of my men managed to escape. They met up with Jensen and we were able to evacuate from the rendezvous point on Christmas Day.

"Did you at any time take prisoners? And if you did, where are they now?" Capt. McMurrey inquired.

"Prisoners? Hell sir, we were fighting for survival. They were out to kill us all, they weren't interested in taking us prisoners, and we had no intention of taking them prisoners, either," Steve replied angrily as he slammed his fist on the table."

This type of interrogation went on for over a week, as the two officers continued asking and repeating the same questions over and over. Steve found it incredibly hard to keep his cool. He could only imagine what Harry was going through. However, his question was answered the next day when evening meals were passed out. As the MP's opened the door to hand Harry his tray, they dumped most of his meal on the floor. Laughing, they began to walk out. Harry called them back, "Hey, I'm not a prisoner of war, nor have I done anything wrong. I'm just here as a witness. So I would appreciate getting my entire meal. Both MP's laughed as one attempted to shove Harry backward. Seconds later, both MP's were lying on the floor. Taking their keys, he began unlocking everyone's door. When several more MP's arrived, the angry paratroopers challenged them to step up to the plate. Instead, they withdrew, seeking assistance from Major Fielding and Capt. McMurrey. The JAG officers arrived, along with Major General Sutton. He was angered by the thought of two combat field grade officers and brave paratroopers being treated with such disrespect. The General ordered Col. Fontaine and Capt. McGlynn transferred to officer's quarters a short distance away. The enlisted men stayed where they were, but were no longer segregated or locked in their rooms, and they were allowed to eat together.

The following week the trial was to begin. However, it was a complete shock to everyone when Col. Manners over powered an MP and committed suicide with his side arm. Because of the incident, the trial of General Booth was delayed one more week to allow the prosecution and defense attorneys to readjust their cases.

General Booth immediately waved his right to an Article 32 hearing, demanding a speedy trial. After two days of haggling between the attorneys, a panel of his peers was finally agreed upon. As General Addle Hopkins, the judge assigned to the case, called the proceedings to order, Major Fielding and Capt. McMurrey had a quick conversation. Stepping forward from the prosecution tables, Major Fielding stated, "The prosecution calls General Booth as our first witness."

Immediately, Col. Charles Andretti, General Booth's attorney jumped up from his chair. "I object, Your Honor. The General is my client, and I do not wish to have him testifying at this time. The prosecution has the right to cross examine after I present my case."

Walking toward the judges stand, Major Fielding began to argue his reasons, "Your Honor, the prosecution has given the defense a list of our witnesses, which includes the General. After all, Your Honor, the General has waved his Article 32 hearing, instead demanding a speedy trial. I see no reason why the prosecution cannot move forward as planned."

Before the judge could respond, Gen. Booth stood up, pushing his counsel aside. "If it please the Court, Your Honor, I have no problem testifying now or later. If the prosecutor wants me on the stand, I am willing to oblige."

Once more, Col. Andretti addressed the judge. "Your Honor, this is highly prejudicial against my case. There is no way I can move forward with my defense if my client testifies at this point in the trial."

"Knock it off, Colonel," Gen. Booth screamed at his counsel. "If I wish to testify I will do so. You can work out the rest later. These people have no case."

Judge Hopkins pondered the matter for a moment. "General Booth, do you understand your rights against self-incrimination under the Uniform Code of Military Justice?"

Glaring back at the judge, Gen. Booth laughed. "I know my rights and I wish to testify. Let's get this over with."

Shaking his head, the judge pointed to the docket. "Have a seat, General."

As Major Fielding approached the docket, Gen. Booth stood up facing the Judge and the assembled panel. "Your Honor, this entire proceeding is a travesty, and a discredit to all my years of service to our nation. I have done nothing wrong, and this constant badgering by these so called attorneys led to the death of Col. Manners. He was a fine man and a good soldier. It is truly despicable for these puppets of the judicial system, to drag the memory of such a great warrior as the Colonel through the mud, in an attempt to fulfill their own grandiose schemes to further their pitiful careers. I ask the Court to throw out all these fabricated and meaningless charges, and let us continue with the execution of this war."

After several moments of silence, Judge Hopkins faced the General. "Sir, with all due respect I must tell you this outburst is not helping your situation. Anything you wish to say must come from your attorney, unless you have decided to defend yourself, which is your right, but I strongly warn you against doing so. However, if that should be the case, then you will have to make a motion prior to such testimony. So General, are you firing your counsel?"

Shaking with rage, Gen. Booth glared toward Judge Hopkins as he slammed his fist against the desk. "No. I am not firing my counsel, and you sir, you are the one that's not helping the situation here. If you were any kind of a judge you would have tossed out this case by now. But I guess the Army has to do something with men that are unfit for combat."

Judge Hopkins slammed his gavel down solidly on his desk. "General, I find you in contempt of court."

Turning to Col. Andretti, he continued. "Sir, if you cannot control your client, then I will ask the JAG Corp for someone who can. I will give you five minutes to speak with him before we continue. But then you damn well better have your client under control."

After a ten minute conversation with Gen. Booth, Col Andretti faced the judge's stand. "Your Honor, we apologize for the outburst. There will be no more such incidents. I request that the court take into consideration what the General has been through these past weeks, and dismiss the contempt ruling. We are ready to proceed."

Judge Hopkins leaned forward in his chair. "I am also ready to proceed. But the contempt charge will remain until the end of this trial. If the General can control his temper and cease his outbursts, I will consider dropping the charges at that point. Now let's move on. Major Fielding you may proceed."

Walking up to the docket, Major Fielding inquired, "How long have you been a General?"

"Six years this coming December, and I have been with Supreme Headquarters since the outbreak of this conflict," Gen. Booth replied calmly, though he was still noticeably angry.

Walking back toward the prosecutors table, the Major picked up a file. "General Booth, this is your outline for the failed mission into North Korea, Operation Piggyback. I have studied your notes, plans of attack, plans of insertion and extraction plans. I have read your detailed report of where General Tenyu was to be housed, and the probable defenses of Kujang. They are very informative and to the point. Who gave you the information for this report and the maps you created?"

"That is all classified information, Major. I cannot release that information without placing a highly trained informant at risk," General Booth explained smugly.

Nodding his head, Major Fielding walked up to the docket. "If that information was accurate, and if your informant was accurate, have you considered that there was a mole in your planning command? Because when our men arrived, General Tenyu was not there, and Kujang was little more than a sleepy North Korean village. A sleepy little village that just happened to be filled to the rafters with enemy soldiers just waiting to spring their trap and slaughter our heavily outnumbered troops. They had to know every aspect of the plan."

General Booth once again slammed his fist on the desk. "Hell no, everyone in our planning network was handpicked. Everyone had the highest clearance, and had worked on many secret missions in the past. You are accusing some very loyal and talented men of treason here, Major."

Staring coldly toward General Booth, Major Fielding inquired. "General, who was your contact at I-Corp?"

"Why, that's top secret of course. You know better. I would be tried for treason if I gave you those names," the General stated, his voice a little less bold.

Nodding his head, Major Fielding turned toward the judge's stand. "Your Honor, I would like to call two other witnesses to testify before I call the General back to the stand."

After the General was seated back with his defense council, Capt. McMurrey called Col. Fontaine to the stand. "Colonel, at any time did you attempt to check with I-Corp regarding the authenticity of Operation Piggyback, or its necessity?"

After taking a deep breath, Col. Fontaine looked over toward the panel. "Yes. On two occasions. Both times I was told that General Booth was operating under orders from Supreme Headquarters, and that we were to cooperate with his needs."

Rubbing his chin, Capt. McMurrey walked across the front of the court room. "Colonel, at any time did you insist that either you or Capt. McGlynn go along on the mission? Did you or the Captain ever push the point with the General or Col. Manner?"

Nodding his head, Col. Fontaine began. "Yes, we argued the point several times. In fact, I told General Booth I wanted to contact Supreme Headquarters myself to make sure an officer would accompany my men, to make sure the tough decisions were handled by a qualified officer."

Looking over at General Booth, Capt. McMurrey inquired, "And what were you told?"

"The last time I insisted, I was told Lt. Silverton from the Mission Planning Group would accompany my men. I was told he had been read into everything dealing with the mission, and that he was jump qualified. At that point I backed off. That proved to be a mistake, and today just like every other day since it happened, I sure as hell wish to God I hadn't," Col. Fontaine replied, hanging his head.

Capt. McMurrey looked at the ceiling for a moment. "Colonel, at any time were you told about a Capt. Corker from I-Corp that was involved in the planning of Operation Piggyback?"

Before the Colonel could answer, Col. Andretti jumped to his feet. "Your Honor, Capt. Corker is neither on the witness list nor was he involved in the planning of this mission. This questioning has no relevance."

Judge Hopkins called the attorneys to the bench. "Captain, what are you planning to prove with this line of questioning. I will not have you destroy another officer's career if he had no involvement in this case."

Capt. McMurrey looked coldly at the Judge. "Your Honor, we have good information that Capt. Corker was indeed involved in the planning of this mission, and may well have been the one that tipped off the North Koreans."

Just as Col. Andretti was about to speak, the Judge raised his hand. "That is a very serious accusation, Captain. Can you back that up with any solid evidence?"

Major Fielding handed a file over to the judge. "Your Honor, we have already contacted representatives in Japan regarding the evidence we have. Capt. Corker has been detained at this point in time pending the outcome of an investigation."

After looking over the file, Judge Hopkins placed it on his desk. "I am ordering a temporary stay on this case until I can contact people in Tokyo. We will resume in forty-eight hours."

Two days later, the court room was packed when the trial continued. Judge Hopkins sat quietly at the desk for several minutes before speaking. "A few days ago, I placed a temporary stay on this trial pending information regarding Capt. Corker from headquarters in Japan, and his role in Operation Piggyback. I will not allow any testimony regarding him or his role in the operation. So Capt. McMurrey, you may continue, but please keep that in mind."

Steve was called to the stand next. After being sworn in, Capt. McMurrey first questioned him regarding his experiences in World War Two. After a slight pause, the Captain turned to face Steve. "Tell me about Lt. Silverton. What kind of man was he? Did he appear to be a capable leader?"

Steve looked over at Gen. Booth with contempt. "Lt. Silverton was no leader. He had no idea of how to command, and no idea what this mission entailed. He was a hot shot Lieutenant looking to make points with the brass for his next promotion. He had no combat experience and couldn't have cared less how many men were killed, as long as it looked good on his fitness report."

Col. Andretti jumped up from his chair, throwing his pen onto the desk. "I object, Your Honor. This testimony is defamatory at best, and the Lieutenant is not here to defend himself."

Judge Hopkins leaned forward from his large leather chair. "Over ruled, I would like to hear what the Sergeant has to say. You may continue Sgt. Kenrude."

Attempting to calm himself, Steve looked up at the ceiling for a moment. "My men were the best. They believed in every mission we went on. However, many of them voiced their concerns to me. They didn't like his care free attitude or what appeared to be a lack of concern. As one of my men said, it was as if he were on his way to a candy store, trying to decide what he should buy. All the way there he was making comments that were upsetting to the men regarding glory in combat and winning ribbons."

Capt. McMurrey walked over to the wall near the docket. "What else was he saying, Sergeant? Did it also bother you?"

Steve shook his head, still in disbelief. "He laughed, stating the mission would be a walk in the park, and that the dumb ass North Koreans wouldn't know what hit them until we were long gone. He said he was going to pimp slap the first North Korean he came across, just to get his attention. The Lieutenant may have been jump qualified, but there was no way he should have been leading men into a life and death struggle such as this. We left a lot of good men behind."

Folding his arms across his chest, Capt. McMurrey looked hard at Steve. "Tell us what happened when you landed?"

Steve's voice cracked as he began to speak. "Sgt. Jensen and his men landed to the east of Kujang. They were to give us fire support, and cover the road so no advancing forces could interfere with our raid. My men were on the west side of town. I had Corporal Kraus set up a rear guard position with two squads. I took Lt. Silverton, along with Cpl. Stebbins and my other two squads up ahead to check out the situation. When we arrived, we found a slight depression we could use for cover. Immediately, it was clear there was no urgency of any sort in the town. There were no guards on the Hostel, and there were very few sentries around the barracks. It was way too quiet for a garrison that was protecting a General. It was obvious, Captain. Nevertheless, the Lieutenant didn't see it that way. He thought the North Koreans were just caught off guard, and that we could just waltz in there and grab the General. I told him no several times, stating that things didn't look right. He was about as pumped up as you could get. He picked up his gun and charged in there. As he began to go, I yelled at him to stay back. However, he ran forward instead. Right toward the Hostel. Gunfire rained down on him from every window in the town. It was a death trap. They knew we were coming and they were ready. The lieutenant must have been hit fifteen, maybe twenty times. I told the men to retreat. Just then, all hell broke loose out east of town. Sgt. Jensen's men were being overwhelmed by a large force. We fell back, but were overwhelmed ourselves just as quickly. We were easily outnumbered five or six to one. It was a trap, pure and simple. The only thing that could save us was the extraction plan, but that was quickly over run by even more North Koreans. They clearly knew every aspect of our plans. At that point, I figured we would all die, but we were determined to go down fighting."

When Steve finished, Judge Hopkins closed the proceedings for the day. Throughout the long night, Steve fought with nightmares of the raid. All he could see were his well-trained men lying dead, staining the snow crimson red. He saw their faces, blue from the cold as frost bite began to burn their skin. They appeared to be asking him over and over, 'Why Steve, why? Awakening, Steve was unsure as to what the prosecution was trying to prove this early in the trial. It just didn't seem to make much sense.

When court resumed the following morning, Major Fielding called a Major Woodman to the stand. "Major, what was your job at Supreme Headquarters in Japan?"

Looking very nervous, and attempting to avoid eye contact with Gen. Booth, he began. "I worked in special operations. Psychological operations."

Slowly walking across the court room, Major Fielding stood in front of the jury panel. "Major, remember now, you are under oath. Did you ever meet General. Booth before today? And if so, what were your dealings with him?"

Major Woodman sat motionless for several moments, as sweat poured down his forehead. Turning to his left, he looked up at Judge Hopkins. "Sir, do I have to answer that question? Or do I have the right to invoke my Fifth Amendment rights?"

Surprised by the question, Judge Hopkins swiftly glanced over to Major Fielding, who was appearing to be enjoying the situation. Turning back toward Major Woodman, who was wiping his brow vigorously with a handkerchief, Judge Hopkins began. "You do have the right to invoke your Fifth Amendment rights. However, I am guessing when this trial is over there may be a much larger investigation brought on by the Defense Department in Washington. You just may want to consider for a moment which side of the fence you want to be on if that should happen."

Lowering his head, Major Woodman began to tremble. "I have known the General for a year or more. Over time, he brought several plans for covert missions to my office. Supreme Headquarters turned them all down for one reason or another. When Col. Manner brought this plan to my office, I basically laughed it off, as it was never a serious plan to begin with. I told him Supreme Headquarters would never allow it, and that we had no new information on the movement of General Tenyu. About a week later, he and Lt. Silverton came back with the same plan with some modifications. I again told them I would not send it up the chain of command. My Intel told me General Tenyu was actually in China, working with the Chinese Military, and thus not anywhere near Kujang. They gave me all their reasons my Intel was wrong. Nevertheless, I turned down their plans. About a week before General Booth set his plan in motion, I was approached by a Lt. Changwie of the South Korean Defense Force, who worked with a Capt. Corker—"

"Stop right there, Major Woodman. I have made it perfectly clear that Capt. Corker is not on trial here, and that his name is to remain out of these proceedings," Judge Hopkins angrily instructed.

Major Fielding turned to face the Judge. "Your Honor, we are not in the process of laying blame or attempting to defame the reputation of Captain Corker. We are simply building a time-line regarding how permission for the raid took place. We can only do that if we are allowed to give the names of the staff at I-Corp who were involved in that time-line."

After a moment of thought, Judge Hopkins nodded his head. "You may resume, Major. But be careful as to where you are taking this line of questioning."

Nodding his head in agreement, Major Fielding replied, "Thank you,

Your Honor. The Court will understand more clearly why this line of questioning is important as we move forward." Turning back toward the docket, the Major stated, "You may continue, Major Woodman."

Lt. Changwie insisted I allow Supreme Headquarters to see the operational plans. I repeatedly refused. He became enraged, punching a hole in my office door and kicking over a chair. He was removed by security forces. That was the last I heard of it until word came down that this attack had taken place. Never did Supreme Headquarters give its approval, because they never saw the operational plan. After the attack, General Booth came to see me. He demanded that I sign off on a copy of the plan or he would see my career ended. He told me again that Captain Corker had approved the plans."

Walking back across the court room, Major Fielding stopped in front of the docket. "Major, did you ever sign the operational plan? And if you did, where are copies of the signed plan located?"

Shaking his head, Major Woodman replied. "I didn't sign them, and I don't know what happened to them after the General left my office."

Walking back to the prosecutor's desk, Capt. McMurrey handed Major Fielding a manila file folder. After removing documents from the folder, Major Fielding walked back to the docket. Handing the papers to Major Woodman, he inquired. "This is a movement order from Supreme Headquarters. Major, is this your signature on these orders?"

Taking a quick look, Major Woodman nodded his head, "Yes, those are orders for the 189th truck battalion to move up near Seoul. I remember working on that plan."

Taking another set of papers from the file, Major Fielding handed them to Major Woodman. "Is this your signature on this order?"

After looking over the last page of the file, Major Woodman handed them back to Major Fielding. "No, that is not my signature. It's a poor replica. I never signed those documents. But I have seen them before. That is the operational plan General Booth asked me to send up the chain of command to Supreme Headquarters."

As Major Fielding prepared to hand the two sets of paperwork to the Judge, General Booth stood up, kicking over his chair. "Look, you ignorant bastard. Neither Supreme Headquarters nor that clothier we call the President in Washington is ever going to win this damn war. If someone doesn't take charge around here, we're going to go down and be under control of the Russians. Only a patriot like me can lead the Allies to victory in Korea. Those other piss ants have their heads up their asses, as does everyone in this court room. Yes, I forged that signature, and yes, I found out after the raid was launched that Captain Corker had been feeding classified information to Lt. Changwie who had by now defected to the North—"

Col. Andretti jumped to his feet. "Your Honor, the General has violated your order not to make charges against Captain Corker. I move his comments be stricken from the record, and I demand a mistrial!"

Judge Hopkins drew in a long breath. "At this point in time I am rescinding my original order. I think it is prudent to hear testimony regarding Captain Corker and just what his involvement was all about. General, you may continue, but understand you are incriminating yourself with every word."

The General nodded his head in agreement. "I could give a damn about self-incrimination, as this entire trial is a bunch of crap. Yes, all the intelligence he gave me was worthless. But damn it, I am the only General in this Theater of Operations that has any balls or enough gumption to win this so called police action. If you send me to Leavenworth, you'll be committing more soldiers to their deaths. You bunch of hypocritical bastards better give birth to your heads and understand who is in charge around here." As the General flipped over the defense attorney's table, three Military Police Officers grabbed a hold of him. As they attempted to place handcuffs on him, the General screamed, “You assholes can cuff me, but you'll find out who the hell you're dealing with.”

Everyone in the court room was standing, attempting to get a glimpse of what was happening. Judge Hopkins slammed his gavel down several times as he yelled out, “Order! Order in this court! Take your seats and be quiet or I'll have the MP's place you under arrest.” When the room quieted down, Judge Hopkins glared at Col. Andretti. “Does the defense have anything they would like to argue in this matter?”

A shaken Col. Andretti stood up, pulling General Booth from the floor. “No your honor, the defense has nothing they wish to argue.”

Breathing heavily, Judge Hopkins looked about his court room. It was obvious that everyone was on the edge of their chairs, just waiting to see what was going to happen next. Looking over at the panel, Judge Hopkins began. “Members of the panel, I understand this has not been the typical type of court martial proceedings we are accustomed to. Nevertheless, I believe enough information has been provided for you to come up with a verdict. I will be speaking with the convening authority once I depart this court room, asking them to add treason to the aforementioned complaint. I am recessing this court for the day. I expect you to do your job, and have a verdict on all charges, including the new charge, as soon as possible.” With that, he slammed his gavel on the desk before departing the court room, with two MP's following swiftly behind him. The General's testimony during his outburst was sobering to everyone in the room. It was evident that the General could be found guilty of treason. If that happened, Judge Hopkins could order him to either be shot by firing squad or hanged.

By noon the next day, the panel had reached a decision. The court room was packed to over flowing as everyone from the Press Corp, and every officer from the base who could attend squeezed into the room. The tension was nearly unbearable as Steve and Harry sat directly behind the prosecution table. Cameras began to click and whirl as General Booth was escorted into the room wearing hand cuffs and leg irons by several new MP's. Moments later, Judge Hopkins entered the courtroom from his chambers. After the room became silent, the judge rolled his chair forward to the microphone. "Before we bring in the panel, I would like to know if either the prosecution or defense has anything they would like to add before we move on."

Major Fielding rose from his chair. "Nothing for the prosecution, Your Honor."

Likewise, Col. Andretti stood, looking intently at the judge. "We have nothing to add, Your Honor. However, we would like to ask the courts indulgence, as it is clearly obvious that the General has suffered some type of mental break down." With that said, the Colonel sat down.

Nodding his head, Judge Hopkins sat quietly for a moment. Turning to the bailiff, he motioned for him to bring in the panel. Once the panel was seated, a noticeably tired and distressed General Hopkins turned to face them. "Has the panel reached a decision?"

Col. Wilcheck, the foreman, stood up. "Yes we have, Your Honor. On the charges of insubordination, we find the defendant guilty. On the charges of authorizing an unapproved mission into North Korea, we find the defendant guilty. On the charges of eighty-eight counts of willful manslaughter, we find the defendant guilty. On the charges of treason, the panel thought it would be better to find him guilty on a lesser charge of dereliction of duty."

Judge Hopkins slowly nodded his head. "So say you all, Colonel?"

Col. Wilcheck looked over at the defeated General Booth for a moment before answering the question. "Yes, Your Honor. The findings on all specifications and charges were unanimous."

Judge Hopkins looked over the panel for a moment. "The Court wishes to thank the panel for their work. You are dismissed."

Steve could tell Judge Hopkins was struggling as to how he should continue with the sentencing. Sending a General to prison had to be the toughest decision he would ever make on the stand.

Steve was still angry with General Booth. Eighty-eight good men had died, nearly two complete platoons wiped out. They were men Steve trained and cared about, all of them lost for nothing, how could their families ever deal with such a loss? Steve wanted to walk over to one of the MP's, grab his weapon and shoot the General where he sat. He deserved little better. The General was every bit the butcher as was Himmler, Sepp Dietrich and Dr. Mengele back in Nazi Germany, and he deserved to die.

After making some notes on a piece of paper, Judge Hopkins closed a manila file. Removing his glasses he peered around the room, stopping momentarily to look at the parents of Private Andrew Sauger, who had been in Harry's platoon. They came all the way to Korea to see how the military would handle the trial of a General. Finally he began to speak. "Col. Andretti, will you and the defendant please stand." Once they were standing, the judge continued. "This will be my final case as a judge for the Army. I handed in my resignation about two hours ago. Although I love the Uniform Code of Military Justice and the law in general, this case has taught me it is time to move on. Never in all my thirty years of serving in the Army JAG Corp, have I witnessed such disregard for the lives of our humble and dedicated service men as I have in this proceeding. Understanding that a decorated General could so blatantly disregard the risks and lives of over eighty men for his own gain saddens me deeply. Our military has a system of checks and balances in its command system that must always be adhered to, in order to ensure prudent decisions, and to prevent mutiny or rebellion among the troops. General Booth has clearly crossed that line. By the powers vested in this office, I have the option to accept or amend the findings of a jury panel. So, I am reinstating the charge of treason in the final findings. I do this without mental reservation or pressures applied from superior officers. General Booth, after hearing the findings of this panel, I sentence you to 200 years of hard labor for all charges and specifications, except for the act of treason. I reduce you down to the rank of private, suspend your pension and any or all military benefits you or your family might have acquired. For the charge of treason, I have already bound over the request for a separate trial to be conducted by the U.S. Attorney General's Office as they see fit, once you arrive at Fort Leavenworth. Your disregard for life and the code every soldier must live by will haunt me forever. May God have mercy on your soul! It is also my duty to inform you that Capt. Corker has been sent back to Leavenworth, Kansas, where he will be tried for treason and espionage. Court is adjourned."

The courtroom was completely quiet for several moments after General Hopkins left the Judges stand. Steve watched as General Booth was removed from the courtroom. The once larger than life, boisterous, angry man had been replaced by a meek and sobbing shadow of his former self. Steve turned toward Harry. "Two hundred years. Why didn't he just say life in prison?"

Harry shook his head. "I'm guessing he did it for effect, Stevie boy. Believe me, it got my attention. And to think he will still be tried for treason. Do you think they will hang him if he's found guilty?"

Steve looked over at Andy Sauger's parents. "Naw, they will just add to the sentence or some goofy thing like that. They'll do it for the record, but they won't execute him. Executing Private Eddie Slovik during World War Two is still haunting them. They'll never execute an officer, especially a General. The military just wants to use this as a teaching moment. You know, to make everyone aware of what can happen if you go off the rails at the end like General Booth did."

Harry nodded in agreement. "Yeah, probably so. Let's get the hell out of here."

After the trial, General Sutton thanked the men for their service to their country, and once more apologized for the way they had been treated. He also thanked them for their assistance in getting justice for all those who were killed.

That last comment did not sit well with any of the men, especially Juarez. He stepped forward, getting within a few feet of the General. "With all due respect, sir. What happened to the General will never make up to the families the loss of their loved ones. Never make up for the loss of the futures of the men he got killed. He can do time in a cell, but that won't heal their pain. Most of those families will never find peace, knowing that the very military their son's went to serve, was negligent and responsible for their senseless deaths."

"Stand down, Juarez!" Col. Fontaine called out, as he stepped forward, pushing Juarez back away from the General. After giving Juarez a disapproving look, the Colonel turned back to Gen. Sutton. "I beg your forgiveness, sir. I'll deal with this man when we get back to the battalion."

Gen. Sutton stood silent for a few moments before turning to face, Juarez. "No need, Colonel, Juarez was completely accurate. What happened in that courtroom, will never take away the grief from the families of those that died. Regrettably, there is nothing that I, or anyone else can do about it. We all have to live with the horror of what happened. Justice, for what it's worth, was served. But even justice falls woefully short in the end. So now, all we can do is go back to work to win this damn war, so we can all go home. I'm proud to have met you men. We need tough resilient soldiers like you and your fellow paratroopers to fight here in Korea. I regret what happened to you and your men in that unlawful raid. I also understand that is little consolation, but that's just the way it is." After shaking hands with each man, Gen. Sutton departed. Later that day the men arrived back with the battalion hoping to put all that had happened behind them.

However, for Steve and Harry it proved to be a bittersweet return. They quickly learned that Franny was being held in the brig for unauthorized use of a military vehicle, and for being AWOL. After appealing to Col. Fontaine, Steve and Harry were granted permission to visit Franny. Entering the visiting area, the men found a very dejected Franny sitting by a table wearing blue prisoner coveralls. Sitting down across from him, Steve looked at his trusted friend. "Franny tell us, what the hell happened while we were gone?"

Shaking his head, Franny looked at his best friends. "You will never believe this. Private Bateman from fourth squad went out for a walk one evening. He discovered a baby Korean girl down by the airfield, next to the parachute rigging shack. He ran into me as he was returning to the company area. He asked what I thought he should do with her. The poor thing was wet from the fog, really malnourished, and coughing up a storm. She didn't look good at all. So we took her over to the aid station. The doctor on duty took one look at her and said to let her die in peace. He said she had pneumonia, she'd never make it and there was nothing we could do for her. Man, I argued like hell with that son-of-a-bitch, but he wouldn't do squat. The bastard said that even the mother gave up on her, so you know it's no use. Then he just walked off while we held that cold, wet and crying baby. Well, we made up a clean diaper from a towel and wrapped her in a dry blanket. Then I liberated a Jeep from outside the aid station, not knowing it belonged to Dr. Heming. We drove her all the way to the hospital at Pusan. It was nearly midnight when we arrived. The first doctor we ran into didn't want to do anything since we had no papers and didn't know who the parents were. Finally, overhearing the baby crying, a nurse came running over. She screamed at the doctor, then took the baby into a treatment room and told us to stay put. About forty-five minutes later, she returned. She asked Bateman if he had any idea who the parents might be. Of course he didn't. But he said his wife would love to have the child, so he offered to adopt her. The nurse rejected the plan, as she knew nothing about those types of things. She figured the baby would make it with nourishment and medication, and thanked us for bringing her in. But the red tape and forms we had to fill out were almost nonstop. We missed roll call of course, since we didn't get back until around 0900 and nobody knew where we were. What made matters worse, was that Dr. Heming's assistant saw us drive off in his Jeep. He told the MP's we stole the damn vehicle, so they wanted our asses when we returned. Good old doctor Heming also filed kidnapping charges on us since we left with the baby without his consent. Then Capt. Manzinni added AWOL charges to the rest of the crap, so here we sit. He told me he wants to see us locked up in Fort Leavenworth. All we did was try to keep that baby alive when no one else would help. What kind of shit is this?"

Harry sat back in his chair after listening to Franny's story. "There's got to be something we can do to get you out of this. When are they planning to take you in for your hearing?"

"I was told they weren't going to do anything until Col. Fontaine returned. So, since he's back it could be any time, I would guess," Franny explained.

"Well now, I have one a hell of a plan Stevie boy. Let's go find Fontaine right now. We need to get moving on this before they take Franny to court," Harry replied, as he shoved his chair back under the table.

The MP's took Franny back to his cell as Steve and Harry left the brig looking for Col. Fontaine. Finding him in the orderly room with Capt. McGlynn, they reiterated Franny's story to the officers. Finishing the explanation, they asked the Colonel what he could do to help their first Sergeant. He explained that his hands were tied because he wasn't the convening authority, so any attempts to interfere would be considered a violation of the code of justice.

Harry began pacing the office floor before speaking. "Colonel, I have a plan, but I need your permission to follow through with it. There is no doubt that this is a total miscarriage of justice. I'd like to contact General Sutton and tell him the entire story. I believe after what happened in that

Court Martial, he might want to get involved. No doubt it's a long shot at best, but I'd really like to try."

Before the Colonel could speak, Capt. McGlynn looked at Harry for a moment. "This entire situation stinks to the high heavens. I did hear the General tell an aid where they were headed after the hearing. So here's my plan. Colonel, why don't you contact the hospital at Pusan. Use your rank to see how the baby is doing. I know how to contact the General. Maybe Jensen's right, the General just might get involved in this. We can't let Franny and Bateman go to Leavenworth over something this ridiculous."

They went to work on the Captain's plan. Several times over the next few days, Col. Fontaine refused to allow the hearings to proceed, sighting investigative privileges. Three days after Capt. McGlynn suggested his plan, Gen. Sutton arrived at Third Battalion Headquarters.

He and his staff interviewed everyone involved, including medical staff at Pusan. No one in the Korean community that worked with the American forces knew of any woman who was either pregnant or had given birth. After a week of pain staking work, Gen. Sutton called a meeting at the brig. "First off, I am appalled at the indifference and lack of compassion displayed by Dr. Heming and his staff. His refusal to render aid to the child was a blatant violation of his Hippocratic Oath. I am ordering him to be sent back to the United States, where he will face a panel of military medical experts for punishment. I am also demoting the doctor at Pusan from Captain down to Lieutenant, and like-wise shipping him state side. I don't care if the patient is American, Korean or Chinese, damn it. They will attended to them, no matter what. Refusing to treat a helpless child is fundamentally un-American and will not be tolerated by Supreme Headquarters in Tokyo or the White House. Sgt. Doogan and Private Bateman are to be released from the brig at once. They will be restored to their former ranks, and given back pay for their time in confinement. Furthermore, I will personally place a letter of commendation in each of their files for the aid they offered that innocent baby, above and beyond the call of duty. As for the decisions made by Lt. Manzinni, I find them to be intolerable. Supreme Headquarters in Tokyo has reduced his rank to second Lieutenant and ordered him back to Fort Benning in Georgia where he will be reevaluated in the Officer Candidate Program. Next, in regard to the child. Normally she would wind up in an orphanage. However, Private Bateman contacted his wife and she has assured the U.S. Government that they would indeed like to adopt the baby in question. My staff is fast tracking the adoption process. Once all the paper work is completed, Private Bateman will fly home with his child and finish his enlistment at a base close to his home. He is not to return to combat duty. Col. Fontaine, you will make the necessary adjustments. And one last item, I am also placing a letter of commendation into the personnel file of Lieutenant Martha Scruggs, for her attention and care given to the baby at the hospital at Pusan. With out her intervention, that child most assuredly would have perished. I think that's everything. This investigation is now closed."

Everyone stood quietly as the General and his staff exited the courtroom. Once the door was closed, Franny and Bateman hugged each other before shaking hands with Harry, Steve and their Officers who had worked so diligently to get General Sutton involved.

Activity in the rest camp began to pick up as all the cadre was present again and on the job. Platoon leaders had to get their new replacements assigned to squads, while also getting them acclimated and ready to operate in combat situations. Aircraft availability and limited numbers of parachutes did not allow for practicing any combat jumps. They were either marched or driven out into the surrounding area, where they operated under simulated war time conditions, capturing bridges or destroying enemy emplacements. The new airborne replacements from Fort Benning were good men and well up to the task at hand.

As rumors began spreading throughout the rear areas of a pending attack, so did the stories of enemy atrocities. While driving north, the First Calvary Division discovered a railway tunnel containing the bodies of sixty-six murdered American soldiers of which a dozen died of torture or malnutrition.

Amazingly, twenty-three men who played dead during the slaughter were found alive, though in bad shape. Additional reports surfaced, explaining how DPRK soldiers murdered large numbers of American POW's along railroad lines. These stories inflamed all the troops in the reserve areas, they wanted nothing more than to be returned to the front, in order to avenge these grievous crimes. They all knew that day was coming soon as their training had heightened to a fevered pitch. On May 18th, the Second, Third and Fourth Battalions moved out of the rest area, headed north to an undisclosed location. Along the way, they joined a task force consisting of the 64th and 72nd Heavy Tank Battalions, the 300th Armored Field Artillery Battalion, a detachment of the 2nd Engineer battalion, a detachment from the 4th Signal Battalion, the 64th Truck Company and a Naval Fire Coordinating Team. The task force was to attack along a line situated just north of the city of Inje, where allied forces had bogged down.

Early on the morning of May 24th, heavy naval guns began softening up DPRK positions, with the added punch of artillery belonging to the 300th AFA Battalion. The ground shook nonstop as tons of high explosives rolled up and down the enemy front lines. The huge shells from naval guns made a terrifying roar as they screamed across the predawn sky. DPRK soldiers attempting to flee the massive barrage were cut to pieces by shrapnel from exploding shells and their own equipment being torn to shreds.

At 0800, the pent up strength of the American task force was unleashed upon the shell-shocked and frightened DPRK soldiers. Most of the survivors fell back to prepared positions farther to the north. Those that chose to stay and fight were quickly overwhelmed by the extreme violence of the Allied assault. Those who chose to stay in foxholes or bunkers were ultimately crushed by swiftly advancing heavy armor, or killed by advancing infantry machine guns. Cannon fire from the advancing tanks, coupled with heavy machine gun fire turned the retreat into a rout. Flaming wreckage of Russian T-34 tanks littered the battlefield, large artillery batteries sat twisted and motionless, and dismembered bodies lay everywhere as the task force moved forward. Although incredible to believe, an unscathed Russian T-34 tank drove through the cloud of dust, setting its sights on an unsuspecting American M-4 Sherman tank. No sooner had the T-34's cannon belched smoke and fire, the Sherman lurched to a stop as fire roared from its turret and engine compartment. With the Sherman out of the way, the Russian commander drove his deadly machine directly toward the advancing infantry. The commander of an American M-46 Patton tank witnessing the battle, turned his machine hard to the west, attempting to overtake the marauding Russian tank. A deadly game of hit and run broke out between the two behemoths. The commander of the T-34 took the first shot, having it fall just to the rear of the advancing Patton. Attempting to avoid that shot, the American commander fired wildly at the churning Russian machine, his shell burst just yards in front of the T-34, covering it with mud and grass. After completing a freakish spin, the T-34 let go a second round, ripping off the left track of the Patton tank. Wounded but not out of action, the gunner of the Patton tank fired his next projectile, striking the T-34 right in front of the turret, shearing off several feet of the deadly cannon. Not able to battle the wounded Patton, the commander of the T-34 wisely chose to retreat north in hopes of fighting another day. Nevertheless, his dreams were cut short, as a second Patton tank approached from the east.

Unable to fight, the T-34's commander began twisting and turning his wounded machine left and right, attempting to make it an impossible target to hit in all the smoke and dust. However, the commander of the second Patton tank anticipated the next turn of the T-34. His shell slammed into the body of the tank, right between the spinning treads. The Russian tank disappeared in a raging fire storm as fuel and spare rounds detonated in unison. Without hesitation, the M-46 Patton spun around quickly, before charging off to the north seeking more targets.

The advancing paratroopers were glad to see the T-34 burning uncontrollably, but they knew inside that burning hulk, men just like them had perished from this earth forever. Through out the first day of combat, Third Battalion saw very few living DPRK soldiers. Those who had survived the incredible onslaught were either seriously wounded or in such total shock were rendered incapable of putting up much resistance. Those that chose to fight were quickly taken out by paratroopers carrying B.A.R.'s who led the way.

After the third day of heavy fighting, torrential rains turned the battlefield into a muddy quagmire. The tired men dug in for the night along a reserve line, just several yards in front of the fuel thirsty tanks. As fueling crews worked feverishly, supply trucks restocked machine gun ammunition and shells for their deadly cannons. Once Harry checked the platoon's formation for the night, he joined Steve and the rest of the Alpha and Baker Company Platoon leaders in the Command tent, which was hastily set up between two tanks. Col. Fontaine had called an important meeting. "Good evening, gentlemen. First off, I've been very impressed with the work you have done the last few days. We have taken a lot of ground and given up very few casualties. That's always good to see. But now we have a special mission."

After his aids rolled out a large map, the Colonel slid his finger along a red line. "This is the line we are holding tonight. We have two battalions in reserve behind us. Tonight at 0100 hours, Alpha and Baker Companies will be pulled off line. We will regroup behind this row of tanks. When I give the order, we'll move out to the east and this set of small hills running east and west. Our goal is the town of Kusingra, in this wide river valley," he explained, while pointing to the spot on his map. "It's the command center for the Third North Korean Infantry Brigade being held in reserve. A Col. Kwan is the commander. Baker Company will move to the west of the town and cut off any retreat to the north. Alpha Company will descend Hill 872, cross the river and take the command center. We want the Colonel alive, any questions?"

Raising his hand Steve spoke up, "How deep is the river and how fast does it flow?"

Col. Fontaine nodded his head. "The river is not more than two feet deep all along this valley during the summer. It's a rather lazy river, so current will not be a problem."

Sgt. Shrider spoke up next. "Sir, what kind of defenses are we going to run into around Hill 872?"

"Navy Sky Raiders have been strafing the hill for the best part of the last few days. They have bombed or rocketed every bunker or emplacement we are aware of. Enemy casualties have been heavy. You should be able to sweep them aside with the help of three tanks we're bringing along from the 64th Tank Battalion," Col. Fontaine explained, looking very confident.

Sgt. Jarvis from Baker Companies second platoon asked, "Sir, are we to avoid contact on the way around Kusingra, or can we engage any DPRK forces we encounter along the way?"

Col. Fontaine smiled. "Well Dave, I would like to tell you to wipe out any enemy forces you see. However, in this case, we want you to reach your position as quietly as possible. But needless to say, fight if you have to." With that, the Colonel dismissed his men to prepare for the move.

At 1250, reserve forces from the rear began replacing Alpha and Baker Company paratroopers. With everyone assembled, they began their ten mile march toward the town of Kusingra at 0130. Three Sherman tanks drove between the two columns, with their gunners sitting high up in the turrets, scanning the countryside for any signs of trouble. Several times during their trek, Allied aircraft raced over their formation, striking at

DPRK forces farther to the north. Distant explosions made the earth vibrate under their tired feet. About 0300, Baker Company broke off to take up their positions to the north. Reaching the base of Hill 872 at 0420, Capt. McGlynn had the company spread out. First and Second Platoons lined up to the west with one tank, while Third and Fourth Platoons circled to the east along with the second tank. The third tank was held back as reserve, if needed. After conferring on the radio with Capt. Blazedale from Baker Company, the drive up Hill 872 began. Only sporadic fire occurred as the men began their assent. Reaching the summit, heavy fire began to emanate from gun pits and bunkers the Navy Sky Raiders had failed to destroy. A heavy Russian machine gun from a well-fortified bunker pinned down First Platoon's attempts at breaching the summit.

Steve slid down the hill a few feet before grabbing the radio handset from his radio man. "Heavy Hitter, this is Blue Fox, do you copy?"

Seconds later, the call was returned, "Blue Fox, this is Heavy Hitter. We see your problem. Do you want H.E. or the juice?"

Steve hated napalm, although it was very effective. After a moment of thought, he replied, "Give them the juice."

The lumbering Sherman rolled several more yards forward before firing. A thick, burning, oily substance shot from the muzzle of the cannon. The bunker exploded into a raging inferno in seconds, allowing First and Second Platoons to begin their descent toward Kusingra. To the east, Steve could see the second Sherman continually firing bursts of napalm at more concealed bunkers, allowing his counterparts to continue their drive.

All four platoons had descended Hill 872 and were in line on the river at 0630. Heavy fighting could be heard to the north of Kusingra, as evacuees were running into Baker Company. With all three Shermans in line behind the paratroopers, Capt. McGlynn gave the order to advance. The tanks immediately began firing on buildings closest to the river, as their machine gunners fired nonstop, keeping down any DPRK soldiers attempting to disrupt the rapid river crossing.

Reaching the far shore, Steve called Eddie Shrider. "Red Fox, this is Blue Fox. Are you set?"

"Blue Fox, we're good to go. We'll follow your lead." Knowing everyone was across, Steve let Second Platoon break loose toward the enemy command post. Sgt. Shrider followed, sending his men toward the north side of the town to encircle the target and prevent any high ranking officials from fleeing. As Third and Fourth Platoons closed the circle, Capt. McGlynn looked over the gated compound.

Taking the hand set from his radio operator, Capt. McGlynn called the lead tank. "Green Giant this is Fox Leader. Crash that gate, but do not, repeat, do not fire your cannon."

Moments later, the third tank smashed the front gate. They spun their turret from side to side to get a better look around the compound before backing out. "Fox Leader, this is Green Giant. It's awful damn quiet in there. Do you want us to shake things up?"

"Negative! Blue Fox, enter from your side. Yellow Fox come on in from the east." Capt. McGlynn called orders over the radio, allowing Second and Third Platoons to enter the compound.

They had barely done so when a white flag appeared in a window on the second floor of what could have been considered the headquarters building.

Steve directed first and second squads to close in on the structure. Moments later, the front door slowly opened. A young Lieutenant walked up to Steve. "Are you the commander of these forces?"

Glaring at the officer, Steve replied, "No. That would be Capt. McGlynn. He is back outside the gate. Do you wish to surrender?"

The Lieutenant spit on Steve's combat boot as he smiled. "We will not surrender to the likes of you or some two bit Captain. Where are your Generals?"

"My general is that large green tank pointing its seventy-five millimeter cannon at your scrawny head. So if you want to play games we'll just blow this place apart, your choice?" Steve replied, with a cocky grin.

Before the Lieutenant could say another word, he was pushed aside by a balding officer wearing the insignia of a North Korean Colonel. "I am Col. Kwan. I wish to surrender my officers to you without further bloodshed. We are ready to lay down our arms if we are assured safe travel back to your headquarters."

Harry stepped in front of the stiff officer, "Oh, so you want assurance from us that you won't be butchered like the American POW's we've been hearing about. Do I understand you correctly?"

Before another word could be exchanged, Capt. McGlynn walked up beside Harry. "Stand down, Sergeant. I'll handle this," the Captain explained with a sly smile on his face.

Unshaken by Harry's attitude, Col. Kwan handed over his side arm to Capt. McGlynn. "I expect we will be treated fairly under the Geneva Convention rules regarding POW's. You appear to be a man of honor, Captain."

Just as Capt. McGlynn was about to speak, the defiant Lieutenant drew his sword as he yelled, "Traitor!" He quickly swung the weapon over his head in the direction of Col. Kwan and Capt. McGlynn. Before he could make contact, Capt. McGlynn pushed the Colonel to the ground. Steve instantly fired a blast from his Thompson into the Lieutenant's mid-section. The angry soldier crumbled to the ground as his sword fell harmlessly at his side.

Helping the Colonel up, Capt. McGlynn angrily shouted to Harry. "Get on that damn tank and go get those trucks. Enough of this crap!"

Several minutes later the tank returned, with ten deuce-and-a-halfs in tow. The surrendering DPRK soldiers occupied two trucks, while paratroopers either crawled into the remaining vehicles or chose to ride back to their lines on top of the three tanks. Once arriving back at headquarters, Col. Kwan and his staff were flown away by helicopters to an undisclosed site.

As a surprise to everyone, Supreme Headquarters in Japan ordered the, 187th Regimental Combat Team to return to Pusan, regardless of what actions they were involved in. Only two days later the men once again occupied the barracks they had departed less than a month earlier. Speculation spread through the camp as to what their next mission would be. But all the rumors and scuttlebutt could have never accurately pinpointed what was going to happen to them next.

On June 26th, orders came down reassigning them to Japan. A cheer went up through the camp as the men celebrated. Of course that sparked new rumors regarding how soon they would be sailing back to the United States. Many of the retreads from World War Two were anxiously expecting to be immediately discharged.

Harry went running up to Steve. “Clearview, Iowa here I come. We’re going home, Stevie boy, we’re going home for good. Our war is finally over. Damn it feels good. What do you think, are you ready to see Karen and the kids?”

Steve gave his best friend a slight smile. “I don’t know about all of this, Harry. We might just be going back to Japan to refit, rest up, and then take on a brand new mission. I’m not getting my hopes up just yet. We might just be held in reserve in case something big blows up. I just can’t let myself get all pumped up and then get deflated when it all goes south.”

Harry nodded his head in agreement. “I understand what you’re saying. But look at the reserves they have now. Where else are they going to need an airborne unit? I think we shove off from Korea, regroup in Japan where the retreads like us get weeded out. Then we head home and the Combat Team goes off to a new base to get replacements and train for whatever comes next. Like a war with Russia. I'm telling you Steve, even Franny and Eddie Shrider think that's the plan."

Two days later a large troop transport sailed into Pusan Harbor. After a meticulous boarding operation was completed, the paratroopers sailed the short trip to the Allied Naval Base at Sasebo, Japan. Trucks and buses waited on the pier to deliver the men to the east side of the base where they would take up residence. What surprised the men most was that no new replacements arrived to fill in for the dead or wounded, and none of the officers could explain why. That just added credence to the notion that they were headed stateside in short order, most likely to Fort Benning Georgia.

Steve didn't dare buy into any of the rumors as it was too hard on his morale. It was good to be away from the war and the death. He had seen plenty, and didn't want anymore. Although Col. Fontaine and Supreme Headquarters did a rather good job of keeping the men occupied, they were beginning to get somewhat rambunctious. On a rainy Saturday evening after writing a long letter home to Karen, Steve strolled over to see Franny and Harry who were involved in a battalion wide pool tournament. He found Harry sitting on a bar stool, drowning his sorrows in a glass of beer.

"Got your butt kicked good, huh buddy?" Steve inquired.

"Hell yeah. You know that tall black dude from Baker Company named Washington? He is kicking everyone's butt. Man, can he play the game. I've never seen anything like it. So, what's up with you tonight? I didn't think I'd see you over here."

After getting a beer Steve had to laugh as Washington polished off Franny in a quick game of eight ball.

"Boredom more than anything, I guess. Col. Fontaine says we can all get passes next weekend. The guys need it bad. They're beginning to go stir crazy. Me too a little. I really thought by now the Army would have made up their minds about what they're going to do with us. I sure as hell would like to go home."

Franny and Eddie Shrider came walking over. After downing a quick beer, Eddie looked at the guys. "Capt. McGlynn says we can get a tour over to Nagasaki next Saturday. I sure would like to go see what it looks like. I know they've had a chance to do some rebuilding, but I'd sort of like to check it out. How many people back home can say they visited a place where an atomic bomb went off? Might be a bit sick, but hey. Any of you guys up for it?"

After several moments of thought, everyone decided it sounded like a pretty good plan.

After a hard week of training, the men boarded the bus Saturday morning for the hour long trip to Nagasaki. The men had seen plenty of devastation in Germany, but they weren't ready for what they were seeing on the north side of the city. It was as if a giant with a huge broom had just swept everything away. No standing chimneys or half walls. No vegetation. Everything was just gone. In the center of the city there was construction going on everywhere you looked. American built cranes, caterpillars and dump trucks were hauling new materials and debris to and from building sights. It was hard for all of them to believe that one single plane, with one single bomb could have caused this much devastation. As the bus stopped to allow other vehicles to pass, Japanese citizens glared at the paratroopers on the bus. Some of them yelled insults in Japanese. After leaving the stricken city, the bus driver traveled on to Kumamoto, where the paratroopers were able to exit the hot bus and stretch their legs. The citizens here were very friendly to American service people. They especially liked the money the G.I.'s spent on food, liquor and souvenirs. Every street corner appeared to be occupied by vendors selling their wares.

Everything from woven silk scarves to jewelry made from coral and other semi-precious stones was available. Many of the men purchased the exquisite jewelry for their wives or girlfriends, since items like these just weren't available back on main street U.S.A. After walking for some time the men turned into a small but busy bar.

After figuring out what was what on the menu with a very patient young Japanese woman who did not speak English very well, they all ordered drinks and some light snacks.

Harry kicked Steve in the leg, "Get anything nice for the wife?"

"Yeah, I did, Harry. I also picked up a few small things for everyone else. It was kind of fun buying some gifts. Odds are we'll never get back here again, and I know they'll appreciate them."

Before anyone else could speak, a blind man came walking up to their table. "Americans, I presume," the man said, with a thick British accent.

"Yes, we are. We are members of the 187th Regimental Combat Team from Sasebo, just returned from Korea," Eddie Shrider explained.

"It's always good to speak to Americans. Do you know why I am blind? Have you even got a clue? Well chaps, I was in Nagasaki when your boys dropped that dreaded bomb. Of course, I never saw the plane that dropped it or the bomb hanging in midair. But I saw that explosion. It was like nothing you could have imagined. Brilliant beyond brilliant. Like the sun, times a thousand, or more. I thought, 'What was that?' My face burned for a moment like I had been out in the sun far too long. Then a tremendous rush of air picked me up, carrying me several blocks back in the direction from which I had just come. I stopped when I bounced off what was left of a power pole. But then I rolled for several more yards before finally coming to a stop. I was shaken beyond belief and couldn't fathom what had just happened. When I was able to get back on my feet, all I could see was dirt and a thick ugly green-gray cloud spreading out over the area. I began to walk back to the north. Where I was going, I am not even sure. Then I passed out. Several days later I awoke under the tent of a makeshift clinic. My face was bandaged, as were my hands. There were screaming people all around me. It went on for days. Day and night, old screams followed by new screams. I am somewhat thankful I was bandaged, so I couldn't see what the horror was all about. About three days later a doctor removed my bandages. He told me I had serious radiation burns from an atom bomb. It was like the one they had dropped days earlier on Hiroshima, but more powerful. My skin peeled off, then grew back fairly well, then peeled off again. The third time it stayed, although slightly redder than it was originally. My eyesight diminished day by day, until I was totally blind. However, I did get a chance to see what was left of beautiful Nagasaki one time. I am thankful I was able to see what that bomb did to the city, since it robbed me of my sight. An American doctor told me that the light of the explosion was like a hundred thousand welding torches. My retinas were destroyed. So, you may ask, what was an Englander doing in Japan since we were at war with her? Well, I was in the Royal Army when Singapore fell. After spending some time in the stockade, the Japanese Army put some of us to work doing civic repair projects, since their men were all off fighting the war. That morning I was headed into Nagasaki with several other men to tend to flower gardens and sweep streets. I guess that project was never completed that day or any day since. I have helped the Supreme Allied Command with interviews and such since the war ended. I haven't returned to England since most of my family died in the Nazis blitzes."

After taking a deep breath the man finished. "I did not wish to make you men uncomfortable. But I thought you might like to know how that damn bomb impacted people other than the enemy we were fighting. I hold no grudges. I just hope you Yanks never drop another one of those blasted contraptions. Well, have a good day and enjoy Kumamoto, a lovely city. I can still smell the flowers you know." With that, the man turned to the west, swinging his cane out in front of him as he strolled down the sidewalk.

The men were silent for a short while before Franny spoke up. "Well, I wasn't counting on that story to be damn sure. But I guess I'll never forget it. What a damn shame. A POW and his eyesight destroyed because of one of our bombs, a damn shame."

Returning to Sasebo that evening, the men were tired and somewhat uncomfortable after listening to the Englishman tell his incredible story.

By October, hopes of being returned to the United States anytime soon were beginning to fall apart. New airborne troops, some from Fort Benning and others returning from hospitals, began arriving to fill the depleted ranks. Near the end of the month, the 187th boarded trains for their former base at Hakata, Japan. Supreme Command understood there was no way to keep this highly trained outfit ready for future combat, unless they could train and jump to keep them proficient. Most of the men had become sluggish, and were beginning to lose the toughness they once possessed to handle the rigors of airborne combat. For the first two weeks at Hakata, the men were put through strenuous physical conditioning for nearly twelve hours a day. No weekend passes were allowed, as Col. Fontaine felt it was best to work the men seven days a week. After weeks of intense training, Third Battalion Officers decided the men were ready for their first jump. Everything went off without a hitch. It was clear the men were beginning to regain the focus and sharp edge the 187th was known for by the Allied Leaders.

Steve sat quietly as the C-47 he rode in gained altitude before reaching the drop zone. After all the jumps he had made in combat, there were no jitters or second thoughts. He was quite simply ready to be under that wide canopy once again. As the jump master ordered them to stand and hook up, a broad smile appeared on his face. There would be no flak, no one shooting up at him, and no dangerous obstacles on the ground placed by enemy combatants. This would just be a jump to enjoy. Exiting the aircraft, Steve's chute snapped open, giving him a fantastic view of the area around Hakata. The refreshing smell of ocean air filled his head. As he descended to the grassy field below, this was by far the most relaxing jump he had ever made. Striking the ground, he ran with his chute for several feet before coming to a stop. After releasing his harness, he blew on the whistle, as Harry was already yelling for his platoon to gather around him. With everyone accounted for, they moved off to the company rendezvous point.

Capt. McGlynn led his men on a three mile march to an area aside a small creek where their cooks had delivered a hot meal. After everyone finished eating, the Captain called Alpha Company together. "Gentlemen, this will be our last day together. Tomorrow, I'll be shipping out to Washington D.C., where I will take up a new job and a promotion to Major." Everyone applauded as Capt. McGlynn smiled. "You will no doubt be happy to know that your new Company Commander will once again be Captain Fargo, as he has recovered from his injuries. Colonel Fontaine pulled a lot of strings to get him back." Another cheer of approval went up from the happy men. "I have one more change to announce. Major Torres is leaving the job as Executive Officer of the Battalion. He's being replaced by a well-trained airborne man who served in Europe during World War Two. Some of you may remember him from the siege of Sainte Mere' Eglise in Normandy. His name is Captain Ronald Lewis. He was supposed to be here today, but was delayed in the Philippines. So, I hope you give him all the help you have given me. Now, let's board the trucks and get the hell out of here." All the men shook hands with Captain McGlynn, as he had led them well.

Major Lewis and Captain Fargo arrived the next day to a warm reception from the happy paratroopers. The reunion between Major Lewis and the men who helped rescue him at Sainte Mere' Eglise was very emotional. The Major had not seen Steve since he had been evacuated from the besieged town in June of 1944. Once again, he praised the men for their outstanding service and bravery during the early days of the invasion of Europe. Before walking off, he looked at Harry. "Has your pit bull attitude improved over all these years?" Steve and Franny had to laugh.

"What the hell, Captain? I put my sorry butt on the line for you and that's all the respect I can get in return?" Harry replied with a smile.

"No Jensen, that was a compliment. Although your snide remarks irritated me at times, I always knew I could depend on that cockiness to get you through the worst the Nazis had to offer. You guys were a hell of a team and I'm glad to be back with you."

Captain Lewis went right to work, putting the paratroopers through many simulated battle situations to heighten their already sharp skills. No one complained, as they knew what they were doing today could spare their lives if and when they returned to Korea.

CHAPTER 15
GLENDALE GROWS UP

Mike's recovery from Wauneta Bainsworth's attack was nearly complete. Glenda had a terribly hard time slowing him down, as he chomped at the bit to return back to his beloved farm. Although she was happy to see her husband's attitude be so positive, she was concerned he might over do things and end up back in the hospital. The Kenrude family was just as excited as the entire town of Glendale when the Bainsworth family sold out their holdings in the bank as well as all the other business enterprises they held in and around town. Following the final business transactions, the Bainsworth family moved to New York City, where they could blend into the upper crust of the financial community, without explaining what happened in Glendale. Everyone asked the same question, 'Who could ever afford to buy the Bainsworth Mansion?' There was certainly no one in the community right now who was able to afford such an elegant home.

However, they didn't have to wait long, as the home was purchased by August Godfrey, a millionaire from the Minneapolis area who bought and sold agricultural products. He also purchased forty acres west of town where construction crews were already building a massive grain terminal.

One morning, as Mike and his father stood beside the barn discussing what to do about their hay baler, two black Cadillac's drove into the yard.

August Godfrey and his legal team approached them from the fancy cars. With a handshake and a smile, the congenial millionaire addressed them. "As you may know by now, my name is August Godfrey. I am the owner of Godfrey Agricultural Concepts. I understand your family owns one of the biggest farms in Kandiyohi County, and from what I've seen driving up the road, you do damn fine work. I fully understand you run a dairy operation as well as cash-cropping. I know operating a dairy farm is rewarding, but at times problematic, so I'm here to offer you a way out of it. You see, I'm building that new grain terminal west of town. I would like you to quit growing hay for your animals, and do nothing but cash cropping for me. You know, corn, soy beans, wheat and oats. I will buy everything you produce. What do you think of the idea?"

Mike looked over at his father for a second before speaking. "I heard you were visiting large farms in the area, and expected to be on your list. Do you have a plan we can look at?"

Godfrey's attorney stepped forward, handing Mike a manila file folder. After looking over the proposed numbers, Alex gasped. "You mean this is what you're willing to pay us for our crops, without growing alfalfa and milking cows?"

"Because, if that's the case, we have an option to purchase another 250 acres over to the west of here. Would you want to buy the products from those acres, also?"

August laughed slightly. "Of course, Mr. Kenrude. Any land you add, we will buy the product." Placing his hand on Alex's shoulder, he continued, "Now, I don't expect you to give me an answer this very minute, although I can see you are interested. I know you have a son serving in Korea that is part of your organization. Go ahead and write to him. Get a family consensus before you contact me. Just remember that I'd like to have your crops in my bins next fall, so we'll need to know in the next few months what to plan for. Please give this some serious thought." After shaking hands once more, Mr. Godfrey and his entourage departed the farm.

Alex and Mike stood quietly, as if in a trance as they looked over the paperwork they had been given. They were startled when Nancy approached from behind. "You two look like you just saw a ghost. What happened? Who were those men? Is everything alright?"

Swallowing hard, Alex looked at his wife. "We need to talk, sweetheart." Taking his bewildered wife by the arm, he led her into the kitchen, with Mike following a few feet behind. He and Mike explained the offer made by Godfrey at some length, including all the changes they would need to make, such as equipment, hiring at least one more employee, and selling off the dairy herd. Mike spoke about purchasing 200 additional acres from the Harmon estate, along with the 250 they already had an agreement on.

After listening to all that had been said, Nancy stood up. "Is this guy on the level, Michael? That proposal is for more money than we normally make in two years. Is it for real? I have seen his name in the Minneapolis paper from time to time. But never in a lifetime did I believe our paths would cross."

Mike smiled at his concerned mother. "Yeah, he's for real. I spoke with Hubbie Gainer from Olivia last week, he farms around 700 acres. He told me Godfrey made him a big offer, plus gave him a signing bonus of three hundred dollars toward seed for next spring. To be honest, I think we need to explain all this to Karen, and write a letter to Steve tonight. I know he would be glad to be rid of the cows; he's actually mentioned it in several letters. Then tomorrow I could go into town, finish the purchase on the 250 acres from old man Redding, and then call Butch Harmon. He told me we had first crack at the land. This is it, Mom and Dad. This is the time we go big, or regret our decision the rest of our lives. Remember, we have three families to support off this operation now. Plus, we have kids coming up that can help with the work."

While holding on to his nervous wife, Alex looked at his trusted son. I have no problem selling off the herd and the rest of the hay, and I know just the guy to talk to. And believe me, I have no problem getting rid of them. I'll write the letter to Steven tonight. You take care of the land acquisitions tomorrow." Turning toward his still nervous wife, he smiled, "I mentioned it once before and you chastised me, but sweetheart, we really aren't poor dirt farmers anymore."

Nancy had to laugh as she looked over her two men. "I believe in you two, and I know Steve will jump at the opportunity. He always said he wanted to turn Kenrude Farms into something big. This will give him something to look forward to when he comes home, but I only have one more thing to add. Like I said before, Mr. Kenrude, we've never been poor dirt farmers. We've always grown two main crops around here that never let us down. Hope and love."

The following day, Mike went to Glendale Realty to work out the arrangement on both pieces of land. As he left the office, he ran into Charlie McGrath from the feed mill.

"Mike, I heard you're going to sign a contract with Godfrey for your crops. I've already lost two other farmers for the same reason. You guys are going to put me out of business. Your dad and I go back over forty years, Mike. You can't do this to me. What will I do if I lose the mill? I'm too old to start another business or go to work for anyone else."

Before Charlie could say another word, Helen Krieding approached the two men, "Michael Kenrude, what are you and your parents doing to our little community? What will we do when my husband has no more grain to haul from Charlie's mill down to Savage? We'll go broke. We'll lose everything. Shame on you, Michael!"

Mike looked off toward the west end of town for a moment before answering, "Look, things are changing all over this country. Every where you look growth is taking place. It was just a matter of time before Glendale felt it's growing pains. Godfrey was just the catalyst. If Dad and I don't sign contracts, other farmers will. I'm sorry you feel the way you do, but we have three families to take care of ourselves, not to mention paying the help we have hired. In fact, we're looking at hiring at least one more man. We have to grow if we're going to stay afloat." After shaking his head for a moment, he continued.

"Even the implement dealer over in Montevideo is expanding. Zenner Construction is hiring help to build the new elevators and storage bins. Things are happening here in Glendale because of Godfrey, and our community will grow and be better because of it."

Stomping her foot, Helen gazed angrily at Mike. "Well, I don't want Glendale to change. I love our community as it is." Before Mike could say another word, she and Charlie walked off in their own directions, leaving him standing all alone.

Before leaving town, Mike drove into Glendale Tire and Auto to fill up his gas tank. Andy , the smiling-est man in town approached the truck.

"Good morning Mr. Kenrude. It's really good to see you again. How are you doing after your run in with Wauneta?"

Climbing out of the truck, Mike placed the nozzle from the pump into his gas tank. "Oh, I'm just fine, Andy. It's been kind of a rough morning. Tensions are running high around town regarding Godfrey's new grain operation. I like the idea, but I don't want to make enemies, either."

Andy leaned against the fender of Mike's truck as he wiped his brow. "Well son, things are happening around here, and it's going to continue whether folks like it or not. I signed an agreement with Godfrey myself. I'm going to supply all his trucks and vehicles with fuel, tires and whatever other lubricants they need. If I don't do it, someone else will. That's just the way it is. I think I'm going to have to hire two new employees, and that will be great for this town. Besides, I'll leave one heck of a legacy for my son and grandchildren. What more could a man ask? Don't think twice about signing on with Godfrey. In the end this town will grow and every family will prosper. Sure, some folks may need to change the way they operate, but hell Mike, when hasn't that happened in this country?"

After paying for the fuel, Mike began climbing back into his truck when Bull Richards drove up. "Say Mike have you got a minute? I have some bad news for you." Slowly Mike stepped out of his truck, walking over to Bull.

"What's happening, Sheriff?" Mike asked nervously.

"I'm sorry to tell you we found Gilly dead in his apartment this morning. According to Doc Mueller, Gilly had some rare type of blood disorder. Like a cancer, I guess. Anyway, we figure he died sometime last night. The only relative we know of is his brother over in Marshall, so we gave him a call. Do you know of any other family?"

Shaking his head, Mike responded. "No, that's the only relative Gilly ever spoke about. We knew he was sick, but he wouldn't talk about what was happening with him. Thanks for the information. I'll let everyone out at the farm know." After waving good bye to Andy and Bull, he drove west out of town.

Parking his truck on the highway near the new grain terminal, Mike watched several surveyors pounding stakes into the ground, as two caterpillars pushed back dirt in an area already surveyed. Farther over, several carpenters he recognized were preparing forms for pouring concrete. Driving forward slowly, he gazed at the huge sign which stood aside of the construction entrance. On it was a list, of all the local construction companies that were applying their trades to complete the project. All the doubt that had been clouding his judgment dissipated. As he drove back home, he knew signing on with Godfrey and expanding their operation was exactly what their farm operation and his community needed. After all, he had seen many good men die over in Europe for the sake of freedom and the ability to live life to the fullest.

CHAPTER 16
DEATH KNOWS NO BOUNDARIES

An almost unnatural calm had spread across the large military base at Hakata, Japan this Christmas morning. Light snow flakes fluttered to the ground as Steve departed the Chapel prior to the conclusion of his Christmas service. The sun was just beginning to break on the eastern horizon as he walked slowly down the path. He thought back to Christmas Eve 1944 at Bastogne. That tiny baby he watched being born would now be seven, if it survived the war and all the hardships its mother would have to endure over the next few years. He wondered about the North Korean couple and their sweet baby daughter that offered him refuge last Christmas, when he was injured and freezing. Were they even alive anymore? Had they been slaughtered by the ruthless North Korean soldiers? He had seen so much brutality on Christmas day over the years. Sometimes he wondered if everyone forgot what the day was really all about. He came to a stop when he heard the sound of someone running up from behind him. Turning back he saw Harry trying to catch up with him.

"Something wrong Steve? All of a sudden you were gone and the service wasn't over yet," Harry inquired as he looked at his best friend.

Shaking his head, Steve looked up at the cloudy sky. "Seemed like the place was closing in on me. I can't explain why. Thought I was going to pass out, so I came to get fresh air. I figured you would catch up with me. I really wanted to be home for Christmas this year so bad. I'm so damn tired of war."

Before either man could say another word, a familiar voice chimed in. "Yes, this is not a blessed Merry Christmas for any of us." Looking to their left, the men saw Fr. O'Heally sitting alone on a park bench by a small garden. Walking over, the men sat beside the humble priest.

Studying the face of his good friend, Steve inquired. "Is there something wrong Padre? You don't look so good?"

After looking at the two men he sighed heavily. "I feel lost today, like I have been abandoned. Though I know God never abandons us. He is always with us in our darkest hours. Yet today of all days, the day of joy and hope, my soul is deeply troubled. You see Steven, I too wish I were back with my congregation in Cincinnati. I feel as if I shall never see them again, or preach from that marvelous oak pulpit. You see, as I said my midnight Mass this morning, I knew it would be my last. I fear there is a bullet in Korea, directly across that channel, that has my name on it. I have prayed to God since my service ended to remove those thoughts from my mind. Yet they persist. Like the heavy hand of death is on my shoulder, as if God is ready to bring me home. I know I'm ready to meet my maker. I have always tried to lead a good life and do his will. But at the same time, I don't understand why it would happen now. Yes, I have heard many boys ask me the question, why me father? Why did this have to happen? I always tried to offer comfort to them. However, none of those words comfort me at all on this blessed morning." Trying to force a small smile the terrified priest stood up. "I think I need to lie down for a few minutes before my sunrise service. You men have a most blessed Christmas, and be sure to write letters home now."

Before he could walk off, Harry rose quickly. "Padre, we're not scheduled to leave here any time soon. Maybe we won't go back at all. I think Supreme Headquarters wants to keep this outfit intact for any future conflicts. Besides Padre, every soldier in this war, and probably every war that has ever been fought, has had the same feeling that you're having today. I have had it, and I know Steve has. I think it's just part of war wearing on your mind. You have to shrug it off and make peace with it, or it will eat you alive."

Understanding Harry was trying desperately to console him, Fr. O'Heally placed his hand on Harry's shoulder. "Thank you son. It is true, that we don't know what Supreme Command has in store for us. I do understand your explanation, and I will try and remember that. Thank you." With that, Fr. O'Heally walked back toward his quarters near the chapel.

A cold chill ran down Steve's spine. The forewarning from the priest was all too similar to the one Archie Davenport had, just before they jumped into Normandy, and he never made it to the ground alive. This was one premonition Steve was not going to let occur. After a moment of thought, Steve scratched his head and looked over at Harry.

"It's Archie all over again. We have to stop him from going back to Korea. I know he would be angry at us for keeping him away from the war, but it has to be done. What do you think, Harry?"

"I don't know, Steve. The man is next to a saint in my book. Do we interfere in God's plan? Or maybe it's just nothing. Maybe he has just seen and heard so much, that his mind is in need of a long rest. He carries the burdens of so many, after all. But on the other hand, I don't want to see him dead either. Yeah, let's talk to the Colonel," Harry responded, as the men began walking back toward their barracks.

Over the next few days they had conversations with Major Lewis and Col. Fontaine. Both officers were very interested in the story. However, Col. Fontaine summed it up best. "Nobody wants to see men get killed. And believe me, the last person I want to see die is that holy man. He has helped so many of us, myself included. That being said, I can't pull everyone out of combat that has a premonition. If I did, there would be no one left to fight when we arrived in battle. True, it is a bit different with the Padre. But I don't have the authority to deny him the right to follow us back to Korea if we are sent. In fact, I would be reprimanded for doing so. I'm sorry men, but that is the long and short of it."

As the New Year began, the war in Korea was on the mind of every American politician and the US Allies abroad. No one wanted to continue spending their treasure of money and lives on a war that appeared to have no end. If they had been fighting just the North Koreans, the war would have been over long ago. But adding the endless manpower of the Russians and Chinese had changed things considerably and the war continued to drag on. President Truman desperately struggled to find a way to end the war through negotiations. Meanwhile in Korea, battles still rolled up and down the peninsula, grinding up men and equipment at an unprecedented rate. Soldiers questioned their superiors, wondering why they would take a hilltop just to give it back, especially after expending so many lives in the battle. Pilots questioned their orders when told they could only bomb the south half of the bridges over the Yalu River being used by Communist Chinese forces to seek safe asylum in Manchuria. None of it made any sense to the common soldier on the ground. Morale, frost bite and trench foot continued to plague the ground troops nearly as much as the constant attacks by the DPRK and the Communist Chinese forces. There just didn't appear to be any well-defined answer to the quagmire the Allies now found themselves firmly entrenched in.

Back in Hakata, Japan, the 187th continued training, simply waiting to see what was going to happen next. Just like the soldiers in Korea who couldn't figure out what was happening from one day to the next, the men of the 187th quit trying to figure out what their fate might be. Every rumor and bit of scuttlebutt continually proved to be wrong. Most superior officers were stunned as well when the typically reliable rumor mills all but dried up.

Steve and Harry were happy to see Fr. O'Heally acting like his old self again. Once more he was officiating basketball games, handing out hilarious penances to players who received fouls. At baseball games, when a batter struck out, the Padre would instantly walk to home plate where he would give the batter a few choice batting tips, then plead with the opposing team to allow the forsaken player just one more chance. Sometimes it appeared the spectators came to the games more often to watch Fr. O'Heally than to enjoy the actual games.

When the Bob Hope U.S.O. show stopped at Hakata, it just seemed natural for Fr. O'Heally to get involved with Mr. Hope on stage. The men in the audience would roar with laughter as the two men along with Jerry Colonna would banter back and forth. The hit of the evening was when their favorite priest sang a duet with recording artist Dinah Shore. It totally brought the house down.

Around mid-February, the rumor mill sprang to life once again, as their training began to include crawling through an infiltration course under live fire. Training sessions went late into the evenings and continued on weekends. Several night combat style jumps were included, which went off without a hitch, but only served to add fuel to the rumors.

On March 20th, orders came down from Supreme Headquarters to prepare for an overseas deployment back to Korea, no later than April 15th. News of the order was kept from the men for security reasons until just prior to the day of transfer. On a cool damp April 10th, the men boarded buses and trucks to be driven to the docks in Hakata, where they would once again load on a transport vessel for the short trip across the Straits of Korea, heading for Pusan.

Col. Fontaine had never seen a more melancholy looking combat force as he did that day. Even in World War Two, he could elicit smiles and smart remarks from the men as they prepared to jump into combat. But not today, as ninety percent of the men ignored his humorous jokes and comments. This was not the type of soldier he wanted to lead into battle. Too many of them would die if they failed to focus on the mission at hand. That's exactly what was happening in Korea right now. After the gang plank was pulled up, the Colonel held a meeting with his Company Commanders and Platoon Leaders.

"Gentlemen, I am very concerned regarding what I observed on the pier today. Although these men are as trained and sharp as any paratroopers I've ever led into combat, their morale has degraded beyond anything I could have imagined. Regrettably, right now I'm not sure how to cope with it. No one on this vessel, including me, wants to return to Korea. But that was not my call. I know we will be held in reserve when we arrive at Pusan. We are not going straight to the line, please make sure your men are aware of that. We will do whatever we can do to keep them occupied and pass the time effectively. Needless to say, your most important job is to keep order and discipline among the men. We all know what can happen if order is lost among combat troops. If you have any questions or problems please get back to me or Major Lewis right away."

Capt. Fargo called a meeting of Alpha Company on the stern of the transport almost immediately. He explained everything the Colonel wanted his men to hear, and although it didn't alleviate every concern, it did make things somewhat better.

Steve and Harry spent every waking hour with their platoon on the short voyage. Sharing friendly conversations and discussing questions the men still had.

Light snow showers greeted the men as they transferred from the troop transport to the waiting trucks. It was heartening to the men to see so many other troops in combat reserve. At least if something transpired where additional combat troops were required, they probably wouldn't be the first to be called up.

Throughout the months of March and April, problems began to escalate at a POW camp located on Geoje Island, which was connected by a bridge to the city of Tongyeong. Many riots had occurred, resulting in the deaths of POW's and South Korean guards. The allied government was working desperately to screen out Communist political prisoners—POW's who chose to be repatriated to the south or Communist North Korean soldiers wanting to return to the north. Tensions ran high between the two groups, as soldiers who believed in the Communist North looked at those who chose repatriation to the South as traitors. Compound 76 was the most violent and problematic of the camp. On May 7th, General Dodd and his adjutant Col. Wilbur Ravens arrived in the compound to hear complaints from Communist prisoners. A quick scuffle ensued in which the General was taken hostage by the prisoners. Col Ravens was able to battle off some of the attackers before being rescued by armed guards. The stand-off lasted seventy-eight hours, during which time Gen. Dodd was held in the center of the camp by armed POW's.

Gen. Colson quickly made his way to the compound to work out a solution to the hostage situation. Not wanting any bloodshed, he agreed to many of the Communist demands. In the end, he signed a document stating that all POW's, especially wounded soldiers, would be treated more humanely in the future, and that all forced screenings would be abolished.

Authorities at Supreme Headquarters were angered, as was President Truman and authorities at the Pentagon. This agreement made it sound like Allied forces had not been treating prisoners properly. Nevertheless, serious problems continued in Compound 76. On May 12th, Lt. Gen. Mark Clark, Chief of United Nations Command, demoted Generals Dodd and Colson, while appointing Brigadier General Haydon Boatner as the new Camp Commander. Boatner immediately removed all refugee camps from around Compound 76, while moving hard-core Communist POW's to smaller, more tightly secured camps around South Korea. For nearly a month tensions and physical assaults fell off dramatically inside the camp. However, everyone knew it was just a matter of time before internees once again began to raise hell. Early on the morning of June 5th, the camp exploded. Communist political prisoners took non-communists, and prison guards hostage. Retaliating, many North Korean soldiers from another part of the camp captured several communist political prisoners, threatening a blood bath. Each attempt at quelling the massive riots was unsuccessful. General Boatner fully understood that the only way to bring about peace to the camp was to bring in actual combat troops. On June 10th, the General ordered the 187th Parachute Combat Regiment, along with several tanks from the 64th Tank Battalion to assault the camp and restore order.

Arriving at Tongyeong with his third battalion, Col. Fontaine was not quite sure how this assault was going to be accomplished. Concerns about a bloodbath inside the camp were a real possibility as combat troops approached the compound. No one in Supreme Command wanted to take responsibility for that outcome. Teams of negotiators moved in on the compound to discuss surrender terms as tanks and infantry moved across the bridge onto the island. Many POW's not involved immediately surrendered and were removed from the compound.

Capt. Fargo assigned Alpha Company to cover the west gate of the camp, along with one M-64 Patton tank, with strict orders not to assault or enter the camp without permission from him or Col. Fontaine.

As dusk fell over the camp, Harry came looking for Steve. "What the hell do you think is going to happen here, Steve? I sure as hell don't want to charge in there like Jack-the-bear and kill unarmed POW's or innocent men. Plus, going after homemade weapons or bayonets with automatic weapons and tanks doesn't make sense. We could end up with the biggest bloodbath in history."

Steve nodded his head in agreement. "We're not even cut out for this. They should have some sort of rapid deployment unit here to put this down. Using our strength is like taking a ton of TNT to take out a squirrels nest. I don't like it either."

As they continued speaking, Franny came walking up to them. "We're set up right behind you guys with some reserves. I don't get it though, reserves to quell a damn POW riot? Do they think they've got tanks and artillery in there? This is a bit out of hand."

"Yeah Franny, Harry and I were just discussing the same thing. None of us likes it, but I guess we'll see what happens in the morning. I suspect that's when all hell will break lose. We figure they're giving these clowns time to digest the amount of force that's leveled against them out here over night. If by morning nothing can be decided, we'll blast our way in and take the camp back with force. It should be a very long and interesting night."

Steve was accurate. Throughout the night, screams and taunts came from inside the compound. POW's carrying weapons, including some semi-automatic rifles roamed the compound freely. Several shots were fired in the direction of the paratroopers throughout the night, without hitting anyone.

Baker Company and a Patton tank had taken up positions on the east gate, as Charlie and Dog Companies with several more tanks stood ready outside the main entrance. It was a worst case scenario for the prisoners at this point. What mattered now was which way they decided to go. Around 0500 hours, a man on a bullhorn near the front gate told the POW's in Korean that they would have until 0700 to throw down their weapons and surrender, or an assault of the camp would commence. The message was repeated every fifteen minutes. About 0645, large groups of POW's began walking toward the main gate. Military Police along with Paratroopers took the prisoners outside the gate in small groups where they were strip searched and redressed in blue coveralls. Things inside the compound tensed up, as the man on the bullhorn gave the holdouts one more chance to surrender safely. The air around the camp was thick with apprehension.

Never did these hard charging combat troops ever think their deadly resources would be used against POW's. But now they would have to do what they were called upon to do. Outside the main gate, Col Fontaine paced back and forth behind the tanks as they warmed up their engines. All he needed now was the order to assault from General Boatner. An order that finally arrived at 0810 hours.

Upon receiving the message to assault, both Alpha and Baker Companies blew through their gates as Charlie Company followed by Dog Company breached the main gate. Instantly, small arms fire erupted from several buildings, Paratroopers with B.A.R's and semiautomatic rifles answered in unison. The highly trained soldiers fired cover volleys as assault squads began entering the somewhat fortified buildings. Hastily erected barricades were quickly torn down as the men rushed forward, searching each room with combat efficiency. From stair wells and blind corners, armed rebels fired upon the advancing paratroopers, only to be quickly cut down. At this point, the Paratroopers were considering the holdout POW's to be nothing more than the enemy, plain and simple. Anyone choosing to surrender was quickly searched before being passed to the rear to waiting Military Police. With rapid efficiency, each floor of the barracks was cleared, allowing the soldiers to quickly move on to the next structure. It was nearly impossible for platoon leaders to keep up with their men, except to point out which building to assault next.

Harry charged forward through the fast moving attack, following third squad into the basement of a large barracks. From behind several tipped over wooden tables, two men fired at the advancing Paratroopers, Harry let go a short blast from his Thompson, as several other men fired into the tables. Both men fell backwards, dropping their weapons to the floor. Leading the sweep of the basement into the northwest corner, Harry suddenly stopped as two men came forward holding a knife to the throat of a third. Keeping his weapon trained on the men, Harry called out. "Throw down your knives. It's all over now. No need to die." Both men looked at each other for a moment as the Paratroopers covered them with about fifteen weapons.

The taller of the two men nodded. "I am Captain Chang. I belong to the Army of the People's Republic of China. I wish to surrender on my own terms. I wish to speak with General Colson."

"General Colson is no longer in charge. I doubt he's even in Korea anymore", Harry informed the frustrated Captain.

"I see you do not treat your hero's well. Then I wish to speak to the new General in charge. You are nothing more than a Sergeant. Go get me the General or this man dies," the arrogant man demanded.

"Look, this is very simple. You kill him, you both die. Look at the weapons that are trained upon you, Captain. Second, I will not get the General. He has washed his hands of this disaster. Whatever I do or say is speaking for the General. End of the line is right here," Harry explained, just as Steve walked in the room to see what was taking so long. Walking up to Harry, he also lowered his weapon on the Captain.

"Do you have more authority than this man?" the irate Captain inquired of Steve.

Shaking his head, he replied. "Sorry. What he says goes, and I really would not want to piss this man off. I'm just here to back him up, or kill you, whatever comes out of this."

"This man I hold is a spy for the south. I will deal with the General only, the Captain replied, tightening his grip on the man's throat.

"Sorry Captain, no deal. Enough is enough. Drop the damn knife," Harry demanded.

Without warning the man to the left of the Captain swung a pistol around the hostage, firing in Steve's direction. As Steve dropped to the floor to evade the shot, Neederman placed a well-aimed round squarely between the eyes of the pistol wielding POW.

The Captain threw down his knife as he called out, "Have mercy on me. I am not North Korean. As I said, I am from Communist China. I have special rights."

Getting up from the floor, Steve grabbed the whining officer, throwing him against the wall. "Savoy, McGee. Strip search this insufferable son-of-a-bitch and march him to the main gate in his underwear. If he hasn't got any underwear he goes bare ass naked. Do I need be any clearer?"

Harry had to laugh as they left the room with the balance of the squad. "Hey Stevie boy, is that covered under the Geneva Convention?"

Still being angry, Steve glared at Harry, "Right about now I can tell you where to shove that damn convention. Just kiss my ass!" Harry and the rest of the squad laughed as they made their way back to the courtyard.

About half an hour later, the search of the yard had been completed. All the internees had been properly searched and moved to waiting trucks. The Chinese Captain, still wearing his dingy underwear, was turned over to General Boatner's men. The man he had been holding hostage was given to representatives from I-Corp, since he had been labeled a South Korean spy. In cleaning out Compound 76, I-Corp reported 31 POW's killed, 131 injured, with one Paratrooper killed. The death toll was much smaller than had been anticipated.

As the men walked back toward the main gate, Steve observed Fr. O'Heally standing near a group of officers. Walking over, he placed his hand on the Padre's shoulder. "What the heck are you doing here, Father? Didn't think we could clean up this mess without you, or what?"

Father O'Heally laughed. "No my son, the Colonel asked me to come along. He thought maybe my presence might help defuse part of the anger in this camp and save lives. Unfortunately, things did not work out that way. But I guess it could have been worse."

As he finished speaking, two shots rang out from a partially opened manhole cover. Instantly, Fr. O'Heally fell forward against Steve, blooding running from two wounds in his chest. Two airborne soldiers, including Andy Sweet, immediately threw back the large iron cover from the snipers nest, dispatching the North Korean soldier with a volley of fire.

A medic standing nearby ran over to offer assistance. "Damn, this is bad," The medic called out as he fought desperately to stop the bleeding.

Father O'Heally brushed the medic's hands away. "Sgt. Kenrude, our friendship has spanned two wars. I know you believe I have always given you strength. But in fact it has been the other way around. I have always been inspired by your courage, your doubts, your faith in God, and your faith in your men."

Steve tried desperately to get the dying priest to stop talking as he encouraged the medic to work harder to save his life. However, each time the medic attempted do anything, Fr. O'Heally stopped him. "I am afraid this is my time, Sergeant. As I told you on Christmas Day, I knew my Father was calling me home soon, and I am ready to go back to him. I have seen too much hate and anger, yet I have witnessed love and compassion from warriors such as you and your friend, Harry." Struggling for air, Fr. O'Heally took hold of Steve's hand. "Make me a promise."

As tears rolled down Steve's face, he nodded. "Name it Padre, anything."

"Don't let them send me back home alone. Come with me, meet my Bishop. Tell him I tried each day to do some good. Tell him I will miss our cribbage games very much." Gasping for breath, once more he looked up at the gathering of men around him. "Will you all join me in the Lord's Prayer one more time?" He began, "Our Father who art in heaven…"

Steve could not say exactly when, but sometime as the solemn prayer was being recited by the sobbing group of rugged paratroopers, Father O'Heally's hand slipped from Steve's grasp, as he closed his eyes forever, slipping into eternity, gone from this troubled world. There was no doubt in Steve's mind that this kind man would never be forgotten by the frightened and desperate men he had counseled.

Without being led, the men prayed the Hail Mary prayer in somber reverence. No one in the group wanted to be the first to leave. They all gazed downward at the dead priest, who had meant so much to each of them. Finally, Capt. Fargo spoke up.

"Men, let's allow the medics to take the Padre's body out of this damn place. He deserves better." One by one the men made the sign of the cross, or knelt down to touch the Padre's arm before they left. Each man walked off mourning the loss of such a great man in their own way.

Steve stood silently beside Harry, Franny and Eddie Shrider as the medics placed Fr. O'Heallys body on a stretcher before loading it into an ambulance. Steve turned toward Harry.

"Did they get the bastard who killed him, or is he still hiding down in the sewers. I'm not going until I know he's one dead son-of-a-bitch."

Franny placed his hand on Steve's shoulder. "He's dead, Steve. Your radio man Sweet was nearby. He kicked the cover back and nailed the bastard three times."

"Good. That's good." Feeling rage build within him, Steve walked up to Capt. Fargo, slamming his Thompson into the man's chest. "I'm done here, arrest me. I'm finished. No more war, no more killing. I won't use this damn thing ever again." Finishing his statement, Steve walked off toward the main gate by himself.

Capt. Fargo looked at Harry. "Any ideas, Jensen? I don't want to have Kenrude arrested. Can you talk with him?"

Taking Steve's Thompson from the Captain Harry nodded his head. "Actually sir, I feel about the same way as Steve. I think we all do. He'll cool down later this evening and we'll have a talk with him. I know he doesn't really want to be court martialed."

The ride back to the base at Pusan was quiet. Steve sat by the tailgate of their truck just staring off into the distance without uttering a word. It was Archie Davenport all over again. Finding Archie hanging in that tree in Normandy with his throat torn wide open by shrapnel, was a sight he would never be able to erase from his mind. Both men had predicted their own deaths, they firmly believed in their premonitions. Archie definitely dwelt on it much more than the Padre had. He had never been able to find peace with it.

Steve remembered telling Archie's English girlfriend about his death. He never realized how serious the two actually were. It had been heart breaking as she wept and screamed. There simply was no way to console the devastated woman. It was the first time he realized what Karen would have gone through if anything happened to him.

About midnight, Harry, Franny and Eddie Shrider found Steve sitting on a bench near the chapel. Eddie sat down beside Steve before Harry could.

"Kenrude, you are a hell of a soldier and one damn good leader. I wish I could be like you. I know how you're feeling. The Padre was a great guy, he really liked you a lot. Do you think he would be happy with you walking away from your responsibilities because of his death? No, I think he would want you to lead your men and do what you have to do to keep them alive. That's what I think, Kenrude. And nobody who heard you this afternoon blames you for what you said. Every one of us has felt like doing exactly what you did at one time or another."

Steve looked up at his friends. "You guys are the greatest, and I thank God every day for your friendship." Smiling at Eddie, Steve continued. "Everything just got to me this afternoon. Like you guys, I want to go home. I'm just tired of war. Come on, walk me over to the orderly room so I can get my Thompson from the Captain."

Franny laughed. "He gave it to me when we arrived back this afternoon. He told me if you couldn't get it any cleaner then it was, he would give you a class on it."

Everyone laughed as Steve stood up. "Let's hit the rack. It's been too long of a day."

As the men reached their barracks, Harry took Eddie by the arm. "Thanks for what you said back there, man. I wasn't exactly sure what to say, but you hit it on the head, Eddie. Thanks."

Things were pretty quiet around the base for the next few days. Some of the infantry reserve companies were working hard in combat maneuvers and sighting in weapons on the range. Finally on the third day, Colonel Fontaine called a battalion formation. Mounting the steps to a small platform the colonel smiled. "Gentlemen, your war is over. Supreme Headquarters in Japan has ordered the 187th back to Hawaii. Upon arrival in Hawaii, all you retreads will be mustered out. We leave for Sasebo at noon tomorrow. I'm not sure of the time for our departure from Japan yet, but it will be soon. Congratulations, men."

A tremendous roar went up from the battalion. Steve stood motionless as the words failed to sink in. It almost felt like a bad joke, since Fr. O'Heally was killed so unfairly that close to going home to the parish he loved so much. After a moment of thought, Steve took off at a dead run to catch up with the colonel.

"Sir, do you know where Fr. O'Heally's body is right now? He asked if I would accompany him back to Cincinnati. Is it possible to actually do that?"

The Colonel smiled at Steve. "Capt. Fargo heard that part of the Padres last request. I had his remains held at the base mortuary. I had heard pretty accurate solid scuttlebutt that we might go home after completing the work at Compound 76. So, we can work things out when we get to Japan."

Steve nodded. "Sir? What would you say if I got five more World War Two guys to volunteer to be pall bearers and escort the Padre all the way back to Cincinnati?"

"Get me a list, Kenrude. Get it to me as soon as you possibly can, so we can get your discharge and travel documents squared away. I think that's a marvelous idea, Sergeant. The Padre would really like that," Col. Fontaine replied, placing his hand on Steve's shoulder.

After saluting his beloved Colonel, Steve took off at a dead run back to the men. There was no problem getting volunteers. Harry, Eddie Shrider, Israel Sanchez, Franny and Gus Rider all jumped at the opportunity.

CHAPTER 17
THE LONG ROAD HOME

Arriving back in Japan, Col. Fontaine and Capt. Fargo worked diligently, sifting through red tape in order to get everything set up for the six men. One of the problems they had to work through was Franny's orders. As he was staying in the Army, they needed to get him leave papers instead of a discharge like the others. The office staff at Supreme Headquarters felt he should stay with the Battalion until they arrived in Hawaii before allowing him to get a leave. It took two days of battling before Franny's leave was approved, and travel orders were finally signed. As the men prepared to leave, Steve walked up to Capt. Fargo.

"Sir, I want to apologize for slamming my weapon into your chest. That was uncalled for, and it should have never happened," Steve explained, holding out his hand to Alpha Company's tough commander.

Shaking hands with Steve, Capt. Fargo smiled. "You caught me off guard, I can say that for a fact. But I knew you wouldn't let down your men, your family, or me, if push came to shove. I understood the mood you were in and I'd seen the frustration growing in you over the last month. I just hoped it wouldn't get the best of you, causing you to make a mistake in judgment and get you or somebody else hurt. You weren't the only one, by the way Kenrude. I had spoken to the Colonel about ten men in the company I was beginning to get worried about. Being called back to fight a second war after being out of the army for so long had to be one hell of a tough blow all the way around. And having a family of your own this time around made it a different deal I'm sure. For me, the Army is my life. I love it, and will eventually retire from it. You guys are just trying to get it done and go home. No Kenrude. I can't imagine what it must have been like for you guys to get that letter, knowing what you were coming back to. So, there are no hard feelings. Thank you for all you did here with your men, and for being such a quality leader I could always count on."

Steve smiled back at the tough paratrooper. "Take care of yourself, Captain. It was a pleasure serving under you. Always stay safe, and don't take any unnecessary chances. I don't want to see you getting hurt again."

That afternoon, the six men boarded a military transport for Tokyo, where they would catch an airliner for the United States. They would stop in Manila, Honolulu, San Francisco, and then finally Cincinnati. The stop over's in Manila and Honolulu were strictly to take on fuel and swap out a few military passengers. The flights from Tokyo to Manila and Hawaii didn't seem so bad, as the men were just excited to be on their way back to the states and flying times within the Pacific were much shorter.

However, the flight from Honolulu across the wide Pacific to San Francisco quickly became boring and tedious, as the men were running out of conversation. Steve could only read or rehash topics for so long before he would nod off to sleep. Making matters worse, the flight across the endless ocean was anything but smooth, so even if he got to sleep, he couldn't stay that way very long. The huge Boeing 377 Stratocruiser bounced endlessly, making Steve wonder how long the big plane could hold together.

As the west coast of the United States came into view, the men were glued to the windows. Sanchez was the first one to call out. "There's the good old Golden Gate Bridge! Damn it guys, were finally home."

Tears of joy ran down their faces, no matter how hard they attempted not to cry. Steve looked over toward Harry. "We did it again, partner. We beat the odds. As we sailed into New York harbor on the Samuel Evans in

1945, I remember talking about how our luck had to run out eventually. So this is it and I don't ever want to try it again. I think this time, we're bound to have reached the end of our luck. The Kenrude's and Jensen's have used up all the luck given any man on this earth. None of us can ever fight another war, the odds would surely be against us." Sitting back in his seat, Steve looked out the window at the city below. Something bothered him. He didn't know what it was, but a terrible feeling overcame him, making him nauseous. It was as if Fr. O'Heally was reaching out from the silver military casket in the hold of their plane, with a premonition he could not yet understand. *What is it, Father? What are you trying to tell me?* Little did Steve know that in just seventeen short years, his son would be fighting a brutal war in a place called Vietnam. Like all American's, that war would have a tremendous effect on the Kenrude family for the rest of their lives. But for today, those feelings would remain a confused mystery, as he was not able to comprehend what could possibly be in store for his family in the future.

As the pilot began his decent, the outboard engine on the left wing suddenly exploded. Flames and black smoke trailed the damaged engine. The aircraft dipped perilously to the left as if it were going to complete a somersault right into San Francisco Bay. Passengers screamed as the Stratocruiser shuddered and rebounded excessively. All the paratroopers knew exactly what would happen to them if they crashed. They had seen the ghastly results on many occasions. Pushing himself back into his seat Steve closed his eyes. He could see the bodies he and Harry discovered after the plane crash in Georgia in 1944. He remembered watching bodies falling to their deaths from exploding planes over Normandy on D-Day. Was this to be their fate after surviving so many battles? No matter how he thought about their predicament, it made him angry. This time there was no open door to escape through; no parachutes to float him down and away from certain death. There was no grassy field waiting below for his feet to touch down on. This impact was going to be deadly for everyone on board, there was no escape for anyone.

A look of complete fear came over Harry's face, something Steve had never seen before, even after all they had been through. He glared out the window at the burning engine, as flames began dancing along the rear edge of the wing. "The fuel tanks, Steve! The fuel line must have ruptured during the explosion. If those flames reach the inboard engine, this thing will blow right out of the sky. Damn it Steve, it just can't end this way!"

As the pilot turned his sluggish plane back out to sea in order to avoid crashing over populated areas, he aimed for a large rain squall that was forming several miles away. The turbulence between the poorly handling aircraft, combined with the updrafts from the growing storm caused the already damaged plane to shake and twist violently. As rain poured over the damaged wing, the flames began to dissipate until they disappeared altogether. However, the added turbulence and gusting winds of the storm, began ripping sections of the engine shroud from the wing. As the pilot attempted to bring his crippled aircraft back toward the airport, added drag from the gaping engine cover caused serious handling problems. Shockingly, the giant prop assembly tore loose from the damaged engine, creating even more handling problems for the crew. As the prop dropped away to the sea below, several smaller parts were sucked into the inboard engine prop, which threw them violently through the thin cabin wall. Three rows in front of Franny and Sanchez, a woman screamed out in pain. Several other passengers screamed as blood sprayed on the ceiling and overhead compartments. Without hesitation, the two men bolted from their seats as the aircraft continued shaking badly.

After surveying the situation for a second, Franny yelled out, "Harry, Steve, get up here, we need your help." Arriving at the seats, Steve was aghast. He had never seen so much destruction to a human being, except for being in combat. The metal parts coming through the fuselage had ripped half the head of a middle aged man completely off. The woman next to him was bleeding profusely from injuries to her neck and shoulder. Sanchez and Harry pulled the man from his seat, handing him to Steve and Eddie Shrider as Franny began attempting to stop the flow of blood from the screaming woman. One of the flight attendants, now completely hysterical, focused on yelling at the men to take their seats, as this was going to be a very rough landing. Gus Rider wrapped his huge arms around the shrieking attendant as she began striking Franny in the back with her fists. Finally, with the flight attendant out of the way, Harry was able to get in beside Franny to help with first aid for the injured woman. Meanwhile, Steve and Eddie provided assistance to two other passengers that had been less seriously injured by flying debris.

Holding a compress on the cheek of a young woman, Steve glanced out the window as the plane began its final approach to the airport. It was apparent the crew was doing everything humanly possible to bring the damaged airliner down in one piece. It was obvious to Steve that the severely damaged airliner was going to miss the runway. Angrily, Steve yelled out, "Listen, we're going to hit hard! Get your heads down and hold on tight!" Closing his eyes, he said a quick prayer as he prepared for the worst.

Seconds later, the ill-fated airliner slammed down hard onto the concrete before skidding off into the grass. Passengers screamed and wept as the plane spun around wildly, ripping the front landing gear free from the undercarriage. The tip of the damaged left wing struck the ground, tearing away everything up to the blown engine pod. After what felt like forever, the skidding and spinning airliner came to a sudden stop. Emergency crews streamed toward the plane, as fire fighters poured thick white foam over the remaining left wing.

Medical crews took over the care of the injured passengers, as police and flight crew members evacuated the rest of the shaken passengers on to buses. Military Officials, waiting there for the six veterans and Fr. O'Heally's casket, came out onto the tarmac with a small bus to gather up the shaken and bloodied soldiers. As soon as the Padre's casket was loaded into an army hearse, the men were whisked away to the Presidio Military Base where they were debriefed on the incident. After showering, fresh clothing and a great meal, the men were given phone privileges to call their loved ones.

Returning to folding laundry after putting her two children in bed, Karen was thinking about some bills for the farm she would have to look at tomorrow, when the phone rang. She never liked late evening phone calls, since they always seemed to bring bad news. Those type's of calls always seemed to bring bad news, something she didn't want to deal with anymore today. With serious trepidation she picked up the receiver.

"Hello, can I help you," she spoke softly into the phone.

The voice on the other end of the phone replied, "Hey beautiful lady, do you have time for a kiss?"

She screamed in a loud voice, "Oh my God! Where are you? I miss you so much."

Hearing his mother scream, Tommy came running from the bedroom. "Is everything alright, Mommy? What's wrong?"

Crying and laughing at the same time, she knelt down on the floor to hug her son. "It's Daddy. He's in the States. Do you want to say hi? Holding the phone to Tommy's ear, Steve and his son had a fun conversation. After Tommy ran off to bed, Karen sat down by the kitchen table. Steve explained everything that happened over the last few hours to his sobbing wife. When he finished, she scolded him, "Listen to me, Mr. Kenrude. You best get home to me and quit all this hero crap. No more! And I mean no more Sergeant Kenrude. And that is an order from the very top brass. Is that understood?"

Steve laughed before explaining their plans for the next couple of days.

As he prepared to hang up, Karen added, "I will see you on Thursday at the airport. Your folks and I are coming to pick you up, no more public transportation for you, soldier."

Steve felt good as he walked out into the damp San Francisco evening. He looked up at the Golden Gate Bridge as traffic streamed across the massive span. A naval cruiser glided slowly under the bridge as the lights of the city twinkled in the distant hills. It was good to be back in America, and far away from the thundering artillery, whining bullets and ever present death. As he stood near the edge of the water, he thought about what it was going to be like to hold Karen in his arms once again, and play with his adorable kids.

The following morning, clad in fresh new uniforms, the men boarded an Air Force aircraft for the final leg of their mission, and thankfully the flight was totally uneventful. About 1700 hours the aircraft touched down in Cincinnati. As the plane slowly rolled up to a National Guard Hanger, Steve could see a Color Guard standing near a black hearse with the rear door already opened. A large crowd of civilians stood behind a rope line, as a large contingent of National Guard soldiers prepared to form a welcoming line from the aircraft to the hearse. When the aircraft stopped, a regular army Colonel came on board to greet the men, and give them instructions as to how they wanted things handled. Departing the aircraft, the men took up positions near the cargo bay door.

Two Air Force Airmen securely draped an American Flag over the silver casket, before helping to lower it down to the waiting soldiers. Taking hold of the side rails, the men turned the casket toward the hanger. With a signal from the Colonel, a Master Sergeant near the hearse called out, "Attention!"

The honor guard and all the National Guard troops instantly snapped to attention as one. A high school band near the hanger began playing a slow funeral march as the Sergeant called out, "Present Arms!"

Everyone in uniform saluted, as the six veterans slowly carried the flag draped casket bearing the remains of Fr. O'Heally forward. Arriving at the hearse, the men reverently slid the casket into the long black Cadillac. As the door was closed, the soldiers entered a military van that followed the hearse. The vehicles pulled in behind two squad cars and a limousine carrying Bishop Timothy Brooks and relatives of Fr. O'Heally. As the procession departed for St. Cecelia's Catholic Church, the Sergeant called out, "Parade Rest!"

About half an hour later the procession arrived in front of the church. Once again the Korean Veterans carried the casket to a special platform near the front of the church. After placing it on the platform and adjusting the flag, the men retired to the side of the church. National Guard Soldiers provided Honor Guard services throughout the evening, as parishioners, politicians and other members of the community filed by, paying their last respects.

The men were driven to a motel several miles from the church where they quietly spent the night.

At 0800 the following morning, the van once again picked up the soldiers for a ride back to the church. The men placed the military casket onto a set of wheels provided by the funeral home. It was then rolled to the back of the church where the Bishop would begin the Catholic Funeral Rite. Steve had never attended a Catholic Funeral before today, and he found it to be very moving. Bishop Brook's homily was very emotional and brought nearly the entire congregation to tears. It was evident that the two men had a very close, deeply religious bond. Many times the Bishop struggled, as he spoke about Fr. O'Heally's war time service. After the funeral, the casket was taken to the parish cemetery where the Color Guard from the airport had assembled. After the Bishop offered the final grave side prayers, the rifle squad prepared to fire a twenty-one gun salute. Steve was amazed to witness the congregation members flinch with each volley, as the six veterans stood frozen in place without moving a muscle. As the service came to an end, the Lieutenant in charge of the Color Guard walked to the head of the casket, calling out orders, as the veterans lifted the flag from the casket, folding it into a tight proper triangle. Slowly the Lieutenant walked over to a small canopy tent where the immediate family was seated. Stopping in front of Fr. O'Heally's weeping sister, he gently placed the flag into her hands as he performed the flag presentation, sharing the appreciation and condolences of the President and a grateful nation.

As the graveside service ended, Bishop Brooks and Fr. O'Heally's sister and family came forward to thank the men for escorting him home.

Mary O'Heally shook hands and kissed each of the men on the cheek. Looking down at the ground she took a deep breath before looking back up at the soldiers. "My brother would have loved nothing more than to have men he served with bring him home. I have read several of his journals he wrote during World War Two. He loved each and every one of you, and felt he could never do enough to make your lives easier. I will miss him very much, but I know he died doing what he loved most. Yes, St. Cecilia was his home parish which he deeply loved, and we loved him. But being with the troops was where he felt most at home, and where he felt he did his most important work. Thank you for bringing him home to us. We will never forget your sacrifice." Before anyone could say a word, Mary grabbed onto the arm of her husband, walking quickly toward their car.

Stepping forward, Bishop Brooks shook hands with the six men. Taking a step back he smiled slightly. "You know, Fr. O'Heally and I have been friends for more years than I care to think about. On more than one occasion it was his wit and humor that pulled me out of a bad mood. I can only imagine what he did for you men when the weight of the free world stood so heavily on your shoulders. Honestly, I don't know if I would have had the fortitude and courage to do what he did. Believe me, everyone here at St. Cecelia's will miss him greatly and mourn his loss for a very long time. Men, may God bless you for what you have done for his family and our grieving parish." After giving them a blessing, Bishop Brooks turned and walked away.

As the paratroopers began to walk away, Steve walked up to the casket one more time. He had always planned to introduce Karen and his children to this wonderful priest who had given him strength during the war, but now that would never happen. Placing his hand on the casket, Steve closed his eyes as he quietly said a prayer for the saintly priest. After taking a deep breath, Steve smiled. "You won't get rid of me this easily, Father. I promise you, I will bring my family here to visit you. I want them all to know what a wonderful man you were. Safe journey home, Father," Steve concluded, as tears rolled down his cheeks. As he turned to leave, something made him turn toward a mausoleum that stood about twenty yards away. There on a marble bench he swore he saw Fr. O'Heally wearing his uniform, waving to him for just a moment.

The following morning at 0800, the men were delivered to the airport. It was another day of high emotions as the men prepared to say goodbye. Israel Sanchez, Gus Rider and Eddie Shrider said their goodbyes after leaving the ticket counter, as their flights were leaving earlier and from a different part of the terminal. The men hugged one another and shook hands as they exchanged comical insults and addresses. Once again Steve felt that nagging hurt in his stomach he experienced after World War Two, as he parted ways with his comrades. He realized he may never see any of them ever again, and in time, letters would become fewer and farther between. That was just the way things always seemed to happen.

He hoped and prayed all of them would return home safely and rebuild their lives once again. Yet somehow he knew he would hear Eddie Shrider doing play by plays for the big leagues down the road. That gave Steve a sense of comfort.

Steve, Franny and Harry walked off toward the far side of the terminal without saying a word, until they arrived at a coffee shop next to Franny's departure gate. After getting coffee, the men sat at a small table. "So, this is it, boys," Franny began. "Once again, we depart. This is almost tougher than when we went our own ways back in Europe. I know we will always be friends, but somehow this really has a finality to it. I know you guys are happy going back to your farms, and I'm ready to get back to Fort Benning, where I can train recruits and be with Darcy every night. Let's all keep in touch now."

Harry laughed as he took a long look at Franny. "What a belligerent jerk you were, when we first met you in Normandy. I could have cared less if we would have left you in Sainte-Mere-Eglise. And today, I hate to see us all break up again. I'm going to miss you, Francis Martin Doogan, the third. You take care of yourself."

After a second call to board Franny's flight came over the loud speakers, the men stood up. Steve gave Franny a big hug. "Franny, you always were a treat, regardless of what Harry said."

The men laughed as Franny slapped Steve hardily on the back. Finishing his good bye, Steve continued. "Stay out of wars for a while my friend. But if you ever need help, you know just the guys to count on. We'll never let you go it alone."

With tears in his eyes, Franny shook hands with his friends once more before walking off to the gate. Before entering the ramp he yelled back, "Stay out of trouble you sad sacks!"

Laughing, the two men continued down the concourse until they arrived at gate G, where Harry would catch his flight for Des Moines. Harry looked around the terminal for a moment before looking at his best friend, "Wow, I really didn't think this would be so tough, and I'm not prepared at all. I know we don't live that far apart, but it feels like it might just as well be thousands of miles. I know it will be a while before I see your ugly mug again, Stevie boy." Shaking his head, he continued. "Hey, did you ever think in your wildest dreams that we would end up in a war again?"

"Never, my friend. I figured we had served our time and any future wars would be fought by the young guys. No, I would have never guessed we'd be called back," Steve replied, as he stared at his best friend. "When problems began in Korea, I had a bad feeling that maybe I wasn't done after all."

"Having you there throughout the entire time made it bearable, Steve. Though there were a few times when I didn't figure we'd be standing here talking about it. Guess I kind of figured we'd be coming back like the Padre. To be honest, there were times I was petrified, and just operated on instinct. That was all I had left," Harry responded shaking his head as a big tear rolled down his cheek. Before picking up his bag, Harry wrapped his strong arms around Steve, giving him a huge hug. "Thanks for everything partner, go home now and make some more kids."

Steve laughed as he slapped Harry on the shoulder. "I'll call you in a few days to see how you're doing. Say hi to Marylyn for me."

Steve stood silently as he watched Harry slowly begin walking toward boarding door, then disappear into the movable ramp. Just as Steve began picking up his bag, Harry came back into the terminal to yell, just as he did when the train pulled out after world war two, "Airborne forever, Stevie boy!"

Quickly Steve spun around, looking back at Harry. Almost in unison the men saluted one another as a flight attendant began pulling Harry toward the plane.

Steve laughed as he shook his head. There was only one Harry, and maybe the world was better off because of it, but Steve knew he was a better person for having known him. Arriving at his gate, Steve found a seat near the window where he could watch airliners coming and going. It seemed strange being all alone, after being continually surrounded by hundreds of men nearly all the time since arriving in Georgia. Perhaps it wasn't such a bad deal, it gave him time to sort through many thoughts and emotions without having someone close by to verify his feelings. As he finally walked down the ramp onto the plane an hour later, he was happy to see the plane was only about three-quarters full, so he could have a seat to himself. He smiled broadly, realizing he really was on his way home, and nothing could stop him now. His phone conversation with Karen in San Francisco had totally prepared him for their reunion. He was excited to see the kids, and find out about all the changes Mike and his Father were making on the farm. He was also happy there would be no more cows to milk twice a day. What a relief that was! Steve enjoyed the smooth flight home. As he peered out the window into the crystal clear day, he thought of all the jumps he had made from so many huge aircraft, responsible for all those men. Now he had no such worries, and all he had to do was watch the cities and town of America, that were never touched by the devastation of war, slowly pass by below.

Two hours later the wheels of the huge airliner touched down at Wold-Chamberlin International Airport in Minneapolis. Walking up the ramp he could see Karen standing next to his mother. She bolted forward, throwing her arms around his neck as she kissed him. Overwhelmed with joy, Steve picked her up spinning her around twice. Laughing, as she called out, "I love you Steven Kenrude!"

Everyone near the gate either laughed or applauded as the happy couple kissed again. Walking to his parents, he was met by his mother, who grabbed her son, giving him a kiss on the cheek before hugging him with all her strength. "No more wars for you, mister. The only thing you'll battle from now on will be weeds in the corn field. Do you understand me?" She whispered it into his ear, so relieved to have him home safe.

Holding on to his mother, he reached one hand out to his father, who said, "Great to have you home, son. We can't wait to have you look over our plans. I think you'll be excited."

With one arm around his mother, and the other around Karen he smiled at his father. "I can't wait to get back to normal with Karen, the kids, the farm, and my entire family. You have no idea how good it is to be home. Let's get the hell out of here, I have children to see."

The ride to Glendale in his parent's new silver 1952 Oldsmobile Dynamic 88 was fun and exciting as everyone exchanged stories and jokes. Steve never thought his parents would splurge on such a nice car, but with the farm doing so well, he was glad they finally indulged themselves a bit.

The yard at his folks place was crammed with cars. People rushed from the house and barn as Alex let go two loud horn blasts as he entered the driveway. Steve barely stepped foot from the car when Tommy and Abigail all but knocked him to the ground. For several minutes he knelt on the ground clutching his children, as tears rolled down his cheeks. Finally able to speak, he looked at his kids. "You have both grown so big. Daddy has missed you so much. I'll never leave you and Mommy like that ever again, I promise."

As soon as he stood up, his sister Christine hugged him tightly as she kissed him on the cheek. Mike shook hands with his big brother as he continued repeating, "Welcome home. Welcome home, brother."

Karen's mother grabbed Steve next. Hugging him, she whispered in his ear. "I want another grandbaby. You have your marching orders, soldier!" Steve laughed as he kissed Janet on the forehead.

The rest of the day was like a whirlwind as people kept coming and going to welcome him home. Eventually, they headed home and it was nearly nine o'clock when he and Karen finally were able to get the kids to settle down and go to bed. A light rain began to fall as the happy couple sat out on the back porch, attempting to catch their breaths. They talked until nearly midnight before finally walking off to their bedroom hand in hand.

The following morning Steve sat by the kitchen table enjoying a cup of coffee with Karen when Mike drove up into the yard. Entering the kitchen he looked at his older brother. "What the hell is going on here? You think you can just come home and sit around here all day doing nothing? Damn, mister there is work to be done here, this farm don't run itself!" Karen tossed a wet dish cloth at her brother-in-law as Steve laughed.

After helping himself to some coffee, Mike sat down at the table smiling at Karen. "Actually, if this pretty lady could spare you for a short time, I would like to run you over to the folk's place. We have some drawings in the barn for new grain bins we would like your opinion on. Plus Dad thinks we need to buy another tractor so you could look over those brochures while we're there. It wouldn't take very long."

Nodding his head, Steve looked over at Karen. "Do you mind, sweetheart? I would be back way before lunch time."

Smiling intently at her husband, Karen replied. "Of course I don't mind. We have a lifetime to be together. And it will be good for you to think about other things besides war for a change."

After kissing Karen, Steve followed Mike out the door. As they reached the truck, they began arguing over who was going to drive. Before Mike could react, Steve shoved him against the front fender, taking the keys away from him. Mike pretended to cry as he stomped his foot against the ground. Karen laughed as she watched the brothers clowning around. She had missed their horse play very much while Steve was away. However, now her loving husband was finally home, and her beautiful family was once again complete. Watching Steve and Mike screw around out in the driveway, she prayed that nothing would ever tear her precious family apart ever again.

Arriving at their parent's home, the boys walked straight into the kitchen, greeting their folks and pouring a cup of coffee. Nancy smiled, giving both of her boys a hug. It was good to have her family back together again, safe and sound.

Sitting down at the table, Alex handed Steve a brochure on the tractor he wanted to purchase. After reading the literature and checking over the proposal Steve nodded his head. "I'm out of the loop a little on current prices, but it seems competitive, and it should do the job you have in mind. Mike told me about the financing plan you have worked out with the bank, so I see no reason we shouldn't go ahead with it."

Alex smiled knowing both his sons were on board with his plans. "I was sure you would agree. It's time to retire the old Massey. It's just not worth putting any more money into it."

"Yeah she is just worn out, and tough to get parts for it. We learned that with the PTO last fall. Plus it's just not powerful enough to pull the big plow and disc we bought. Sad to say, but it needs to go."

Pulling some papers from a file, Alex handed them to Steve. "This is the field lay out we have figured on for planting next spring, and the remodeling we want to do on the machine shop on the old Welch property. We're wanting a place to store fertilizer and equipment so we don't have to pull it all so far. That would save a lot of wear on the equipment. Any ideas Steve?"

After studying the drawings Steve shook his head. "You guys have really done your homework, and this all looks good to me. Let's try it for a year, and if it doesn't work we can always change things down the road. Thank you for showing me all of this. It feels good to be part of something other than war plans. What else do you want me to look over since I am here?"

Mike handed Steve several legal documents from an envelope Nancy handed him when they first entered the kitchen. These are the documents of incorporation for Kenrude Farms, Inc. You will notice you are Chief Operational Officer, I am Assistant Operational Officer, Karen is Chief Financial Officer and Dad is considered the Trust Officer. We all agreed on this months ago as you can see by the signatures and dates, so all we needed was your signature to make it all legal. It's open ended so we can add our boys to the corporation when they get older. What do you think, Steve?"

Shaking his head, Steve looked at his parents. "Wow! I knew we were expanding big time, but I wasn't ready for this. If this is what you all want, I would be honored, to be in charge of this entire operation, considering Mike and Dad continue to have a voice in all the decisions we make."

Alex held out his hand. "Shake hands, son. All of that was discussed and agreed upon. Sign the documents and we are on our way. Karen can file them with the attorney's this week."

Steve walked out into the yard after all the business was taken care of. For the first time since leaving home, he felt a sense of calm flow throughout his body. This is what he had hoped could happen with the farm someday. With a renewed sense of purpose, Steve and Mike climbed into the truck to take a tour of the land and buildings they had acquired over the last eighteen months.

Meanwhile, all was not well at the old Donnelly Residence. As Karen began cleaning her brightly decorated kitchen, a strange feeling came over her. Sitting down at the table she tried to make sense of it, but there just didn't appear to be any reason for the foreboding fear that was attempting to consume her soul. The kids were safe at her mother's home, and Steve was with Mike at their parent's house. There just didn't seem to be any reason for this suffocating torture she was feeling. After taking a deep breath, Karen rose from the chair to look out the back door. The yard seemed way too quiet since Steve and Mike had driven off. She looked down at Missy, their playful cat that had just laid down in front of the screen door. "Well Missy, I guess it's you and me against the world today. Do you think everything is going to be alright now that Steven is home?"

Surprisingly, the cat stood up and looked at her before meowing in an almost menacing manner. "Well, what has gotten into you this morning?" Karen inquired, as she approached the screen door. Instantly, the cat jumped up, growling and hissing at her, something it had never done before. Karen stood motionless as she watched Missy's disturbing actions. "What is it, girl? What's wrong with you today?"

After backing away from the door, Missy walked over toward Tommy's baseball glove that he left lay by the wash line pole last night. After sniffing it a few seconds she laid down in the pocket of the glove and whined.

Karen felt herself tremble as it appeared that simple barn cat was trying to tell her something she couldn't understand. Retreating back into the house, she felt a chill run down her spine. Her world appeared to be out of control, but she couldn't put her finger on any one item making her feel that way. Not able to figure out what was going on, she decided to get on with her morning chores. After walking upstairs to change the sheets on Tommy's bed, she peered out the north window for a moment. Everything was quiet on the Kenrude Farm as best as she could see, so what could be upsetting her so much?

After a few moments of thought she walked into Tommy's room. Like most boys, his room was usually anything but neat. After picking up some clothing off the floor, she walked past the small writing desk Alex had made for him. She observed sheets of paper sticking out of the book on modern day aircraft Mike had given him for Christmas. Sitting down at the desk, Karen opened the book to see what was on the sheets of paper. Pulling out the first sheet, she placed her hands over her mouth and gasped. Tommy had drawn a picture of an army helicopter landing in a grassy field with a soldier jumping off. Under the soldier he had written, 'Tommy.'

The next piece of paper depicted a crashed helicopter on fire, with soldiers running in different directions. Again, one of the soldiers was labeled 'Tommy.' The third picture frightened her the most.

There was a helicopter sitting on the ground, as two men loaded a stretcher into it. The soldier on the stretcher was apparently wounded very bad, as Tommy colored in several red splotches on the man. However, in this picture, none of the men were labeled with Tommy's name.

Karen looked over the papers for several moments before placing them neatly back into the book. Fear clutched her heart. There was no way she was ever going to allow her sweet little boy to be involved in a war. The Kenrude's had done enough fighting for their country, and there would be no more.

Rising from the desk, Karen stripped the sheets from the bed, and began replacing them with clean linens. But no matter how hard she tried to ignore the book on Tommy's desk, her eyes kept returning to it. Sitting down on the edge of the bed she closed her eyes. "Dear God, my family has sacrificed a lot for this great country. And we appreciate all you have done for us, and we are truly grateful. But please let my son live in peace. Let him know life and love the way it was meant to be. Don't ever allow him to experience the horrors of war as his father and uncle were forced to do."

Little could she comprehend as she sat on Tommy's bed that morning, that just 1500 miles away in Washington D.C., President Eisenhower was seriously attempting to disperse storm clouds that were already gathering over the horizon in Southeast Asia, in an unknown country called Vietnam. On this splendid summer day in 1952, it didn't seem possible that those ominous dark clouds could unleash their wrath upon her family twenty years into the future. Much less like a plains tornado, devastating the happiness of her family forever.

EPILOGUE

As the war ended for Alpha Company, the living returned home to restart their lives the best way they could. Here is a short synopsis of what happened to the brave warriors of Alpha Company.

*Pvt. Andrew Rausch was convicted of murdering Pvt. John Warner. He received 30 years at hard labor in Leavenworth. He was then tried in Georgia for the murder of the fourteen year old girl he tossed down a man hole, receiving a life sentence. He was murdered in prison in 1960.

*Andrew Tormay returned home to Burlington, Illinois after Rausch's trial. He drove bus for the city transit service until he retired in 1977. He disappeared while swimming in Lake Michigan in 1986.

*Jimmy Whitebear, killed in action, buried in the National Cemetery of the Pacific in Hawaii.

*Arnie Stebbins, returned to Detroit and his job at Chevrolet. Months later he married a school teacher and had two children. He passed away in 2013.

*Gus Rider returned home to Plano, Texas where he became an insurance agent. He passed away from cancer in 2001.

*Jack Albert returned home to Portland, Oregon. No record of what happened to him.

*Dave Seaton returned home to Devil's Lake, North Dakota. Worked on a road maintenance crew until July 1992 when he was struck by a speeding motorist.

*Manuel Juarez returned home to Phoenix, Arizona, where he worked with his father in the family lumber business. He died of natural causes in 2014.

*Dave Taggered returned home to Cleveland, Ohio where he went to college on the GI Bill to become a dentist. He has his own clinic in Branson, Missouri, and is still alive as of this writing.

*John Neederman returned to Omaha, Nebraska, becoming a Catholic Priest. He served two tours of service in Vietnam as an Army Chaplain. He was killed by Hamas snipers bullet while visiting Israel in 1995.

*Earl Sweet, killed in action during the Imjin River Defense. He is buried in his hometown of Ozark, Missouri. With the help of Fr. John Neederman, Earl's daughter Flo, who he never knew, traveled to Korea in 1980 to place a wreath near the Imjin River, where her father was killed.

*Devin Kraus, returned home to Kissimmee, Florida where he and his wife operated a successful Pizza franchise. He passed away in 2015.

*Capt. Fargo retired from the Army in 1969 at the rank of Lt. Colonel, after serving two tours of duty in Vietnam. After his 28 years in the Army, he sold real estate in Seattle. He passed away in 2000.

*Israel Sanchez, returned to his small home town in the desert southwest where he became a minister. He is still alive as of this writing.

*Wally Umberto, killed in action, buried in Youngstown, Ohio.

*Conroy Dayton, killed by the North Korean Terror attack is buried in Arlington National Cemetery.

*Eddie Shrider returned home, becoming a television sports announcer and reporter in Philadelphia. He became a popular football broadcaster for several TV Networks as Steve predicted. He passed away in 2010.

*Craig Dymetrie, killed in action, buried in the National Cemetery of the Pacific in Hawaii.

*Hector Gomez, killed in action buried in Chicago, Illinois.

*Victor Martinez, killed in action, buried in Bull Head City, Arizona.

*Kelly Trost, killed in action, buried in Bangor, Maine.

*Steve Donahue returned to Clinton, Oklahoma. Found murdered in a parking lot in 1954.

*George Dinsmore killed in action. Buried in Hampton, Iowa.

*Mitch Hagen went home on hardship discharge when his father died. He ran the family farm until his sons took over in 1995. He is retired and living in Las Vegas as of this writing.

*Capt. McGlynn retired from the army in 1965 at the rank of Lt. Colonel. He owned and ran a hardware store in Frankfort, Illinois until his death in 1987.

* Col. Fontaine also served in Vietnam. After retirement from the army he worked as an import-export broker until his death from a heart attack in 1983.

*Harry Jenson returned to Clearview, Iowa, continuing his work with the family beef raising operation. He and Marylyn visited Steve and Karen every chance they could. Harry passed away while touring World War Two battle sights in Europe in 2011.

*Francis Martin Doogan, III (Franny) went on to serve in Vietnam. He retired at the rank of Sergeant Major to his home in Florida. He served two terms in the state legislature before retiring to write. He wrote several novels and a historical account of his war experiences. He passed away in 2009.

*Fr. Timothy O'Heally, killed in action, was buried in Cincinnati, Ohio with full Military Honors. Many war veterans from World War Two and Korea have journeyed there to visit his grave.

*Capt. McMurrey resigned his commission in 1960. He opened his own law office in Fargo, North Dakota, he passed away in 2011

*Major Fielding retired from the army in 1977 after 32 years. He served four years in the Indiana State House before becoming a contributor to a national law review magazine. He passed away in 2014.

*Gen. Addle Hopkins returned to New York City where he became a stock broker. He passed away in 1966.

*Col. Charles Andretti resigned his commission in 1955 after 23 years. He joined a prestigious law firm in Los Angeles. He was killed in an automobile accident in 1966.

*General Booth died in Leavenworth Military Prison in 1973 after a severe heart attack.

*Lt. Silverton's remains were never returned by the North Korean's. He is listed as MIA.

* Col. Manner died in 1999. He is buried in Selma, Alabama.

*Pvt. Sam Bateman returned home with the Korean girl he and Franny saved. He and his wife adopted two more Korean orphans over the next three years. Sam died from cancer in 1999.

* Pvt. Dennis Scott who helped rescue the kidnapped Korean baby, attended Southern Christian University where he studied theology, becoming a Baptist Minister. He is still alive as of this writing.

* Sheriff Waylon 'Bull' Richards, retired in 1980 after serving sixteen years as Sheriff. He enjoyed living out his life in Glendale, passing away in 1995.

* Deputy Stu Johnson was elected Sheriff when Bull Richards retired. He served as Sheriff until 1992 when he retired. He was killed in a boating accident in 1996.

* Oswald Timer, the Bainsworth's attorney, became a prominent Wall Street Attorney before passing away in 1990.
* Florence Bainsworth, aunt to Grant and Wauneta, finished selling off all their financial holdings in Central Minnesota and Illinois in 1954. She and her husband, Wallace Cooper III, moved to Long Island, New York where they were welcomed into the wealthy financial community.
* Stan Mullins was sentenced to 25 years in prison for the death of Grant Bainsworth. He hanged himself in his cell at Stillwater State Prison in 1960.
* Frank Schuster Kenrude's hired foreman worked for the family until 1995 when he retired. He passed away in 2005.
* Janet Donnelly, Karen's mother, continued helping Karen with the children and the farm's paper work. She passed away from cancer in 1965.
* Tommy Kenrude, Steve and Karen's oldest son would attend the University of Minnesota's Medical School, where he studied to become a doctor.
* Abigail (Kenrude) Lyons, Steve and Karen's daughter, attended college at St. Benedict's College in St. Joseph, MN. Majoring in Accounting. She married a doctor and still lives near St. Cloud, MN.
* Steve Kenrude returned to Glendale, Minnesota where he continued working with Kenrude Farms, Inc. He and Karen had one more son named Peter. Steve passed away in 2012 while sitting on his back porch while reading the newspaper.
* Karen (Donnelly) Kenrude enjoyed adding one more child to their family. She loved raising her children and helping with book work for the farm, as well as helping with the PTA and church functions. She is still alive, living in a nursing home in Willmar, Minnesota.
* Christine Simmons (Kenrude) still lives in Minneapolis, MN. She

and her husband had four children who were all very successful. Christine and her husband are retired. They are both alive as of this writing. They visit Glendale and Willmar on a regular basis.

* Mike Kenrude, Steve's younger brother enjoyed operating the farm with the family. He and Glenda had four children. Greg and Matthew took over the operation and still run it today. Mike passed away in 2011.
* Glenda (Ramsdale) Kenrude, enjoyed raising her four children on the farm. She helped Karen with paper work and served two terms on the Glendale School District Board. She moved to Willmar, MN after Mike's death to be with her eldest daughter Anna. She is still alive as of this writing.
* Alex Kenrude passed away in 1972.
* Nancy (Abbott) Kenrude passed away in 1974.
* The remains of the men killed in the failed raid into North Korea have never been returned to the United States, as the North Korean Government refuses to admit the raid ever happened. The United Nations and the Pentagon continue to classify all documents on the raid as Top Secret.

CPSIA information can be obtained
at www.ICGtesting.com
Printed in the USA
LVHW041945180723
752479LV00004B/628

9 780578 453873